Zoë Barnes   gend has it
her skirt once fell off during a school performance of 'Dido and Aeneas'.
According to her family, she has been making an exhibition of herself ever

SP
SF   aried career has included stints as a hearing-aid technician,
E   board operator, shorthand teacher, French translator, and the worst
T   nts clerk in the entire world. When not writing her own novels, she
            ates other people's and also works as a semi-professional singer.

            ugh not in the least bit posh, Zoë now lives in Cheltenham where
          of her novels are set. She shares a home with her husband Simon, and
         d rather like to be a writer when she grows up.

         Barnes is the author of seven best-selling novels including BUMPS
       HITCHED. The others are HOT PROPERTY, BOUNCING BACK,
     APPEAL, LOVE BUG, JUST MARRIED, SPLIT ENDS and BE MY
     BY, also published by Piatkus. Zoë loves to hear from her readers.
      te to her c/o Piatkus Books, 5 Windmill Street, London, W1T 2JA or
      email at zoebarnes@bookfactory.fsnet.co.uk

Wedding Belles

Zoë Barnes

PIATKUS

Visit the Piatkus website!

Piatkus publishes a wide range of best-selling fiction and non-fiction, including books on health, mind, body & spirit, sex, self-help, cookery, biography and the paranormal.

If you want to:

- read descriptions of our popular titles
-
-
-
-

v ..... co.uk

All the characters in this book are fictitious and any resemblance to real persons, living or dead, is entirely coincidental.

First published in Great Britain in 2006 by
Piatkus Books Ltd of
5 Windmill Street, London W1T 2JA
email: info@piatkus.co.uk

This edition published 2007

The moral right of the author has been asserted

A catalogue record for this book is available from the British Library

ISBN 978 0 7499 3788 1

Set in Times by Phoenix Photosetting, Chatham, Kent
www.phoenixphotosetting.co.uk

Printed and bound in Great Britain by
Clays Ltd, St Ives PLC

For Dawn Clark, the best mate anyone could have.
And with special thanks to The Falcon's Nest, Port Erin, Isle of Man,
my favourite place in all the world

Prologue

Cheltenham, just before Christmas

Annabelle Craine paused in the doorway to her father's home office, and contemplated her mother with growing bemusement. 'Mum, what exactly are you doing?'

Brenda Craine – vicar's wife, organising genius and pillar of the parish of St Jude's – had been hogging her husband's office telephone for most of the morning. At the sound of her daughter's voice she glanced round, smiled, shushed her into silence, and continued chatting animatedly to someone on the other end of the line. 'Yes, that's right: in one of those neat little boxes with the tasteful edging, and you will make sure you spell "Craine" correctly, won't you? C-R-A- . . . yes, that's right. It's an old Manx name, you know. Many thanks for your help, goodbye!'

Curiosity got the better of Belle, and she rested the cardboard box full of Christmas decorations on a teetering pile of old books just inside the door. 'Mum. . .'

Brenda spun round in Gerry's beloved bosun's chair. There was a definite sparkle in her baby-blue eyes, and two pink dots of excitement marked the centre of her cheeks, making her look more than ever like a petite porcelain doll. What with Belle's almost raven hair and altogether more generous curves, not many people would have guessed that they were mother and daughter.

'I'm phoning round all the newspapers, dear,' breezed Brenda, as though it was something she did every day.

'Why? Is something happening at the church?' Probably some kind of New Year fundraising event, thought Belle; though this did seem like overkill for a charity bring and buy sale.

Brenda let out a peal of laughter. 'Something? Honestly, Annabelle – only your own wedding! Or have you forgotten already?'

1

'But that's not till next summer!' protested Belle. 'Kieran only proposed last week.'

A faraway look came into her mother's eyes. 'I wish I could say I'd been proposed to on a horse-drawn sleigh ride through Prague,' she mused. 'Your father popped the question on a Christian youth camp in North Wales. I was frying sausages at the time.'

'It was a lovely romantic surprise,' admitted Belle, recollecting the shiver of excitement when Kieran, her boyfriend of three years, slipped a gorgeous solitaire ring onto her finger. 'But what's our wedding got to do with the papers?'

Brenda shook her head – still naturally blonde at forty-five – and gave a long-suffering sigh. 'Sweetheart, these things take months to plan. You'll be amazed how the time flies by. Before you know it the banns will be read and you'll be gliding up the aisle. And in the meantime, your father and I want to make sure that everybody knows how proud we are that you and Kieran have decided to get engaged. At long last,' she added, with just the faintest hint of reproach. 'Three years is long time to be courting, don't you think?'

Belle might well have answered that not everybody these days wanted to be wedded, bedded and divorced by twenty-five; but she was far more concerned with this newspaper business. She just plain hated any sort of limelight. 'Let me get this straight,' she said slowly. 'You're announcing our engagement in the *Cheltenham Courant*?'

'Not just the *Courant*, all the papers! You know, the nationals. Well, all the ones that matter. I didn't bother with the tabloids.'

'But Mum, that's just silly!' Belle was aghast. 'Why would anybody outside Cheltenham – or outside our family for that matter – want to know about me getting engaged to Kieran? I'm hardly Paris Hilton, am I? I'm a shop assistant!'

Her mother just smiled and shook her head, like one who had lived and knew these things. 'Don't be silly Annabelle, you're a senior retail adviser; and you want things to be done properly don't you?' Without giving Belle a chance to say no, actually she didn't, Brenda added, 'And think how exciting it's going to be, seeing your names in *The Times*.' She ignored the look of horror on her daughter's face, and went on, 'Besides, I'm sure lots of people will be interested when they see the announcement. Just you wait and see.'

Somewhere on the other side of the world, scarlet fingernails were tip-tapping on a computer keyboard, providing a rhythmic accompaniment to the typist's humming.

It wasn't the most melodic of sounds, but the only audience was a brightly coloured parakeet, preening its plumage in the golden summer sunshine, and it didn't seem to mind in the least.

The optical mouse glided across the mat and the screen scrolled through the pages of the newspaper website.

'Nothing much in the news today, Rita. Same old boring people, doing the same old boring stuff.' The parakeet cocked its head on one side. 'Maybe I'll give up and get some lunch.' But the screen still beckoned. 'Or maybe I'll just take a quick look back at the old family homestead. That's always good for a laugh.'

Sure enough, a couple of clicks brought up the *Cheltenham Courant* website, and the headline: STROUD MAN ATE MY GOLDFISH.

'What a country, Rita. And they call us uncivilised! Just look at all this – cheese rolling, a beauty contest for snails . . .' A sudden intake of breath. 'Oh my God. That's him!'

It was the *Courant*'s Births, Marriages and Deaths section. At the very top, a photograph smiled out, nicely presented in its own decorative box: it showed a middle-aged man in a dog collar, with one arm around a young woman and the other on the shoulder of a rather buff young guy. The girl was smiling and flashing an engagement ring. The caption read: 'Local vicar's daughter to marry: Annabelle Craine, daughter of Brenda and the Reverend Gerry Craine of St Jude's, Cheltenham, is to marry local journalist Kieran Sawyer on . . .'

Well.

Rita the parakeet broke the silence with a questioning squawk, but there was no response.

'Well, well, Gerry.' A glossy red fingernail tapped at the smiling face on the screen. 'A big family wedding. I hope you remember to send me an invitation. Otherwise, I might just have to remind you.'

Chapter 1

St Jude's vicarage, one chilly evening in January ...

'I know you'll think I'm a silly old fool,' said Gerry Craine, 'but you two are certain this is what you want, aren't you? I mean, absolutely certain?'

Belle Craine looked into her father's eyes and saw an awful lot of love, and just a little concern. 'Of course we don't think you're silly, Dad,' she answered in surprise. 'But you know we're sure about getting married.'

She and Kieran exchanged loving looks. 'We're meant to be together, Mr Craine,' said Kieran. 'Always have been, always will be.'

Belle and Kieran were sitting on squishy floor cushions in the front room at the vicarage, drinking hot chocolate with marshmallows and vaguely helping Brenda to sort out the wedding invitations. Outside the windows, a few fat snowflakes were drifting lazily down onto the wet January earth.

'Gerry, love, do try and stop worrying,' urged Brenda, who was working her way laboriously through a pile of old address books, in search of any relatives and friends who might have slipped through the net. 'You'll make the poor girl neurotic and give yourself another ulcer.'

Now in his forties, Gerry Craine was still the best-looking reverend in Cheltenham: tall and broad-shouldered, with amiable brown eyes and near-black hair that was only just beginning to show a few distinguished streaks of grey. He was also a man who could worry for Britain.

'I just want to them to be absolutely certain they're making the right decision,' he told his wife. 'They're both still very young, you know. And marriage is a very big commitment.'

'Come on love, you're not running one of your marriage preparation classes now. This is Annabelle and Kieran you're talking about, not some pair of daft teenagers.' Brenda finished jotting down the names of some distant cousins in Perth, then looked up. 'Anyway, marrying young didn't do us any harm, did it?' she pointed out. 'Or are you saying we should've waited?'

'No, of course I'm not, I'm just . . .' Gerry threw up his hands. 'I'm just doing my job, I guess,' he said with a rueful smile.

'We've given this an awful lot of thought,' stressed Kieran. 'In fact, I think we've known ever since the day we met that this was going to be for ever. Haven't we, Belle?'

Belle answered this unusually intense declaration with a coy smile. 'Well, the day *after* the day we met anyway,' she quipped. 'The day we met, all I could think was that you must be the worst newspaper reporter in the world, because you kept coming back to the shop to ask me all these really peculiar questions.'

Everybody laughed at the familiar story, and even Kieran chuckled. Sent by his editor to Belle's shop to do a feature on cosmetics for men, he'd taken one look at Belle and fallen hard. He'd spent the rest of the day trying to think up reasons to go back and talk to her again. He'd bought four different kinds of moisturiser before he finally plucked up the courage to ask her out.

'Hey, it's not easy being a bloke,' he protested good-naturedly. 'The minute you meet the girl of your dreams, you can't think of a sensible word to say, because all you really want to say is "marry me".' He gazed adoringly at his fiancée. 'Well, I plucked up the courage in the end. And lucky for me, she said yes.' He turned back to Gerry. 'I promise I'll take good care of her. Always.'

'He knows that, don't you, Dad?' Belle, who was sitting by her father's armchair, reached up and took his hand. His clasp felt reassuring and strong, a token of the deep emotional bond that had grown up between Gerry and his elder daughter. 'He's just trying to protect me. But Dad, we're not kids and we've been going out for nearly three years. It's not as if Kieran was my first boyfriend, is it? And don't forget he's a few years older than I am.'

'And what's the point of waiting,' Kieran added, 'when you know you've found the person you want to spend the rest of your life with?'

Gerry looked at the semi-circle of faces, hesitated for a moment, and then smiled. 'I know, I know, I'm just being an overprotective dad. You can't blame me though, in my job I see far too many marriages go wrong.'

Belle's promise was firm and unafraid. 'Ours won't be like that. We won't let it.'

He smiled down at the pair of them. 'I just want the best for you,' he said. 'Both of you.'

'We know.' Belle squeezed her dad's hand. We're so alike, she thought. Same hair, same features, same personality; it was no wonder they'd been so close ever since she was a baby. 'But Kieran is the best, so you can stop worrying, can't you?'

'Yes,' echoed Brenda with a chuckle. 'You can, can't you?'

Gerry laughed softly. 'Well . . . if you put it like that.'

Brenda was muttering to herself as she shuffled books and papers on the coffee table. 'Great-Aunt Margot, Cyril . . . oh no, not Cyril. Can't really leave him out though, he's a cousin. Emma and John – wait a minute though, wasn't it John who ran off with the au pair, or was that Andy and Jane?'

Belle got up and went over to her mum. 'Need a hand?'

'Several,' replied Brenda, raking harassed fingers through her hair and leaving her fringe standing on end. 'Please, somebody sort out this guest list,' she implored. 'I'm sure I've put some of these people down twice. And I've a nasty feeling a couple of them might be dead.'

Kieran's eyebrows shot up at the sight of Brenda's enormous hand-written list. 'Good grief, how many guests? Blimey, I know I don't have much in the way of family, but the Craines sure make up for it.'

Belle felt for Kieran; knew that the light-hearted comment concealed a deep sadness. He had accumulated plenty of good friends along the way, but when it came to family, he was definitely the poor relation compared to Belle. His father had left home before he was born, and his mother – unable to cope on her own – had allowed him and his sister to be taken into care. Their childhood and adolescence had been a succession of foster homes, sometimes together, sometimes apart, but always longing for something that they could call 'family'. Belle had always thought it was remarkable that Kieran was so well adjusted, with nobody but a sister who lived at the opposite end of the country, but as Belle and Kieran had grown closer he'd confided that he'd always felt there was something missing in his life, until he'd found her. And now, through Belle, he had found that precious something.

'I thought we'd agreed to keep it just to family and close friends,' Gerry remarked.

'These are family and close friends, dear! And this is only about two-thirds of the total. I haven't included all the people who are just coming to the evening do.'

Belle swallowed. 'Mum—'

But Brenda just ploughed on regardless. 'You can't invite one family member without the rest of them, can you? And Belle has family all over the place, don't you dear? And then there's all your friends, Kieran . . .'

Seeing all those names written down made Belle's head spin. All those people, she thought. All those people, coming to the church to stare at me and Kieran! The very idea made her feel queasy. When Brenda paused to take a breath, Belle cut in. 'Mum, do we really have to invite all of them?'

'Yes, of course we do!' laughed Brenda as if this was the funniest thing she'd ever heard.

'Why?'

'I told you, dear: because they're family!' Brenda explained with infant-school patience. 'And we don't want to upset anybody, do we?'

'Hm. I suppose.' Belle glanced down the list. 'But I don't even recognise some of these names! Who on earth is Gregory Ansell-Smith? And you can't possibly invite that awful Marion woman – isn't she the one who dropped Jax in the font and nearly split her head open?'

Brenda sighed. 'Trust me, when you're older you'll understand. It's all about being diplomatic. Take Cousin Les – we've no choice but to invite him. And if we invite him, we'll have to invite all the rest of the Liverpool Craines as well.'

'What, even that creep Sebastian?' shuddered Belle.

Brenda laughed uneasily. 'Don't worry dear, I'll keep him away from the bridesmaids. And the ... er ... pageboys. Then there are all your father's Church contacts. We absolutely can't avoid inviting the bishop ...'

'But couldn't we just—?'

'Just what?' enquired Kieran.

'Like you said, keep it small,' said Belle, feeling almost apologetic, which was rather ridiculous seeing as this was supposed to be her wedding.

'This is –'

'No, Mum, I mean really small. And, well, affordable. I mean, you and Dad aren't exactly millionaires, and neither are Kieran and I. Why don't we just invite a handful of guests who really mean a lot to us?'

'That might be nice,' pondered Gerry. 'Intimate and meaningful.'

'No, it wouldn't,' Brenda replied sharply. 'This is your wedding, Annabelle, your once-in-a-lifetime day, and we're going to do it properly.'

'Oh dear,' said Belle. 'I was afraid of that.'

It was halfway through the evening when Belle's sister Jax finally stomped home in her big black boots with the soles like car tyres and her favourite ripped combats, low-slung to show off the silver skull dangling from her belly button.

She was followed into the front room by a boulder-shaped youth with so many facial piercings that he jingled when he walked.

'Oh look,' Kieran nudged Belle in the ribs. 'It's Frankenstein and the monster.'

'Kieran!' she hissed back. 'Don't be so mean.' Belle tried to stifle a laugh, but only succeeded in getting mulled wine up her nose. 'Now look what you've made me do,' she scolded him, half-laughing and half-coughing.

Jax threw her elder sister a look of severe suspicion. 'If you two are taking the piss out of me, you're going to die,' she said, matter-of-factly.

'Don't use language like that, dear,' called Brenda from the hall, where she was struggling to hang up Razor's huge ankle-length leather trench-coat. She said it more as a kind of reflex than in any serious attempt to modify her daughter's behaviour. Even Brenda wasn't that much of an optimist.

'Where's Dad?' demanded Jax, once a natural blonde like her mother but currently sporting a fetching royal-blue crop that bore more than a passing resemblance to the new carpet in the doctor's surgery.

'He's visiting the sick,' replied Belle. 'Why?'

'What!' Jax was considerably less than impressed. 'He's out? Again? But me and Razor wanted him to give us a lift to Cirencester.' She lowered her voice to an irritable whisper, out of earshot of her keen-eared mother. 'There's an all-nighter in the big tithe barn, bring your own sleeping bag.'

Belle didn't normally get involved in her sister's social life, but this was just preposterous. 'Oh come on,' she cut in. 'You know Dad would never let you go to something like that!'

Jax folded her arms and scowled. 'He would if he thought we were going to spend the night at Razor's Auntie Jen's,' she retorted.

'You'd lie to Dad?'

'And you wouldn't?'

'No.'

'Liar.'

The two sisters glared at each other from opposite sides of the room. It was Jax's boyfriend, the rock-like Razor, who broke the silence. From the look of him, you'd have expected him to have the sort of voice that came from eating gravel; but when he did speak, it was in the embarrassing public school accent he just knew he was never going to be able to get rid of. Wealthy parents could be such a bummer. 'Hello Mrs Craine,' he said, clearing his throat as she walked into the room, a little flushed after her tussle with the two-ton coat. 'You're looking very nice this evening.'

'Thank you, Marcus,' smiled Brenda, who couldn't and wouldn't come to terms with calling anybody Razor. She peered a little more closely at his face. 'Is your eyebrow all right, dear? It looks awfully sore.'

Razor flushed slightly and gingerly prodded it. 'Actually I think it might be going a bit septic, Mrs C,' he admitted sheepishly. 'I s'pose I should've sterilised the needle or something.'

'Oh Marcus, you silly, silly boy. I hope you're up to date with your tetanus injections. Come along, you'd better let me clean it up.' Abandoning her pile of address books, Brenda got to her feet and chivvied Razor in the direction of the nearest first aid kit.

That left just Belle, Kieran and a very disgruntled Jax.

'Poor Razor,' commented Kieran, for want of anything else to say.

Jax glowered. 'Razor's a prat.'

'That's not a very nice thing to say about your boyfriend,' commented Belle.

'Shut up. You're a prat too. You're all prats.'

'Don't worry Jax, you'll grow out of being unpleasant,' observed Kieran impishly; 'right now you can't help yourself – it's just the hormones.' For all her hard exterior, Jax blushed crimson, and couldn't think of a single clever thing to say in reply. Blushing and going all squishy-brained was something that often happened when Kieran spoke to her, though of course she'd die rather than admit it to anyone else. Especially Kieran himself.

Belle shut Kieran up with a poke in the ribs. She'd promised herself – and her mother – that she and her little sister were going to be on good terms for the next six months if it killed them. And the way things were going, somebody was certainly going to die. 'We've been planning a few things for the wedding,' she said with a conscious effort at niceness as Jax flung herself into her father's armchair.

'So?'

'So we were wondering if there's anybody you'd like to invite, weren't we Kieran?'

This time it was a well-placed elbow that jolted Kieran into responding. 'We were? Oh. Yes, definitely. I'm sure there must be somebody you'd like to have along. Razor, perhaps?'

'No, there isn't, OK?'

'We're really looking forward to having you there,' Belle went on.

'Yeah, right! Like you think I'll fit right in with all your boring friends.'

'We do very much want you there, really we do. And actually, I was sort of hoping . . .' She remembered what her mother had said, only the other day: 'I'd so love it dear, it'd make my day complete,' and forced herself to be convincingly enthusiastic. 'Kieran and I were sort of hoping you'd be a bridesmaid.'

For a moment, Jax just stared open-mouthed at her sister, momentarily deprived of the power of speech. Then she threw back her head and laughed until her mascara ran.

Unlike sporty Kieran, Belle had never been one for exercise: in fact she absolutely despised it. Running around in the mud or jumping up and down for no good reason had always struck her as uniquely pointless. Being rubbish at ball games at school hadn't helped either. On the last day of school she'd made a bonfire of all her PE kit and sworn a silent oath never to set foot in a sports centre again.

So the New You Fitness Club wasn't perhaps the first place you'd expect to find her – but nevertheless she was there, spending an hour of her precious day off lifting weights and pounding tedious miles on a treadmill – all in aid of New You's special 'Buff Bride' exercise course. The course was a series of punishing one-hour sessions, spread out over a couple of months and supervised by an instructor. It wasn't just a lot of jumping around, either; there was a diet to follow too. Not that Belle was doing very well on it. As she took a breather with her best friend Ros she was nibbling on a contraband Snickers bar.

It was good having fitness fanatic Ros along, to give her a bit of moral support. In fact, Belle seriously doubted if she'd ever have got past the front door of the gym without Ros to egg her on.

'You know, I think it's starting to work,' said Ros, cheerfully flicking glossy brown hair out of her eyes. 'You're really beginning to get some definition in those lower-body muscles.'

Belle contemplated her thighs, quivering like two sweaty pink jellies after twenty minutes of pumping up and down on the pedals of an exercise bike. 'It's OK, Ros, you don't have to lie,' she declared bravely. 'I'm a lardy lump and I know it.'

'You're not lardy and you're not a lump!' retorted Ros with a squeal of laughter. 'You're just . . . curvy.'

'Fat,' Belle corrected her.

'Shapely.'

'Tubby.'

'Well-proportioned.'

'The human blimp.'

'Don't talk rubbish! At least you're woman-shaped.' Ros stopped eating raw carrot sticks for a moment and jiggled her upper half; or rather, tried to. 'Look at my boobs – if you've got a microscope handy. They're like two aspirins on an ironing board.'

They shared a giggle and a couple of bites of the chocolate bar Belle had smuggled in. 'OK, point taken. Nobody's perfect. But at this rate I'm never going to be a Buff Bride, am I? And with you buggering off to see the world for the best part of a year, who's going to motivate me to stick at it?'

'You are! Just think of the look on Kieran's face when he sees you on your wedding day. And if I'm flying back from the other side of the world just to be your chief bridesmaid, I'm expecting you to be nothing less than drop-dead gorgeous for Kieran.'

Belle shrugged. 'Oh, everybody looks good in a wedding dress anyway.'

Ros winked. 'I didn't mean with your dress on.'

God I'm going to miss you, Ros, thought Belle as they chatted. The two of them had been mates on and off ever since their last year at school, when they were both desperate to get out of uniform and into the world of work. But Ros had grown bored with her office job, and had just inherited a bit of money, so what better time to take a year off and see the world? Why did it have to be now though, with the wedding looming on the horizon and Belle struggling to stick to her new exercise regime?

'I've come to a decision,' she announced. 'You can't go. You've got to cancel everything and stay here with me. Otherwise I'll stuff myself with cake and explode long before I ever get up the aisle.'

'Sorry mate, I've already bought the tickets.' Ros's expression turned thoughtful. 'Tell you what though – why don't you escape from all this and come with me?'

'What? Aagh.' Belle spluttered as a peanut went down the wrong way.

Ros patted her on the back. 'I'm serious, Belle. If all of this is getting you down, say "sod it", pack a bag and take some time out, just for yourself. Why shouldn't you? It's your life – not your mother's, or Kieran's, or anybody else's.'

For a fleeting second, the prospect seemed curiously appealing. No pressure, no limelight, no silly pretentious announcements in *The Times*; new things to see, new challenges ... But even before that second had passed, Belle knew it was just a silly fantasy, and not for her in a million years. Quite apart from anything else, it was way, way, way too scary for somebody like her. 'Nice idea, Ros, but no thanks.'

'You're chicken!'

'No, I'm not,' she protested. 'Well OK, maybe I am a bit. But that's not the point. Kieran makes me happy and I'm going to marry him in six months' time, and we're going to have a home together, and that's what I want. It's what I've always wanted, more than anything – you of all people know that.' Her eyes sought Ros's, urging her to understand. 'I'm not an adventurer like you. Not a go-getter. I'm just ... I don't know ... one of life's ordinary people.'

Ros shook her head and tutted. 'No such thing as ordinary.'

'You wouldn't say that if you were me.'

'Ah well, you can't say I didn't try. Anyway, come rain or shine I'm going to be on that plane next week, so you're just going to have to stick to the plan all on your own. You can do it!'

'If you say so ... Couldn't you stay just a few more weeks? I need you

11

here to keep me sane! And stop me murdering my sister,' she added under her breath.

'Jax? What's little sis done now?' Ros enquired.

'I asked her if she'd be a bridesmaid – just to please Mum – and I asked her nicely, honestly I did. Anyhow, when she'd finished laughing, she said she'd rather stuff a live wasp up her nose.'

'Not a definite yes, then?' Ros shrugged. 'Never mind, it's her loss. I bet you've got tons of cousins and nieces and what-have-you who'd love to be bridesmaids. And you've got to admit, she wouldn't exactly ... blend in.'

Belle sighed. 'True. But there's only one Jax. And she may be a pain in the bum sometimes, but it would mean a lot to Mum to see her following me up the aisle in a pretty dress.'

'Jax? In a dress?' Ros considered the concept. 'No, it's no good, I just can't see it.'

'Me neither,' lamented Belle. 'So what do I do? Give up?'

'Half an hour on the weights,' replied Ros. 'And then on to the treadmill. You want to be a buff bride for this perfect husband of yours, don't you?'

Chapter 2

It was a quiet Monday morning in early January at Green Goddess, with nothing much for the staff to do. But Waylon Smith the store manager could always find something to occupy them, even if it was just counting bars of soap. Belle had been swift to learn the art of looking busy.

'I really don't know why you're complaining,' said Lily Broome, doggedly reassembling a pyramid of bath bombs that a customer with a double buggy had just ploughed straight through. 'I really don't. God, Belle, I wish my Rick wanted to spend a load of money on me. Mind you,' she admitted thoughtfully, tossing a brown plait over her shoulder, 'I wouldn't want him to spend it on a wedding. I think we'd both rather have a Honda Goldwing ... though I guess we'd end up saving it for when we have sprogs. You have to be a millionaire these days to have kids.'

'Or stage a wedding,' interjected Belle. 'And believe me, my parents are anything but millionaires. I mean, OK, the dressmaker's doing the job for free because she's a friend, and there's a caterer in the congregation who's giving them a big discount on the buffet. But – two hundred and fifty guests, I ask you! Bye-bye Mum and Dad's holiday budget for the next twenty years.'

She sighed, shook her head in incomprehension and went back to totting-up the weekend's sales figures, laboriously recording every sale, exchange and return. Green Goddess might have impeccable organic credentials, but its administrative procedures were still firmly stuck in the nineteenth century. Hair gel was up, foot cream was down and that black liquorice face mask still wasn't shifting, even with thirty per cent off.

Being sales supervisor in an organic toiletries shop might not be the big time, but Belle didn't just enjoy it: she took it seriously too. In fact she tended to take most things seriously, which was probably at least partly the result of having a vicar for a dad. Not that Belle was what people might call 'religious', not if that meant going to church a lot and name-checking God at every possible opportunity. Having been brought up surrounded by people for whom faith was a natural part of everyday life, it had quite simply never been a big issue for her. Jax might make a song and dance about rejecting conventional religion; but it was a part of Belle, something she seldom mentioned but would have felt very strange without.

'I don't get this,' said Lily, a solidly built girl who raced motorbikes and sidecars at the weekends, with her long-time partner Rick. 'I thought you wanted to get married. You've been going on about it for months.'

'I do, I really do!' Belle threw down her pen and ruffled her shoulder-length dark hair, making it even more tangled. 'I'm just a bit worried, that's all. Mum and Dad aren't that well off. They can't afford to go wasting money on my dream wedding.'

'Well no, I guess not. But some parents are obsessed with doing things properly, whether they can afford it or not. And you and Kieran haven't got pots of money either, have you?'

'Too right we haven't,' agreed Belle gloomily. 'Especially now we're house-hunting. And now Mum's got this weird idea that the whole world wants to know her daughter's getting married, like we're posh or something. She even put an ad in *The Times*, can you believe that? I nearly died of embarrassment.'

Lily wrinkled her freckled nose. 'You know, each to their own and all that. If you're not happy, can't you just put your foot down and tell her that's not what you want?'

'It's a bit late now.' Belle fiddled with her biro. 'Besides, I was going to ask Mum to tone it all down a bit,' she admitted, 'but then she started saying how organising her daughter's wedding is going to be the most fulfilling thing she's ever done, and I simply couldn't.' She shrugged wearily. 'I only hope the caterer gives them a *really* big discount.'

'You've got a younger sister haven't you?' Lily pointed out, deftly catching a bath bomb as it rolled towards the end of the line. 'Can't your mum wait a bit and then organise her wedding instead?'

Belle laughed so hard her head nearly fell off. 'Jax? Get married? Sell her soul to a mere male? Give me a break, Lily, my little sister thinks being asked to sling a pizza in the microwave is slave labour.'

Very slowly and cautiously, Lily eased herself away from the sweetly scented pyramid and admired her handiwork. 'Looks like you'll just have to shut up and enjoy all the attention then,' she concluded.

'That's the trouble,' admitted Belle. 'I don't. Being the centre of attention isn't me at all, you know that. Jax is the diva of the family. Me, I prefer the back row of the chorus line every time.'

'Too bad.' Lily studied the perfect symmetry of her creation. 'Ah, who says shopwork's not rewarding? Look at that for a pyramid.'

'Very nice,' agreed Belle. 'But if that third row of bath bombs is supposed to be all white, why's there a pink one,' she pointed, 'there?'

'Shit, you weren't supposed to notice that,' said Lily, who had only just noticed it herself. She advanced a hand gingerly towards the rogue rose-coloured sphere. 'I'll have to take it out now.'

'Good God no, don't do that!' urged Belle. 'You'll have the whole lot over again. Just ignore it.'

'But I know it's there now! I can't stop looking at it.'

'Then stick something in front of it! A point-of-sale display or something.'

They both looked round the shop for something suitable. Then Lily pounced. 'Ha! The very thing.' She dragged over last year's large plywood cut-out of a smiling bride from behind the wedding cosmetics display, blew off a film of dust and plonked it right in front of the pyramid, almost square on to the front door of the shop. 'There you go, boss, now every time you look up from the till you'll be reminded of your forthcoming special day.'

'Gee thanks.' Belle pulled a face, and would probably have said something extremely rude if Waylon the branch manager hadn't chosen that moment to push through the door from the Regent Arcade, bottom first and dragging a laden trolley behind him.

'A bit of help would be nice.' He swung round and eyed his staff suspiciously. 'I hope you two haven't just been standing around doing nothing while I've been gone.'

'Of course not. We've been . . . merchandising, haven't we Lily.'

'Yeah, merchandising. Lots of it, all over the place.'

Waylon caught sight of the cut-out bride. 'Well, well, you're on the ball, I'll give you that,' he commented. Blank looks returned his gaze. 'How did you know I was going to get you to move that somewhere more visible? Had a call from the Gloucester office, have we?'

'Er . . .'

'About the new seasonal in-store promotion? Come on girls, help me get this lot into the stockroom before a customer trips over it. Idiot driver delivered it to the arcade manager's office instead of round the back to the delivery entrance.'

'What new promotion?' enquired Belle as the three of them lugged the stock off the sales floor.

'Spring Brides,' replied Waylon, brushing Peachy Pink talc-free dusting powder off his black shirt and trousers. 'Cosmetics and toiletries for spring weddings, all that stuff. They're even sending us a beautician for a couple of days, to do in-store bridal facials.'

Belle groaned. Was there no escape from the world of weddings? 'But it's not spring, it's only January!' she protested.

15

Lily chuckled and patted Belle on the shoulder. 'Ah, but when there's love in your heart it's always spring. You should know that, Belle.'

Jacqueline Craine had not answered to the full version of her name since at the age of twelve she had pierced her ears with two ice cubes and a needle, hacked at her hair with her dad's garden shears and announced to the world that henceforth she was to be known as Jax.

It was ironic really. Brenda Craine had put an awful lot of thought into making sure her daughters had nice, middle-class names that would ease their passage in society, in a way that being called Brenda had never done for her. And what did the two of them do? They promptly mangled those nice names beyond recognition and metamorphosed into Jax and Belle.

With Belle though, shortening her name was mostly a matter of convenience; there'd never been much of the rebel about her. But with Jax, it was a ferocious style statement. If Jax had ever met her alter ego Jacqueline in the street, they'd both have run a mile.

It was lunchtime at St Jude's – one of Cheltenham's longest-established private schools – and the senior students were packing the common room to eat their Fair Trade granola bars and yoghurts. Nobody would've been seen dead eating school dinners. Rumour had it that if you did eat one, your arteries would instantly fur up and you'd keel over anyway. St Jude's set great store by the public-school tradition of horrible food and sport in all weathers.

Scholarship girl Jax settled on a chair, swung her heavily booted feet up onto the table, and made an announcement: 'I bloody hate my sister.'

Her boyfriend Razor, aka Marcus Stamford-Jones, gingerly negotiated a way round his new lip piercing with a mouthful of crusty baguette. There was a high price to pay in pain if you wanted to achieve the perfect anti-Establishment look. 'Has she been bullying you again?'

Jax gave him a look she'd borrowed from Medusa. 'Bullying? Get real, Razor, do you really think I'd let anyone bully me? Especially Princess Goody Two-Shoes?'

'Sorry, I didn't think.'

'So what's new?' Jax leaned over and helped herself to a large bite from her boyfriend's baguette. 'But if you mean, has she been going on about that stupid wedding of hers, then yes.' She chewed irritably. 'It's like she thinks the whole world revolves around her or something.'

Razor shrugged. 'Women are like that though, aren't they?'

'Like what?'

Razor blundered on. 'A bit, you know, obsessed with big frilly dresses and all that stuff.'

'I'm not!' snapped Jax.

'N-no, of course not, I mean you're not a – a—'

'A what? A woman?' She threw him a withering look. 'Well thank you very much, Casanova.'

Razor sighed. He loved Jax dearly but this was a game he could never win. When she was in one of her argumentative moods, he could have suggested that water was wet and she'd have disagreed with him. 'I meant, you know, you're only just seventeen aren't you? You might change your mind when you're as old as your sister is.'

'Twenty-four?' Jax shuddered. 'God, I don't even want to think about that, it's practically thirty. And anyway, my precious sister came out of the womb middle-aged. Well, she might not care about selling herself into bondage, but as far as I'm concerned, you can stuff marriage. In fact, they ought to ban it,' she added with the self-righteous recklessness of the young and frighteningly inexperienced.

'Oh,' said Razor.

'Oh what?' demanded Jax.

'Just ... oh. So you're not going to go along with Belle's wedding plans then?'

Jax smiled savagely. 'What do you think?'

There was no such thing as a quiet day at the offices of the *Cheltenham Courant*. Like every other local paper in every other provincial town, it was understaffed, underfunded and over budget. And for a young journalist like Kieran Sawyer who was hankering to pen prize-winning features about politics and major world issues, it was depressing to know that the *Courant* always sold twice as many copies when there was a cute kid or a furry animal on the front page. And this was 'intellectual' Cheltenham: town of famous literary festivals, and more authors per square inch than there were fleas on a hedgehog.

On this particular Monday, Kieran was doing his best to finish up a profile of a woman who habitually did all her Christmas shopping for the following year on Boxing Day. It wasn't much of a feature really, but then again this was January, when traditionally nothing ever happened. The woman in question was going to be pictured in glorious colour on the front page of the Saturday magazine with her fluffy little shih-tzu, both wearing furry reindeer antlers and loaded up with next year's presents. If that didn't boost sales, nothing would.

His boss, Sandra the features editor, walked by and leaned over the back of his PC, tapping the screen to get his attention.

Kieran started. 'What? Oh, sorry, I was miles away.'

'How's the mad woman story coming along?'

'Nearly there, just need a few more quotes to jazz it up. Mind if I disappear for an hour or so this afternoon?'

A knowing smile crept across Sandra's lips. They were rather scary lips: Sandra favoured the sort of lipsticks that made her mouth look like a bloody slash in the middle of her face. It was the sort of face that people seldom said 'no' to. 'What is it this time – somebody give you free tickets to that new lap-dancing joint in Gloucester?'

'No! Well, yes,' Kieran admitted, turning a little pink, 'but I gave them to Colin on the news desk. It's Belle,' he confessed. 'Or, her mother really. I sort of almost promised I might pop in sometime this afternoon to lend her a bit of moral support.'

'Moral support? Why, what's she doing – auditioning as a pole dancer?'

It occurred to Kieran that something of that order might actually be easier to handle. 'No,' he replied with a hint of pure dread in his voice, 'Belle and Jax are talking bridesmaids' dresses.'

Belle turned the corner into St Jude's Square and headed for the vicarage. It was the only home she'd ever known, if you didn't count her own little studio flat in town, and it was strange to think that when Gerry retired, he and Belle's mum would have to move away.

Like her dad, she wasn't a big fan of change; if things were OK already, why do something that might make them worse? This was one of the few areas where she and Kieran disagreed. He was all for taking chances, reaching for the top, even if it meant accepting the risk that he might fall. Belle knew she was a chronic underachiever, but basically she kind of liked it that way.

St Jude's vicarage was a three-storey, cream-rendered house built in the 1850s, back in the days when vicars had huge families to accommodate. Nowadays it was a bit on the big side, but its location was ideal: right opposite the church and its encircling horse chestnut trees, complete with a prime view of fluffy-tailed squirrels scampering around in the early-morning sunshine.

With just the faintest twinge of apprehension, Belle pushed open the wrought iron gate and walked up the path to the front door. The old pull-out doorbell set into the wall still worked, but Belle had her own key so she just walked straight in. Oh dear, she thought as she turned the key; I hope she's in a better mood today. That Godzilla act of hers is seriously stress-inducing.

Good mood or not, it was pretty obvious that Jax was at home, because loud music was thundering down the stairs from her room and her beloved clumpy black boots were lying discarded halfway down the hall, for her mother to clear up or her father to fall over. Belle nudged them out of the way with her toe. She drew the line at tidying up after her sister, even if she did want to ask her a favour today.

Brenda and Kieran were downstairs in the basement kitchen, where Brenda was busy baking fruit scones for the next church social and Kieran was equally busy eating them.

'Kieran – you made it!'

'Greetings, comely wench. Didn't I promise I'd leave work early if I could?' Kieran stood up, wrapped his arms round his fiancée and gave her a big buttery, crumby kiss, and Belle felt her heart grow light as candyfloss and start fluttering in her chest, the selfsame way it had fluttered on their very first date at the pizza restaurant, when Belle had been terrified to eat or drink in case she spilled it down her front and spoiled everything. What you've got here truly is the real thing, she reminded herself, never forget that. You've always known marrying Kieran is the right thing to do, so stop worrying about stuff that doesn't matter.

'Hello, darling.' She licked butter off her lips. 'I hope you're not expecting home-baked scones every day when we're married.'

Kieran's hazel eyes twinkled. 'Of course I am. And home-made strawberry jam, but make sure there aren't any bits in it.'

Belle folded her arms. 'Anything else?' she enquired with a smile.

'Well, while you're at it, Wife-to-Be, you might as well learn how to churn your own butter, and maybe brew a few kegs of— Why are you looking at me like that? Belle?' He dodged aside but he wasn't quick enough. 'Ow, get off! Stop tickling me!'

He backed away, but Belle pursued him round the table, laughing even more than he was. 'I'll stop tickling when you stop behaving like Henry the Eighth!'

'Get your elbows out of my scone mix!' scolded Brenda with a smile, whipping the bowl away before Kieran could trail the sleeve of his jumper in it. 'I thought you two were here to sort out Jacqueline's bridesmaid's dress, not get in my way.'

The tickling stopped, and the hilarity faded from Kieran's face. 'Aw, Mrs C, did you have to mention that?'

'I can't imagine why you're worried about talking to Jacqueline,' breezed Brenda. 'I know she can be a little bit prickly sometimes, but she's already said she'll do it. I can't wait to see her all dressed up and gorgeous; it'll be a real treat, I can tell you.'

Not so much a treat as a miracle, thought Belle, who was still slightly suspicious of Jax's sudden acceptance. 'Come on then, Tiger,' she said, taking Kieran by the hand, 'I guess we'd better go up and see the Empress of Grump.'

'She's your bridesmaid, not mine,' Kieran pointed out hopefully. 'Are you quite sure you need me to come up too?'

'Nice try,' Belle commended him. 'Now get up those stairs before I spank you.'

For a moment, Kieran considered putting up some serious resistance. After all, it was the best offer he'd had all day.

Standing on the landing outside Jax's closed door, Belle experienced the not-so-dulcet tones of Machine Head as they thudded into her soles of her feet through the floorboards. It felt a bit like a rather brutal kind of reflexology. She had to raise her voice to twice its normal volume before Kieran could make out what she was saying.

'I reckon you should go in first,' she said with the sweetest of smiles. 'After all, she's only saying she'll do it because of you.'

'Me?' Kieran was aghast. 'What have I got to do with it?'

Belle laughed. 'Oh come on darling, you know she fancies you like mad. Why do you think she's so snotty to me all the time?'

'I thought it was just a sister thing.'

'Well ... yes. That too. But this is definitely a bad case of the green-eyed monster. Face it Kieran, you're irresistible to seventeen-year-old heavy metal freaks with a blue hair complex.'

'I'm ... honoured.'

In the end it was Belle who hammered on the door, waited the requisite ten seconds and then walked in.

Jax was sitting at her PC, silently headbanging along to the CD as she did her History homework. When she realised she wasn't alone, she swung round on her chair, turned red at the sight of Kieran, and hammered the 'eject' button on the CD drive. 'I never said you could come in! Did I say you could come in?'

'I've no idea,' replied Belle. 'Would we have heard you if you had?'

Jax scowled.

'Anyway, we're here now,' pointed out Kieran. 'And you did say we could talk about you being a bridesmaid.'

Just the merest hint of a smirk crept across Jax's face and then slunk away again. 'Oh yes, I did, didn't I?'

Belle scented imminent disaster. 'Oh Jax, you haven't changed your mind, have you? You're not going to mess us about? You know how much it means to Mum.'

'No, I'll do it all right,' replied Jax. 'I'll walk down your poxy aisle.' Kieran's face relaxed into a broad smile. Belle ought to have been relieved too, but she had a nasty feeling there was a great big 'but' coming up. And she was right. 'But ... I'll only do it on one condition.'

I knew it, thought Belle. I just knew it. 'What condition?' she demanded.

Jax savoured the moment, and made it last. Right now she had them both in the palm of her hand, and she was absolutely loving it.

'Jax,' urged Kieran. And she finally took pity on him.

'I want to choose my own outfit,' she announced.

'Oh.' Belle exchanged looks of relief with Kieran. She'd been expecting something much, much worse than that. Like being allowed to ride a motorbike up the aisle, or substitute 'Love divine, all loves excelling' with 'Bring your daughter to the slaughter'. 'Well, of course you do.' She rummaged in her bag. 'In fact we've bought a whole load of pictures of dresses to show you, from lots of different catalogues, so you can pick the one you like best. We were thinking maybe aubergine and cream, but if you—'

'No, you don't get it,' cut in Jax. 'I want to really choose it myself, not just pick it from some crap list of boring stuff you've provided.'

'Oh,' said Belle and Kieran in unison.

Jax crossed her legs, smiled and sat back in her chair. 'And I'm absolutely, definitely NOT wearing a dress. Not for anybody.'

Chapter 3

As the radio alarm assaulted her ears with the Chelt FM breakfast show, Belle opened one eye, yawned, stretched and became aware of something rather odd. She'd just woken up in her own bed. Alone.

As she slid her feet into her fluffy mules and padded off to the bathroom, she tried to remember the last time she'd spent the night at her own flat, without Kieran. It was probably only a few weeks ago, but it felt like years. In the normal world they'd probably have been living together for ages by now, but the world wasn't normal when your dad was a vicar. Belle knew her dad would never actually condemn them for 'living in sin', but she also knew it would make things difficult for him. Not to mention her mother's inevitable diatribe about never being able to hold her head up in public again. All things considered, it was just a whole lot easier to at least pretend to be living separate lives until they got married.

Throughout their three years together, the relationship had always been potentially permanent but, in recent months, the process had somehow accelerated. All the same, Belle had been genuinely stunned when Kieran finally proposed on that magical weekend away. Marriage was no longer something that would probably happen someday; suddenly, it was about to happen any minute – and the feeling was both exhilarating and scary.

Although not living together, the two of them had fallen into a routine that made perfect sense, spending most nights at Kieran's place. For a start, Kieran's flat was so much nicer than Belle's: part of a development in chi-chi Montpellier, just across Imperial Gardens from Belle's mum and dad in St Jude's. And to say it was a bit bigger than Belle's was like saying King Kong was a teensy bit larger than the average ape.

Belle's euphemistically named 'studio flat' was more of a converted boxroom with pretensions. The way the developer had managed to squeeze in a shower room and a kitchenette was a miracle of miniaturisation, even if the wall-mounted, fold-down bed did have to play the role of sofa as well, because there simply wasn't room for one. Add to this the fact that the flat was in a part of town known locally as 'Ambush Alley', and it wasn't really that surprising that Belle and Kieran usually ended up round his place at the end of the evening. Nor that Kieran kept nagging her to terminate her lease and move into his place until the wedding, whatever her mum and dad – or the bishop – might say.

Stepping out of the shower and into a nice warm bathrobe, Belle looked around her and knew, for all practical purposes, he was right. Everything he said about rent being 'dead money' made perfect sense. And why insist on living all the way out here, when she could be with Kieran, and so much more conveniently situated for work as well as her family?

She wriggled the corner of a towel into her waterlogged ear. If she rang the agency today, she could be out of the flat and into Kieran's in a month. No more rent, no more turning on the TV and seeing the man next door on *Crimewatch*, no more arguments with the landlord about repairs that never got done. She and Kieran could quite simply spend the next few months living together, while they looked around for the right property to buy. But however sensible it might be, she just couldn't do it; though if she was completely honest with herself, she couldn't be certain that it was just because of vague moral misgivings, or worries about what her parents might think.

Still, hey, why worry? In six months' time the whole question would be academic, since once they were married she'd hardly need her own pad to scuttle back to.

Would she?

As she got dressed, to a soundtrack of the couple overhead having a blazing row, Belle mentally listed the thousand and one reasons for moving out. But even when she'd finished, there was a curious, inexplicable reluctance buried deep in the pit of her stomach. Surely I can't be feeling nostalgic about this hole, she thought. So what's going on? Am I trying to hold onto something else? My independence, maybe?

Belle laughed aloud at that thought. All she'd ever wanted, since she was a little girl, was to get married and have a happy family life, the same as her mum and dad. It might be old-fashioned, like her insistence on not living together, and Jax might think it was downright traitorous to the female sex, but it was just the way she was. Work she'd always regarded as a way of marking time, not a bid for the pinnacle of success. It was nice to do well sometimes, but it didn't matter to her enough to screw up her life for a few extra quid a week. And as for her independence . . . well, that had never really been on the agenda. Or at least, it never had before she started thinking about letting it go.

Pull yourself together Belle, she told herself sternly. You're getting married, it's going to be the best thing you've ever done, and it's about time you made that call to the agency. Get a move on with mapping out your future. Or are you planning to move Kieran in here and squeeze a couple of hundred wedding guests into a six-by-ten kitchenette?

If nothing else, it was an entertaining thought.

When it came to independence, Jax had it all worked out. In fact it was one of her favourite words, along with expressions like 'it's not fair', 'whatever!', 'you can't make me' and 'I need you to give me some more money.' But this morning things weren't going all her way.

'Why do I have to do it?' moaned Jax as her mother thrust a mop and a bottle of bathroom cleaner into her hands.

'Because you made the mess,' replied Brenda, turning back to the washing up.

'But—'

'You're the one who got blue hair dye all over the tiles, so you can clear it up.' The corners of Jax's mouth turned down and she glared at her mother's back. 'And don't scowl at me like that, dear, it makes you look like a constipated frog.'

Jax's scowl only deepened. 'But it's not fair!' she protested. 'I've got to get to school, it's my AS level mocks in a fortnight's time, you know.'

As if anybody could forget. Somehow, Jax had managed to turn her forthcoming exams into the perfect, all-purpose excuse for not doing anything she didn't want to do. There was just one fly in the ointment: the only person who fell for it was Dad. Other people were prone to pointing out that she spent more time shaving patterns into her eyebrows or writing lyrics for Throbbing Viscera, Razor's new goth-metal band, than she did actually studying. Then again, Jax didn't need to study much; she was irritatingly, sickeningly bright.

'You've got a free period first thing,' her mother reminded her, scrubbing industriously at a rock-hard blob of muesli on a breakfast bowl. 'So you've got plenty of time to clean up before you go.' She looked back at her daughter over her shoulder. 'Off you go then, Jacqueline.' Jax didn't move. 'The sooner you start, the sooner you'll be done.'

With extremely bad grace, Jax stomped off upstairs, hoping to get away with a quick flick of the J-Cloth and a squirt of air-freshener. But two minutes later her mother followed her up, and stood in the bathroom doorway chatting while Jax went about her task with the kind of malevolence that only adolescents can muster.

'Oh, your cousin Trixie was on the phone last night, did I tell you?'

Jax's back stiffened like the hackles on a very pissed-off Rottweiler. 'That cow? What did she want?'

'Now, now, Jacqueline. She's not a cow, she's your cousin. I know she's a bit ... well ... different from you, but you're almost the same age. There's absolutely no reason why you two shouldn't be really good friends.'

'No – apart from the fact that she's a conniving bitch and I trust her about as far as I could throw her.' Jax attacked the bathroom tiles with the full force of her venom, raising a froth of blue bubbles. 'Which is about six inches,' she muttered as an afterthought, 'seeing as she's such a fat cow.'

Her mum sighed and cocked her head on one side. 'You're not still angry about that boyfriend thing, are you? I'm sure it was just a misunderstanding.'

Jax flung her screwed-up cloth into the bucket. 'Mum! Why do you always have to think the best of people? How many boyfriends have I had in the last two years? Three. And how many has she stolen off me? Two!'

Brenda frowned. 'Don't you think you're being a little overdramatic?'

'Overdramatic? Mum, she's poison! She steals them off me just because she can, then gets bored with them in about five minutes and gives them the push.' Jax straightened up and regarded her handiwork. 'Well, I've got Razor now and she's not making a hat-trick out of him and that's all there is to it.'

'I'm sure she wouldn't—'

'Oh yes she would.' Jax's expression altered from hostility to suspicion. 'So what did she want anyway?'

'Oh, nothing special. She just rang to thank us for her invitation. She's really looking forward to the wedding.'

'I bet she is,' said Jax darkly. 'They have men at weddings.'

'And she sends you her love and says she ... er ... can't wait to see you in your bridesmaid's dress.'

This produced a grunt. 'Then she'll wait a long time, won't she?'

There was a look of baffled despair on Brenda Craine's face. She came into the room and perched on the edge of the bath. 'Jacqueline love, you're not going to keep this up long, are you?'

'Keep what up?'

'This nonsense about not wearing a dress at your sister's wedding.'

Jax's mouth set into a defiant line. 'It's not nonsense. Sorry, Mum, but I'm not compromising my principles just so Trixie can have a good laugh at me looking like a pink blancmange.'

'Principles?' Brenda scratched her head and looked puzzled. 'Actually I'm a bit hazy on that. What principles are you talking about, exactly?'

Her daughter grabbed her bucket, drew herself up to her full height (five feet five, plus three inches extra with the platform boots) and declared: 'Just principles, OK?'

Then she headed for the door before her mother ground her down and forced her to admit that when it came to principles, Jacqueline Craine didn't really have any.

It was lunchtime in the Everyman Theatre coffee bar, and Kieran had sneaked away from his desk at the *Courant* for half an hour.

He liked to get out of the office at lunchtime whenever he could, and he was gradually working his way round all the cafés, pubs and wine bars in Cheltenham: you never knew when you might pick up a bit of gossip or an idea for a story, just from a spot of idle eavesdropping. Besides, it gave him a chance to catch up on the news with his old mate Oz.

Kieran had known Oz Hepplewhite ever since secondary school, where the two of them had developed a mutually beneficial relationship. Oz helped Kieran with his maths homework and fed him the answers in class, and Kieran beat up anybody who thought that Oswald was a stupid name that merited its owner a good kicking behind the bike-sheds.

Indeed, it was Kieran who had persuaded him to start calling himself Oz when they went to university, on the grounds that Oswald's name was terminally uncool – rather like the rest of him. Unfortunately, that was where the great transformation had stalled in its tracks. A decade or so later, Oz was just the same as he'd always been; it was just that he and his home-knit jumpers and faded jeans were a little bit older.

'Looking good, Oz,' commented Kieran jauntily, as he returned to the table with a brace of cappuccinos, a couple of chocolate muffins and a huge plate of cheese-smothered nachos.

'Yeah, looks delicious,' agreed Oz, helping himself to a tortilla chip.

'Not the food – you,' retorted Kieran, sitting down.

'Ha ha, very funny.'

'No, I mean it. That patterned shirt of yours is so retro it's back in fashion. And those glasses are pure John Lennon. You're turning into a dude without even trying.'

Oz grimaced. 'I really hate it when you take the piss. I can never think of anything clever to say back until about two hours later. Anyhow, what's got you looking so perky on a cold Monday?'

Kieran sipped reflectively at his coffee. 'Oh . . . I don't know. Life just feels good, I guess.' His eyes strayed across the café to a corner table, where an infant in a blue woolly hat and mittens was gurgling delightedly in its buggy as its mother fed it fromage frais, aeroplane-style. 'Aaah, look. Over there.'

Oz followed his gaze and winced. 'God, roll on the day when they start fitting babies with silencers.'

'Aw, don't be mean, he's just happy.' Kieran's face adopted a goofy expression. 'He's so cute. Look, he's kicking his little legs.'

'Astounding,' replied Oz from the depths of his coffee cup.

Kieran swivelled back to the table. 'Just think. In a year and a bit from now, I could have one of those,' he declared.

'A chocolate chip muffin?'

'A baby, stupid!'

'Oh. One of those.'

'A little baby boy with dimples ... I could take him to football matches. Or a little girl, I don't really mind which,' he added earnestly. 'Just as long as I'm a daddy. Do you think that's a reasonable thing to expect in a year?'

Oz munched steadily. 'Don't ask me, I'm an entomologist. I only do bugs. But it sounds like you've got it all worked out. So, what does Belle say about this great breeding programme of yours?'

The silly grin faded from Kieran's face. 'I'm not really sure,' he admitted. 'She says she wants kids. And I know she loves them.'

'That's good then.'

'But whenever I say, "Let's start a family as soon as we're married," she goes all vague on me and says she wants to wait a while. Why would she do that?'

'God knows.'

'Exactly! I mean, it's not like she's got some amazing high-powered career and she's afraid to take a break from it, is it?'

Oz shrugged. 'Maybe there's other stuff she wants to do before she has kids.'

'What other stuff?'

'I dunno. Girl stuff. And she's a bit younger than you, too.'

Kieran scratched his head. 'So?'

'So ... maybe her biological thingy isn't, you know, ticking or whatever yet. I don't know!' Oz gave up trying to offer his friend any sensible explanations. 'Kieran, I'm a nerd, my co-workers mostly have six legs and all the women have moustaches, girls run off screaming when I tell them what I do for a living, and just to make me a real catch, I'm still living at home with my mum. Why the hell are you asking me about relationship stuff?'

'Because ... you're my best mate.'

27

Oz's amiable face relaxed into an open smile. 'Just as well I am – can't see anybody else putting up with you. Belle must have been hypnotised or something.'

'True,' agreed Kieran ruefully.

'So ... um.' Oz leaned across the table and lowered his voice. 'Seeing as I'm your all-time bestest mate ... could I ask you the usual favour?'

Kieran grinned dirtily. 'Well, well, you dark horse. That's twice in six months. What night?'

'Thursday, if that's convenient.'

The request was greeted with a broad wink. 'I guess I can make it convenient. I'll stay over at Belle's place that night. I'm assuming you'll be wanting my flat for the entire night?'

Oz coloured up to the roots of his unmanageably wiry hair. 'I hardly think so! I only met Eve last week. I just want somewhere nice and quiet for the evening so we can get to know each other.'

Kieran wiggled his eyebrows. 'You sex god, you.'

'Oh shut up. I hate asking to borrow your flat, but believe me, you'd need somewhere to go if you were living with my mother.'

'So move!'

Oz squirmed. 'I sort of ... well ... it's a bit too much trouble, isn't it? And I'm not that good at being on my own, and my mum does do a top steak and kidney.' He sighed. 'You're such a lucky bastard, you know. Sexy job, beautiful fiancée, good looks, personality ... I ought to hate you.'

'Don't worry, my editor does that for you.'

'I'd give up my entire collection of South American Lepidoptera for a chance to be you for a day.'

Kieran thought for a moment, and then nodded. 'Yeah mate,' he agreed. 'So would I – if I was somebody else.' He grinned. 'And I'm so glad I'm not.'

It was Thursday night, the lights were dimmed in Belle's flat, nobody was murdering anybody else in the street outside, and there was a freshly opened bottle of Rioja on the table.

But romance was off the menu. Belle was not happy. Frankly, she felt like tipping her home-made goulash over Kieran's head.

'Oh Kieran!' She glared away his excuses. 'You promised you'd sort Jax out *properly* this week. You promised!'

'It's not the end of the week yet,' Kieran pointed out lamely.

'You've had loads of chances to talk to her.'

'Yes, but who's to say she'll listen to me if I do?'

Belle flumped down on the end of the pull-down bed, which gave an alarming twang of protesting springs. She half expected that one day it would spring back into the wall, taking her with it. 'We discussed this,' she reminded him. 'And you agreed that the best bet was for you to talk to her, because she's got this thing for you, and you can wrap her round your little finger.'

'I wouldn't quite put it like that,' protested Kieran, sitting cautiously beside her.

'Oh come on! What about that time Dad asked her to help out at the mother and toddler group, and she wasn't having any of it until you came along and said what a nice idea it was, and what a natural she was with kids. And all of a sudden it was "yes Kieran, no Kieran, three bags full, Kieran"! I'd never have believed my sister could flutter her eyelashes, but she did that day. And then there was that poem I asked her to write for Nanna Craine's birthday card. Would she do it? No way – not until Gorgeous Kieran asked her to.'

She finally paused for breath, surprised by her own anger. Was she really this jealous of her little sister's adolescent crush on her fiancé? Could she really be so insecure about his feelings for her that she'd worry about Jax luring him away from her? Jax, of all people?

No, of course she couldn't. She was just being incredibly silly.

'Look, I'm sorry,' she began. 'It's just that I'm a bit tired, and—'

Kieran squeezed her hand. 'It's OK, you're right. I have been avoiding talking to her. Every time I step into her room I feel like the fly inviting itself for dinner with the spider.'

Belle giggled at the mental image. Dressed in all that black, Jax did look a bit like a giant arachnid with a blue head. 'Oh God Kieran, why do I let her wind me up like this?'

'Don't ask me, my sister's very nearly normal. But there was this lad at school who used to piss me off on a regular basis. When we went on a school trip to the Lake District and had to sleep in bunks, Gary saved up his sweaty football socks specially, so he could drop them on my face when I was asleep.'

'Ugh.'

'It's OK, I got my own back. Cling-film over the toilet is a terrible thing.'

'You villain! If you're bad enough to do that, surely you can face up to one harmless little sister?'

'Hm. Harmless eh?'

'Nearly harmless.'

'And you're not afraid your sister might drag me back to her lair, rip me limb from limb and devour my still-quivering remains?'

Belle laughed and returned his kiss with enthusiasm. 'I guess I'll have to take that chance.'

They were just about to sit down to dinner when the doorbell rang. With a groan, Belle went to open the door. Outside she found her mother.

'Mum! This is a surprise.'

'Yes dear . . .' Brenda made a rather tentative entrance. 'Kieran's here isn't he? I wouldn't want to . . . you know . . . burst in on anything. I know what it's like being young and in love,' she added, in a way that made it sound like a very far-off memory.

Kieran snorted with laughter. 'Hi, Brenda. Sorry to disappoint you, but the only thing we're getting up to is eating this goulash. Pull up a chair, there's plenty for three.'

'It does smell nice,' admitted Brenda, sniffing the air. 'But I've got the remains of last night's cottage pie to heat up and I just know Jacqueline won't have made a start on the carrots.'

Belle refrained from saying anything, but exchanged looks with Kieran.

'Anyhow,' Brenda went on, 'I only popped in to find out if you've got anywhere with Jax over her not wanting to wear a proper bridesmaid's dress and all that nonsense.'

Belle looked at Kieran. Kieran blustered. 'I . . . er . . . well . . . not exactly. Yet.'

'Only if you haven't,' continued Brenda with a smile, 'I've had an idea.'

When she got home, Brenda found Jax slouched in the living room, watching a DVD, and a big pile of unpeeled carrots on the kitchen work-top.

'You didn't get round to doing the carrots then?' she enquired.

'I was busy.' Jax didn't bother turning round. 'Assignments and stuff.'

'Oh, I see.' Brenda took a deep breath. 'Well, at least I've managed to relieve you of one worry.'

Jax glanced up. 'What?'

'I just rang your cousin Trixie, and she says if you don't want to do it, she'd be more than delighted to be Annabelle's bridesmaid. And she's quite happy to wear the dress. Isn't that nice?'

Jax's mouth fell open. 'Trixie!'

'That's right. She seems really keen to do it, I was quite surprised. So, shall I ring her back and tell her yes?'

Belle and Kieran were snuggled up together on the bed, watching TV, when the phone rang. Belle reached out for the receiver.

'Belle, it's me.'

'Hi, Mum. Any news?'

Brenda chuckled softly. 'Let's just say Jacqueline is suddenly very happy to be your bridesmaid, dear. Oh – and she wants to know when her first dress fitting will be.'

Chapter 4

'Thanks mate, keep the change.'

The taxi drew away and disappeared into College Road, leaving its passenger alone on the pavement amid a heap of assorted luggage. Shouldering the rucksack, she distributed the other bags between both hands and crossed the road by St Jude's church.

'God I'm cold,' she thought with a shiver. 'Doesn't it ever get warm in England?'

It was early evening and the area was astonishingly quiet – too late for the teatime rush, and too early for anyone to be on their way out for the evening. The click-clack of her high-heeled mules on the pavement sounded like pistol shots as she headed for her destination.

She didn't need to check the *A to Z* guide, or the address details she'd printed off the Internet. You couldn't miss St Jude's vicarage. Even among the other mid-Victorian houses in the road it was imposing, dramatically lit by the sulphur-orange street lamps, and with a sweep of tree-lined drive that just cried out for a grand entrance by horse and carriage.

But on this occasion, good old-fashioned walking would have to do.

'Well, well, Gerry,' she murmured to herself, 'aren't you living in fine style? Regular pillar of the community, I'll bet.'

Tossing back her lustrous blonde hair, she stepped through the gate, strode confidently down the path and climbed the three front steps, rang the doorbell, and waited.

Belle didn't normally spend her evenings round at her mum and dad's. But on this particular evening she'd dropped round to have a rummage through some of her old stuff that had been gathering dust in the loft ever since she moved into her own place. She'd been putting it off for far too long, and now that she was getting married, her mum felt it really was high time she decided which parts of her old life were worth keeping, and which ought to be consigned to the shredder.

She was kneeling on the floor in the family living room, surrounded by the contents of an upturned cardboard box labelled SCHOOL STUFF. The loft was filthy, and after crawling around up there for an hour, there were cobwebs in her hair, a big black smudge on her nose, and all she'd managed to jettison so far were a couple of old crisp packets and a crumpled birthday card from somebody she could only vaguely remember, but she was having big, nostalgic fun. It was taking ages though, much longer than she'd expected. Every photo, every yellowing cutting from the *Courant*, every embarrassing or flattering school report had a tale to tell. It was impossible not to linger over all of them.

An old class photo showed her a couple of months before she left school: a gawky sixteen-year-old with braces and a thick, dark fringe that obscured her eyes. She was grinning like a maniac at the camera, and she remembered why: she'd just found out that she'd been offered her first full-time job in retail – and that meant no more school and no more exams. Ever. For sheer exhilaration, that day almost ranked right up there alongside the day Kieran had proposed. She smiled as she also remembered that the night before at the school dance, she'd finally caught the eye of seventeen year-old Max Levenshulme, the sixth form's brightest and sexiest star. Max had been Belle's first serious boyfriend but what she'd felt for him paled next to her feelings for Kieran.

Of course, Mum and Dad had hoped she'd go to university, she knew that, and she could probably have managed it if she'd tried; but A levels just weren't her thing, let alone uni. Besides, Jax was the smart one, and everybody knew you could only have one decent set of brains per generation. Not that Jax used them any more than she had to.

As she slid the photo back inside its envelope, the doorbell rang.

'Mum! Door!'

Belle listened for a while, expecting to hear her mother's footsteps scurrying down the stairs, but nothing happened. She hesitated. Then the doorbell rang again, with just a hint of impatience.

She got up, patting dust from the knees of her jeans, went into the hall and called up the stairs, reluctant to open the door herself looking like she'd just swept next-door's chimney. 'Mum?' Nothing. Must be in the bath or something. And it was no use calling for Dad, since he was out somewhere, doing whatever arcane things vicars did on weekday evenings.

So, wiping a grubby hand on the seat of her jeans, Belle walked to the front door and opened it. It was most probably the bell-ringers wanting the key to the church, or one of the homeless people who periodically stopped by to ask for money and a meal.

But the young woman on the doorstep didn't look much like either, even if she did have a rucksack slung over one shoulder. It was a designer rucksack and she was tall, blonde, shapely, and healthily beautiful in a way that made her look as though she'd been rolled in sunshine and then lightly toasted.

'Hi.' She beamed, switching on a smile that could sell a million tubes of toothpaste.

'Hello,' said Belle, marvelling at the way Mother Nature seemed to give some people all the breaks and wishing she was wearing something a bit less scruffy.

'Hey – you must be Jacqueline.' The voice was clear and just a little strident, the accent unmistakeable to anyone who'd ever watched an Australian soap opera. 'Jacqueline Craine, am I right?'

'Jacqueline? No, Jax is my sister. I'm—'

'Of course – Annabelle, you're Annabelle. Pleased to meet you, I've been looking forward to it.' She proffered a hand whose grip was bone-crunchingly firm. She might look feminine, but this was the kind of woman who had muscles on her toenails. 'Would you mind fetching your dad for me?'

'You want to see the vicar? Is he expecting you?'

'Not . . . exactly, but I reckon he'll see me.'

'I'm afraid he's out at the moment.'

'Will he be long?'

Belle vacillated. 'If it's important, I guess you could come in and wait, and I'll phone him on his mobile.'

'Oh, it's important all right.'

'Well . . . OK. Who should I say wants to see him?'

The smile turned ever so slightly coy . . . or was that sly? 'My name's Mona Starr,' she purred, 'but just you tell him it's his eldest daughter.'

Gerry was having an average sort of Wednesday evening: an hour or so of visiting the sick, followed by the usual argumentative parochial church council meeting in St Jude's Hall. This week, Mrs Armitage was up in arms about plans to build a toilet onto the back of the vestry on the grounds that it was ungodly for people to perform their bodily functions on consecrated ground, Len the groundsman was complaining about an invasion of moles in the churchyard, and half a dozen members of the congregation were making noises about switching their allegiance to All Saints' if the new curate turned out to be a woman. All the usual parish wrangling.

It wasn't the most exciting way to spend an evening, but Gerry enjoyed his weekly tussles. He'd been at St Jude's a long time now, had become part of the furniture, and these days even when nobody agreed with him it felt no worse than a minor family spat. Other vicars might feel a need to set themselves new challenges, seek out new horizons, but Gerry wasn't the pioneering kind. He'd got that pioneering, crusading thing out of his system during his gap year, working for the youth ministry in Australia – and even then you couldn't really have called him adventurous. These days, it was nice just to feel accepted. He supposed that must mean he was now officially middle-aged and boring.

The members of the PCC had arranged themselves around the table in the vestry, and were drinking instant coffee and discussing the refreshments for the bishop's forthcoming visit when Gerry's mobile rang.

The fearsome Mrs Armitage fixed him with a look that could freeze lava. 'Really, Vicar. You, of all people. And in the middle of important parish business.'

'Yes, Jean, I'm sorry, I know how much you hate meetings being disturbed.' He tried not to feel too much like a scolded schoolboy as he rummaged for the phone in the depths of his briefcase. 'But I can hardly switch off my mobile – what if I'm needed urgently?' He put the phone cautiously to his ear. 'Hello? Annabelle? I told you, dear, not when I'm in the middle of . . . What? Who? Oh my goodness, no. Perhaps I'd better . . . yes, right away.'

Nobody could fail to notice that his hand was shaking as he dropped the phone back into his case; not even old Mr Grundy with the pebble glasses.

'Are you all right, Vicar?'

'You're looking very pale. Is it bad news?'

'I bet it's that old dear from the sheltered flats. Dorothy said she wasn't looking at all well . . .'

'I'm dreadfully sorry, everybody,' announced Gerry, grabbing his briefcase and making for the door without further explanation, 'but we'll have to adjourn our meeting until tomorrow night. Something rather . . . unexpected has just come up.'

Kieran was working late at the *Courant* when he got the call from Belle. It came as such a shock that he bit the eraser off the end of his pencil.

'She said she's his what! Is this girl some kind of nutter or something?'

Belle winced. 'Keep your voice down, she's only in the next room.'

'But she can't be his daughter! That's ridiculous. And besides, you said she was Australian.'

'So?'

'So the whole thing's nonsense. How can your dad have a daughter who's Australian? If you ask me, she's escaped from the local psychiatric

35

unit. Does she have a dustbin on her head? She probably thinks she's Ned Kelly as well.'

Belle wished she could be so sure. 'Dad did go to Australia once,' she said quietly.

'Oh,' said Kieran, some of the wind knocked out of his sails.

'It was years and years ago, before he and Mum got married. I saw the photos.'

'Yeah, but all the same. I mean, if you had a kid ... you'd know, wouldn't you?'

Belle voiced the unspeakable. 'Perhaps he did know.'

'What – all this time? And he kept it to himself? You're kidding Belle, your dad's not like that.'

Is he or isn't he? wondered Belle. Can a person you've known and adored and admired all your life suddenly turn out to be somebody completely different? 'Look,' she said, 'all I know is, ten minutes after I called him he turned up here looking as white as a sheet, took this Mona woman and Mum into the office and closed the door, and that was nearly an hour ago.'

She could imagine Kieran thinking at the other end of the phone line. 'What about Jax?' he asked. 'What does she make of all this?'

'She's not here, thank God. You know what she's like – acts first and thinks later.' A nameless panic rose in Belle's throat. 'What's going on, Kieran? I need someone to tell me what the hell's going on.'

Belle waited, and then she waited some more.

The last thing Kieran had said to her before he rang off was, 'It's OK darling, chin up and don't panic. In fact don't do anything, just wait till I get there and we'll sort it out together,' and she did wait, for what seemed like hours and hours even though it could only have been twenty minutes. But when the grandfather clock in the hall chimed the half-hour and he still hadn't arrived, Belle knew she couldn't wait any longer.

Cautiously, she crossed the hall and followed the worn-down strip of Wilton carpet that led to the door of her father's office. The door was solid oak and thick with it; even up close, all she could hear was an indistinct blur of voices, like an untuned radio with the batteries running down.

She raised a hand to knock; changed her mind; took a deep breath and this time went through with it. Grasping the doorknob, she gave it a twist and pushed the door open.

It swung slowly away from her, gradually revealing a kind of frozen tableau. Dad's face, solemn and concerned. Mum's, taut with shock. And Mona Starr, sitting there between them, still bloody well smiling – as if there was anything to smile about.

36

Belle took a step forward. 'I'm sorry I barged in, but I was worried. You've been in here an awful long time.' She paused, before saying determinedly, 'I want to know what's going on.'

Gerry and Brenda exchanged looks, and Gerry opened his mouth as if to say something, but it was Mona who actually spoke.

'Why don't you come in, Annabelle? Your mum and dad and I are just having a bit of a friendly chat, you know, about family stuff.' She reached out and actually patted Gerry's hand as if he was her dad and not Belle's at all, and Belle felt deeply, creepily uncomfortable. 'Now we've finally found each other, I want us all to be really close.'

A cold, trickly feeling ran down Belle's back, like that feeling you get when somebody shoves a half-melted snowball down the back of your neck. She shuddered. This felt wrong, horribly wrong. None of it was real. People didn't just turn up from the other side of the world and announce that they were part of your family. Unless they were lying. But then again, why would anybody want to lie about something like that? She wished with all her heart that this made sense.

'Dad,' she said slowly.

His eyes looked tired and maybe just a little ashamed, like he blamed himself for all of this. 'Yes love?'

'Is . . . she . . .' her eyes lighted on Mona, 'really your daughter?'

She could see Gerry willing Brenda to look at him, but she turned away. He forced a half-smile. 'Yes love, Mona's my daughter and. . .er. . .your half-sister. But I had no idea that she existed until today, really and truly I didn't.'

'Mum wrote to you after you left Australia,' said Mona, not smiling quite so brightly. 'She wrote to tell you she was having a baby.'

Gerry shook his head. 'I never got any letters. I wrote to your mother too, but I never got a reply. You do believe me, don't you?'

Mona didn't say anything, and Belle couldn't really blame her. It all sounded like complete and utter rubbish – missing letters, secret children suddenly appearing. It was the stuff of melodramas.

Something in her normally placid disposition rebelled. 'Oh come on!' she bridled. 'This is totally stupid. How could you not know you had a daughter?'

'I told you, love, I never received anything from Australia, and . . .' Gerry lowered his eyes. 'Can we talk about this later? I'm so very sorry, this has come as a big shock to all of us.'

But Belle wasn't in the mood to let it drop. 'You're a vicar, Dad! Even back then you knew you were going to be one. And vicars aren't supposed to . . . to do that sort of thing! You preach about it in church all the time!'

'I know love, I know.' Gerry looked absolutely mortified. 'But I knew Mona's mother very briefly . . . It was a long time ago.'

Belle wanted to sympathise, but all she felt was angry and disappointed. And jealous of the blonde bombshell who had exploded into their cosy, settled lives. Mona Starr, she said silently, I hate you – even if we are related.

'But how can you be sure that she's your daughter?' Belle asked pointedly. 'She could be absolutely anybody. It could be some sort of . . . I don't know . . . trick, or – or something.'

'I know it's hard for you,' said Mona sympathetically. 'Does this help?' She reached out to the pile of papers on Gerry's desk and handed Belle a birth certificate. Under 'father's name', it read 'Gerald Craine, Theological Student, Cheltenham, UK'. 'I know it's not much but it's real,' she said.

Brenda raked the hair back off her forehead. She was still refusing – or unable – to look Gerry in the face. 'It doesn't really hit you, does it?' she said quietly. 'Not until you see it in black and white.'

Belle's mouth suddenly dried up and she could hardly swallow. 'Dad . . . Come on Dad, tell me this isn't true! This is some kind of spectacularly bad joke, right?'

His eyes met hers. 'I'm so sorry, Belle. But I've talked to Mona for a long time, and looked at the letters and papers she's brought with her, and I'm convinced it's true.'

'It's OK to feel angry, you know.' To Belle's horror, Mona took hold of her hand and gave it a sympathetic squeeze. She had a horrible feeling that Mona was enjoying every second of this. 'You're bound to feel a bit off for a while – it came as a pretty big shock to me too, you know, when Mum told me I had another family in England.'

'And when was that?' demanded Belle.

'Not till a few years ago, when I needed my birth certificate to renew my passport. Before that, when I still lived at home, Mum used to sort everything out for me.'

Belle stared at her. 'You've known all about this for years? And you waited until now to do this to us?'

For the first time Mona was on the defensive. 'Hey, it was hard for me too, you know. I wasn't sure what I should do – get in touch or try and forget.'

Anger and hurt stirred Belle into snapping back: 'So you waited all this time and then just descended on us without so much as a letter, a phone call, nothing?'

There was a short, uncomfortable silence, punctuated by the incongruous gurgle of the ancient central heating pipes. Then Mona's smile sprang right back onto her face. 'Hey, look on the bright side: we've both just found ourselves a new sister! Isn't that just great? I'm so excited, finding my English family!'

'A sister?' demanded a caustic voice from the hallway. 'What's all this crap about new sisters? And who's she?'

Belle turned round. Jax was standing in the hall, the whiteness of her face exaggerated by her heavy black eye make-up. Behind her loomed Razor, as ever in attendance like some benevolent troll. Jax's eyes moved from one face to another, lingered for a few critical seconds on Mona and then decided that her father was the best bet for an answer.

'Look, is somebody going to explain this to me, or is it some kind of guessing game? 'Cause if it is, I'm not playing.'

Later than evening, when Mona had been shown to the guest room, on the grounds that no member of the family was going to be consigned to some nasty cheap guest house, not to mention minimising the chances of the scandal getting out, Belle sat down halfway up the stairs, gathered up her knees under her chin, and let the full force of the shock hit her.

She felt exhausted, bedraggled, shipwrecked. In one unremarkable evening, Mona Starr had appeared from nowhere, and with one careless flick of her shapely wrist turned the cosy little snow-dome of her existence upside down. And now everything was just a blinding swirl of whiteness, obscuring everything that had once been familiar.

You're overreacting Belle, she told herself. You should lighten up a bit. But she'd never been any good at taking her own advice. So she just sat there on the stairs and wilted, staring blankly at her own toes, as if she feared they might play tricks on her too if she took her eyes off them for a moment.

And what kind of a name was 'Mona Starr' in any case? It sounded fake and if her name was fake, was it possible her claims of paternity were equally dubious? Belle desperately wanted to believe so.

'Hey gorgeous, what are you doing out here all on your own?' asked Kieran, appearing at the bottom of the stairs. 'Sorry I'm so late, big story came up just as I was leaving.'

She looked up and shrugged. 'Dunno what I'm doing really,' she admitted. 'Vegetating.'

'Room for a little one?' he enquired.

'You're not little.'

'OK, a medium-sized one then.'

The ghost of a smile flitted across Belle's face. 'Well . . . go on, seeing as it's you.'

'Budge up then.'

He eased in beside her on the step. It felt good to have him next to her, warm and reassuringly real. He at least would never let her down. 'It's been quite a night,' he commented.

'I never want another one like it, that's for sure.' Belle straightened up and looked at him. 'Do you think it's really true? Is she my sister?'

'Half-sister, you mean.'

'What's the difference? It still means Dad and some Australian woman . . . Oh God.' She shuddered. 'It doesn't bear thinking about.'

'Well, nobody can cope with the idea of their parents having sex, can they?' he pointed out. 'It always seems a bit disgusting if you try visualising it.'

'Yes, but this isn't actually about my parents, is it?' Belle's face creased into a grimace. 'Kieran, I do not want to visualise my dad – who in case you've forgotten is a vicar – consorting with some bimbo, and fathering a child. And just think what it must be doing to poor Mum.' She passed a hand across her perspiring brow. 'When I think of how upset he was when he found out that I was having sex, not to mention Jax . . . And all this time . . . It's no good, I just can't get my head round it!'

'Shh,' urged Kieran. 'Mona's only upstairs, she might hear you.'

'I don't care if she does. Anyway, does she have to be so bloody pleased about all of this? All this "I love everybody and isn't everything wonderful" stuff. It's not . . . normal.'

Kieran chuckled. 'Hey, you're not, are you?'

Belle frowned. 'Not what?'

'Jealous of your new big sister.' A grin spread across his face. 'Oh Belle, you are!'

'Don't be stupid. Why would I be jealous of her?'

Kieran rubbed his chin, now rather stubbly after a long day's work. 'Well,' he mused, 'it's not every day you get a new half-sister who's a six-foot blonde fashion model with big blue eyes and legs that—'

Belle interrupted him in his reverie. He was enjoying it far too much. 'Yes, thanks Kieran, you can stop there, I've got the picture. And no, I am not jealous of her. I'm not jealous of anyone,' she added firmly, 'because I'm quite happy being me.'

'Good,' said Kieran.

'There's no need to sound so surprised. Being me's not the worst thing in the world, you know!'

'I'm very glad to hear it.'

'So no matter how much you try to wind me up by going on about how gorgeous she is, you're not going to make me jealous. OK?'

'Absolutely.' He winked. 'Nice bum though.'

'Kieran!'

'Not hers – yours.' He made a playful grab for it, and Belle laughed for the first time that day. 'God but you're easy to tease.'

'Sure you wouldn't rather have her bum? I'm sure it's been on all sorts of exciting magazine covers.'

He took her in his arms and rolled her into an untidy heap on the stairs. 'Don't be daft, yours is much sexier. If I've got yours, how could I possibly want anybody else's?'

After a long and shell-shocked evening, Belle had finally gone off to spend the night at Kieran's flat. Mona was reposing in crisp new sheets in the guest room, Jax lay curled up under her black duvet cover, and Gerry had finally drifted off to sleep, his face as serenely untroubled as a medieval martyr's.

It was very late. So late in fact that it was bordering on early. The clock in the church tower across the road struck a single, mournful note that seemed to drift endlessly on the chill, misty air.

Brenda wasn't asleep. She was standing by the bedroom window in her dressing gown, holding the curtain aside and gazing out into the night. Everything was muffled, motionless and ever so slightly unreal, as if all she could see in the square before her had been secretly replaced with life-size cardboard cut-outs.

Mona seems like a nice girl, she told herself again. Cheerful, polite. A very nice girl. Tall, blonde, dark, eyes the image of Gerry's. Yes. Nice.

A lone car drifted by in slow motion, its headlights sweeping lazily across the front of the vicarage and then disappearing into the darkness.

Brenda's fingers tightened about the edge of the curtain, twisting and crumpling the heavy fabric. And as she stood there, a single tear crept from beneath her eyelid and slipped away along the curve of her cheek.

'How could you do this to me, Gerry?' she whispered. 'How could you?'

Chapter 5

Since the whole of Cheltenham could have fitted quite snugly into a small corner of New York City and still left room for a nice set of built-in wardrobes, the parish of St Jude's was not exactly the throbbing hub of a mighty metropolis.

On the other hand – despite the fact that it was only a five-minute walk from the centre of town – it did possess all the essential characteristics of a village: it was close-knit, boasted about its 'community spirit', had one shop that sold everything … and if you lived there, you'd be lucky to keep anything secret for more than five minutes. Nobody could be born, married, die or indeed scratch their bottom in St Jude's without the event raising considerable local interest. And since hardly anything significant ever happened there, insignificant things tended to swell to enormous proportions to fill the vacuum.

Which was how rumours got started. And with a postie like Welsh Dave on the job, they didn't take much starting …

Welsh Dave – who had acquired his nickname as a means of differentiating him from the other six Daves down at the sorting office – hummed to himself as he did his rounds. Country and Western mostly, with a smattering of Eighties standards. He loved his job. It allowed him to indulge both of his main passions: healthy exercise and unhealthy curiosity. For Welsh Dave was easily the nosiest man east of Abergavenny. What was more, he didn't just pry into people's business for the sake of it. Oh no. Generous soul that he was, Dave firmly believed in sharing his discoveries with as many people as possible. You could say it was his way of providing a service to the community.

On this particular crisp February morning, he was halfway through 'Wake Me Up Before You Go-Go' when he jogged up to number 28, St Jude's Place, a groaning satchel of post across either shoulder. No bicycles or cissy trolleys for Welsh Dave. He was the only postman in the whole of Gloucestershire who actually looked forward to the Christmas post.

Sheaf of letters in hand, he rang the bell. Sure enough, a few seconds later the door opened to reveal one of the winsome quartet of nurses who shared the house, mug of coffee in hand and dressing gown gaping enticingly at the front.

'Oh, it's you.' She rubbed a hand across her eyes. 'Morning Dave.'

Dave leered appreciatively 'Morning, Miss Sadie, and a lovely one it is, though not as lovely as you. One to sign for here if you'd be so kind.' He leaned closer as she signed. 'News about your poor dad's will, is it? Only I couldn't help noticing the Scottish postmark.'

She half smiled at him. 'Oh, you know. Probably.' She yawned. 'I don't know how you post office types manage to get up at four in the morning. I miss a bit of sleep for one night and already I'm half dead.'

Dave's ears pricked up. 'Had a disturbed night, did you? Oh, that's a shame. Trouble in the neighbourhood, was there?'

'Not trouble exactly. It's just that I've only just got off nights, so I'm not sleeping properly anyway, and I tried to get an early night. And then there were some comings and goings over the road . . .'

'What, at number twenty-seven, you mean? Bit of a rowdy bunch, those kids.'

'No, the vicarage.'

Dave's eyebrows embraced his hairline. 'Never!'

'Yeah. They had some girl visiting, drop-dead gorgeous too damn her. Anyway, the lights were on till really late, God knows why.'

Armed with this nugget of interesting information, plus a pleasant mental image of Nurse Sadie's cleavage, Welsh Dave continued on his journey round the square. At number 32, he learned that a drop-dead gorgeous girl had indeed entered the vicarage the previous evening, round about half-past eight, just about the time – according to the woman at number 23 – that the vicar had come scurrying across from the church hall as if his cassock was on fire. The elderly couple two doors down from her were as positive as everybody else that they'd never seen the girl before. You didn't forget a good-looking girl like that, they said. Looked good enough to be one of those film actresses or something.

Well, well. Welsh Dave licked his lips in anticipation. An unknown beauty at the vicarage, of all places. Everybody had seen her go in. And even more interesting, nobody had seen her come out again.

He hurried on his way to Mrs Armitage's house, round the corner in St Jude's Place. If there was one person who knew more about what was going on round here than Welsh Dave, it was Jean Armitage. And nobody in the world was fonder than Jean of a nice bit of fresh, juicy gossip.

*

43

Over at Green Goddess, the day's trading had barely started and already Belle had Lily worried.

Belle's teenage customer seemed a bit flummoxed too. She watched, wide-eyed, as Belle stuffed handfuls of mini soaps mechanically into a gold silk gift bag.

She'd probably have carried on doing it until the bag split if Lily hadn't nudged her elbow and hissed, 'What are you doing? It's nine soaps per bag, not ninety! And you've forgotten the complimentary ceramic sea-horse.'

Belle blinked, shook herself and came back to her senses. 'What? Oh. Whoops.' The young customer looked most disappointed as two-thirds of the starfish-shaped soaps came back out of the bag and into the display, to be replaced by a very small green pottery seahorse. 'Sorry about that, miss, I was miles away.' Belle reached for the box of oddments she always kept under the counter. 'Here – have a free sample of Gorgeous Goddess foot cream, with our compliments. Oh, and a sachet of Damson Hair Jam.'

Lily gave Belle the strangest of looks as the customer exited the shop and disappeared into the arcade with her purchases. 'Is there something the matter?' she demanded, modulating her voice to the sort of whisper that carries across canyons, 'Hey – you're not on drugs are you?'

'Drugs?' squeaked Belle, not sure whether to be horrified or amused. 'Of course I'm not on drugs!' She realised that she'd spoken a little too loudly when a middle-aged lady in a symphony of brown corduroy turned round and threw her a look of utter disgust. She smiled back in what she hoped was an unconcerned manner, and dropped her voice a few decibels. 'What on earth are you on about?'

'I've never seen you like this before,' insisted Lily. 'You've been acting all ... I dunno ... spaced-out,' protested Lily. 'Like our Mark's dog when it drank that half-bottle of Bailey's.'

'Gee, thanks! I've always wanted to be compared to a drunken dog.'

As Belle had often found, Lily wasn't one to climb down if she thought she was in the right. 'What am I supposed to think, Belle? You've not been right since you got here.'

Belle was beginning to feel distinctly picked-on. 'Don't exaggerate,' she snapped, rearranging things that didn't need rearranging. 'And ... tidy that display.'

Lily stuck to her like glue as she made her way round the shop. 'I already tidied it twice. Belle, you're not yourself. Take that man in the Save The Penguins T-shirt.'

Belle swung round to face her in exasperation. 'What about him?'

'If I hadn't stepped in, you'd have sold him aloe vera toothpaste instead of hair gel. And that's really, really, really not like you.'

'I'm fine,' said Belle, so feebly that not even she believed it was true.

'So why's your cardi on inside out then?'

'Oh . . . bum.' Belle glanced down and saw that Lily was right. 'It's lucky, everybody knows that.'

'Well yes, seeing as you did it without realising,' agreed Lily. 'I did try and tell you,' she added as Belle wrestled out of the cardigan and into it again, this time the right way round, 'only you haven't listened to a word anybody's said since you got here. Is it your period?' she asked in the self-same, hideously embarrassing stage-whisper that had already alerted every browser in the store to Belle's alleged drugs problem. 'I've got some paracetamol in the restroom.'

Belle fetched up against the plywood Spring Bride, took one look at her maniacal grin, and gave a sigh of capitulation. 'No it's not my period, no I'm not on drugs, and yes I've got something on my mind but it's nothing. Honest. So can we just get on and do our jobs please?'

Lily folded her arms and leaned her bum against the front of the counter. 'It's a good job Waylon's not in, you know what he's like. He'd have you in his office giving you the third degree.'

'What – like you are, you mean? Just leave it will you, Lily?'

'No.'

'Not even if I bribe you?'

'Nope. Come on, spill the beans to Auntie Lily and you'll feel a whole lot better. Come on, I need the practice for when I'm a parent and I've got nightmare teenagers to sort out.'

'My God, whatever happened to blind obedience and people knowing their place?' Belle felt her resistance collapse like an unsuccessful soufflé. 'All right, all right.' She poked an admonitory finger at Lily's nose. 'But if you breathe a word about this to anybody else, I swear I'll take those two lavender Bath Bombs over there and shove them right up your nostrils.'

In the wake of her doorstep pow-wow with Welsh Dave, Jean Armitage was fairly crackling with energy and bursting with inquisitiveness. Whatever was afoot at the vicarage, she was going to get to the bottom of it. After all, in a very real way Mrs Armitage was the nearest thing St Jude's had to an information superhighway, and what good was a highway, super or otherwise, if it didn't have any traffic on it?

A telephone poll of a few local friends produced some interesting hypotheses. One – a retired midwife – was convinced that the real reason why the vicar's wife had been putting on weight around her middle wasn't an excess of Christmas pudding, but because she was secretly pregnant; and that the young stranger was consequently a live-in nanny. Jean

45

thought this highly unlikely, given she knew that Brenda Craine had had a hysterectomy two years previously, but made a mental note to keep an eye on young Annabelle's figure over the next couple of months, and liaise with the manageress of the bridal boutique in the High Street – just in case.

Greta from the Thursday night bridge club thought it was all down to money. What with his paltry stipend, Jax set on university and a big wedding to pay for, Gerry was purely and simply hard up. And that was why he'd decided to rent out Annabelle's old room.

'You mean ... she's a lodger? But why's he being so secretive about it?' pondered Jean.

'Because he's embarrassed,' replied Greta. 'Wouldn't you be?'

Jean had to admit this made a kind of tedious sense, though it wasn't half as entertaining as the explanation proffered by her husband, George. According to him, it was all patently obvious to anyone with half a brain. The blonde stranger was clearly Kieran's secret mistress, who – having heard about the forthcoming wedding – had turned up at his fiancée's parents' home the previous evening for a big showdown.

'Don't be silly, George,' Jean scoffed. 'If that young woman went in there last night just to cause a scene, why hasn't she come back out again?'

George responded with a macabre wink. 'You'll find out soon enough,' he promised, in his lugubrious Gloucestershire drawl. 'When the police turn up and start digging up the garden for bones.'

'George, that's horrible! You can't say things like that about the vicar!' But all the same, she laughed. Now that really would be a coup, she mused; to be able to say one had lived next door to the Vicarage Murderer.

While she washed up the breakfast dishes she abandoned herself to pleasant reveries, in which she was being interviewed about her experiences for a tasteful but hard-hitting documentary on BBC 2 ('Well yes, Mr Paxman, I always suspected there was something not quite right about next door ...') when George cut in and spoiled it all.

'Of course, you know who she really is, don't you?'

'Hm?' asked Jean, absent-mindedly. 'Who who is?'

'That girl next door.' He picked reflectively at his teeth with a matchstick. 'I reckon she's the new curate.'

His wife turned pale at the thought. A female priest, at St Jude's? A parish that had held out for years against the forces of trendy religion? The thought was simply unbearable. 'No!' she gasped.

George grinned. 'A very nice-looking woman, if I do say so.'

'But ... a woman curate? Here? The bishop knows we won't accept it.

Gerry knows we won't. He wouldn't do a thing like that behind our backs.' Her face darkened. 'Would he?'

George settled himself back in his chair and picked up his newspaper. 'Well if he has, it's going to put a few cats among the pigeons, don't you reckon?'

'This is so kind of you,' purred Mona as Kieran came down the front steps of the *Courant's* HQ and joined her on the pavement amid the other lunchtime escapees from neighbouring office buildings. 'It's really hard, you know, not knowing anybody and everything.'

Kieran shrugged modestly and thrust his hands deep into the pockets of his fleece. 'Oh, that's no problem. I mean, somebody needs to show you round, help you get your bearings, so why not me?' He didn't let on to Mona that he'd sort of promised Brenda he'd keep her away from as many people as possible. He had a feeling Mona wouldn't appreciate it.

'Well, I think you're a regular knight in shining armour.'

'Don't you believe it. I just thought everybody else was being a bit ... backward in coming forward.'

She smiled ruefully, and he noticed that two little dimples appeared in her cheeks. 'Let's be honest, there weren't going to be any other volunteers. I mean, if looks could kill I'd never have made it out of that vicarage alive.' She let out a wide-eyed, helpless sigh. 'But it's not as if I have anywhere else to go . . .'

'Oh, it's not that bad, I'm sure,' he protested gamely. 'I expect they're just, you know, shaken up. It was all a bit sudden, that's all.'

'I guess,' Mona conceded. 'But then that's me all over,' she grinned, 'Little Miss Impulsive..I mull something over for ages without doing anything and then bang! Suddenly I'm doing it.'

They stood in the street in silence for a few seconds, dodging about to keep out of people's way. There was no doubt about it, Mona Starr was one heck of an attractive girl. And not ill-looking and bony like your average model, either. This was a woman whose chest was strictly convex.

It was Kieran who broke the silence. 'Right then – where do you fancy for lunch?'

Mona giggled. 'I don't know anything about anywhere round here, remember? Original stranger in a strange land, that's me. Anywhere you like, as long as it's not chips with everything.'

'Ah – so you've tried our pub grub then?'

Mona pulled a face. 'I thought we Aussies were bad with our big steaks and our barbies, but you guys would deep-fry custard if you could get it to stick together. I'm not big on grease. Anyhow, got to watch my figure.' She gave a playful wiggle that almost sent a cyclist crashing into a lamp post. 'Nobody wants a fat arse on the cover of *Australian Cosmo*, do they?'

Kieran wouldn't have described Mona's rear end as fat in a million years, but the very thought of it was a little too distracting to be comfortable and he swiftly changed the subject. 'Come on, let's try the Vaults,' he proposed, setting off across the road to an old converted church. 'It's a wine bar but it's not too snobby. And they do some great healthy snacks.'

Mona was only an inch or so shorter than Kieran, and kept up easily with his long, loping strides. 'You like healthy food too, then?' she asked as they stepped through the door into a cavernous space lined with recovered oak and furnished with recycled church pews.

'When I can get it, yeah. I come in here sometimes after I've been for a swim or a run.' He chose a table and handed Mona a menu.

'You like running?' Mona beamed delightedly. 'Me too. What's your best time over a mile?'

'Hey, whoa – I don't take it quite that seriously! I just enjoy keeping myself fit,' he patted his stomach, 'and keeping this down.'

'Does Annabelle go running with you? It can get a bit boring if you don't have a running partner.'

Kieran burst out laughing: 'Belle, go running?'

'Should I take that as a no?' enquired Mona.

'Let's just say Belle thinks people who take exercise when they don't have to need their heads examining.'

'Oh, that's a shame,' sympathised Mona. Her face brightened again. 'What about sports? Do you surf?'

'Never tried,' Kieran admitted. 'In case you haven't noticed, there's a serious shortage of coastline round here. Mind you,' he mused, popping an olive into his mouth, 'some people rave about the Severn Bore.'

'The Severn Bore?' Mona's nose wrinkled. 'Sounds like some really tedious old guy...'

Kieran smiled, then explained that the Bore was a what rather than a who. 'You're right, you really do have a lot to learn about round here,' he agreed.

Mona's pimpernel-blue eyes twinkled. 'That's OK, I've got you here to teach me. So how can I possibly go wrong?'

She looked at him. He looked at her. And they exchanged smiles. A few moments later, the ever-so-slightly embarrassed silence was broken by a familiar voice.

'Kieran? What are you doing here? I thought you always went to the Swan and Anchor on Tuesdays ... oh!' Oz's bespectacled gaze met Mona's cool one and he blinked. 'Sorry, didn't realise you had company. I'll ... um ... see you later then, shall I?'

The look on Oz's face said it all. He'd caught his soon-to-be-married best friend in a compromising situation with a breathtaking blonde, and was manfully trying not to be shocked.

Kieran made a grab for his hapless mate as he backed away and – right on cue – tripped over the leg of a chair. 'Come back here you idiot, and say hello to Mona. Mona Starr, this is Oswald Hepplewhite, but we're not sadists so we call him Oz. Oz, this is Mona. She's over from Australia, and...erm... she's staying at the vicarage for a few nights. I'm showing her the sights of historic Cheltenham.'

'Oh,' said Oz, battling the crimson blush that was creeping upwards from his neck to his ears. 'Sorry, I thought ... I mean, I didn't actually think, but I ... er ... might have done if—'

Mona threw back her blonde head and gave a raucous laugh. 'Shut up and take the weight off your feet, Oz. What's your poison?'

Oz shuffled uneasily on his chair. 'Well, I've got to go back to work in the lab after this, so you'd better make it a tonic water with ice and no lemon, please.'

Kieran got to his feet, rummaging in his back pocket for a tenner. 'You'll have a half of lager and like it, young man. Australians don't drink tonic water – do they, Mona?'

'Absolutely not. Oh, and make mine a nice cold pint, Kieran.'

'Right you are,' said Kieran.

'Well all right then,' said Oz, a tinge of panic adding to the embarrassment on his face as Kieran headed off to the bar. 'You won't be long, will you?' he called back over his shoulder.

Mona sat back on her pew and contemplated Oz. 'You're not scared of me, are you?'

Oz swallowed. 'Of course not.'

'Are you always that bad at lying?'

He hung his head. 'I'm afraid so. Sorry, I'm not really the social type. Kieran's the party animal round here.'

She cocked her head on one side. 'So why's that then?'

'I haven't got any conversation, for a start off. Unless you like bugs?' he ventured without much hope.

'I'm not sure "like" is quite the word, but I could tell you a few stories about them,' she replied. 'We've got some monster bugs back home – great huge dunny spiders, the lot. So, are you some kind of bug exterminator or something then?'

'Er ... sort of. I'm a lecturer in entomology at the university here.'

It was Mona's turn to look embarrassed. 'Sorry Oz, I guess I haven't met many university types.'

'And he hasn't met many models,' cut in Kieran, returning from the bar with three glasses.

'You're a model?' Oz hadn't looked so impressed since one of his colleagues nurtured his own head lice for the purposes of experimentation. 'Wow.'

Mona waved his admiration aside. 'Oh, it's not really all that "wow", not when you've done it for a good few years like I have. I'm sure it's much more interesting working in a university – or being a journalist,' she added, directing a smile at Kieran. 'You know, I've always wanted to write.'

'Well, Kieran's the man to show you how,' said Oz. 'Don't suppose you've a yen to learn about the physiology of Sri Lankan hissing cockroaches? Or termites? They're my speciality.'

Mona licked her lips in a way calculated to tease any man to distraction. 'Well you never can tell, Oz. Never say never, that's my motto.'

Mrs Armitage could bear it no longer.

It was past lunchtime and she still didn't know for certain what was going on inside the vicarage. She'd even tried phoning the bishop's office to ask about the new curate, but had been thwarted by the kind of tight-lipped PA who couldn't even have been persuaded to admit that it was Tuesday. And a call to the news desk at the *Courant* had drawn a blank too. Women curates were a long way down their list of exciting news topics, somewhere behind five-legged sheep and people who circumnavigated the globe in bathtubs.

There was nothing for it. It was time for drastic measures.

Five minutes later, she was ringing Gerry Craine's doorbell.

To her disappointment it wasn't Gerry who answered, but Brenda. Jean had always been able to extract information from Gerry without much trouble; Brenda was a somewhat tougher cookie.

'Hello, Jean.'

Jean flashed a mouth full of immaculately whitened dentures. 'Brenda, darling. How are you? You're looking tired.'

This was perfectly true. Brenda's face was even paler than normal, and the tiny lines around her eyes had deepened into a darker web. 'Oh, I'm fine thank you, Jean. Gerry and I just didn't sleep too well last night, that's all.'

Jean's ears pricked up. 'Really? Any particular reason?'

If Mrs Armitage had been hoping for an invitation into the front room, followed by a cup of tea and a prompt confession, she was in for a disappointment. 'No, not really. Was there anything in particular you wanted, only I'm a little bit busy just at the moment.'

'It was just about last night's PCC meeting,' said Jean. 'Gerry rushed away so quickly, we didn't really make any arrangements to finish going through the agenda. Incidentally, he is all right, isn't he? We were so concerned when he left like that, it's just not like him.'

'No,' said Brenda with the ghost of a sigh; and for a split second Jean thought she might be getting somewhere. 'But he's fine, thank you, it was nothing serious. If that's all, I'll get Gerry to phone you when he gets in.'

She was about to close the door when Jean made a last, desperate bid for information. 'The postman happened to mention you've got a guest staying with you,' she blurted out.

Brenda's expression was inscrutable. 'Oh yes?'

'A very attractive young woman, apparently.'

'Hm?'

This was like getting blood out of the proverbial stone. 'I and the other PCC members were just wondering if she'll be staying long enough for us to get to meet her,' fished Mrs Armitage.

'I really don't know,' replied Brenda. 'I couldn't say.'

'Oh. So she's not someone who's moving here permanently then? Like . . . like a new curate, for example?'

There was a short moment of suspense, and then Brenda smiled coldly. 'Not that it's any of your business but. . .let's just say she's a friend of the family, Jean. Now if you don't mind, I really must get back to my work.'

Back at his desk in the *Courant*'s offices, Kieran popped a couple of Polo Mints into his mouth to damp down the smell of beer and garlic, and went back to his feature on 'Cotswold Park Benches of Yesteryear' for the weekly supplement. What with the drink, the food and Oz's conversation, it was a tough job keeping awake, let alone generating any enthusiasm.

Just as he was getting into his stride, Sandra the features editor hove into view, dominatrix-like in spiky Victorian-style boots, a tight black slit skirt and lipstick so red it made Kieran's eyes hurt.

'Hello, stranger. Had a nice lunch out, did we?'

He looked up. 'Yes thanks. And don't worry, I'll stay late to make up the time.' Not that I don't always work late anyway, he added silently. He couldn't remember the last time he'd actually worked the hours set out in his contract but hey, that was the price you paid if you wanted to be a big-shot feature writer some day.

'Good boy.' Sandra perched her bottom on the corner of his workstation.

'Was there something else? Only I'm a bit busy,' he hinted.

'Ah yes, the park benches.' Sandra's mouth gave an ironic twist. 'Fascinating stuff, how I envy you. There was just one little thing, actually.'

'What's that then?'

'Rosie on the news desk had a call this morning from some funny woman in St Jude's. It was hard to make out what she was on about, but apparently she's convinced there's something going on at the vicarage. Load of old rubbish, I suppose?'

Kieran took a close interest in his keyboard. 'How would I know?'

'Well, you are marrying the vicar's daughter,' Sandra pointed out sweetly. 'So you'd be bound to know about any funny business, wouldn't you? Hm?'

'Not necessarily,' he parried. 'Anyway, you said it yourself – it was just some funny woman. We get dozens of calls from nutters every day.'

He moaned inwardly. The last thing he wanted was to let Sandra and the *Courant* in on the Craine family's bombshell – or to let Belle down. Already he could imagine the reception Belle would have in store for him if he did. But his boss was a woman of rare perception and even rarer persistence.

Sandra tilted her head down until she was looking him square in the face – albeit from a rather strange angle – and he could no longer avoid her gaze. 'It's no good, Kieran, I can read you like a book.'

'Drop it, Sandra. I really don't want to talk about it.'

'So! Rosie's hunch was right – there is something going on.' She rubbed her hands with glee. 'Out with it, boy, and I want all the gory details.'

Chapter 6

Away from the vicarage and St Jude's, it was really quite easy to believe that nothing untoward had happened; that the biggest item of local news was Mr Jarvis's new conservatory; and that Mona Starr simply didn't exist.

It was breakfast time, and as usual Belle was busy burning toast while Kieran was in the bathroom, trying to persuade his stubbly face that it really didn't want to grow a beard. A stream of curses issued forth through the half-open door as he cut himself, just like he always did. Kieran occasionally stayed the night at Belle's place, although it was a good deal too bijou for a man of his dimensions. He invariably bumped his elbows on the bathroom cabinet, got cramp sitting at the tiny breakfast bar, or hit his head on the pull-down bed.

'You know, I don't care what kind of property we end up buying,' he called through the gap, 'as long as it's got plenty of space. You couldn't swing a bloody ant in here, let alone a cat.'

'Assuming you'd want to,' Belle pointed out, blowing on her fingers as she prised hot slices out of the toaster. 'Which I truly hope you don't.'

'You know what I mean.' He emerged from the tiny bathroom with bits of bloodstained loo roll dotted all over his manly jaw. 'Remind me never to stay the night here again, or I'll end up looking like Quasimodo before I'm forty.'

'Never again? That's what you said last time,' Belle reminded him, fetching the butter and jam from the fridge. 'And the fourteen times before that. Or is it fifteen? And after I showed you my new Agent Provocateur undies, you didn't seem that keen on going home.'

Kieran stuck out his tongue at her. 'Is it my fault if you're a wicked seductress and I'm a mere weak-willed male who just can't say no?' He seized her by the waist and swung her round into an embrace that squeezed all the breath out of her but left her tingling deliciously. 'See? Even when you're wearing those pyjamas I can't keep my hands off you.'

Belle looked down at herself. 'What's wrong with these pyjamas?'

'Oh – nothing. Except the fact that you're wearing them.' He grinned lasciviously. 'But we can soon put that right.'

She giggled in his arms as he attacked her buttons with his teeth. 'Hey, tiger, some of us can't afford to be late for work,' she reminded him. 'Not since head office gave Waylon that stupid timecard system.'

'Sod Waylon,' snorted Kieran, his words slightly muffled by a mouthful of pyjama. 'How's about I tell him where to stick his system? You can have a full-time position pandering to my every whim.'

'Not unless you pander to mine too,' Belle replied sweetly, then she whispered seductively in his ear, 'Darling, I think your toast's going cold.'

It's unlikely that Kieran would have been deterred just by the thought of cold, rubbery toast; but the metallic snap of the letter box did manage to penetrate his consciousness. 'Hey – the post. Could be some more house details to look at.'

Belle groaned. Ever since Kieran had decided it 'made sense' for everything to come to her address because she had 'more free time' to sort through it all, she'd been gradually sinking beneath a slew of paper. Still, he was right about the need for them to find somewhere to buy. If they didn't, they might have to move into Kieran's place, and that was something that didn't bear thinking about. No way did Belle want to start her married life as an optional add-on to Kieran's bachelor life. They needed somewhere that would give them both a fresh start, otherwise Belle knew she could never hold her own, or build something that was uniquely theirs.

'The post? Well, that's just great!' protested Belle, as Kieran trotted off to the front door. 'First you diss my pyjamas, and now I'm playing second fiddle to the postman! What happened to you ravishing me over the breakfast table?'

He blew her a kiss over his shoulder. 'Just hold that thought, darling, I'll be right back.'

'Anything worth getting excited about?' Belle enquired as she slapped a dollop of butter onto a round of charcoal-rimmed toast. She reached out for the mail but Kieran ploughed straight past, opening it as he went. Typical.

'Let's see . . . What looks like a bank statement . . .' He chucked it at her and she caught it. 'Junk, more junk.' They went straight into the bin. 'Gas bill, phone bill, more junk . . . aha! Couple of bulky letters postmarked Gloucester – that'll be the latest batch of stuff from the estate agents.' Discarding the rest, he seized his prize and went to sit on the end of the bed.

'So much for *my* post.' Belle said pointedly as she gathered up the rest, but Kieran was far too absorbed to notice. 'Hey, you never said there was a postcard from Ros!' She waved it in front of his face. 'Wow, look – she's in Hawaii. How glam is that?'

Kieran grunted non-committally, and went on leafing through the sheaf of house details.

'Hawaii.' The word exited Belle's mouth like a plaintive sigh. Jacking in a secure job and bumming around the world with a backpack might not be her style, but Hawaii certainly did look awfully nice on the postcard: all waving palms and gorgeous sunsets. She tried to imagine what it must be like, wriggling your toes into all that soft, warm, golden sand and shaking your booty in a grass skirt, but the best comparison she had was with wading about in shorts on the mudflats at Weston-super-Mare, and she had a pretty good idea it wasn't anything like that at all. She'd have to ask Ros to relive it all in gorgeous Technicolor detail as soon as she got back – if she ever did. Wedding or no wedding, Belle had serious doubts that Ros would ever be able to bring herself to give up her new life of adventure and come back to nice, safe, ordinary Cheltenham, where the theft of a concrete bollard was front-page news.

There was no avoiding the truth: Belle had simply never been the unconventional type. As a small child, she'd been the kind that adults described as 'wise beyond her years', when what they really meant was 'boring and a bit timid'. On one memorable birthday, it had taken her dad six attempts to get her to go down the big slide in Pittville Park, and even then she'd got stuck halfway down and ripped a big hole in her shorts. But right now, when it felt like the sky was falling in big grey chunks all around her and there was nothing she could do but stand by and let it happen, Belle was just beginning to comprehend the appeal of being footloose, carrying your home in your rucksack and never staying in one place long enough to get too comfortable. Hm, bit like Mona in a way, she pondered. All that swanning around between glamorous assignments. It must be nice to be able to move on whenever you felt like it but even so, Belle doubted she could ever be like that herself. She'd spend all her time worrying about whether she'd left the iron on, and how the shop was getting on without her.

She turned over the postcard to see what Ros had written. It was a short message, but to the point:

Having a great time, but missing you.
WISH YOU WERE HERE?
Bet you do, lots of love, Ros xxx

Belle smiled to herself. Ros was a woman of few words, but they were mostly worth listening to. Belle could just imagine her sitting there outside some beach bar, drinking something alcoholic out of a coconut shell and thinking how best to wind up her best mate from half a world away.

'Well, it's nice to see somebody enjoying themselves,' she commented out loud as she wriggled into her Green Goddess work clothes, a crisp, white T-shirt and dark green trousers, and stuffed the matching apron into her handbag.

Kieran looked up briefly from his sheaf of house details. 'Hm?'

'Ros. She's obviously having a good time in Hawaii.'

'Oh, right. Good for her.' Kieran went on reading, clearly on autopilot.

'A damn sight better time than we're having, anyway – thanks to you know who.' Belle felt her skin prickling with muted fury as Mona Starr's smiling face came back into her mind again. If I was a cat, she thought to herself, every hair on my back would be standing on end. As it was, her jaw was aching from clenching her teeth so hard.

A few supportive words from her fiancé would have been nice, but it was pretty obvious they weren't forthcoming. 'Are you listening?' she demanded, making him budge up a bit so that she could sit down next to him.

He glanced up again. 'What's that? Yes, of course you look nice, you always look nice.' He went on before Belle could think of a suitable reply. 'Ah well, there's nothing much in this latest batch for us, not unless you're into massive DIY or one of those houses with the metal shutters on the Bluebell Estate.' He put an arm round her shoulders and gave her a hug. 'Chin up kid, we'll find something, don't worry.'

The hug was a nice one, and Belle decided to forgive him for not listening. Besides, Kieran had set her thoughts off on a different tack. 'Is that really the best we can afford?'

'Well . . . no,' he admitted. 'I'm exaggerating a bit. But the way prices are at the moment, we may have to set our sights lower and go for an apartment to start off with. Maybe even move into my place . . .'

'Surely we'll find somewhere by the time we get married.' Belle felt a pang of anxiety.

'Yes – if we don't mind settling for a flat. Pity though . . . once the babies start arriving, we'll have to move again to get more space. So we'll hardly be in the place ten minutes before we're having to go through the whole house-hunting process all over again.'

'I suppose so,' said Belle, not altogether comfortable with the new direction the conversation was taking. 'But it's not like we're starting a family the minute we get married . . . I mean it's not as if there's any tearing hurry . . .'

'Tell you one thing though.' Kieran's gaze took in the entire studio apartment in one sweep. 'It's a real pity you're renting this place, and didn't buy it, like I bought mine. You've been living here a long time now, and prices have really shot up. Think of the extra capital we could have had from the sale if you'd just listened to me. All that wasted rent.'

Money talk always made Belle feel queasy. It might have had something to do with having a vicar as a dad, but on the whole it was more that Belle Craine and money didn't talk the same language. Everything in her financial world was determinedly small-scale. As far as she was concerned, dazzling financial success meant keeping within her overdraft limit for more than two months running, and career success meant earning enough money to buy the things she needed. And what was wrong with that?

Even worse, Kieran's critical tone pressed all the wrong buttons. Belle might be mild-mannered, but she sure as hell wasn't a doormat. 'Well, darling,' she replied with acid in her voice, 'some of us waste our money on rent, and others waste it on paintballing weekends in the Scottish Highlands and belonging to the most expensive gym in Cheltenham. Don't they?'

'Keeping fit's very important,' he sniffed. 'Plus it's my hobby. And anyway, you should have bought yourself somewhere for your own sake, it's a much better investment than renting. Everyone knows that. Renting's about as sensible as . . . as dropping your money out of an aeroplane.'

Belle was getting more than a bit fed up with being lectured like a naughty schoolgirl. 'Come on, Kieran, not everybody's like you. People have different values. You're a journalist, you should know that.' She glanced across at the glossy postcard, with its smiling people in leis and its waving palms, and she could almost smell the salt and spices in the air. 'Who's to say one person's way of living isn't just as good as another's, even if it is a bit different?'

There was a short silence, then light dawned on Kieran. 'Am I being a pain in the backside again? I am, aren't I?'

'Just a bit,' Belle agreed. 'That "Uncle Kieran knows best" routine of yours is wearing a bit thin.'

'I'm sorry sweetheart, I didn't mean to sound like a bank manager with a stick up his backside. I just care about our future together, that's all.'

'I know. But so do I. I just do it in a different way.' He should understand that by now, her subconscious added, but Belle didn't say it out loud. She reckoned she'd got her point across, so what was the point of more aggro?

He tossed the papers to one side. 'Never mind, we'll look in the property supplement on Thursday, and just keep on looking until we find our dream pad.' He yawned until his jaw clicked. 'By the way, did Mona tell you about her place in Melbourne? It sounds like really something.'

Belle felt the icy tension creep into her neck and shoulders. 'No,' she said quietly. 'She didn't.'

'Three-bedroom bungalow, garden, garage with those cool electric doors . . . and less than half of what you'd pay here. She even has a swimming pool in the back yard.'

'Really.' Belle could hardly believe the way he was going on. He was already talking about Mona as if she was a real member of the family, not a cuckoo who was pulling the adoptive nest apart. Why did he have to be the one to show her round Cheltenham and keep her out of people's way? Why did anybody, if it came to that? And why did he have to enjoy her company so much? She sniffed. 'Everybody in Australia has a pool in the back yard. Haven't you ever seen *Neighbours*?'

'Now that's a girl whose feet are on the ground,' Kieran went on without paying the slightest heed, nodding to himself approvingly. 'Soon as she earned a decent amount from modelling, she put all her money into property. Obviously got a good head on her shoulders.'

When Belle spoke it was between clenched teeth. 'Obviously much better than mine, at any rate.'

The sarcasm bounced right off Kieran. 'Oh, I wouldn't necessarily go that far,' he replied, rubbing his chin. 'I mean, you've got a lot of common sense. But she certainly thinks things out clearly, you can tell that just from talking to her.'

This was just too much for Belle. 'Thinks things out! Oh yeah, it really takes brains to make sure you turn up for your grand entrance on the other side of the world, without a word of warning, and announce that you're some poor guy's illegitimate daughter. Oh – and to make sure you turn up just in time to mess up his legitimate daughter's wedding plans. You're right, she must be smart – because that's what I call perfect timing!'

'Oh.' Kieran blinked at her in surprise. 'I didn't realise you still felt so negative towards her,' he said. 'I mean, I know it was a shock and that it's hard for you and your family at the moment, but once you've all got used to the idea and—'

Belle turned on him. 'No Kieran, you don't know. You don't have the faintest idea how hard it is!'

'It's going to be OK though, I'm sure,' said Kieran. 'Mona's a nice girl, you know. She really is.'

Belle felt like screaming. How was it that supposedly intelligent men like Kieran invariably had a blind-spot the size of Everest whenever an attractive woman stole centre stage? Mona Starr could have been the

Sydney Strangler or the Woomera Wolf Woman, and he'd still have looked surprised and said, 'But she's such a nice girl.'

'Yes, well, you'd know, wouldn't you?' snapped Belle. 'The amount of time you've been spending with her over the last couple of days, you should know her entire bloody life story by now.'

'I've only been showing her round, you know that. Even your dad agreed it was a good idea. And I thought I was keeping her out of your mum's way until she got used to the idea. . . Look, it's not like any of the rest of you have done anything to make her feel welcome, is it?'

A great silent scream filled Belle's head. 'That's because she isn't welcome! Would you welcome some tart if she turned up and started destroying your dad's life, his career, his reputation – everything?'

'I haven't got a dad,' Kieran reminded her quietly. 'If you remember, I don't have much of a family.'

Belle felt fleetingly guilty. 'Sorry. I didn't think.'

'And Mona's not a tart either,' Kieran went on. 'OK, maybe I wouldn't welcome her,' he admitted. 'But she's not trying to destroy anything. And it's hardly her fault that she is who she is.'

'Possibly – unless this is some huge scam – but it is her fault she didn't even warn us, just wafted into Cheltenham and made her big announcement, like she thinks she's the Angel Gabriel or something.'

Belle realised that she was panting, and her whole body was sticky with sweat. Mona Starr really had got well and truly under her skin.

'Blimey,' said Kieran, 'I had no idea you were still so hostile.'

'And I had no idea you could be so insensitive.'

On her way out of the flat, Belle took a last look at Ros's postcard. 'Wish you were here?' Yes Ros, thought Belle. You know, I bloody well do.

There was nothing quite like a mother and daughter Saturday shopping expedition for rekindling old arguments.

'Mona reckons I'd look good in Empire line,' announced Jax as she and her mother sorted through the rails of bridesmaids' dresses at the Bridal Fayre boutique. 'Seeing as I'm so tall and slim,' she added with more than a hint of smugness.

'Does she, now?' Brenda muttered something inaudible under her breath. 'Well, I'm sure Annabelle will be happy if we can just get you into a dress. What about this lovely one?' She plucked it off the rail. 'It's very feminine.'

Jax's pierced nose wrinkled in disgust. 'Feminine? Oh Mum! I wouldn't be seen dead in pink.' She pushed dresses along the rail, one by one. 'In fact I wouldn't be seen dead in any of these, full stop.'

Brenda silently counted to ten, and reminded herself that family weddings were supposed to be joyous affairs. 'Don't be silly, Jacqueline, you've only looked at a few dresses. I'm sure there's something here that'll suit you. They have the biggest selection in the whole of Gloucestershire,' she added, quoting from the brochure. Just as well; it looked as if they were going to need it.

Right on cue, a pleasant-faced, middle-aged assistant glided forward. She had the permanently fixed smile of someone who spent her entire working life dealing with tears, tantrums and unrealistic demands, and was clearly suffering from politeness overload. Brenda recognised a fellow-sufferer instantly. Having to be nice to obnoxious people was something a vicar's wife had to do most days of the week. This poor woman probably went straight home and kicked hell out of the nearest inanimate object – unless her husband got in the way first.

'I'm Amanda, can I help at all?' enquired the assistant.

'No,' replied Jax.

'Yes, please,' replied Brenda, at precisely the same moment, with a hard stare at her intransigent daughter. 'As you can see, Jacqueline isn't really a dresses sort of person, so we're looking for something really—'

'Different,' cut in Jax firmly. 'Nothing like this load of old cr—'

Brenda stopped her in the nick of time with a sharp, 'Jacqueline!', then turned back to the assistant with a polite smile. 'Something feminine but not too flouncy, if you get my meaning.'

'And definitely not pink,' added Jax, eager as ever to have the last word.

'What kind of style will the bride be wearing?'

'Meringue, probably,' grunted Jax. 'Something that makes her look like one of those crocheted dollies you stick on top of toilet rolls.'

Over in the opposite corner of the showroom, another customer sniggered into the merchandise. Brenda's blood pressure climbed high enough to blast the pigeons off the store roof. 'Annabelle hasn't made her final choice yet,' she said. 'But it will be simple and elegant. And definitely not a meringue.'

'And the colour?'

'Ivory, I think.' The fact that Brenda knew that Belle was currently favouring a less traditional pale gold was neither here nor there. If she couldn't persuade Belle into virginal white, ivory was as far as she was willing to compromise. A mother had standards to maintain, particularly when that mother was also a vicar's wife.

Amanda beckoned them over to another rail of multicoloured frocks. 'Any of these would look good with ivory,' she assured them. 'And the boning in this one would add curves to madame's ... er ... gamine figure.'

'Are you saying I'm too skinny?' demanded Jax, with a murderous look.

'No, of course not, madame,' Amanda replied, hastily replacing the gown on the rail. 'But every young lady likes to make the most of her assets. And I'm sure you'll want to show off your lovely slim figure.'

Vaguely mollified, Jax perused the frocks one by one. 'Boring, too frilly, very boring, oh my God no, yuk pink again, boring, boring ... Nope, there's nothing here,' she announced.

Brenda threw Amanda a desperate look. Amanda responded with an understanding smile. Brenda wondered whether she kept a cricket bat under the counter for the really difficult customers.

'Well, we do offer a full range of colours,' Amanda went on. 'So if you wanted, say ... this one, you could have it in burgundy, or yellow, or even electric blue if that was what you fancied.'

'Electric blue?' Jax's face brightened. 'That's more like it.'

'And then there's our Special Collection catalogue.' Amanda fetched it out from underneath a pile of tiaras. 'Cutting-edge designs by today's top young designers. Of course, they do come a little more expensive ...'

Brenda strove not to think about her crumbling budget. Her daughter was going to be a bridesmaid; that was what mattered. For once in her life, Jacqueline Craine was going to look as beautiful as nature intended, and they would all be together: one happy family.

'Go on then,' said Jax. 'Let's cop a look.' She flicked through the first few pages. 'Hmph, I wouldn't call that cutting edge, I saw one just like it in Debenhams last week. Besides, Mona said I ought to avoid green, 'cause it'd make my complexion look sallow.'

'Is Mona another of your sisters, then?' enquired Amanda, making friendly conversation.

'Yes,' declared Jax, at the very same moment that Brenda snapped, 'No.'

Jax pouted. 'Half-sister,' she insisted defiantly.

'Well, she has absolutely nothing to do with this,' retorted Brenda, covering the feeling of deep upset that she suddenly felt with a veneer of anger. How could her younger daughter just accept this Mona girl as a member of the family? How could Gerry appear so calm, when she, his wife of a quarter-century, was weeping inside? She could barely even cope with thinking about the girl, let alone talking about her. And when she did enter her thoughts, those thoughts amounted to only one thing: wondering when she would get out of their spare bedroom, move on, and leave them all in peace.

'Mona is a fashion model,' sniffed Jax. 'So she must know what she's talking about.'

Good grief, thought Brenda, pondering the fickleness of teenagers. One minute the radical feminist, the next, starry-eyed over some six-foot Australian Barbie doll. Brenda wasn't altogether sure which version of Jax was the worse.

Her eyes narrowed. 'Just choose something, Jacqueline. Or I'll get back on the phone to Cousin Trixie.'

That was all the motivation Jax needed to take a serious look at the catalogue. Settling her combat-clad bottom on a gold brocade chaise longue, she perused every single page. 'Hm, guess this one's not *too* bad, but . . . Ooh Mum, this one's great! Can I have this one, can I?'

Astounded by such a display of enthusiasm, Brenda and Amanda both craned their necks to look at the picture. It showed a bride, groom and bridesmaids all clad in black, with little touches of blood-red lace. The groom was even wearing an old-fashioned undertaker's hat, with a veil down the back, while the bride was sporting black lipstick and nail polish, and a crimson velvet choker that made her look as if her throat had been cut.

All of Brenda's resolutions, to accept whatever her daughter chose, flew out of the window; and Jax's hopeful expression was met by a wall of absolute horror. The look of hostility on her mother's face was so ferocious that she didn't have to utter a single word.

'Aw, why not?' whined Jax. 'You're all fascists, that's what you are. Why give me the catalogue to look at it if I can't choose what I want?' Jax retreated into full-on sulk mode.

'We . . . er . . . find that old-fashioned gothic look is a little out of favour with our more fashion-conscious customers at the moment,' said Amanda. Jax looked up. 'They seem to find it rather passé. But if you just turn to page eighty-seven, I think you might find something that both you and your mum can live with.'

The look on page 87 wasn't exactly classical. Then again, it wasn't unspeakably outrageous either – and there wasn't a hint of black. It was definitely more Gwen Stefani than Marilyn Manson. Admittedly the slit up the front climbed so high that it very nearly met the neckline on its downward plunge, and crimson sequins weren't everybody's idea of bridal wear, but at least it was a dress. And Jax didn't stick her finger down her throat or immediately turn the page.

'That's the one,' announced Brenda.

'I haven't told you the price yet,' pointed out the assistant.

'I don't care.'

'I haven't even told you if I like it yet!' protested Jax.

Damn, thought Brenda. 'Well?' she demanded.

'It's . . . OK . . . I guess.'

'Right, that's it then. We'll have some lunch, then we'll go and see your sister at work. And if she thinks it's all right, we're having it.' She glanced at Jax, for once open-mouthed. 'And before you change your mind, Amanda can get you measured up. Oh, and do close your mouth Jacqueline, you look like the village idiot.'

Belle was working this Saturday, but she didn't mind. In fact she enjoyed her one Saturday in four behind the till, and not just because she got a day off in the week when everybody else was slaving away in their offices; it was because they were busy, and however lazy she might be when it came to the gym, Belle loved nothing better than a big queue of customers and products flying off the shelves.

There was only one down side to Saturdays – well, three really. Their names were Millie, Dan and Waylon. Millie and Dan were the latest clueless duo of sixteen year-old Saturday assistants, who invariably caused more work than they actually did. It wouldn't have been so bad if they'd just been the usual schoolkids with no interest in shop work and a big breeze between the ears; this pair weren't just daft, they were mad keen to please . . . and to make matters much, much worse, they were utterly, nauseatingly in love. It was like working with a couple of Care Bears. Sometimes Belle found it sweet, sometimes funny; but on a busy Saturday with the store full to bursting, Belle felt her time would have been better spent spotting shoplifters than sorting out their muddles.

Then there was Waylon. For some reason, whenever Belle was working Saturdays, the manager was working too. She was starting to get quite paranoid about it. Did he really think she was so incapable that he had to be around? It didn't make sense. After all, he often left her and Lily to fend for themselves on weekdays – putting Belle effectively in charge of the shop. There was only one answer: he didn't think she could cope with a busy Saturday, and he was just waiting for her to make a mistake so that he could give her the boot.

Needless to say, Lily had a different theory. She reckoned Waylon was secretly in love with Belle, and only came in on a Saturday so that he could ogle her at his leisure among the talcum powders and foot balms. Belle thought this highly unlikely, but was nevertheless a bit miffed when Kieran fell about laughing at the idea. After all, why shouldn't men worship her from afar – even if they were short, bald paintballing fanatics whose real name was rumoured to be Arnold?

'Thank you sir, thank you madam, do call again.' Belle served a young couple with a selection of organic baby products and excused herself from Waylon and the counter for a moment so that she could dive into the stockroom and prise Millie and Dan apart. 'Are you two planning to do any work today, or are you just going to spend the whole day eating each other's faces off?' she demanded.

Two crimson faces looked at her apologetically. 'Sorry Belle,' giggled Millie. 'Dan was just showing me how to price up these gift boxes, and I got all muddled up, didn't I, Dan?'

'Looks more like you both got muddled up,' observed Belle drily as she took in an array of undone buttons. 'Look, you'd better sort yourselves out or Mr Smith will be down on you like a ton of bricks.'

'Sorry, Belle. I'll get right on with those soaps.' Dan stepped backwards, crushed a gift set with his size ten shoe and fell over.

'Ooh Dan, are you all right?' Millie leapt to help him to his feet. 'Let me feel you all over in case you've broken something.'

Belle groaned, gave up and retreated to the counter.

Waylon handed over change to the last person in the queue, and slammed the cash drawer shut. 'Now it's quietened down a bit,' he said, 'I'd like a private word with you, young lady.'

Belle's heart turned to a lead weight in her chest. 'Oh,' she said. 'I was afraid you might.' She swallowed hard. 'To be honest, I've been racking my brains for weeks to think what it is I've been doing wrong, but I just can't fathom it out.'

Waylon scratched his freckled pate, sparsely furnished here and there with the remains of a full head of carroty-red hair. 'What are you on about, Belle?' he demanded.

'About you keeping an eye on me to see what mistakes I've been making.'

'I don't know where you got that idea from,' said Waylon. 'This isn't about you doing anything wrong.'

Another thought, a very crazy one, flashed briefly into Belle's head. Surely Lily couldn't be right about the manager fancying her? She was practically a married woman, and she loathed running about in forests, splattering people with emulsion! And if he did like her in that way . . . well, quite frankly Belle didn't know whether to feel flattered, embarrassed or just a bit nauseous. 'Oh?' she ventured, afraid to utter anything more specific in case she got it all wrong again.

'Well, OK, I admit I have been watching you,' conceded Waylon, 'but only so that I could be sure.'

'Sure? About what?'

'About how you cope with running the store on busy days – staff management, prioritising your tasks, merchandising, paperwork . . . Anyhow, I'm pleased to say that you've been doing very well. In fact I'd say you have real management potential.'

'Oh!' Belle knew she sounded idiotic, but she was so taken aback by these rare words of praise that she hadn't the faintest idea what else to say.

Waylon leaned his elbows on the counter. 'The thing is, Belle, head office wants flagship store managers like, ahem,' he coughed modestly, 'me to spend more time out in the field, motivating staff in the less successful outlets. You've probably noticed that I've been away from the store quite a lot lately, and that's going to increase. So I need someone to rely on back here, someone who I know will take good care of the store. Someone like you.'

'Me!'

'Don't look so surprised, Belle. We haven't had a deputy manager since Tony had his breakdown, so you've been filling in a lot for me as it is. Let's just say this is a chance to make things more formal. And of course, there'll be an appropriate increase in salary to go with the job title. Have a think about it and let me know what you think.'

Belle was so flabbergasted that she didn't know what to say. Whether she would have come up with any kind of sensible response, she was never to discover; because a customer had just approached the counter.

'Excuse me, Belle,' said a familiar voice. As Belle turned round her heart stopped.

'M-mona.' She had trouble getting the word out.

But Mona looked, as ever, cool as a cucumber. 'Could you spare a couple of minutes?' she asked with a smile. 'Only I could really use some good advice about organic moisturiser.'

Kieran didn't normally work Saturdays. As a feature writer, he had the luxury of a Monday-to-Friday job, though the hours could be so long on occasion that the days tended to run into each other.

This particular Saturday was a bit special, though. He'd been summoned to Bassett Hall, in the middle of the Gloucestershire countryside, to interview Mad Dog McKindrick, veteran bass-player of the legendary rock group Afterlife. Mad Dog didn't give interviews, every journalist knew that. He was a total recluse except when he and the band were on tour, and these days even that wasn't very often. That was why when Kieran got the call – even though it was Saturday – he jumped straight into his car and headed off to the Cotswold village of Ampney Bassett.

He didn't even have time to do any research. So when the big electric gates at Bassett Hall swung open to admit him, Kieran was just a tad worried about putting his foot in it. Certain lurid tales regarding Mr McKindrick tended to stick in the mind: like the time a newspaper had spelled his name wrong, and he'd mailed the editor a crate of live, poisonous South American frogs. Kieran certainly wasn't prepared for the positively polite welcome he received.

'Hi, Kieran?' Mad Dog, instantly recognisable by his substance-ravaged features, red bandanna and Wolverhampton accent, was there in the entrance hall to greet him. 'Good to meet ya. Fancy a bevvy?'

'Er ... great.' Better not say no, thought Kieran, but then again he didn't want to get arrested. 'Thanks. It'd better be a small one though, I'm driving.'

Mad Dog laughed. Actually it was more of a vulpine howl, but there was humour in it. 'I was thinking of tea,' he explained. 'I've kicked the booze and drugs, you know. Cleaned up my whole life.'

Kieran's eyebrows shot up to meet his hairline. 'Really. Wow.' Shit, he thought; that's the kind of thing I should have known. I'm never going to get my entrée to Fleet Street if I don't make more of these chances. 'Congratulations, Mr McKindrick.'

'Call me Mad Dog.' It was more of a command than an invitation. Mad Dog led him into a huge sitting room, opulently furnished in a Moroccan style that blended surprisingly well with the Tudor architecture. 'Take a seat,' he growled amiably, and Kieran obediently sat, half-vanishing into the depths of a very sumptuous pile of floor cushions. 'It's OK, you don't have to look like you already knew about me getting clean,' he continued. 'You're the first to get the story. I decided, why let those London wankers in on the act? What've they ever done for me? This is where I live now; keep it local. That's why I rang your editor.'

Kieran mentally punched the air. 'I'm really glad you did.'

'Of course, I made him promise to send me the best man he had.' Mad Dog paused for effect. 'But you were the only one he could contact.' He waited until Kieran's face had fallen down to his boots, then burst out laughing again. 'Sorry mate, I couldn't resist it. Wicked sense of humour, me.'

'Wicked,' agreed Kieran, though he was thinking something rather different.

Mad Dog rubbed his hands together in anticipation. 'Right, where shall we start?'

'How about the day you first realised you had a problem with booze and drugs?' suggested Kieran. Nothing ventured, nothing gained, he told himself.

'Ah, yeah.' Mad Dog nodded as he reminisced. 'Well, I reckon that'd be the day I was trying to mend my boots and I was so out of it I nailed my foot to the floor. Fancy a couple of HobNobs with that cup of char?'

A couple of hours later, and full of tea, biscuits and exclusive information, Kieran was on his way back to Cheltenham, whistling all the way. The interview had gone well. So well, in fact, that Mad Dog had given him a handful of invitations to a big 'Coming Clean' party he was holding in a few weeks' time. Belle's going to love this, thought Kieran, thinking of all the megastars who'd probably be there. And I might even get another exclusive out of it . . .

It was just as he was driving into the centre of Cheltenham that his day took a turn for the worse. As he passed by, he couldn't help noticing the newspaper-sellers with their mobile stands, hawking the final edition of the Saturday *Courant*. Wonder what the big story is today, he mused. MYSTERY FUNGUS ATTACKS MAYOR'S SPROUTS, perhaps? Or CHELTENHAM GRANNY CAMPAIGNS AGAINST EVILS OF CHEWING GUM?

He was smiling to himself at the thought when he caught sight of one of the posters displayed on the stands . . . and the smile slid from his face like ice off a roof in April.

A moment later he was accelerating through Cheltenham towards the *Courant*'s offices. He had to see the editor; but he feared it was much, much too late. They waited till I was out of the office, he thought to himself with growing fury. They knew I'd kick up a stink about them publishing the story, so they made sure I couldn't put a spanner in the works. The total bastards.

But even as he railed against his fellow journos, he couldn't help admitting the truth; in their place, he'd have done exactly the same.

Mona and Belle were standing in the corner by the organic moisturisers.

'Are you dry, greasy or combination?' demanded Belle, determined to keep this as professional as possible.

Mona looked momentarily puzzled, then chuckled. 'Oh, skin you mean! Look, I don't actually want any moisturiser, I just came in 'cause we haven't really got off on the right foot.'

'You could say that,' agreed Belle.

'Well, I thought maybe if I came and had a chat, I could make you see that all I want is for everybody to be happy.'

Belle held in her anger, but with difficulty. 'Mona, if you wanted us to be happy, you wouldn't have turned up out of nowhere, without so much as a phone call, a letter – nothing.'

Mona sighed. 'I know it was a bit insensitive,' she admitted, 'but you have to believe me . . . this all came as a huge shock to me, too. Mum wouldn't tell me anything about my dad for years and years. I thought Eddie – my stepdad – was my real father. And when she finally told me about my dad being a trainee vicar, and coming from Cheltenham, I couldn't resist trying to find out about him on the Net. Can you blame me for that?'

'No, I suppose not. But why didn't you warn us? Have you any idea what this is doing to my mum and dad? Have you any idea how selfish it is, turning up out of the blue and just . . . just announcing that you've arrived to turn our world upside down?'

'Jeez, when you put it like that it does sound bad,' conceded Mona. 'But it didn't seem that way at the time. I was confused, you know. I didn't know where to turn, not since my stepdad died. And I was excited too – I'd just found out I had a real family on the other side of the world, and I wanted to meet them all right away. You can understand that, can't you?' Then, just as Belle was almost prepared to admit that possibly she could, Mona made a big mistake by adding smugly, 'Kieran understands. Him not having a family and all that.'

'Oh yes,' flared Belle, 'I'm sure Kieran understands! In fact I'm starting to think he understands just a bit too well.'

'Oh Belle, surely you don't resent him spending a little bit of time showing me round the place?'

'As long as that's all he shows you.' A moment later, Belle realised she'd gone a little over the top with that remark. 'Look,' she said wearily, 'I don't mind if Kieran gives you the grand tour or whatever, that's fine. But it's no use you thinking we can all be big buddies overnight, 'cause that's just not going to happen. It's going to take a long time for Mum and Dad to get over this, and I hope to God it doesn't get round the parish . . .'

'Well, I wouldn't say anything to anybody,' replied Mona, looking wounded. 'Tell you what, kid, can you and me start all over again? And I'll try and get it right this time?'

Belle looked suspiciously at the proffered hand, hesitated and then briefly took it. 'Well, we can try. I guess.'

'That Kieran of yours is a real catch, you know. A totally nice guy.'

'I know,' replied Belle smartly. 'That's why I'm marrying him.' And don't you forget it, she added under her breath.

At about the same time as Kieran was racing across Cheltenham, Brenda and Jax were strolling leisurely up the Regent Arcade after a nice lunch and a relaxing head massage at the new beauty parlour. All wasn't exactly right with the world, but it was certainly an improvement on a few hours ago. Jax was behaving almost like a normal human being, and Brenda was sure that Belle could be persuaded to like – or at least tolerate – her choice of bridesmaid's dress. Compromise, that was the key to family life; just plain, old-fashioned compromise.

As they neared Green Goddess, Brenda extracted the catalogue from her shopping bag. 'Now, we are sure, aren't we?'

Jax gave a long-suffering sigh. 'Yes Mum, we are sure. I suppose.'

'Good. Because I don't want any more silly messing about. Got that?'

Jax gave a grunt that might have been a yes, and Brenda left it at that. Best not push her younger daughter too far.

A breathtaking barrage of scents assailed them as they walked through the door of the shop. Even Jax's eyes watered, and she liked to spend her leisure hours surrounded by joss sticks. 'God,' she coughed, 'I don't know how anyone can work in this place.'

Brenda looked round for Belle in the crowd of shoppers, but at first didn't see her. 'Oh dear, I do hope she's not on her break. Ah, there she is, over there in the corner, talking to—' She came to an abrupt halt. 'Oh. Maybe we'd better come back later.'

'Mum?' Jax followed her mother's eyeline. 'Oh Mum, it's only Mona. Hi, Mona! Over here!'

Reluctantly, Brenda trailed her daughter across the shop floor. Everybody looked at everybody else.

'Hi!' breezed Mona, flashing her electric smile. 'Isn't this great? Almost the whole family together!'

Brenda might well have come up with something caustic in reply, if Kieran hadn't exploded through the door at that very moment, his hair tousled, his face red and sweaty, and his expression positively doom-laden. There was a copy of the *Cheltenham Courant* under his arm.

'Kieran!' Belle smiled with relief. At last, an escape from Mona. 'I wasn't expecting to see you until ... What's the matter?'

Kieran swallowed very hard. 'I had to get here and show you this,' he said, unfolding the newspaper with trembling hands, 'before somebody else did.'

'What are you talking about?'

'Just read it.'

There wasn't a lot to the headline, but it was in large capitals that ran right across the front page; and it read: ST JUDE'S VICAR IN SECRET LOVE-CHILD SHOCK. Nobody really needed to read the rest.

Jax stood open-mouthed and pale. Brenda squeezed her eyes tight shut to hold back the tears. And Belle felt the whole world lurch on its axis, destroying every certainty, every feeling of security she had ever known. She raised her eyes slowly to Kieran's. 'You ... promised,' she whispered. 'You promised this wouldn't happen.'

Kieran raked distracted fingers through his hair. 'I know I did ... and I told her – I told Sandra, this mustn't go any further, it's just between me and you.'

Belle felt the cold hand of betrayal clutching at her heart. 'You did what? You told her?'

'Oh Kieran,' sobbed Brenda, 'how could you?'

He looked from one to the other in bewilderment and despair. 'She already knew, I don't know how. I was just confirming what somebody else had already told her. But she swore to me she'd keep it out of the paper.'

'I'm sure he tried,' cut in Mona, oozing sympathy. 'I'm sure you did your best, Kieran.'

But Belle wasn't listening. She was just staring up at Kieran, trying to believe that the man she loved would do this to her family. 'You promised,' she repeated; all at once the tears started to fall, and she was running ... out of the shop, into the arcade, and then just running. Running until she could make the pain stop.

Chapter 7

'Mind where you're going . . . bloody hell, young people today! No manners at all.'

Belle just kept on running, oblivious to the comments as she pushed her way through the heaving Saturday-afternoon crowds. She didn't really know where she was going, just that she had to get as far away from here – and all these people – as possible. And she would have kept on until her breath failed her, if the end of the arcade hadn't loomed up, its doors opening out into a big rectangle of cold, wintry daylight.

'Are you all right, love?' asked a kindly woman struggling with a couple of boisterous toddlers, as Belle walked out into the open air, her face still streaming with tears.

'I . . . I'm fine thanks, I'm absolutely fine.' If there was one thing harder to bear than what Kieran had done, it was the spontaneous kindness of people who didn't even know her. And to make things infinitely worse, right opposite the entrance to the Regent Arcade stood a newspaper stand, proclaiming to all the world that Gerry Craine, vicar of St Jude's, had a secret illegitimate daughter.

Her cheeks burned as she read the words over and over, unable to tear her eyes away. Ridiculous it might be, but Belle felt as though every single pair of eyes in Cheltenham High Street was trained upon her; that even the people who appeared to be looking the other way, deep in conversation or reading their newspapers, were really covertly spying on her and sniggering behind their hands. Some were probably looking at her with pitying smiles: 'Her father's disgraced his family you know – not to mention the Church.'

Laying her cheek against one of the concrete pillars, she closed her eyes and forced herself to breathe properly. Calm down, Belle, she commanded. This may be bad, but it's not the end of the world. You have to believe that, for your mum and dad's sake.

A hand touched her lightly on the shoulder and she almost jumped out of her skin.

'Belle – oh thank God, I thought I'd lost you.' As the words left his lips, Kieran realised their double meaning. 'I'm so sorry, Belle, oh God, you look terrible.'

She turned to look at him and the tears started coming again, and she hated herself for her weakness. 'Go away,' she said dully.

'You don't mean that, you're just upset.'

'Please, just go away and leave me alone.'

'You 'eard the lady,' intervened a burly man standing nearby. 'She don't want none of yer, so sling yer 'ook.'

For a second, Kieran almost did that very thing. But that would've been like admitting defeat, and – much worse – it would have meant leaving Belle standing there, all alone and looking unhappier than he had ever known her. Recklessly, he swung round and glared at the burly interloper. 'Push off and mind your own business. My fiancée's just had some very bad news.'

Grunting and grumbling, the man bottled out and pushed off; and the other passers-by gradually lost interest in the minor domestic scene.

Belle stopped staring disconsolately at the toes of her shoes, gave a long sniff and looked up at Kieran. 'You haven't gone away,' she commented.

'No,' he admitted. 'But I will now, if you still want me to.'

She thought about that for a long time. Half of her wanted to kick him into the middle of next week, but the other half craved the warmth and affection that only he could give. 'If this was a soap opera,' she said, 'I'd have smacked your face by now.'

'You can if you like.'

'It's not the same if you want me to.' She walked out of the doorway of the arcade, and across the pedestrianised street towards one of the benches outside Marks & Spencer.

'*Big Issue*, love?' enquired the hopeful man who stood there every day of the week with his dog Toby, come rain or shine.

'Next time, John, for sure.' She managed something approaching a smile as she turned away from him and sat down at one end of the empty bench. Her face felt hot, puffy and embarrassing. Why did women have to cry? Why couldn't they get angry and punch people, the way men did? She supposed some women would. Mona Starr for example.

'Can I?' asked Kieran, indicating the empty seat next to her. She didn't answer, so he sat down anyway. 'I'm really sorry, Belle,' he said sincerely. It sounded so inadequate. 'I was out of the office working all day – the first I knew was when I saw the story in the paper. I would have done anything to avoid this happening.'

'But you didn't, did you?' Belle's temper flared into open malice, so vehement that it surprised even her. 'You just blabbed the whole story to your mate Sandra, so you could keep in her good books and make sure you get a really good reference when you go for your next promotion.'

Kieran's mouth dropped open. 'You really believe that? My God, Belle, what kind of guy do you think I am?'

'An ambitious one.'

'Ambitious, maybe – but do you really, honestly, truly think I'd willingly do that?'

Belle's anger subsided just a little, tempered by a breath of reason. 'I never would have thought so,' she admitted, 'not ever. But you did, didn't you?'

Kieran took a deep breath. He could've thrown a wobbly and stormed off, but that wasn't his style. Besides, all he wanted to do was calm Belle down and make her understand, so things could get back to normal between them. He reached out for her hand, and felt mildly encouraged when she didn't instantly snatch it away. 'Can I explain?' Belle nodded. 'OK, well this is what happened. I got to work the other day and Sandra came up to me and told me she'd had this phone call from some woman—'

'Let me guess – Mona Starr?'

'No. Belle, not Mona. Some "interfering old biddy from St Jude's" who didn't give her name, apparently. Sounds a lot more like that bloody awful Armitage woman to me. Anyhow, whoever it was told Sandra they'd seen this glamorous blonde was staying at the vicarage, and was trying to find out if she was – wait for it – the new curate.'

'What – Mona?'

'Yeah, I know. Anyway, Sandra gave me the Gestapo treatment and in the end she got the truth out of me.'

'Why the hell didn't you lie?' demanded Belle.

'And say what? I did try. Look, I know I should've told her it was none of her business . . .'

'But you didn't.'

'No.' He squeezed her hand very tightly. 'And I'm so, so sorry Belle, really I am. But it'll be OK, you know. The *Courant*'s only a local paper, and errant vicars are two-a-penny these days.' He saw from Belle's face that he'd said the wrong thing, and hastily continued, 'I'm not saying your dad's not important, of course he is. But give it a day or two and people will have forgotten. It'll all be lining somebody's hamster cage and it'll be some other poor bugger's turn.'

Belle considered this. She wanted to believe it was true, and maybe it was. After all, there had been all sorts of local scandals over the years, but she'd have been hard-pressed to recall any of them now. Time did fade memories – it was just a question of how much time.

Her silence worried Kieran. 'It would most probably have come out in the end anyway,' he went on. 'With women like Mrs Armitage around.'

Belle wiped a weary hand across her sore eyes. 'Yeah, maybe.' Then she pulled herself up straight. 'I have to go and see Dad. He's been doing weddings all day, maybe I can get to him before the paper does.'

'I'll come with you,' volunteered Kieran.

'I think you've quite done enough for one day, don't you?'

'But—'

'Just go and explain to Waylon, will you?' She managed the ghost of a laugh. 'I can't believe this started as a good day. God knows what's going to happen next.'

The second wedding of the afternoon was drawing to a close at St Jude's, and cohorts of friends and relatives were piling out of the church onto the lawns to be photographed in their new outfits. Very nice outfits they were too; or, at least, very expensive, which wasn't necessarily the same thing. Sixty-year-old Mrs Farringdon-Thynne's pink fur minidress had certainly raised one or two eyebrows, and the bride's mother's hat looked as though half a dozen tropical birds had crash-landed on it and conveniently expired.

This wedding was, after all, one of the social highlights of the winter months, with the bride's father something big in the Army and the groom's father one of the bishop's golfing buddies. To Gerry Craine, however, it was just another wedding – and he had always enjoyed officiating at weddings, big and small, rich and poor. Like christenings, they were one of the more joyful parts of his job. Today though, he had found his thoughts intermittently distracted by flashbacks to what had happened over the last few days, and his very personal reminder that not all children were born in or even within shouting distance of wedlock.

All the same, he was smiling as he allowed Mrs Farringdon-Thynne to drag him into the family photographs, protesting mildly, 'I hope it won't take too long, only I have another wedding this afternoon.' Things, he had learned, generally worked out for the best; and he wasn't about to abandon that belief now. No, it was Brenda he was worried about. She was trying to put on a brave face, but every time he caught her unawares, he found her gazing silently into space; and he knew for a fact that she'd barely eaten a morsel since Mona arrived at the vicarage. They would have to have a heart-to-heart, very soon. A man couldn't afford to gain a daughter only to lose a wife.

'Just a little to the right, Reverend, that's the ticket,' chirped Roy the photographer, a red-faced man who was sweating profusely in his brown checked suit even though the temperature was hovering just above zero.

'Now, where's our lovely mum-in-law? That's right, you go on one side and Mum on the other with her dead parrots – oh, and where's Grandma gone? Not done a runner on her Zimmer frame, has she?'

While Roy was cheerily arranging elderly relatives, some of the younger ushers were getting a bit restless.

'How much longer is this going to go on, Wills?' demanded a young man whose rugby-playing physique looked as if it had been poured into his morning suit and then sealed in with super-glue. Even so, an explosion seemed on the cards. 'We should be at the reception by now. I'm bloody starving.'

Wills shrugged. 'God knows. Fancy nipping round to that pub on Bath Road for a swift one?'

'Better not, there'll be hell to pay if they notice. Tell you what though, I'm going to that shop over there for some fags and a Mars Bar.'

'Righty-ho, Giles. Get me some mints or something.'

Giles was not gone long – just long enough for Grandma to be tracked down and dragooned into a photograph with the husband who'd left her for the chauffeur, forty years previously. But Giles's attentions were not on Grandma, or even on his rumbling stomach. He was devouring the front page of the *Cheltenham Courant*, every so often lowering it to steal a sly look at the vicar.

'What have you got there, Giles, another girly mag?' joshed Wills.

'Better than that – here, look at this.' He handed him the paper.

'Bloody hell, the randy sod! Here, Nigel, you'll never guess what a certain somebody's been up to . . .'

It's amazing how fast news can spread through a group of people, even when half of those people aren't on speaking terms with the other half. Within minutes, the *Courant* had done the rounds of the wedding guests and the choirboys were tittering over it in the porch as they waited for the next wedding party to arrive. The photographer couldn't believe it: normally he'd have had this lot eating out of his hand, but all of a sudden they just didn't seem interested in being photographed any more.

'Come along, folks! Bridesmaids and ushers, let's be having you.'

But nobody moved, or at least not towards the photographer. They were all staring in the selfsame direction.

And to his absolute horror, Gerry Craine suddenly realised that the thing they were all staring at was him.

It was only a ten-minute walk from the arcade to the church, but it felt like an hour. Belle kept checking her watch as she hurried along: coming up to half-past, the wedding will only just be over. With a bit of luck they'll still be doing the photos and Dad won't know yet. With a bit of luck . . .

But that vital spark of luck didn't choose to make an appearance. As she neared the church, she saw a crowd of wedding guests, apparently arguing about something, a photographer failing dismally to organise them . . . but no sign of her father. Her heart missed a beat. And as she got even closer, her worst fears were confirmed: there was a copy of the *Courant* lying abandoned on the churchyard wall, with its damning headline for all the world to see.

'Well, I think it's absolutely disgusting,' screeched a horsey-looking woman. 'He's defiled my poor niece's wedding, that's what he's done.'

'Don't talk rubbish, woman,' snorted a fat, tweedy man who appeared to be her husband. 'The man's only flesh and blood. Primeval needs and all that, what?'

'I might have guessed you'd see it that way.'

Belle pressed through the throng, trying to close her ears to all the chatter. Spotting the photographer packing everything back into his camera bag, she went up to him. 'Excuse me, where can I find the vicar?'

He looked her up and down, winked and accompanied it with a dirty chuckle. 'Here, you're not her are you? The one in the paper?'

Belle gave him the coldest of cold stares. 'The vicar? Please?'

Roy shrugged. 'In the church, I 'spect. Once they saw the story, this lot got a bit too hot to handle. Best of luck with him,' he added over his shoulder. 'I'm off home.'

The interior of St Jude's church was like something out of a pre-Raphaelite painting, or one of the lusher Burne-Jones tapestries: jewel-bright stained glass and enamelling, richly coloured tiles and graceful painted saints. It made a fine setting for all the pomp and pageantry of a society wedding, but a sad one for Gerry Craine, sitting alone in the front pew, his eyes closed and his pale face impassive.

Belle ran up the aisle. 'Oh Dad, I'm sorry.'

Gerry opened his eyes and gave his daughter a quizzical look. 'Sorry? Whatever for?'

She slid onto the pew, beside him. 'I thought if I could get here before you found out, I could be the one to tell you and maybe it wouldn't hurt so much if . . . if you weren't alone.'

He smiled and put his arm round her shoulders. 'You worry far too much, you know. It's bad for someone as young as you.' He ruffled her hair. 'You'll go grey before your time, and then what'll Kieran say?'

Belle's lips pursed. 'All of this is his fault, you know. His boss got him to tell her all about it – of course, being him, he believed her when she promised she wouldn't publish it.'

'Ah well. It would be bad if we could never allow ourselves to believe or trust anyone,' Gerry reflected. 'And maybe it was meant to happen.'

'Oh Dad,' protested Belle, 'you're not going to say it again, are you?'

'Say what, Tadpole?'

An involuntary laugh escaped from her. 'Tadpole? You haven't called me that since I was at primary school!'

'Well, you'll always be my little Tadpole to me. Say what?'

'"Everything works out for the best in the end", just like you always do.'

He raised an eyebrow. 'And doesn't it?'

'I don't know. I'd have to see everything first, wouldn't I? Or else how would I tell? And besides,' she went on, her animation waning, 'it's pretty hard to see anything good coming out of this.'

The sounds of affected coughing and the creak of the vestry door announced that Jean Armitage had finished sweeping up the latest drift of confetti, counting up the proceeds from the collection plate and putting away the vestments. 'The next wedding party should be here soon, Vicar,' she said, appearing in the vestry doorway.

'You're still here, Jean? I thought you'd long gone.'

Of course she's still here, thought Belle. She's loving every second of it. There's enough gossip in this to keep her going for the next decade.

'Oh, you know, things to do.' She hovered. 'Sure there's nothing else you'd like me to do?'

'No, you be off now. And thanks for your help.'

'I could buff up those brasses? That lectern's looking a little tarnished.'

'No, thank you,' he replied firmly. 'Goodbye, Jean, don't forget to close the vestry door behind you. I'll see you at Sunday service.'

There was just the faintest sign of hesitation on Jean's face, then she said, 'Well . . . yes. I expect so,' and was gone.

'You do realise she's a poisonous old witch, Dad?' said Belle.

'Oh, I think that's a bit strong, don't you?'

'No, actually.'

He laughed. 'It's all right, Belle, you don't have to defend me from the world, much as I appreciate your wanting to. I'm a grown-up now, you know. Not a very good one perhaps, but a grown-up. I have to take responsibility for my own actions, and I expect things'll be a bit sticky round here for a while. But then that's my fault, isn't it? It's only what I deserve.'

Belle wanted to protest that no, he was her beloved daddy and he didn't deserve anything of the sort, but she knew it wouldn't change the way he felt or what he believed. In some ways it was the strength of his convictions that made her love him so. Just as Kieran's principled strength had strengthened her love for him. Only now, a tiny, hairline crack had appeared in the golden wall of her love, and she was afraid she might not find the means to mend it.

That was silly though. Every couple had bad moments. Every human being had weaknesses. And nobody more than me, thought Belle. So who am I to criticise?

'You're very quiet,' observed her father.

'Dad,' she said slowly, 'you've never really told us what happened in Australia. I mean . . . *exactly*. It's all a bit, well, vague.'

'There's not much to tell.' He heaved a sigh. 'As you know, I was a kid just out of school, working on a youth mission project outside Melbourne. Rena – Mona's mother – and I became friendly. She was living in the area with her widowed mother, and life got a bit dull for her sometimes I think. We enjoyed each other's company.'

'Yes,' said Belle. 'Obviously you did. Quite a lot.'

'Well . . . apparently,' replied Gerry, with an embarrassed cough. 'The thing is, it was really only the one time that we. . . erm. . . There was this last-night barbecue that we all went to, and somebody must have spiked the non-alcoholic punch, because when we all woke up the next morning we had the mother of all hangovers and most of us couldn't remember a lot about the night before.'

Belle's brow furrowed. 'So what about Mona's mum and. . .you know?'

'We were both a bit tipsy and let's just say we ended up spending the night together.'

'Oh,' said Belle, suddenly more embarrassed than she'd ever been in her life before. Imagining your parents having sex was awkward enough, but imagining them having adolescent, drunken fumbling sex with other people. 'Oh, dear.'

'Anyway, in the morning we were both a little embarrassed – well, rather more than embarrassed in my case – but we parted in good spirits and promised we'd keep in touch.'

'But you didn't.'

'Well, I did. I wrote to her every day for weeks, but I never got a reply. Eventually I thought she'd lost interest in me, so I stopped. I never had the faintest idea she was pregnant, let alone that Mona had been born.'

Belle scratched her head. 'But according to Mona, her mum wrote to you but she never got a reply either.' Somebody's lying here, she told her-self, and I'm one hundred per cent sure that someone isn't my dad.

She was going to ask him more, but then the main door of the church opened and Jean Armitage's face appeared, wreathed in the smuggest of smiles. 'Oh Gerry, I was just on my way out. . .'

He sighed. 'Yes?'

'And I bumped into a gentleman by the lych gate. He says he's from the *Cotswold Mail*, and he's terribly insistent on talking to you. I told him I was sure you'd want to talk to him right away.'

A few days later, Brenda sat alone in the huge kitchen at the vicarage, a lonely figure surrounded by cold cups of tea and newspapers she couldn't bring herself to read. Yes, it was only a few paragraphs in a couple of regional newspapers, and like everybody said, the whole thing would blow over in a day or two, of course it would. She had repeated the mantra to herself often enough, but somehow she still couldn't quite believe it. From where she was sitting, the whole world seemed to have taken a sudden lurch into darkness; and ordinary, boring, precious normality seemed impossibly far away, down the wrong end of the telescope.

Her eyes strayed to the selection of family photographs on the shelf above the old range. There she was, all dressed up to the nines and smiling proudly as she clung to her husband's arm at the bishop's garden party. How many garden party invitations are we going to get now? she wondered gloomily. I can't even bring myself to go to the local shop in case I meet somebody I know.

Over the years, Brenda had made it her business to know everybody. Born on the iffy side of the tracks, she had worked like crazy to claw her way into respectability. When she met Gerry, she could hardly believe that someone so good-looking, polite, well-spoken and downright nice could be interested in a girl whose male relatives mostly sported missing teeth, multiple aliases and a prison record as long as her arm. Gerry had been so different that she could hardly have resisted falling in love with him. She'd never met anyone like him before. He even inspired her to take an interest in the church that meant such a lot to him, and gradually she'd begun to share his faith until it became a part of her life, too.

In all the intervening years, she'd never seriously questioned that faith. But right now, Brenda was fighting down bitter regrets; regrets she was deeply ashamed of, but which would not be suppressed. If she hadn't married him, hadn't devoted her entire life to his home and his career, she wouldn't be in this position now. OK, so she might be a lot worse off, like some of the girls she'd gone to school with ... but then again ... She sighed into her teacup. So much for being different. It seemed that when you got down to the heart of things, men were all the same – mix alcohol and testosterone, and there you had it: a bomb just waiting to explode. And maybe she couldn't escape her destiny, either.

Footsteps on the stairs announced the arrival of somebody in big boots. Brenda breathed a sigh of relief: at least it wasn't Mona, the smirking phantom who seemed to dog her every step and inhabit every corner of the house. She straightened up and tried to look as though she was reading the horoscopes.

'Jacqueline, love. Shouldn't you be at school by now?'

Jax shuffled her platform soles on the quarry-tiled floor and avoided eye-contact. 'I'm a bit . . . scared, Mum.'

Brenda couldn't recall the last time her younger daughter had admitted to being scared of anything, if indeed she ever had. As a little girl, she'd always been the one who dragged her big sister head first down the water chute, or jumped into the deep end before she remembered she couldn't swim. And she hadn't changed much over the years.

'Scared, love? What about?' As if I don't know, thought Brenda.

'People keep staring at me.'

'That's never bothered you before,' pointed out Brenda, eyeing her daughter's latest PVC and lace ensemble.

'But before they weren't staring at me because of Dad, were they?' Jax sat down at the kitchen table, opposite her mum. 'Well OK, the kids at school used to tease me a bit about having a vicar for a dad, but that was different. That was just . . . stupid kids' stuff.'

Being a vicar's daughter had never seriously impacted on Jax's life before. Whereas Belle had always kept her head down at school, done her best to be invisible, Jax had made darned sure that having a dad in a dog collar was the least interesting thing about her. Now, for the first time, her very visibility made her feel horribly vulnerable; she could feel her bravado ebbing away, and she hadn't a clue how to handle that feeling.

She glanced at the table top. 'That tea's cold.'

'Yes, dear, I know.'

Jax's bright, beady eyes scrutinised her mother's pale, tense face. There seemed to be fine lines around the eyes and mouth that hadn't been there a day or two before. 'You're scared too, aren't you, Mum?'

'Don't be silly, of course I'm not.' I can't let this happen, thought Brenda. I can't let this family fall apart because of my husband's stupid mistake. Summoning up all the steely determination that had dragged her out of the gutter all those years ago, she fixed her daughter with an unwavering gaze. 'And neither are you.'

A look of surprise appeared on Jax's face. 'Yes, I am, I just told you so.'

'No you're not, you're not going to let yourself be frightened of anything, do you hear? Annabelle and your father have both gone to work – they're not afraid, are they?'

'I bet they are.'

'Maybe they are underneath,' Brenda conceded, 'but they're not going to let anybody else see that they are.' She breathed deeply. 'And neither am I. This family has nothing to be ashamed of, and if people want to stare at us, we'll just stare right back.' Pushing back her chair, she stood up and grabbed her handbag. 'Come on, I'm going to the shops and you're going to school.' Her voice strengthened as a spark of the old Brenda resurfaced. 'And if anybody dares say one word out of turn, I'll smack them right into the middle of next week.'

There they were, all fired up and ready to go, when another set of foot-steps sounded on the stairs; and a few seconds later, a long-limbed blonde goddess stepped through the door into the kitchen. Brenda's heart sank.

'Hi there,' chirped Mona, with a smile that seemed overfull of glittering teeth. 'Did I hear you say you were going out? Hold on while I get my coat, and I'll come with you.'

Belle was having problems adjusting, too. She might have forgiven Kieran for what happened at the *Courant*, but forgiving wasn't the same as forgetting, and there wasn't much chance of forgetting when your dad was being dubbed 'the randy rector' and made the subject of a thousand and one bad jokes.

'I don't know how Gerry keeps going,' said Kieran that evening, as he and Belle walked across town to the vicarage. Since the story broke, they had got into the habit of eating dinner with the family every night. It just felt like the right thing to do. To all intents and purposes they were his family, and he wanted to share what they were going through. 'All the phone calls, the comments . . . it'd finish me. And the things some of his parishioners have been saying! All those malicious lies. People who've known him for the best part of twenty years.'

'Dad seems to think he deserves it,' replied Belle, trudging along with her head down and her hands thrust deep in the pockets of her overcoat.

'But that's ludicrous!'

'I know it is, but I think it's his way of coping. If he sees it as some kind of punishment for something bad he's done, he can take it. But if he thought it was just God being horrible to him for no reason . . . well, that's when he'd find it hard to accept.'

'Hm,' said Kieran dubiously. 'Trouble is, it's not just your dad who's being punished, is it? How does he rationalise that?'

'I don't know,' Belle admitted. 'I don't imagine he can. I'd never seen him cry in my life before this week.' Her hands clenched into fists. 'Of course, we all know whose fault it really is, don't we?'

Kieran stopped her with a hand on her arm. 'Not Mona again! Belle, you know you're just being silly. She's never said one word to the press, you know.'

'Yeah, yeah, OK, I know.' Belle started walking again, her breath forming little clouds of steam in the lamplit, frosty air. 'Maybe you're right and I've been unfair to her all along. But it doesn't change the fact that if she'd stayed in Australia, nobody would've been any the wiser.'

'But you wouldn't have gained another sister,' pointed out Kieran.

Belle gave a grim chuckle. 'I think I could live without that.'

Kieran slid his fingers into Belle's pocket and clasped her hand. 'You're all cold,' he said. 'Come on, let me warm you up.'

The warmth and strength of his hand, enfolding hers, made her feel safer and more secure than she had done for days, and she began to relax. 'I guess I ought to get to know Mona a bit better,' she admitted reluctantly.

'She is your sister,' Kieran agreed.

'Hm. Well, half of her is. But I can't help feeling I'll like her an awful lot more once she's gone back to Australia.' She caught Kieran's eye. 'All right, don't look at me like that – I'll try.'

But I still can't wait to see the back of her, she thought to herself. And that's the unvarnished truth.

Dinner was nothing out of the ordinary, just a casserole Brenda had taken out of the freezer and reheated, but everyone knew that the food didn't matter, because that wasn't really what they were there for.

'Perhaps we could unplug the phone,' mused Brenda.

'You know that's out of the question, darling,' replied Gerry. 'If there's an emergency, people need to be able to contact me right away. I have to make myself available at all times – it comes with the job.'

'What about call screening then?' ventured Belle. 'It would be good to know who's calling before you pick up the phone.'

'Well ... maybe.' Gerry rubbed a hand across his tired eyes. 'We'll see.'

Mona spooned a little more mashed potato onto her plate. For a fashion model, thought Belle, she sure knows how to eat. Actually though, that was one of her more endearing features. 'Things won't always be like this,' she said, with complete assurance. 'Everything will work out fine, just you wait and see.'

'I hope you're right,' said Brenda, forcing herself to add 'dear. Have some carrots.'

'Thanks, I will.' Serving spoon poised in the air, Mona continued. 'Things always blow over, people have such short attention spans. I remember the time when my friend Arlene ...' She giggled and stopped. 'Well, maybe I'll save that story for another time, it's a little raunchy. But suffice to say, it all worked out fine in the end, though the koala's in

82

therapy.' Her face arranged itself into a solemn expression. 'I'm just sorry I started all of this trouble for you.'

Belle gritted her teeth. Brenda stared down at the carrots. Kieran opened his mouth then thought better of it. But Jax was swift to defend her new role model. 'Oh it wasn't your fault, Mona. Was it, Dad?'

'Nobody's blaming anybody,' Gerry assured her. 'We're all just really glad to have you as part of our family, aren't we?'

Nobody said anything.

Undeterred, Mona simply carried on. 'I'm so glad about that, you know, because I've got a bit of an announcement to make.' A pink flush of excitement highlighted her perfect cheekbones as she milked the suspense for all it was worth.

'You're going home?' enquired Brenda, trying not to sound too eager.

Mona smiled. 'Well, I was going to . . . but then, when I realised how well we're all getting on and everything, I thought how can I possibly abandon my lovely new family, especially when they're going through such a difficult time? The least I can do is be supportive.'

Oh no, thought Belle, anticipating only too clearly what was coming next. Please let me be wrong.

But of course, she wasn't.

'And that's why I decided to get my visa extended,' beamed Mona, 'so I can find a job and stick around for a while. Won't that be great? We'll have loads of time to get to know each other really well, and best of all, Belle, I'll be around for your wedding!'

Chapter 8

Right now it felt a bit lonely, being Belle Craine.

Maybe that was a self-indulgent way of looking at it, but if she couldn't be a bit self-indulgent now, when could she? Her parents were understandably preoccupied, Jax wasn't interested in anything unless Mona said it, Kieran was still falling over himself to be the perfect host, and her best friend was thousands of miles away. Belle had never expected life to be exactly fair, but she did wish it wouldn't take quite such evident delight in tripping her up.

At least Ros's sporadic emails from across the Atlantic provided some light relief, and instant messaging was bliss. Belle was certain it must have been designed specifically with her and Ros in mind.

Sitting at Kieran's laptop, late at night, she keyed in: 'Hiya Ros how u doin? How's New York?', sat back and waited for the reponse.

'Gr8 thanx, but what's going on in Chelt? Logged on to the local news and your dad was all over it!'

Belle's two typing fingers busied themselves with the sorry tale of Dad, Rena, and the Australian cuckoo in the spare room. 'Now half Dad's parishioners won't speak 2 him. But at least there aren't so many phone calls now.'

There was a short hiatus while Ros digested this information, then: 'God poor Gerry and poor u. How's the others?'

'Mum's upset but she won't admit it. Jax thinks the sun shines out of M's butt. Kieran thinks I should be nicer 2 her.'

'2 Jax???'

'Mona, u prat. I am trying but she's hard work. Mind u, K's being nice enough 4 both of us if u ask me.'

As if alerted by some weird telepathy that only worked between engaged people, Kieran loomed up behind Belle's chair. 'Hey, time for bed, Princess. Don't want you turning back into a pumpkin.' He leaned forward over her shoulder and read what was on the screen. 'Here, what's that about me?'

84

'Nothing,' she replied, obliterating the words with one press of the backspace key. 'Anyway, it's rude to read other people's emails.'

'Ah, but this isn't email, it's instant messaging. Budge over, I want a go.'

'Shan't!'

'In that case you're in for a good tickling, wench!'

They play-fought for possession of the one small wooden chair, and ended up having to share it, with one buttock on it apiece. Words scrolled across the screen. 'U still there Belle?'

Kieran scrabbled for the keyboard and got there first. 'Yes she is and everything she says about me is all lies! Kxx.'

'So u r not Chelt's premier sex god then?'

He cursed and typed back, 'Damn.'

Eventually Belle managed to get back possession of the laptop. 'What r u doing over there in NY?'

'Got a job!' Ros replied. 'Working in a deli. Strictly illegal, cash in hand. Seeing life! Not as exciting as life in Chelt tho by sound of it.'

Belle sat back and gazed at the screen, with its lonely little procession of words. It was really good, being able to keep in touch with Ros like this, but sometimes it seemed almost worse than not having any contact at all. Every conversation was so stilted; things never really got beyond the superficial, no matter how long they remained online. Yet if they'd been in the same room together, with a bottle of wine and a tube of Pringles, they'd have put the whole world to rights in half an hour. Her shoulders drooped. 'Miss u, Ros.'

'Miss u 2.'

'Got 2 go now, K's wearing his come 2 bed look.'

'Lucky u. Nite.'

'Nite.'

With a sideways shuffle of his bum, Kieran deftly unseated Belle from the chair and followed her unceremoniously down onto the kitchen floor. Kneeling astride her, he reached down and gently stroked the hair from her eyes. God but he's beautiful, thought Belle, with one of those sudden surges of lust and emotion that reminded her just why she was about to tie herself to this guy for ever and ever, Amen. She savoured the warmth and hardness of his body against her belly. Beautiful and sooo sexy.

She grabbed his face and pulled it down to hers, engulfing his mouth in a voracious kiss. An age later, he pulled back, gasping for breath. 'Like I said, Princess Annabelle, it's definitely time for bed.'

'Who needs a bed?' whispered Belle. And right there on the kitchen floor, she proceeded to show him precisely why they didn't.

*

85

A few evenings later, Jax, Razor and a couple of their mates were indulging in that favourite teenage pastime: under-age drinking.

Not that the Hairy Newt gave a damn about its patrons' age. Its brief was cheap drinks all night long, shatter-proof furniture, and no questions asked. Binge-drinking was nothing new to the Newt. They'd been championing it ever since the bar's original incarnation, as a genuine Irish boozer, back in the mists of time. And the modern teenage generation, Irish or otherwise, was quite happy to uphold the tradition.

'Another half of cider, Snooker?' enquired Razor. Snooker had acquired his nickname several years earlier, when his adolescent acne had blossomed into a boil so huge and crimson that it looked exactly like a red snooker ball: the kind of boil about which legends are written.

'Your round, is it?' Snooker emitted a reflective belch. 'Reckon I'll move on to Snakebite, thanks mate.'

'That's another quid you owe him then,' cut in Jax, never one to see her affable boyfriend ripped off.

Reluctantly, Snooker dug into the pockets of his low-slung jeans, and extracted a fluff-covered pound coin.

'Me and Jax will have another Archers, won't we, Jax?' announced Demi, a diminutive redhead in skater gear who could just about pass for thirteen if she wore a bit of make-up, but who was in fact the same age as Jax. ''Cause some of us are really sophisticated.' She flopped against the back of the bench seat, stifling a giggle.

'Some of us,' remarked Jax, 'are a bit pissed.' She raised her glass and emptied it in one. 'Still, who cares eh? Get them in, Razor, let's make a night of it.'

'What about your mum and dad?' asked Snooker while Razor was at the bar. 'Don't they mind you coming home mullered?'

Jax sniffed, in an attempt to look like she didn't much care what they thought. 'Dad's got a lot on his plate and Mum just mooches about,' she admitted. 'Anyhow, I said I was staying with you tonight, Demi.'

'Oh. OK.' Demi rooted for her mobile. 'I'll just phone Mum and tell her.'

'Don't be daft,' laughed Jax as Razor plonked a tray of drinks down on the table. 'I'm not really staying with you.' She exchanged looks with Razor. 'Razor's mum and dad have gone to Wales for a couple of days, haven't they, Razor? And his brother's away at uni. And when the cat's away . . .'

Razor looked ever so slightly uncomfortable. 'I just hope they don't come back early.'

Jax punched him. 'God Razor, anybody'd think you didn't want to shag me.'

Demi tittered, Snooker sniggered, and Razor turned the colour of vintage claret. But under the table, Jax caught his hand and gave it a squeeze of encouragement. Razor realised with surprise that her hand was trembling – ever so slightly, but trembling all the same. She'd never admit it, he thought, but Jax just hasn't been the same since all the trouble started.

'If I stayed out all night I'd be bound to get caught,' said Demi regretfully.

'Well, you've got to live a bit, take a few chances,' replied Jax recklessly. 'That's what my sister Mona says.'

'Hm, so she's your sister now, is it?' Snooker took a gulp of Snakebite and wiped his mouth with the back of his hand. 'I'd have thought you'd all hate her, what with all the trouble she's caused.'

'It's been difficult for Jax at school,' agreed Razor. 'Well, you know what some of the other kids have been like.'

'And one or two of the teachers, come to that,' interjected Demi.

'It's nothing I can't handle,' insisted Jax. 'Besides, it's not Mona's fault. Mona can't help who she is, any more than I can. It's the evil capitalist press who are to blame. They're the ones who've turned it into a circus.' She turned her bottle of Archers round in her hand. 'Mona's cool.'

'Would she still be so cool,' wondered Razor, 'if she wasn't a model?'

Jax sniffed dismissively. 'Of course she would, she's my sister. We have natural empathy.'

'Half-sister,' her boyfriend reminded her helpfully. 'Belle's your proper sister, and you never agree with her about anything.'

'Belle ... Belle wears cardigans, Razor! Need I say more?'

The look on Jax's face spelled out 'shut up' like a neon sign in Piccadilly Circus, but Razor didn't feel he could. He certainly didn't relish the job of agent provocateur, but he had a highly developed sense of what was right and what was wrong; and there was something about Jax's slavish devotion to Mona Starr that tasted as bad as the half of stale lager in his glass. 'I thought you hated models,' he recalled. 'Didn't you say they were the empty-headed pawns of the global fashion dictators, and that fashion was just another way of enslaving the masses?'

'No,' snapped Jax.

'I'm sure you did.'

She rounded on him with eyes of fire. 'If you don't shut the fuck up, Razor, I'll never speak to you again.'

He sighed. Crusading had its limits, even for him, and terminally pissing off his beloved Jax was too high a price to pay. 'Sorry. Anybody want a hickory-roasted peanut?'

Everybody did, and peace was restored as the packet did the rounds.

'I wonder what Australia's like,' pondered Demi. 'It always looks really great on TV ... except for the bits about man-eating crocodiles and backpackers being murdered, and stuff. I'd love to cuddle a koala bear.'

'They're not bears,' said Jax, with the air of one who knew these things. 'They're marsupials. And Mona says they've got really bad tempers – they aren't cuddly at all.'

'Well, I still wouldn't mind going,' replied Demi defiantly.

'Me neither,' added Snooker.

Jax looked smug. 'Well, if I play my cards right I reckon I can get myself an invitation,' she declared. 'After all, Mona and I are getting along really well, aren't we? And she'll have to go back to Oz eventually. I'm aiming to get her to take me with her.'

Razor choked on a peanut, and had to be slapped forcefully between the shoulder blades. 'You never said anything about going to Australia! What about uni?'

'Have you never heard of a gap year, cretin? Assuming I don't get spotted by one of Mona's contacts and decide to stay on there ... She says I have an unusual look that's really now,' she added proudly.

Although normally placid, Razor felt a surge of anger and upset. 'Oh I see, so that's why you're all over her. Not because she's your sister, but because you want her to take you to Australia. Nice one.'

'I think so,' replied Jax, failing to appreciate her boyfriend's sarcasm.

'Just one question,' he went on. 'Is there any place for me in this grand plan of yours?'

'Don't be paranoid you big div, of course there is.'

But based on all the evidence so far, Razor wasn't so sure.

As Belle, Kieran and Mona walked through the mean streets of Cheltenham in the evening drizzle in search of a 'real English pub', they happened to pass the front of the crowded Hairy Newt.

'Looks lively in there,' commented Mona enthusiastically.

Kieran and Belle burst out laughing.

'What did I say?' Mona protested, clearly mystified.

'Nothing really,' Kieran assured her as the laughter died down. 'It's just that the last time my mate Oz went there, he came back with fleas.'

'Big ones,' agreed Belle.

'Jeez, poor guy,' grimaced Mona. 'Well maybe not there then.'

A couple of steps further on, Belle did a double take, stopped in her tracks and half-turned.

'What's up?' asked Kieran, retracing his steps to join her outside the Newt.

Belle squashed her face up against the glass. 'I'm sure I saw Jax in there.'

'Nah, couldn't have been.'

'How many girls in Cheltenham have electric blue hair?'

'More than one, I'm sure,' said Mona.

'Jax is staying over at her friend's tonight,' Kieran reminded Belle. 'Besides, she's under-age.'

Belle gave him a pitying look. 'You what? Oh, and that stopped you getting drunk when you were sixteen, did it?'

'Well ... no,' he admitted. 'So ... do you want to go in and drag her out then?'

'I really ought to.' Belle hesitated for a moment, conjuring up the consequences in her mind: the big scene, the pouting, the loud abuse and general unpleasantness; and thought, No thanks. She gave a shrug. 'Oh sod it. But I'm not covering for her when she rolls in at four am stinking of alcopops.'

'That's the spirit,' said Mona encouragingly. 'Let the kid learn from her own mistakes.'

'I suppose that's what you did, is it?' enquired Belle, adding before she could stop herself a spiky 'or don't glamorous fashion models make mistakes?'

This was clearly the funniest thing Mona had heard in a long time. 'No mistakes? Belle, you have got to be kidding! Men, money, fashion, more men ... believe me, I've screwed them in more ways than one, if you get my drift.' Her irritating laugh ricocheted off the surrounding buildings, causing heads to turn. 'You name a mistake, I've made it. Mind you,' she confided, 'I'm not sure I've learned anything from them. It's like I told you, I'm just so impetuous, you see. I'm always doing things and then thinking about them after.'

Oh great, thought Belle. What a brilliant role model for my sister. With her impulsiveness and Jax's inventiveness, there's no end to the trouble they could get into or the chaos they might cause. All the same, she reflected, I'm not her mother and she's not a little kid any more. I should probably just stand back and let her get on with it. The trouble was, she couldn't help worrying about her – which was silly really, seeing as the politest thing Jax tended to say to her from one day to the next was, 'Lend us ten quid.' But somebody had to keep an eye on her and Belle suspected her mum and dad had enough on their plate at the moment, just keeping going from one day to the next.

After a few more minutes' walking, during which time the streets grew gradually grottier, Kieran pointed to a ramshackle building on the other side of the road. A tattered Union Jack dangled from a flagpole over the door, and a peeling sign proclaimed: 'Royal Shakespeare Tavern' with 'Formerly "Ye Olde Dog and Duck"' in small letters underneath. The stench of beer and fags was apparent even from ten yards away. 'There you go, can't get much more authentically English than that.'

'Fab!' Mona clapped her hands in girlish enthusiasm. 'You guys are so great, taking me out on the town like this, showing me all these terrific places I'd never find on my own.'

Terrific? Wait till you get inside, thought Belle; but she followed Kieran in, wondering just how long she could hold her breath.

Sean the barman was a man of few words and many tattoos. 'What you drinking?' he demanded before the trio had got halfway through the door. Mind you, he wasn't exactly overworked. Apart from a couple of old blokes playing dominoes in the corner, and a scruffy terrier fast asleep on the pool table, the bar was just about deserted. Judging from the layer of dust on everything, it was often that way.

'Wow, atmospheric,' enthused Mona.

Belle and Kieran looked at each other and made a concerted effort not to laugh. That barman didn't look like he'd appreciate it. 'Very ... authentic,' agreed Belle.

'I'll get these,' volunteered Mona. 'Lager is it, Kieran?' He nodded. 'Right, couple of nice cold lagers and ... what about you, Belle?'

'Small white wine please – no, second thoughts, make it a big one.'

'Lager's off and we don't do wine,' grunted the barman. 'This is an ale house, not a poncy wine bar.'

'Oh. Well, what have you got then?'

'Mild or bitter.'

Mona looked to Kieran for inspiration. 'Better make it three pints of best bitter,' he counselled. 'Can we get some sandwiches or a pie or something?' he added hopefully. 'I'm starving.'

Sean pointed to a half a dozen bags of pork scratchings, hanging on a faded card above the bar. 'We don't do food.'

'How did I know you were going to say that?'

The three of them chose a corner table to skulk at, and sat down. 'Sorry about this,' said Kieran. 'We'll drink up and go and find somewhere nicer.'

'Yes please,' Belle seconded him. 'I've only been here two minutes, and I can't stop itching.'

'No, no, this is great, honest!' protested Mona. 'I've never been anywhere like this before. It's so ... real. OK, so it's a bit quiet, but all it needs is a little livening up.' She sipped at her tepid bitter. 'I think their fridge must be on the fritz,' she confided. 'This beer's all warm.'

Belle put her straight. 'It's meant to be like that. Yes, I know it's disgusting, but that's how British blokes like it.' She thrust a bag under Mona's nose. 'Pork scratching?'

'Thanks.' She crunched away gamely. 'Very tasty, aren't they? What exactly did you say they're made of?'

Kieran steered the conversation away from deep-fried, over salted pig skin and lumps of fat. 'I bet you're used to much more glamorous places than this,' he said, 'what with being in the modelling business.'

Mona smiled and set down her pint. 'Yes and no,' she admitted. 'I've done the swankiest clubs and restaurants in Sydney, and I've done photo shoots in the middle of the Outback with a bucket for a dunny. To tell you the truth, I'm not a ballgowns kind of a girl. What I'm really into is the great outdoors: surfing, running, climbing, beach volleyball, even soccer.' She tossed back her golden mane and wiggled her chest, and one of the old domino players started dribbling into his beer. 'I'm just hooked on the great feeling you get when your body's really in top condition, know what I mean?'

Belle could see that Kieran definitely knew what Mona meant. He was hanging on her every word, like a spaniel hoping forlornly for a doggy treat. Accidentally on purpose, she stepped on his toes as she leaned over for another bag of pork scratchings. 'Oh sorry darling, was that your foot?'

'Belle's no athlete, are you sweetheart?' said Kieran with a rueful grin as he rubbed his crushed metatarsals.

'Not at all,' she agreed. 'I've got much better things to do with my time.' She hoped Mona never found out about the Buff Bride programme, or she'd never hear the end of it. 'I don't know, all that pointless running about – you could be doing something interesting!'

'It is interesting!' laughed Mona. 'It's more than that, it's a drug. Kieran understands, don't you Kieran?'

'Oh yes,' he replied with a beatific smile. 'Absolutely. Fancy another pint?'

'Not for me, thanks.' Belle was having enough trouble getting through the one she'd got.

But Mona was up and ready with an empty glass. 'Give me your glass, Kieran, I'll get them in.'

While she was up at the bar, Belle had a short but meaningful conversation with her fiancé. 'Kieran darling?'

'Hm?'

'You really like Mona, don't you?'

'What makes you say that?'

'Put it this way, love,' Belle explained sweetly. 'If your tongue hangs out any more than it is doing, you'll trip over it next time you go to the Gents'.'

'Oh,' said Kieran, somewhat sheepish. 'Is it that obvious? Sorry darling.' He leaned over and kissed her. 'You're the only one for me, you know that. It's just . . . well, she is a bit gorgeous, isn't she?'

Belle didn't reply.

When Mona returned with the drinks, she launched into tales of life on and off the modelling circuit. Even Belle had to admit that it was all pretty interesting. One thing puzzled her though. 'Why haven't I heard of you over here?' she asked.

'Oh, you know. Most of my work's been in Australia or South-East Asia. I didn't actually get a passport until a few years back.' Was that the tiniest hint of a crack in Mona's composure? 'And when I'm made up you probably wouldn't recognise me from my picture anyway. Besides, I'm kind of semi-retired from it now.'

'Your life sounds so exciting,' said Kieran.

'Yeah, kind of, but it's hard work too. I love all the travelling though – I must be a nomad at heart.'

'Me too,' agreed Kieran. 'Not Belle though.' He gave her a squeeze. 'Belle's a real homebody, aren't you, darling? Not really into excitement.'

'Gee thanks,' retorted Belle, feeling more than a tad patronised. 'You make "homebody" sound like "mentally defective"! And who says I don't like excitement?'

'Sorry darling, but it's true,' Kieran insisted gently. 'You've never been one for danger, or big challenges or any stuff like that.'

'Are you saying I'm boring?'

'Of course not, you just like it when things stay the same all the time, don't you?'

'If you know everything about me already,' she snapped back, by now thoroughly riled, 'why are you bothering to ask?'

Mona intervened. 'Hey, you two, calm down. Is it really that important? The world wouldn't be very interesting if everybody was the same.'

'Exactly,' agreed Kieran. 'The way Belle is, is the reason I love her so much. She's going to make a wonderful wife and mother.'

All at once, the future flashed across Belle's brain – and she didn't much like the look of it. 'Now you're making me sound like a . . . a brood mare!' she protested.

'Don't be silly, love.'

Belle was on her feet now, for once in her life thoroughly overreacting and finding it a liberating experience. 'Well, at least one person thinks there's a bit more to me than that,' she declared. 'Waylon wants to make me up to deputy manager. He started talking about it a couple of weeks ago, but then everything went mad and it got forgotten about.'

'Well done,' said Mona.

'Actually I was all set to tell him no, seeing as I've got so much on with the wedding, and setting up home and all that. But thanks to you, Kieran, I've changed my mind.'

'Oh,' said Kieran.

'It'll mean longer hours and more responsibility of course, and working every Saturday instead of one in four, but so what?'

Kieran tried to take her hand but she shook him off. 'Oh come on, darling, you don't have to prove anything to me. Does she, Mona?'

Belle looked him straight in the eye. 'Unfortunately, it looks like I do.'

You couldn't exactly say that Brenda was getting back to normal, but on the surface, at any rate, she was starting to slip back into her ordinary daily routine. A bit of housework in the morning, maybe some paperwork for Gerry, and voluntary work a couple of afternoons a week. At one time she'd dreamed of running a posh dress shop, but she'd married young and wasn't actually qualified for anything; and if she did go out and get a part-time job, what would she do? To Brenda's mind at least, there was something a little undignified about a vicar's wife working on a supermarket checkout. If it was a toss-up between money and gentility, Brenda would opt for gentility every time.

Deep down though, the last couple of weeks had torn open wounds that hadn't even begun to heal; that might never heal at all. She still felt the eyes of the locals on her whenever she left the house, and there were still letters about her husband in the local paper, almost all castigating him for his 'disgusting behaviour'. Several parishioners had left St Jude's and defected to other parishes, that Armitage woman was continuing to spread her web of nasty, inaccurate gossip, and Mona Starr was still residing in the spare room. Perhaps worst of all, Gerry just wouldn't talk about any of it; not even to her, his wife.

One thing was certain: there wouldn't be any forgetting, not any time soon.

Brenda was dusting around the piles of paper on Gerry's desk when the phone rang. She'd always enjoyed answering the phone, acting out the role of Gerry's PA and masterminding everything from church fêtes to funerals. But now her heart twisted in her chest whenever she heard its distinctive call.

She cleared her throat. 'St Jude's vicarage, can I help you?'

A rather constipated-sounding male voice answered her. 'Tom Anthony here, Bishop Grove's personal assistant. May I speak with the vicar?'

'I'm sorry, Gerry is out on parish business at the moment, but I'm his wife – can I help?'

There was a brief pause. 'I'm afraid not, Mrs Craine. Could you ask your husband to phone the bishop's office as soon as he returns home? The bishop wishes to speak with him as a matter of some urgency.'

Chapter 9

With all the potential party outfits she'd hung up on every available hook and shelf, ready for Mad Dog McKindrick's 'Coming Clean' extravaganza, there was even less space than usual in Belle's tiny studio flat.

But for once, Belle didn't give a damn about that. Why? Because this very pokiness meant that she had a watertight excuse for not inviting Mona to come and stay with her. Not that Kieran necessarily saw things that way.

'I'm dying,' he moaned as he lay spreadeagled and fully clothed on top of Belle's pull-down bed. It was early afternoon on Belle's day off, and Kieran had staggered round to her place after a punishing lunchtime session of circuit training at the gym.

'Don't expect me to feel sorry for you,' replied Belle, returning from the fridge with a tub of ice cream. 'It's your own fault for trying to compete with her.'

He half sat up, propping himself up on his elbows. 'I'm not competing!'

Belle smiled as she dug her spoon into the ice cream. 'Oh come off it! What's with all this extra training, if you're not competing? Typical man – can't bear to be beaten by a woman.' Wary though she still was of Mona, there was something highly impressive about the way she effortlessly outdid him in every physical challenge he attempted – and something very endearing about Kieran's desperate attempts to find something he was better at than she was.

'She won't beat me,' retorted Kieran. 'Not again. Next time we go out running, my body's going to be in the peak of condition.' He held out an arm. 'Here, feel that.'

Belle did. 'Ooh, all soft and squidgy,' she teased.

'It is not!' He grabbed her and overbalanced her on top of him. 'There's nothing soft and squidgy about me, you cheeky little madam. Come here and I'll prove it.'

'Promises, promises ...'

Belle wriggled delightedly as he fiddled with the buttons on her blouse. Then all at once, he stopped. Instead of burying his face in her welcoming chest, he was looking over her shoulder. 'I've been thinking,' he announced suddenly, rolling sideways and sitting up, and leaving Belle sprawled on her back on the duvet. 'About that built-in wardrobe over there.'

'Nice to know you still find me so irresistible,' remarked Belle with a twist of acid, the moment well and truly destroyed. 'What about the stupid wardrobe?'

'It's easily big enough to store one of those folding mattresses in during the daytime.'

Not this again, groaned Belle. 'Let me see, that wouldn't be for Mona by any chance?'

'It wouldn't get in the way, and if she disturbed you at night you could always drag the mattress into the kitchenette or something.'

Belle rolled her eyes to the ceiling. 'For the last time, Kieran, I am not sharing my flat with Mona. And before you suggest it,' she added as a hasty afterthought, 'you're not sharing yours with her, either, sonny boy.'

He looked quite wounded. 'As if I'd suggest it.'

'Well you're obviously gaga about her. And to be honest I'm starting to get really pissed off.'

'But Mona's not—'

'Not with Mona! With you.'

'I'm only trying to find a solution so she can have somewhere to stay without paying the earth, and some of the pressure gets taken off your mum,' Kieran protested as Belle ordered him into the kitchen to make coffee by way of penance.

'If Mona's such a big-shot fashion model, why does she need somewhere cheap to live, anyway?' Belle demanded. 'Why can't she just rent a penthouse in Century Court, or a wing of Liz Hurley's country pile?'

Kieran's voice answered from the depths of the fridge. 'Belle love, there's successful and there's mega-successful. And she's only a name in Australia. Plus she spent most of her savings on cancer treatment for her stepdad, remember?'

'Hm. So she says.'

'God you're suspicious. You can tell by the way she talks about her stepdad that she loved him to bits. I bet you think the moon landing was a hoax and Dale Winton's an alien.'

'Don't you? It would explain a lot.'

'OK, so Dale Winton's a bad example,' conceded Kieran. 'But you have to admit, having Mona to stay with you would be a really nice, sisterly thing to do. Think how well you could get to know each other.'

'We can do that without bonding in the bathroom, thanks.'

A moment later Kieran stuck his head back into the main room. 'Hang on, I've had an even better idea.'

Inevitably, thought Belle. 'Go on,' she said cautiously.

'You're going to give up this place soon anyway. Why don't you just move in with me now, and let Mona take over the tenancy here?'

'I've told you before, Kieran, I'm not "living in sin" with you. I'm not being a miserable old prude, it'd just upset Mum and Dad too much.'

'But it'd be perfect for Mona,' wheedled Kieran. 'And she'd never get another place this cheap round here.'

This might be true, but there was no way Belle was going along with Kieran's plan, no matter how much he hovered in optimistic anticipation.

'I'm not ready yet, anyway,' she said firmly. 'I want to keep the flat on a bit longer.'

'But . . . why? In four or five months' time it'll be totally irrelevant anyway, 'cause we'll have our own place.'

'So I'll give it up then,' she said promptly.

'You know, sometimes I really don't understand you. Is this just because you've got it in for Mona?'

'No,' she replied with perfect honesty. 'I told you, I'm just not ready. And I don't much like being told what to do, even by you.'

'You never used to be this awkward,' grumbled Kieran. He disappeared back into the kitchenette. 'I suppose this is the new, supercharged Belle Craine, is it? God knows what you'll be like if you ever get to be manager of that bloody shop. You'll be chaining me to the bed with furry handcuffs and demanding your conjugal rights.'

Belle chuckled as she lay back on the bed and arranged herself seductively. 'You should be so lucky, Tiger. Now, are we having that coffee, or something a bit more interesting?'

Jax was even more annoyed than usual. And she was making sure that everyone in the senior common room knew about it.

'It's so unfair,' she complained. 'I know he's got three invitations. So why won't he give one to me?'

'Didn't he say why?' asked Demi, licking hummus off a celery stick.

The painful memory of a humiliating moment clouded Jax's blue eyes. 'According to him, Mum says I'm too young,' she muttered. 'And she doesn't want me getting into trouble. Can you believe that?'

'Yeah,' nodded Snooker. 'I can. Mums are all paranoid.'

'Perhaps he's given the third invitation to Mona,' suggested Demi.

Jax hrrumphed into her lunchtime salad bap. 'Yeah, well, he was going to, then my precious other sister tells him she's not going to the party if Mona's going, 'cause she's "not playing gooseberry". Selfish cow.'

'Actually I'm not sure I'd want to, either,' confessed Demi. 'I mean, it doesn't matter how much trouble you take getting all dressed up, you can't compete with a fashion model, can you? You're going to trail around all evening feeling like the fat ugly mate nobody fancies.'

'It's not Mona's fault if she's got class.' Jax bit savagely into her bap. 'Anyway, it didn't matter in the end, 'cause Mona told me she went backstage at an Afterlife gig when they were on tour in Australia, and she got on really well with the band. So if she wants to go to Mad Dog's party, all she has to do is turn up. I hope she does,' she added with a malevolent smile. 'That'd really piss Belle off.'

'So what's with the third invitation then?' cut in Snooker. 'If she's not got it and neither have you, who has?'

Jax grimaced. 'Oz. That nerdy mate of Kieran's who works with bugs and stuff. Apparently he needs cheering up 'cause his latest shag's just dumped him. Pathetic or what?'

Snooker rubbed his chin, resplendent with no fewer than three downy ginger hairs. 'Bugs, eh? Didn't the rhythm guitarist of Afterlife get done once for eating live cockroaches on stage? If you ask me, this Oz guy's going to fit right in.'

'Women,' lamented a gloomy voice from the back of Kieran's car. 'At least you know where you are with invertebrates.'

'Put a sock in it, Oz,' pleaded Kieran. 'There are going to be loads of fit women at this party, and if you don't take advantage, I'll punch your head in.'

'Take no notice,' advised Belle rather more gently. 'He's only trying to wind you up. Just relax and try and enjoy yourself. Me, I'm going to eat myself silly and have a good stare at all the famous people.'

'And eavesdrop on their private conversations,' prompted Kieran with a grin, 'just in case there's a nice juicy story in it for me.'

'Kieran, is there ever a time when you're not thinking about the scoop of the century?' enquired Oz.

'There'd better be,' replied Belle; 'or else he can find somebody else to sleep with.'

'Ow, stop tickling me woman!' squawked Kieran as she went for his ribs. 'I think that's our turning coming up.'

They turned off the main road towards the village of Ampney Bassett, and followed the increasingly narrow, winding lane between a double row of impossibly cute stone-built cottages. Oz navigated with difficulty by the light of a pen torch, as lamp-posts became a thing of the past and the car's suspension laboured over lumps and into potholes.

'Where next?' asked Kieran impatiently. 'Come along, trusty navigator.'

Oz scratched his head with the torch. 'You tell me, you've been here before.'

'Ah, but it was light then. Everything looks completely different in the dark.'

'Hang on.' Oz wrestled with an acre of paper. 'I think I may just have the map the wrong way up.'

Kieran groaned. Belle twisted round in her seat and squinted at the map. 'Hold the torch still, Oz . . . is that Bassett Hall, the thing you've drawn a ring round?' She glanced at their darkened surroundings and just made out a turning to the right. 'Next right and then across the ford,' she announced. 'Then straight up the lane and we're there. Who says women are crap at reading maps?'

'We're not there yet,' pointed out Kieran.

'Oh shut up and drive!'

At just about the same time as Belle, Kieran and Oz were driving up the tree-lined driveway towards the grand facade of Bassett Hall, a shadowy figure emerged from a clump of rhododendron bushes at the rear of the building.

'Bloody guest lists,' Mona muttered under her breath.

True to her word, Mona had sailed up to the front door at the appointed hour, looking only marginally less magnificent than the Queen of Sheba in gold sequins and killer heels, and fully expecting to walk straight in.

One of the shaved gorillas on duty was brandishing a clipboard. 'Name?'

'Mona Starr, but you won't find my name on there,' she purred.

'If you're not on the list, you don't get in,' replied the gorilla.

'Ah, but I'm a close friend of the band. Could you let Mr McKindrick know I'm here?'

The gorilla looked her up and down suspiciously, pondered for a moment and decided he'd better go through the motions. 'All right miss, but you wait over there, right? And you don't move a muscle.'

Mona waited obediently beside one of the six-foot carved stone griffins, occasionally flashing a twenty-four-carat smile at one of the male guests on his way in. Some of them were decidedly toothsome, and once she got inside, she just might get to know them a whole lot better. Never miss an opportunity to connect with people; that was definitely one of her mottos. And she'd found that if she showed enough of the right bits, people were generally pretty interested in connecting right back.

The gorilla returned, black hairy monobrow overhanging deep-set, beady eyes. 'Says he's never heard of you,' he announced, cracking his knuckles with relish. 'Now, are you going quietly, or shall I escort you off the premises myself?'

It had all been rather humiliating, but Mona Starr was not a girl to call it quits. So, ten minutes after she'd driven off down the drive, she sneaked her borrowed car round the back of Bassett Hall and parked in the lane, conveniently close to the back wall of Mad Dog McKindrick's estate. It was twelve feet high but that didn't pose any problems for a girl of Mona's athletic abilities, though she did have to tuck her sequinned minidress into her thong and carry her strappy shoes in her teeth.

A couple of minutes later she was on the other side of the wall and heading for the sounds of revelry coming from the gardens. And five minutes after that, she was enjoying canapés and champagne in the ballroom, admiring the erotic ceiling paintings and planning her next move.

'Oh . . . wow!' Once she, Kieran and Oz had made it past the two gorillas, Belle stood in the marble entrance hall and turned slowly round, giddy with the sensory overload. 'Just look at this place!'

Kieran joined her. 'I know, great isn't it?' He craned his head back and gazed up at the glass dome above them. 'Wouldn't fancy cleaning the windows though.'

'I dunno – trust you to think about something like that.'

The three of them followed the sounds of music and laughter, and came out into a huge ballroom smothered with wall paintings and gilding. This isn't a person's house, she found herself thinking; it's an art gallery. She giggled to herself.

'What's so funny?' asked Kieran.

'Oh, I was just imagining lounging on that day bed over there in my jim-jams, eating Coco Pops and watching *Coronation Street*. Between you and me, I don't think I'm cut out for the aristocratic lifestyle.'

'Oh man,' said Oz, belatedly shuffling up like a man who felt sorely out of his depth, 'have you seen the lavs? The seats are gold plated! Do you suppose if you sat on one and some of the gold came off on your bum, they could do you for theft?'

Kieran gave him a funny look. Belle just laughed. 'This place is incredible.' She grabbed Kieran and smacked a big kiss on his lips. 'And you're very clever for getting us invited. Isn't he, Oz?'

But Oz had wandered off across the room, totally ignoring two of the Sugababes, a Pussycat Doll and the really fit one from Girls Aloud, and currently had his beaky nose and glasses pressed up against a glass case containing rare butterflies picked up by a long-forgotten chum of Charles Darwin, somewhere up the Amazon.

'That's him happy for the night then.' Belle smiled.

'But that's no good!' protested Kieran. 'Honestly, I despair of that boy. You bring him to Gloucestershire's finest selection of top-notch totty, and all he wants to do is ogle dead butterflies.'

'Oh, let him be. What does it matter if he's happy?' Belle was certainly enjoying herself. She practically dragged Kieran towards the buffet table for nibbles and champagne. 'I thought Mad Dog was celebrating going on the wagon,' she commented as she knocked back the Krug.

'He is. That's him over there, with the pint mug of orange juice.'

'Gosh, he's huge. And talk about hairy . . .'

'He probably didn't think anybody'd come if he didn't serve any booze,' said Kieran. 'Not to mention – you know – other substances.'

'Not come?' Belle laughed out loud. 'Anybody'd kill for an invitation to this. Look – over there! Isn't that. . .'

'Yes, I do believe you're right. Don't forget to curtsey if she says hello.'

At that moment, an all-too familiar voice sounded right behind them; and it wasn't the kind of voice you could ignore. 'It's OK guys, you don't have to curtsey to me!'

'Oh bugger,' said Belle under her breath, making sure there was a smile firmly adhering to her face before slowly turning to face the speaker. 'Mona, hi! You decided to come after all then? Last I heard from Jax, you were planning on giving it a miss.'

'Well, you know.' Mona picked a bit of olive from between her teeth with a cocktail stick. 'I don't do that many showbiz parties these days, but I thought, seeing as it's my old mate Mad Dog I might as well show up and say hello.' She waved to him from across the room and blew a kiss, and he responded with an appreciative thumbs-up. What the hell if he couldn't remember who she was? He could soon find out – and by the look of her she'd prove well worth the effort. Mona gave a little twirl and struck a pose. 'What do you reckon to the outfit then?'

'Great,' nodded Kieran.

'Very . . . subtle,' said Belle, half-blinded by the glare from all those gold sequins.

Mona hesitated for a moment, then slapped her half-sister hard on the back and burst into peals of raucous laughter. 'You're a real scream you are, sis!' Glancing across the room she saw a couple of starlets moving in on Mad Dog. 'Oh, sorry guys – you don't mind if I love you and leave you for a bit? Only I think Mad Dog's calling me over for an intimate little chat.'

This was, without a shadow of a doubt, one of the weirdest evenings in Belle's life. Not that her life so far had been all that weird, admittedly; and pretty much all of its weirdness had been concentrated into the last few weeks. But by anybody's standards, it took some beating.

Not many parties had naked fire-eaters, or male belly dancers, or Sting popping in to sing a spot of karaoke with the host. Maybe the chocolate fountain was a little passé, but the other fountain, carved entirely from a single block of ice and cascading pink champagne, was straight out of a fairy tale. Even if I never do anything else interesting for the rest of my life, thought Belle, I'll remember this. And she marvelled at the fact that some people – people like Mona – apparently lived like this all the time. It wouldn't do for me, she thought; but then again maybe it would, if she had time to get used to it. And she really quite fancied getting used to regular doses of ice-cold champagne.

Some of the other guests were, admittedly, a little strange; and she wasn't entirely comfortable with the small French foot-fetishist who had been following her round all evening, asking if he could stroke her instep. But all the same, when midnight struck and the party was in full swing, Belle was at the heart of it – disco-dancing with a camp guy in a cowboy outfit, and having the time of her life.

'Kieran,' said Oz as the two of them propped themselves up against Mad Dog's silver Steinway grand piano.

Kieran struggled to get his friend in focus. 'What?'

'Are we a bit . . . pished?'

'Search me.'

'Thought you weren't drinking tonight.'

Kieran contemplated his swaying glass and burped. 'Haven't had much.'

'Where's Belle and Mona?'

Kieran swung round unsteadily. He had the vaguest of vague memories regarding Mona, Mad Dog and something about a water bed. 'Dunno. Can't remember.'

'Kieran?'

'What?'

'Is that Belle over there, with that cowboy in the pink trousers?'

'Yeah.' Kieran nodded morosely. She should be here with me, he thought, not going off dancing with camp cowboys. She should always be with me, she's mine. 'I'm bored,' he announced, peering into his empty glass. 'Let's have another drink.'

That's exactly what they did.

An hour or so later, when Belle's energy started to wane and she went looking for them, she found them sound asleep under the Steinway, dead drunk and snoring like a pair of Old Spot porkers.

Thanks, Kieran – so much for you driving me home, she thought ruefully; and she got out her mobile and dialled up a very expensive taxi ride. Which Kieran would be paying for in due course.

Chapter 10

Justice not always being the even-handed thing it is supposed to be, it was Belle who had the killer hangover next morning, whereas Kieran merely awoke with a raging thirst and an appetite for bacon, sausage, egg and fried bread.

Belle edged her way painfully around the kitchen of his flat, trying not to move too fast or breathe in through her nose. One more sniff of frying chipolatas, and she would have to rush to the bathroom again.

'This is what happens when you can't take your drink,' Kieran explained, merrily attacking his breakfast like a man who hadn't eaten for a week.

'But I only had a few glasses of champagne! And I thought it was only cheap champagne that gave people hangovers, not the good stuff.'

Kieran chewed. 'Nah, that's just what they say to make you buy the expensive stuff. Face it love, you and alcohol don't really mix. I mean,' he went on, waving his knife for emphasis, 'that much was pretty obvious from the way you were cavorting about last night.'

'Cavorting!' Belle winced with pain as she spun round too quickly to stare at him in disbelief. 'I've never cavorted in my life. What on earth are you on about?'

'You, at the party,' he replied through a mouthful of food. 'You, hurling yourself around the place with every bloke in sight, like you'd got St Vitus's Dance or something.'

'Oh, you mean enjoying myself?'

'That's one way of describing it,' he conceded. 'But it looked more like cavorting to me. Like I said, that's what happens when the drink gets to you. You little women can't take it you see, not like us big-framed men.'

He sounded so pompous that Belle almost choked laughing. 'Of course,' she nodded understandingly, 'so when I found you and Oz lying underneath the piano you were . . .'

'Resting our eyes,' Kieran replied promptly. 'Any more sausages, darling?'

Holding her breath, she resisted the urge to shove the remaining banger up Kieran's nostril, and flipped it onto his plate. 'Resting your eyes,' she repeated. 'So you weren't blind drunk and completely out of it then?'

He grinned. 'Perish the thought.'

'You've got cheek, I'll give you that,' laughed Belle, rummaging in her jeans pocket for a slip of paper. 'Well, I've only got one thing to say to you, Kieran Sawyer.'

He looked up at her. 'What?'

'Thirty-two pounds fifty.' She slapped the receipt down on the table, right in the middle of a pool of tomato ketchup. 'That's what you owe me for the taxi.'

A couple of hours and two Nurofen later, Belle and Kieran threw on some clothes and headed across the park towards St Jude's.

Kieran was still making the most of Belle's discomfiture. After all, it wasn't often that he got a chance to tease her about a hangover – it was generally the other way round. 'Ooh, Yorkshire pudding,' he declared, sniffing the air greedily. 'I'm sure I can smell one of your mum's roasts cooking.'

Belle looked at him pityingly and tried not to think about her unsettled stomach. 'No you can't, we're not halfway across the park yet!'

'Ah well, extra-sensitive nose, that's what I've got.' He tapped it for emphasis.

'Yeah, right.'

'It's true,' he insisted. 'Right now I can smell rare roast beef and home-made gravy and carrots and sticky toffee pudding and custard.'

'That's funny,' remarked Belle, ''cause Mum said she was doing fish pie for lunch today.'

At least that shut him up for a few minutes, until they were turning into St Jude's Place. But then he started going on about a particularly smelly fish pie he'd once been served in Cornwall, with the fish heads sticking up in the air, and Belle had to slug him with her handbag.

'Ow!'

'Serves you right!' giggled Belle.

Kieran played it up for all he was worth. 'Help, help, I'm being attacked by this crazy woman!'

Belle caught a swish of curtain in Mrs Armitage's front window. 'Shh, people are staring!'

They were still play-fighting when the vicarage loomed into view.

'Now now, behave yourself, woman,' ordered Kieran sternly.

She stuck out her tongue at him, and would probably have pinched his bottom too if they hadn't both been brought up short by the sight of an enormous car, parked on the street outside the vicarage gates.

It wasn't the sort of car you'd expect to find in St Jude's – not unless there was some kind of theme wedding on at the church. There wasn't much call locally for gold vintage Rolls-Royces, particularly ones with a pop-eyed golden bulldog as a hood mascot and the registration MAD 2OG.

'Hey.' Kieran squinted at the number plate. 'Isn't that—'

Before Belle had time to reply that yes, it was indeed Mad Dog McKindrick, sitting behind the wheel of his infamous 'Mad Wagon', a figure in close-fitting pink leisure gear came skipping down the vicarage drive. It was Mona, and she was carrying a very tightly packed holdall.

Just for the briefest of moments, Belle's heart soared. She's moving out! Mona's moving out to shack up with Mad Dog McKindrick!

'Hi guys,' Mona called out, blowing Mad Dog a kiss through the windscreen. 'Slept it off then, Kieran?'

Kieran coloured up. 'I don't know what you're talking about! Anyway, where are you off to? Eloping to Gretna Green?'

Mona exploded with laughter and dealt Kieran such a hearty blow to the stomach that it knocked all the wind out of him. 'I just love your English sense of humour!'

'Not eloping then?' Belle asked wistfully.

'Hardly. Mad Dog asked me to stop over with him for a few days, that's all.' She must have noticed Belle's crestfallen expression, as she added, 'Don't worry sis, I'll be back for your dress fitting.'

'M-my . . .?' stammered Belle.

'That fitting you're having next week. I knew you'd want me to come and give you a bit of moral support, so I got Brenda to give me all the details. Besides, got to get back here and do a spot of job-hunting, eh?'

'And flat-hunting,' Belle reminded her.

'Oh, actually no. Your mum and dad just told me I can stay at the vicarage as long as I like. Isn't that lovely? I've got to admit, I wasn't really looking forward to moving out.'

At that moment, Mad Dog parped his horn and a peculiar electronic barking noise came out of the bulldog's golden mouth.

'Oh dear, looks like he's getting a bit impatient. Hold on sweetie, I'll be right there.' Mona picked up her holdall and swung it over her shoulder as though it weighed nothing at all. 'See you later guys, don't do anything I wouldn't!'

That doesn't limit us much, thought Belle maliciously as Mona leapt into the passenger seat and the golden monstrosity glided away into the distance.

*

If Jax was her normal self at lunchtime, Brenda and Gerry certainly weren't. Brenda's overcooked pie tasted like fishy rubber, and her legendary sticky toffee pudding was so sticky that most of it couldn't be persuaded to part company with the basin. She spent the major part of the meal answering questions in monosyllables and asking everyone if they wanted more – which not surprisingly they didn't. It was pretty obvious that Brenda Craine was not a happy bunny.

The really awful thing was the aura of defeat that surrounded her. In normal circumstances, this was a woman who'd fight to her last drop of blood for her home and her family; but these weren't normal circumstances. And if Brenda had been her usual self, Belle was sure she'd never have simply flung wide the door and invited Mona to take over.

As for Gerry, he put up a good enough show. You couldn't spend twenty-odd years as a parish priest without developing the ability to keep going for other people's sake, even if you couldn't be bothered about your own. But Belle knew her dad just about as well as anybody did, and she'd never seen him so restless and distracted.

The contrast with Sunday lunches of her childhood was almost painful. She recalled times when she and her father had driven her mother to despair with their improvised games of table football. Vegetable football to be precise; with goalposts made from roasted parsnips and a sprout for a ball. It was a good job that they'd had wipe-down tablecloths in those days, Belle recalled. And of course, wipe-down children came as standard.

Dad was an awful lot different now though, Belle reflected, looking at his careworn face and then recalling the mad footballing mastermind, dribbling his sprout past the mint sauce with a look of gleeful determination. Physically impossible though it might be, Dad seemed to have shrunk, as if all the cares of the last few weeks had crushed him so hard that he had collapsed in upon himself.

When he got up from the table and went to his study, Belle followed. 'Dad.'

Gerry turned to her with a questioning look. 'Yes, love?'

'Can we talk?'

'Of course we can. Come in and tell me what's wrong. Is it something to do with you and Kieran?'

He closed the door behind her, sat down in his bosun's chair, folded his hands in his lap and waited patiently for her to say something.

'It's not me, Dad,' she said. 'It's you.'

'Me?'

'I'm worried sick about you, Dad. Every time I see you, you look more upset and miserable. And Mum's in a terrible state too, that's obvious.'

Gerry chose his words carefully. 'Well, I'm not going to say that everything is fine,' he admitted.

'Good.'

'Your mother and I have had some difficult times just lately. There have been . . . challenges we weren't expecting.' He rubbed a hand across tired eyes. 'And I have been finding it difficult to come to terms with the pain I've inflicted on your mother. All of this is especially hard for her. The comments . . . people talking in the street . . .'

Belle reached out and took her father's hand. 'Dad, you've never deliberately hurt Mum in your life, I know you haven't. I can't imagine you ever wanting to hurt anybody.'

He smiled, perhaps at the naivety of her trust. 'Perhaps. But I have hurt her, and there's no escaping that.' He sighed, but said no more.

'There's something else though, Dad, isn't there?' insisted Belle. 'Something's happened and you're not telling me what.'

'It's not important. It's not something any of us can do anything about.'

'I'd still like to know. Please, Dad.'

Gerry gave her a long and penetrating look. 'You're a very persistent young woman Belle, do you know that?'

'I take after my dad.'

'All right.' Gerry glanced up at the walls, where dozens of photographs chronicled his life as vicar of St Jude's. All those years. And he'd been proud of what he'd achieved here – perhaps a bit too proud. 'Your mother had a phone call from the bishop's office the other day. He wants to see me.'

'Oh.' Belle swallowed. 'When?'

'Next week. His PA's going to call me to confirm the time. It was bound to happen, love. I'm surprised it hasn't happened sooner.'

'But what does he want to see you about?' ventured Belle, though with hindsight it seemed like a pretty stupid question.

'I think it's fair to say it won't be about the next church fête,' Gerry replied ruefully. 'But until he actually gets me in his office and tells me, what's the point of dwelling on it?' He squeezed his daughter's hand. 'All we can do is live for today – and for each other.'

In due course, Mona returned to the vicarage like a well-crafted boomerang – a boomerang sporting several expensive new items of jewellery and regaling anyone who would listen with anecdotes about sharing the sauna with Duran Duran and midnight helicopter flights to Deauville.

Belle stayed out of her way as much as she could. It wasn't that she exactly hated Mona – though actually liking her was a bit of a tall order –

but spending a lot of time with her inevitably stirred up all her latent worries about her dad. And Mona didn't quite seem to appreciate what a big deal it was when you got a summons from the bishop.

'I don't see how anyone can take him seriously,' reasoned Mona. 'I mean, he's only some grumpy old guy in a dress.'

'Some guy in a dress who happens to be Gerry's boss,' Kieran reminded her as they pounded the streets of Cheltenham one murky morning.

Mona's attractive nose wrinkled. 'Vicars don't really have bosses, do they? Being men of the cloth and all that.'

'They do these days,' Kieran assured her. 'And they can get the sack too.'

'Can they really? Oh God.' She clamped a hand to her mouth and giggled self-consciously. 'Oops, bad joke. It just slipped out.'

'As the model said to the bishop?'

'Kieran Sawyer, your filthy mind!'

They jogged on through the grey dawn, past the boys' public school to Cox's Meadow, and then back down towards London Road. The fine drizzle that had been misting the air was now turning to persistent rain, but Kieran and Mona didn't even notice. If you really cared about your running, that kind of thing just didn't enter into the equation.

'Kieran,' said Mona, a little further on.

'Yeah?'

'You're sure Belle doesn't mind you spending time with me?'

'Oh, she's fine with it,' replied Kieran. 'She was a bit jumpy at first, but now she can see we just have a lot of shared interests, she really doesn't mind. Besides, she has a lot on with the shop at the moment,' he added, not without a hint of resentment. 'I dunno, all that extra hassle for a few more quid a week. It was bad enough when she was working one Saturday a month; now it's every bloody Saturday and when I do get to see her, she's knackered.'

'Belle must think it's worth it,' Mona pointed out.

'God knows why. It's not like it's anything wonderful, it's just a job in a shop. And when I get my promotion ... Oh hell, it'll work itself out I guess.'

Mona waited a moment, then went on. 'So ... if Belle's OK with us running and stuff, do you think she'd mind you helping me a bit with my writing?'

Kieran turned and looked at her. 'What writing? You never told me you wrote seriously.'

For the first time he could remember, Mona actually blushed. 'I don't really,' she admitted shyly, 'or at least, I do, but I don't expect it's very

109

good. The thing is though, I've always wanted to be a writer, and so I wondered . . .'

They came to the edge of the road and jogged on the spot as they waited for the lights to change. 'I guess I could take a look at some of your stuff,' suggested Kieran. 'Maybe give you a few hints or whatever.'

Mona's face lit up. 'That'd be just great. And I was sort of wondering . . .'

'Yeah?'

'Do you think you could maybe take me out with you when you do some of your interviews? I'd be no trouble.' She fluttered her long, silky eyelashes. 'And you did say Belle wouldn't mind.'

Whether Belle minded or not seemed to have become something of an irrelevance. At least, that was how Belle was beginning to feel.

I miss you, Kieran, she said to herself as she sat on a bench outside the arcade, sharing her lunch with a lone pigeon. I miss sharing my cheese and pickle with you, and telling you about my morning.

All right, so it was a childish way to feel. After all, she'd spent the whole night with Kieran and would be spending tonight with him too, and she could tell him anything she wanted then. They weren't joined at the hip. There was no law that said he had to walk over from the newspaper offices every lunchtime, just to share a bench and a sandwich with her. Besides, there had been lots of times in the past when he'd had to go off and do an interview, or pursue a story halfway across the county, and they hadn't had lunch together then, either.

Ah, but then he hadn't been sharing it with Mona, had he?

She sighed into her cheese and pickle. I shouldn't really be jealous, she told herself. It's not as if anything's going on between them. Kieran had explained to her about Mona's dream of being a journalist, and Belle had to admit that Mona seemed really sincere about it. And Kieran was just a downright nice bloke. If he could help people, he did. So what was wrong or unusual about him helping Mona?

All of this made perfect, logical sense to Belle but didn't actually make her feel much better. Dispensing the last few crumbs to the pigeon, she rummaged at the bottom of her handbag. It was still there! A little squashed and misshapen from having melted when she put it by the radiator, but it was there all right. Her emergency bar of chocolate. It didn't actually say 'in case of emergency remove wrapper and eat', but she'd been carrying it round with her ever since she'd started the 'Buff Bride' course, just in case her willpower gave out.

And it just had. Suddenly the whole idea of toning herself up to get married seemed utterly ludicrous. Would Kieran go on a diet of chocolate muffins and lard if she told him she'd prefer him fatter? Of course he wouldn't; he was far too vain. Well, thought Belle, I quite like my bottom the way it is – so there.

Just as her teeth homed in on the first square of chocolate, a familiar voice halted her in mid-bite.

'Belle? It is you, isn't it? I nearly didn't recognise you with your hair like that.'

The face was friendly, freckled and framed by long curls of gingery-blonde hair that would have defied the finest hair-straighteners in the world. The eyes were grey and the mouth was made for smiling.

'Clare!'

Clare Levenshulme sat down next to her on the bench, crossing one curvaceous leg over the other. 'My God, how long has it been? Must be three years at least.'

'Nearer four,' Belle corrected her. 'Since just after . . . you know.' She looked down in slight embarrassment. It wasn't every day you were confronted by a girl who'd been one of your closest friends until you split up with her brother.

'Just after you broke up with Max? Yeah.'

'Is he doing OK?'

'Oh, you know. Much the same as ever. Still counselling heroin addicts in Haringey.' There was an awkward pause until Clare breezily changed the subject. 'And then my company sent me to the Strasbourg office, and I only got back in Cheltenham last month. I meant to stay in touch, you know.'

'Me too. It's just . . . stuff got in the way somehow.'

'I know. How's things?'

'Well, fine I guess. I got promoted to deputy manager at the shop.'

'Brilliant!'

'Oh, and I'm . . . er . . . getting married in the summer.' She almost winced as she said it. The break-up from Max had not been easy, for either of them, and even now there were fleeting moments, when she was tired or upset or lonely, when she found herself wondering if she had done the right thing. But that was a long time ago, and the past ought to stay that way. On the other hand, Clare had once been a wonderful friend, and with Ros out of the country Belle could really use that friendship.

Clare's smile didn't waver. 'I'm really pleased for you,' she said. 'So who's the lucky guy?'

'Kieran. He's a journalist.'

'Nice one. You must be thrilled.'

'Er . . . yes.'

Clare cocked her head on one side. 'You are thrilled, aren't you?'

'Of course I am.' Belle snapped the chocolate bar in half and offered one piece to Clare. 'You haven't gone all sophisticated and given up chocolate, I hope?'

Clare threw back her head and let out one of her explosive guffaws. Every pigeon within earshot headed for the hills. 'You are joking? Give it here, I'm starving.'

Belle stretched out her legs, leaned back and took a big bite of chocolate. 'Boy but this tastes good,' she sighed.

'First one in a while?' enquired Clare. 'Been on a diet, have we?'

'Been going to the gym.'

'Madness,' declared Clare. 'Love your curves, that's what I say. Now, finish that and let's head for the nearest coffee shop. I want to hear all your news.'

Chapter 11

The new manager of the Royal Shakespeare Tavern looked Mona up and down. 'I'm looking for experienced bar staff, you know. Done pub work before, have you?'

'Plenty,' she lied with a beaming smile. 'Back in Oz, that is. I mean, I'm not that familiar with British pubs but I'm a quick learner ... Mr Crenshaw, isn't it?'

'That's David to you.' He glanced around the dilapidated, nicotine-stained décor. 'Now, you do realise I have six months to drag this God-awful place into profit, and hardly any budget? Otherwise the brewery closes us down and we're all out of a job.'

Mona nodded. Perched on her bar stool, she contrived to expose as much smooth thigh as possible without actually looking tarty. 'Don't worry, Mr Crenshaw, I'm not afraid of hard work. In fact, I quite like things hard,' she added with just the right amount of innuendo.

To her satisfaction, a faint crimson blush appeared above his shirt collar and he cleared his throat noisily. 'Yes, well, I'm sure you'll do your ... um ... best to fit in.'

'You can count on it,' she breathed. 'Does that mean I get the job?'

David Crenshaw gave Mona another thorough look. Yes, she looked like one of his more lurid dreams come true, but was that really going to count for anything? How on earth would a blonde in stilettos cope when the bar erupted into one of its regular Saturday-night brawls?

On the other hand, he hadn't exactly been deluged with applicants. As he shifted his foot, he found the sole of his shoe had stuck to something nasty on the beer-soaked carpet. 'I suppose it does,' he replied, scratching his ear and hoping for the best. 'You'd better meet our head barman. He's the one you'll be working with most of the time.' He stuck his head through the door behind the bar and called down the stairs. 'Sean, have you got a minute?'

Rather more than a minute later, Sean the barman came lumbering up the stairs from the cellar, where he'd been reading girlie magazines while

113

pretending to put on a new barrel. 'What?' he grunted at the new manager.

'This is Mona, the new barmaid. She starts Saturday.'

Mona and Sean looked at each other and realisation dawned. 'Hi, Sean!' chirped Mona. 'We've already met, haven't we?'

His concrete features splintered into a frown. 'You were with those prats who wanted food the other week. Bunch of tossers.'

David Crenshaw looked distinctly uncomfortable. 'Yes, well, there'll be no more of that attitude thank you, Sean. From now on we'll be serving delicious bar snacks all day and the customer is always right.' He turned his attentions back to Mona. 'You know, your face is awfully familiar. I'm sure I've seen you somewhere before. You haven't been in the local paper have you?'

She gave in gracefully. 'Well, you might have seen a fuzzy telephoto picture of me a few weeks back. There was this story about the ... er ... vicar of St Jude's.'

Both Sean and David's eyes widened. 'Oh,' said the manager, with quickening interest. 'That was you, was it?'

''Fraid so.'

'Well, like they say, any publicity is good publicity,' mused David Crenshaw. 'And if I recognised you, I bet other people will too.' He treated Mona to a practised, professional smile and the firmest of handshakes. 'Welcome to the Royal Shakespeare Tavern, Mona, you're hired.'

Mona glanced around, taking in the full horror of her foetid surroundings without a single flicker of disgust. 'Never mind,' she said, beaming, 'us Aussies like a challenge.'

When Mona arrived back at the vicarage that evening, she had not one but two surprises.

'Oh my ... what on earth is that?' Brenda nearly dropped the roast chicken on the floor when she saw what Mona had on the end of a piece of string. Not that the creature would have minded. It looked as though it hadn't eaten in a fortnight.

'It's a dog,' said Mona helpfully. The mutt sat down on its hairy backside and scratched an ear with its back leg. It was so painfully thin that it didn't look capable of very much else.

'It can't do that in here!' squeaked Brenda. 'There's food around and it's bound to be full of fleas! And what on earth are you doing with it anyway?'

'I found him,' Mona replied, bending to scratch the poor dog's scabby head. 'Round the back of that cut-price supermarket. I think he's got a skin disease,' she added.

Brenda could not have looked more horrified if she'd been offered a plate of fried grasshoppers. 'Oh my ...' She snapped into efficiency mode. 'I'll get the number of the animal shelter,' she said. 'If he shows the slightest sign of tiddling, take him straight outside.'

'Animal shelter?' Ignoring Brenda's instructions, Mona followed her out of the kitchen, with the dog trailing her obediently on the end of its tatty string.

'Yes dear, of course.' Brenda gave her an 'I know you're foreign but do you have to be stupid as well' look. 'That's where all the stray animals go, till somebody adopts them.'

Mona bent down and scooped the dog up in her arms. He was light as a feather; nothing to him but bones and fur. 'We can't do that to him!' she protested. 'They'll put him down for sure. Who in their right mind would adopt a dog like him?'

'You said it,' replied Brenda.

The two women stood looking in silence at the hairy grey mongrel, its pink tongue lolling and every ounce of its energy going into wagging its tail.

'Come on, Brenda,' pleaded Mona. 'I'm sure it's the Christian thing to do.'

'That dog is a heathen if ever I saw one.'

As though he sensed that his life hung in the balance, the dog stretched forward and started licking Brenda's hand. 'You see? He likes you already.'

Brenda was marshalling all her waning strength into one big 'no' when Jax walked in. And the moment her younger daughter set eyes on the stray, she knew the battle was all but lost.

'Hey Mona, you've got a dog! Cool!' Jax metamorphosed from surly adolescent to soppy girl in two seconds flat. 'Oh the poor thing, he's so thin! Where did you find him? Can I hold him? What are we going to call him?'

Brenda let out a silent groan of despair, rolled up her sleeves and headed for the bathroom to see if they had anything that might serve as doggie shampoo. 'Just don't expect me to fork out any money for his vet's bills,' she called back over her shoulder.

But as usual, nobody was listening.

Clare was laughing so hard that her mascara had started to run, and Belle had to find a tissue to dab away the black streaks.

'Engelbert?' gasped Clare when she could get some of her breath back. 'This girl Mona's got a dog called Engelbert? Belle, you are so having me on.'

'Actually I'm so not,' replied Belle, reclining back on Clare's plump old leather sofa and helping herself to another chocolate truffle from the box at her elbow. 'She's told us that's what we have to call him from now on.'

She'd been more than a little nervous about accepting Clare's invitation to spend an evening round at her flat, after so much water had flowed under the bridge, but so far she was feeling unexpectedly comfortable in her company. They seemed to be slotting straight back into each other's lives, and it was hard to believe they'd lost contact with each other a good year before she even met Kieran.

Even Clare's flat looked the same. True, it was a completely different flat in a more upmarket part of town, but just about every detail of the décor was the way Belle remembered it from her old place. The clutter of CD cases on the Moroccan inlaid coffee table. The antique Persian rug with the burn hole in it, masked by a three-foot-tall ceramic elephant. Everything down to the neutral walls, transformed into a multicoloured mosaic by dozens and dozens of prints, photographs, postcards and paintings. If there was such a thing as the 'maximalist' look, this was it; and Belle had the feeling that, no matter where Clare might settle, her bedsit or apartment or palace would end up looking the same.

In that respect, thought Belle, Clare's a lot like me: a creature of habit. Someone who only feels comfortable and secure when she's surrounded by all the pieces that make up her life.

And she found herself wondering: maybe that's why I feel so insecure when I'm not seeing much of Kieran. Maybe it's not about him being with Mona all day, it's just about him not being with me; and if we were together more, I'd feel calmer about the future. And once we're married we will be together more. Won't we?

Clare interrupted Belle's reverie with a shake of her auburn head. 'Engelbert? Yeah, right. Pull the other one.'

'I'm telling you, it's true!' Belle insisted. 'Gosh these choccies are a bit special – are you sure you don't mind if I have another one?'

'Go ahead, help yourself.' Clare leaned forward, still dabbing at her eyes. 'Engelbert? Really?'

'Cross my heart and hope to die. Mona reckons he likes singing along to Engelbert Humperdinck records, but believe me, you wouldn't call it singing. And when it comes to looks, he's more like Iggy Pop on a really bad hair day. Goodness knows how she got round Mum to let her keep him. His head's all scabby and he's got more fleas than fur.'

'Now I know you're exaggerating!'

'Only a little bit. You should have seen the colour of the water after

116

they gave him a bath, not to mention the flood all over the kitchen floor. And you know how house-proud my mum is.'

'I certainly do,' reminisced Clare, topping up two glasses of Zinfandel. 'Do you remember that day Max fell in the pond? She made him take all his clothes off in the porch before she'd let him in.' She giggled. 'I don't think I've ever seen him look so embarrassed.'

I have, thought Belle, smiling as a door opened in a dusty corner of her mind, and one by one the thousand and one memories came tumbling out of long-term storage. Happy memories of the times they'd had before it all went so catastrophically wrong. 'Ah well,' she countered, 'that's because you weren't there the night Mum and Dad came home early from the theatre, and Max had to get dressed so fast, he put his trousers on back to front. My God,' she added after a moment's thought, 'that seems like decades ago, and it was only, what – five years? No, six at least! But it's so fresh in my mind.'

'Back before you turned into an old married lady, you mean? Ah, happy days, eh Grandma?'

Belle grunted unappreciatively. 'Well, I can't say I'm sorry I'm not a teenager any more. There's nothing glamorous about being spotty or having clandestine encounters in the cemetery because it's either there or the number ninety-four bus shelter.'

Clare stifled a squeal of delighted disbelief. 'You and Max – in the cemetery? And you the vicar's daughter? You never did!'

Belle chuckled. 'Don't even think about broadcasting it to the world,' she warned, 'cause I still haven't forgotten about you and Sebastian and what you got up to in that theatre lighting booth when Max was in that show at the Playhouse. You know, just before he went up to uni.'

'It was all a vicious lie!' Clare shook with laughter. 'It wasn't our fault all the lights fused in the middle of *Brigadoon*. And you've got to admit, it's really difficult to see where you're putting your hands when it's completely dark.'

'True,' conceded Belle, through a mouthful of chocolate, 'but all the same, you never did really explain how your knickers got jammed in the wind machine.'

'No, and I'm not going to, either!'

When they'd laughed themselves silly, they lapsed into a comfortable, meditative silence, punctuated by the odd 'Do you remember?' and 'Was it really that long ago?' It was surprising how many experiences they'd shared, over the formative years – from sixteen to nineteen – when Belle had dated Max.

'I'm really glad you came,' declared Clare, opening a second bottle of wine. 'You know, I didn't realise how much I've missed you.'

'Me too.' Belle nodded. 'Why didn't we stay in touch?'

'I dunno. Jobs, moving about. Stuff.'

'Yeah.'

There was a short silence. Then they looked each other in the eye and Belle said: 'It was Max, wasn't it? That's why. You were angry and I was embarrassed. I felt guilty.'

'But it wasn't your fault, was it?' said Clare, topping up Belle's glass with an unsteady hand.

Belle took another gulp of wine. Her head was starting to feel a bit fuzzy, but for once she didn't care. 'It felt like it was,' she replied. 'You said it was.'

Clare winced at the reminder. 'Yeah, OK, you're right, I was angry. It still wasn't your fault, though, whatever I said back then.'

'But I always knew Max was very sensitive,' countered Belle, perversely attempting to prove her own guilt.

'It's not the same thing,' said Clare firmly. 'There's no way you could've known he'd take the break-up so badly and jack in university like that. In fact, if you really want to know,' she went on, 'I don't think it had anything to do with him being sensitive or vulnerable or any of that stuff. I think it was just because he loved you so much.' She shrugged. 'It's hard losing somebody you care about. Anybody could've reacted the way Max did.'

Some of the old misery of those past times started oozing back into Belle's thoughts. She remembered now why she'd made such a determined effort to blank out everything to do with Max – his obsessive pursuit of her, his oppressive love, so suffocating that in the end she just couldn't take it any more. Even though she'd had to end the affair for the sake of her own sanity, it still felt bad after all this time, knowing she'd hurt him so much. But like Clare said, how could she have predicted he'd take it so badly? How could anyone have guessed that he'd leave university and abandon what promised to be a brilliant medical career? Still it seemed he'd found his true vocation as a drug support worker in London.

She thought about Kieran, who was so different, so self-sufficient. Kieran, who'd have been less than impressed if she'd told him who she was seeing tonight; because according to him, Max was a 'nutter' and Clare a 'grade-A bitch', and that was all there was to it. Life according to Kieran did not contain any provision for agonising about the past, or feeling guilty about things you couldn't change. Belle often wished it could be that simple for her, too.

'What do you think?' asked Clare, interrupting her train of thought.

'About Max?' Belle really didn't know what to say. 'I . . . don't remember that clearly,' she lied. 'It was all so long ago.'

Clare drained her glass and sat up straight in her chair, as though she'd come to some sort of decision. 'Yes, you're right Belle, and I'm sorry. I didn't ask you here just so we could drink too much and get maudlin or so I could make you feel bad about the past.'

Belle smiled ruefully. 'No?'

'No! I just wanted a chance to catch up, and hear all about this wedding of yours.'

Belle pulled a face. 'You don't want to hear about all that,' she protested. 'Other people's weddings are so boring! Besides, it's been taking a back seat since all the local press started camping out on Mum and Dad's doorstep.'

'It must have been terrible,' sympathised Clare. 'I mean . . . you read about this kind of thing in the papers, but you never imagine what it must be like when it happens to you.'

'Oh, I'm OK – I've got Kieran. It's Mum and Dad I worry about.' She twiddled the stem of her wine glass between her fingers, watching the dark red liquid sloshing about lazily inside the bowl. 'Look, do you mind if we talk about something else? What about Strasbourg – was it exciting? Did you meet any gorgeous French guys?'

'Just the one,' admitted Clare. 'Only trouble is, he's already attached, which is a bit of a bummer. Still,' she added with a wink, 'when the cat's away . . .'

'Clare!'

'Oh come on, everybody's doing it these days. Look, I'll tell you all about Pierre-Yves if you spill the beans about Kieran. Go on, tell me. I want to know exactly what he's like.'

Belle had a mental image of Kieran eternally charging round Gloucestershire in pursuit of the ultimate scoop, his faithful apprentice Mona by his side, 'To be honest,' she admitted, 'I'm not exactly sure any more.'

'Having to be apart sometimes is one thing; but if he's neglecting you, that's just not right.' Try as she might, Belle couldn't get Clare's final words out of her head. Every time she looked at Kieran and Mona, huddled together over his latest interview notes or a piece she'd written, she found herself thinking: why aren't you spending this time with me? Why do I have to share you with her, just because she likes sport and thinks she's some kind of journalist?

And why does she have to be so much prettier than me?

But the funny thing about this peevishness or resentment, or whatever you wanted to call it, was that its main target wasn't Mona; it was Kieran. Somehow, without her being aware of it, Belle's feelings had undergone a subtle change.

119

As she and Kieran sat in the lounge bar of the Royal Shakespeare Tavern, watching Mona zipping around, practically running the place single-handed while Sean collected the occasional empty glass, Belle couldn't help but feel impressed. She knew how hard it was carrying the shop on her own, and she'd had loads of experience. Here was Mona, who cheerfully admitted she'd never pulled a pint in her life, taking on a horrible pub on the other side of the world and dealing with every insult, proposition, bottom pinch and brawl as if she'd been doing it all her life.

And smiling.

'Why does she do it?' Belle asked out loud.

Kieran looked up from the stack of property details they were trying to narrow down to a short list. 'What?'

'Why does Mona work here? Why doesn't she get herself some modelling work and make life easy for herself?'

He buried his head back in the details. 'She says modelling's behind her, and she wants some new challenges.'

'Well she's certainly picked herself a big one here.' Belle watched Mona bustling off towards the pub kitchen with a stack of empty plates, while Engelbert hovered hungrily around the tables, hoping for the odd chip to fall into his open mouth. 'Doesn't the manager mind her bringing the dog to work?'

'Shouldn't think so, he's cleaner than most of the customers.' Kieran extracted one sheet from among the others and laid it on the table in front of Belle. 'What do you reckon to this one? Two-bed Regency conversion, off Lansdown Road. It's got a nice new kitchen for you, and there's even an option on a parking space.'

Belle scanned the sheet. The pictures showed one of those immaculately anodyne conversion jobs you find everywhere, transforming one nice roomy house into twenty poky flats with the aid of MDF and a lake of magnolia emulsion. 'It's a bit . . . boring,' she hazarded.

'Neutral,' Kieran corrected her, jabbing his finger at the pictures. 'Nice and neutral so we can decorate it however we want, you know, put our stamp on it. You'll enjoy that,' he added, as if this was something that might not have occurred to her. 'And just look at that kitchen.'

Belle looked. It was indeed a nice kitchen, considering the size and price of the apartment. She could even imagine them hosting little dinner parties in it, swapping recipes and baby-rearing tips over one of those antique pine tables. For some reason, the idea profoundly depressed her.

'Yes,' she said, doing her best to sound enthusiastic. 'It's nice. But I still think the flat's a little on the dull side.'

Kieran took a deep breath and began one of his very patient explanations. 'I know it's not perfect, darling,' he conceded, 'but it's got space, the location's good and most important, we can afford it. So – shall I add it to the viewing pile then?'

'Yes' was obviously the answer she was supposed to give, so she nodded her compliance.

Mona came racing up with double steak and chips, and offloaded them at the next table. 'Really good of you guys to come over and give me a little moral support,' she said cheerfully, wiping her hands on her apron. 'And to be honest, I can use a bit. My feet are killing me.'

'I'm not surprised,' said Belle, looking over to where Sean was standing, propping up the bar. 'Does he ever do any work?'

Mona followed her gaze. 'Not if he can help it. And between you and me, I think he's been watering down the vodka. What've you got here?'

'Just some flats we're thinking of looking at,' replied Belle.

'Right!' Mona bent to look at the property details and immediately picked on Kieran's favourite. 'Jeez, this one's like a dentist's waiting room.'

'It just needs a touch of colour,' said Kieran defensively.

'It's not that big either, is it?'

'Yes, well, property's expensive in Cheltenham.'

'I'm just hoping he doesn't end up getting a job in London,' Belle confided. 'We'd be lucky to afford the rent on a garden shed.'

'Yeah,' sympathised Mona, 'I've heard house prices down there are really going crazy. I mean, how do people live?'

'Don't be silly Belle,' cut in Kieran. 'If we move to London it'll be because I've got a much better job and we'll be able to afford somewhere really nice. But for the time being,' he pointed to the papers on the table, 'it's one of these or nothing. And I reckon that one's definitely got potential.'

'Hm,' said Mona, ignoring Sean's signals to come back and serve at the bar. Turning her back on him, she sat down at the table next to Belle. 'How's things at the shop?'

'Good,' replied Belle. 'Turnover's up nearly ten per cent since I reorganised the shelving plan.'

'Ten per cent? Go, girl. Clark Kent here must be really proud of you.' She nudged Kieran. 'Aren't you?'

'Aren't I what?'

'Proud of how well Belle's doing at the shop.'

'Oh, that. Yeah. Look Belle, what about this one? It's got a boxroom we can turn into a nursery.'

Oz pocketed the key to Kieran's flat as though it unlocked the gates of heaven, which, as far as he was concerned, it possibly did. For a bloke like Oz, a peck on the cheek and a glimpse of ankle was depressingly close to his own personal Nirvana.

'I'm not going to ask who she is,' said Kieran, spearing a cube of quiche. 'All I ask is no soiled underwear left in embarrassing places, and no curly hairs in the bath.'

'Aw, Kieran!' Oz pulled a face. 'That's disgusting.'

'Yes, well, I know what you entomologists are like,' replied Kieran, managing to keep a straight face. 'Lotharios to a man. Oh, and while we're at it, no poisonous spiders or unusual larvae, either.' He took in Oz's mortified expression and grinned. 'For God's sake man, I'm just taking the piss. Enjoy yourself.'

It was just after one, and the two had escaped from their respective duties to share a quick lunch at the theatre café, just up the road from the *Courant* offices.

'So . . . how's things?' asked Oz, picking a stringy bit of bacon out from between his teeth.

'Good. Me and Belle are viewing some flats on Saturday.' He laughed. 'Not as exciting as what Mona's getting up to next week, mind you. That Mad Dog bloke of hers is only flying her to some party on the Isle of Wight in his private helicopter! I mean . . . wow!'

'Wow,' echoed Oz.

'And she's got him wrapped right round her little finger, you know. She's even persuaded him to drag some of his celebrity mates down to the Royal Shakespeare, to bring the punters in. And there's talk about her organising some kind of theme evening.' He shook his head. 'What a woman. And then there's the writing.'

'What writing?' enquired Oz.

'She wants me to help her sharpen up her journalistic skills – not that she's got any, mind you. But she's one hell of a determined woman. If anybody can be successful through sheer bloody-mindedness, she can.' He rubbed his chin. 'I might see if I can do an article on her for the weekend supplement sometime.'

'And what about Belle?' asked Oz, rather pointedly. 'You know – the woman you're marrying? The one you're madly in love with?'

Kieran gave Oz a hard look. 'Yes, I'm quite aware of that, thank you.'

'Only I thought maybe you'd forgotten all about her, seeing as you spend most of your time talking about Mona.'

'I do not!'

'Actually, you do.'

'Oh shut up, Oz. You spend all your time going on about the mating habits of fruit flies, but I don't accuse you of having an affair with them, do I?'

Oz munched on unconcernedly. 'It wasn't an accusation, just an observation. Anyway, how is Belle?'

'She's fine. Why wouldn't she be?'

'God knows,' replied Oz. 'You tell me.'

Whether she was fine or not, Belle wasn't entirely sure. She'd been feeling strangely unsettled all week.

Still, maybe that wasn't such a strange thing, bearing in mind all the trouble at home. In a way, being so close to her father just made things worse for her: it was as though she could feel every agonised second of suspense just as acutely as he did. And the sight of her mother, with all the fight drained out of her, was almost more than Belle could bear. She couldn't walk through St Jude's any more without thinking about the poison pen letters her dad had been getting, and wondering just how many of the smiles she encountered were genuine. This was supposed to be her home, but it didn't feel that way any more.

And now she didn't even feel she could heap all the blame onto Mona. The more she got to know her, the more Belle was forced to admit that there was a lot to admire about her new half-sister: her energy, her determination, her cheerful resilience. She didn't have to share Jax's starry-eyed view of her to recognise her good qualities. It was no good casting Mona in the role of the wicked witch just because it was emotionally convenient; life was a lot more complicated than that.

And not just in ways that related to Mona Starr.

'Get a move on, Belle,' urged Kieran, slamming the car door and striding off across the road. 'We've got another five flats to see before lunch.'

Belle gazed wistfully through a nearby café window. Inside, people were drinking hot chocolate with marshmallows, and luxuriating in a warm fug of cosy camaraderie. Out here, the gunmetal-grey skies were dripping sleet onto slippery, slithery pavements and even the pigeons looked miserable. She shivered. 'OK, I'm coming.'

She scuttled across the carriageway to join Kieran on the opposite pavement. 'It's very ... urban round here,' she commented, taking in the metal shutters on the window of the local newsagent's. The Bluebell Estate might sound verdant and delightful, but the nearest it got to lush greenery was its abundance of home-grown cannabis plants.

He gave her a long-suffering look. 'It's an up and coming area,' he reminded her.

'Well it's got an awful long way up to go.'

'Come on, you can't keep judging properties before you've even seen them.'

Oh yes I can, thought Belle, noting the wheel-less hulk of a Ford Fiesta on a nearby street corner, and the group of youths eyeing her up from the vandalised bus shelter. The words 'over my dead body' were already forming on her lips before she'd crossed the threshold of what the estate agent had dubbed 'a top investment opportunity for the DIY enthusiast'.

As it happened, Kieran got there first. 'Never in a million years,' he announced, after the two-minute tour that politeness demanded, instinctively scratching himself as he emerged into daylight, as though something nasty might have hitched a ride.

'I think it's absolutely perfect,' declared Belle.

'You what?' The look on Kieran's face was priceless. So much so that she left it several seconds before putting him out of his misery.

'Joke,' she revealed.

'Thank God for that,' said Kieran humourlessly, obviously not getting it. 'I thought you'd lost your mind. That place is a slum.'

'Did you see that kitchen? I swear there were mushrooms growing in that cupboard under the sink,' Belle recollected. 'And what was that funny smell in the living room?'

'I don't even want to think about that, thank you.' Kieran was evidently relieved to see that the car hadn't vanished while they were inside.

'Mind you,' Belle teased, 'it is "competitively priced for a quick sale".'

'Not to me it isn't.'

'Don't you mean "us"?'

He waved away her correction as he put the car in gear. 'That's what I meant. Now let's get out of here while we've still got an engine. We're going to find a flat to buy today if it kills me.'

By the fourth flat, things were starting to get decidedly tetchy.

'There was nothing wrong with that last one,' complained Kieran as they sat in the car and compared notes.

'It was ghastly and you know it.'

'I've told you before, we can't have everything.'

'So we have a choice between an overpriced cupboard in Montpellier or a bug-infested slum?'

'Or my place,' Kieran reminded her.

'I've already told you, I'm not starting my married life in your old bachelor flat! It's got to be somewhere that's new for both of us. Somewhere that's ours.'

Kieran let out a little explosion of breath. 'Why do you have to see things in such a negative way?'

'I don't!' protested Belle, who was starting to feel severely fed up with the whole house-hunting business. 'But if buying a flat means shelling out a fortune to live somewhere neither of us likes, I'd rather stick with renting, thanks.'

As a rule, Kieran wasn't one to lose his temper, but Belle knew as soon as she'd opened her mouth that she'd said precisely the wrong thing. What's more, she didn't care.

'Oh, I get it,' snapped Kieran, rounding on her. 'This is all an excuse to get out of buying anything at all. I should've guessed. I mean, you won't even get rid of your flat and move in with me.'

'Don't be silly, of course it isn't an excuse. And you know Dad would be upset if we started living together before we're married.'

'Well it sounds like an excuse to me! I mean, your dad can hardly preach abstinence after his youthful sexploits have been all over the local papers, can he?'

'Kieran, that's not fair and you know it!'

'Admit it, Belle, you've been funny about this house-hunting business all along. Every time I suggest going to see somewhere, it's, "Oh, I think I'm doing something else that day," or "A friend's asked me round".'

'Can I help it if you arrange all the times to suit you, without even bothering to check if I'm free?' countered Belle, who was definitely not in the mood for a lecture. Today had started off badly and got worse, and turned into a complete waste of a perfectly good, positively precious Saturday off. 'I am supposed to be part of this too, you know!'

Kieran had the good grace to look fleetingly embarrassed, but then came back with 'Well, at the end of the day I'm the one with the capital, darling.'

'You pompous git!' Belle had a sudden strong urge to smack him. Hard. But why should she lower herself? 'So this is all about money, is it? You earn more than I do so you should be allowed to choose where we live?'

'No, of course not, you stupid—' He stopped in his tracks. 'Of course it's not.'

'Oh, so I'm stupid as well am I? Or is it just that I'm not the obedient little girlie you thought you were marrying? Go on, admit it. You've been pissed off with me ever since I took that promotion, haven't you?'

Kieran let out a sort of frustrated growl. 'If you mean, am I fed up that you hardly have any time for me any more, then yes I bloody well am. Not to mention the fact that it now seems as if you're not even that keen on setting up home with me any more!'

'Now who's the stupid one! Just because I've found one thing I'm good at doing. Just because I care about Mum and Dad's feelings, and I don't want to waste our money . . .'

Silence fell like the stage curtain at the end of a crucial Act. It was punctuated only by the swish-swish-swish of the windscreen wipers, parting the sleet on the windscreen of the stationary car.

'I think we got a bit carried away there,' said Kieran soberly.

125

'Yes.' Belle could feel her heart thudding ludicrously fast inside her chest.

'I'm ... um ... sorry if I went over the top.'

'Me too,' said Belle; though it was more of a reflex than a real apology, because deep down she knew that all she'd done was say what she really felt. And what good was a relationship if only one of you could be honest?

'You're right about the flats,' Kieran went on. 'None of them were right for us. And as for this lot,' he indicated the sheaf of property details poking out of the glove compartment, 'they're definitely the bottom of the barrel.'

'What are we going to do then?' asked Belle.

'Tell you what.' He reached for his mobile. 'Why don't I phone the agents and cancel the rest of the viewings? Then we can go off somewhere and have a nice late lunch, just the two of us?'

She received his kiss with as much gratitude as passion. 'Yes please,' she murmured. 'That's the most sensible thing you've said all day.'

Belle couldn't sleep on Sunday night. As she lay there in bed, watching her alarm clock project the vanishing seconds onto her bedroom ceiling, she hugged her pillow and wondered about tomorrow.

She'd never in her life suffered from feelings of uncertainty: not until now. She'd always known that Mum and Dad were there to shield her from bad stuff until, one day, she'd marry her ideal husband and he'd take over. Why didn't she feel that way any more? Why, when she thought about giving up her bedsit, getting married and setting up home with Kieran, did she feel as much fear as she did anticipation? Was she really using her dad's principles as a convenient excuse?

It wasn't just her own tomorrows she was worrying about. Curling up with her knees to her chest, she thought about her parents. Poor Dad, hounded by gossip and heading for the bishop's office tomorrow. Poor Mum, who'd invested so much strength and determination in becoming the kind of woman she'd always longed to be. Poor Mum, so afraid of falling.

I wonder if they're awake too, thought Belle, instantly wishing she'd decided to spend tonight at the vicarage to keep her mum company as she sat at the kitchen table in the small hours, drinking warm milk and doing Sudoku puzzles. Maybe I should get up and go over there now.

But tiredness overtook her, and a few seconds later Belle was fast asleep.

Chapter 12

At breakfast the following morning, Jax was her normal self even if nobody else at the vicarage was.

'Mum, there's no cereal left except Shredded Wheat!' She banged the kitchen cupboard shut in disgust. 'You know I hate Shredded Wheat.'

Standing at the sink, Brenda swore under her breath as a soapy cup slipped out of her shaking fingers. 'I haven't had a chance to go to the supermarket,' she said irritably, without turning round. 'If that's all there is, you'll just have to like it or lump it.'

'That's not fair,' whined Jax. 'You always—'

'No, Jacqueline.' Brenda turned to face her daughter, too harassed to rein in her temper. 'What isn't fair is that I have to stand here and listen to you complaining, today of all days.'

'Talk about overreacting.' Jax sloped off to the bread bin, rooted around inside and finally found something that would do. 'I don't know what all the fuss is about,' she muttered, disdainfully picking all the raisins out of a slice of fruit bread. 'Dad's only going to see the bishop. So what? He's always going to see the bishop.'

'You know perfectly well this is different.'

Jax shrugged. 'Well, I'm sure he'll be fine. And I bet Mona agrees with me, don't you, Mona? Mona told me she thinks you're going right over the top,' she added, perhaps unwisely.

'Oh, did she really?' Brenda wiped her hands on a tea towel and slung it onto the worktop. 'Well that's a great comfort to us all, I'm sure – having an amateur psychiatrist in the house.'

Mona gave Jax a 'thanks for nothing' look, but as usual the teenager was immune. It took something really important, like her favourite death metal band breaking up, to really rattle Jax. 'I didn't actually say that,' Mona protested. 'All I said was, I think everybody here's been under a lot of strain lately.' She oozed sincerity as her eyes met Brenda's.

Brenda laughed humourlessly. 'Yes, you'd know all about that.'

127

The pointed comment struck home, and Mona coloured slightly. 'And I just wanted to say, I'm really, really sorry if I've been the cause of some of it.'

At the words 'some of it', Brenda made some kind of non-committal sound that might have been 'huh'. 'Frankly Mona,' she replied, 'I personally might be under marginally less strain if you didn't fill the house with smelly animals that use my lounge carpet as a toilet.'

'Sorry.' Mona took a look at the tatty mongrel, sleeping unconcernedly underneath the kitchen table. 'He's only had a *few* little accidents.'

'Plus barking at all hours of the day and night and depositing his hair all over the place.' Brenda was in full flow now, grateful to have something to complain about, as an outlet for the unbearable tension she felt. 'And have you seen the damage he's done to the wallpaper in the lounge?'

'I'm sure he'll improve,' said Mona sweetly. 'In time.'

Jax sprung swiftly to Engelbert's defence. 'It's not his fault he's not properly house-trained, Mum, he had a bad start in life.'

Brenda might have come back with: 'So what's your excuse then?', but managed to resist. 'Well just you keep him out of my way today,' she warned. 'One more puddle and it's curtains for Engelbert.'

Footsteps outside the kitchen door announced the arrival of Gerry. Tall, handsome and rangy in his best grey suit, he looked more like a harassed middle manager or a middle-aged catalogue model than a vicar, though the harsh, cold light from the kitchen window aged him, deepening the dark shadows beneath his kindly eyes.

'Shredded Wheat, darling?' enquired Brenda, instantly energetic and smiling for his benefit. 'Or would you rather have eggs and bacon? You could do with a good breakfast inside you.'

He poured himself a cup of coffee from the pot on the table and tossed it down his throat. 'Nothing, thank you, darling, I think I'll just get on my way.'

'But you'll be ridiculously early,' she protested.

'Well, better that than hanging around Cheltenham, kicking my heels,' he replied with an effort at a smile. He kissed his wife on the cheek, let her adjust his tie and then picked up his car keys and headed for the door. 'See you all later then.'

Mona smiled encouragingly through a mouthful of cereal. 'Good luck . . . Dad.'

Brenda glared sharply at Mona. Gerry looked secretly pleased. Jax merely glanced up and echoed, 'Yeah, whatever. Not that you'll need it.'

Welsh Dave was in his element. St Jude's hadn't provided him with such a rich vein of gossip in years, not since the house of ill-repute on

Elmstone Avenue had been closed down, and as a rule there wasn't a single detail of local life that got past him.

Jean Armitage did still manage to catch him on the hop occasionally though, much to his annoyance.

'Today's the day of judgement,' she announced as he handed over her morning mail on the front doorstep after discreetly reading the picture postcard from Madeira, 'you mark my words.'

He leaned closer, with a conspiratorial glance to right and left, just in case anyone else was up and listening in. 'Vicar off to see the boss, is he? How'd you find out – did he announce it to the PCC or something?'

The St Jude's oracle looked slightly disappointed. 'Well, no,' she admitted. 'Evidently he didn't deem us sufficiently important to be told – which is typical of the man, in my humble opinion. To be quite frank, he's been keeping this whole business disgracefully close to his chest.' Her stern expression softened to a sly smile. 'But one has one's reliable sources.'

'Good for you, Mrs A. Up for the high jump then, you reckon?'

'Well, a sharp rap on the knuckles anyway, I'm quite sure of that. And not a moment too soon.'

Welsh Dave reached into his satchel and brought out a crumpled notebook and pencil. 'Don't suppose I could interest you in a little wager on the outcome?' he enquired. When he saw the look of uncertainty on Mrs Armitage's face he added, 'All in aid of church funds, of course.'

'Well, I might be persuaded to a small flutter.' Mrs Armitage smiled, and fetched her handbag right away.

'Ah, Reverend Craine.' The snooty male PA indicated a door to his right. 'Go straight in, the bishop is expecting you.'

Bishop Thaddeus Grove's office was not at all as might have been depicted in the pages of a Trollope novel, either by Anthony or Joanna. There was no age-mellowed oak panelling or Victorian stained glass and not a hint of a discreet but well-stocked drinks cabinet. On the contrary, it boasted smooth-lined Habitat furnishings and a flat-screen computer, and the previous incumbent's monogrammed Wilton carpet had been replaced by easy-clean maple-effect laminate.

The overall look was functional, and the ambience just a tad chilly. But all of this austerity wouldn't have mattered if the bishop had exuded his usual fraternal warmth. Unfortunately, the moment Bishop Grove deigned to look up from signing papers at his glass and chrome desk, Gerry knew there would be no chatting about golf handicaps this time, no sherry, not even a cup of lukewarm tea.

'Craine,' he growled, tetchy as a grizzly bear awakened too soon from its hibernation.

Since the bishop seemed disinclined to shake hands, Gerry nodded respectfully. 'Bishop.'

'Right. Close the door and sit down. You've a great deal of explaining to do.'

David Crenshaw was cock-a-hoop; Sean the barman, less so.

'Well done, Mona,' Crenshaw said, beaming, with a pat on the back so hearty it would have sent a lesser woman scudding face first through the door to the Ladies'. 'I don't know what I ever did without you.' Then he turned to the scowling Sean. 'Head barman? I dunno, Sean. All these years you've been here, and you can't even tell when someone's got their hand in the till.'

'Weren't my fault,' Sean grunted. 'I've got to go down the cellar and see to my barrels, I can't be in two places at once, can I?'

Crenshaw sniffed. 'More likely you were ogling that temporary barmaid's cleavage while she was pocketing my profit.'

Mona soaked up the appreciation graciously, while Engelbert panted lovingly up at her, filling the bar with his fragrant breath. 'Don't be too hard on him, Mr Crenshaw,' she urged.

His well-tended smile positively gleamed. 'Call me David.'

At this, Sean glowered even more malevolently. All this time, and he'd never got past 'sir'.

'Well – David – like Sean says, he's really good with the cellar work and he doesn't have a chance to keep an eye on the tills all the time, like I do. And the girl did have an accomplice – it was quite a clever little scam,' she added, as though she was an expert rather than someone who'd got lucky, nabbed the main culprit pocketing a wad of tenners and extracted a full confession on the spot.

'I'm not thick you know,' growled Sean. 'I've got exams.'

'Nobody's saying you are!' Mona assured him, as though the very thought was anathema.

'Well I am,' Crenshaw objected. 'And I think it's time for a few changes around here. From now on,' he announced, pointing at Mona, 'this girl here is head barman – I mean woman. Got that?'

Sean's lower lip did something nobody had ever seen it do before. It wobbled. 'B-but . . . what does that make me?'

'Unemployed,' replied the manager.

Before the spurned barman had a chance to dig his own grave by swearing colourfully and decking Crenshaw, Mona interceded. 'Don't do that, David,' she pleaded. 'Sean is so talented with all those pipes and valves and things. He has a real flair for the work.'

'I do?' Sean's gloom lifted fractionally. 'Yeah, she's right. As a matter of fact I do.'

'So couldn't you maybe make him head cellarman or something?' she hinted. 'And keep him on the same salary, of course.'

'Head cellarman?' David Crenshaw scratched his head. 'But there's only him down there.'

'Maybe you could get him an apprentice? There's a lot of work and you did say we're still short of staff.'

Crenshaw shook his head and sighed. 'I don't know why I'm listening to you, Mona, but maybe it's because you're the only one here with any brains – me included. OK Sean, get your pinny on, get down that cellar and thank your lucky stars you've still got a job.'

A little later in the day, Mona found David Crenshaw in the pub's back room, poring over sheets of figures.

'Not adding up?' she enquired.

He rubbed his eyes and sat back in his chair. 'Not yet, but it's my job to make them. What can I do for you?'

Mona closed the door, came in and sat down at the table, opposite the manager. 'You know you were asking if we had any ideas for drumming up trade? Well I was wondering about a theme night.'

He chuckled. 'Don't tell me – Aussie Nite, complete with plenty of lager and those hats with the corks round the brim? Actually,' he mused, 'that might not be such a bad idea. And I do know this guy in Worcester who's got a stuffed kangaroo. Know any more expat Aussies round here, do you?'

Mona winced at the cartoon image of Australian life he was painting. Any minute now, he'd be volunteering Sean to dress up as Dame Edna Everage, hurling gladioli and calling everybody Possum.

'Actually no,' she revealed. 'I mean, that kind of theme's not quite right for a place like this, is it?'

'Come on.' He nodded towards the public bar. 'Give that bunch of piss-heads in there enough beer to drown themselves in, and they're happy.'

'Ah, but we want to draw in new customers, don't we? Not just them. They'd come if all we had was beer and sawdust.' She looked around her, taking in the ancient, wobbly walls and worm-eaten beams. 'And you've really got something special here, you know.'

'Oh yeah – and what would that be? Our own strain of bubonic plague?'

'History, David! This place stinks of it.' That wasn't all it stank of, but Mona was too carried away with her own enthusiasm to mind. She got up from the table and started pacing the room. 'You know how old this pub is? Hundreds of years! Do you realise there was a pub on this spot before the first European set foot in Australia?"

'Fascinating, but what about this theme night of yours?'

Mona tried not to grind her teeth in frustration. 'That's what I'm talking about – a historical theme night! This place isn't called the Royal Shakespeare Tavern for nothing, you know. I've been doing a spot of research down the public library. There's a legend that says Shakespeare himself actually spent three days here, recovering from gut rot after a pint of bad ale.'

Crenshaw chuckled. 'So it was still a dive, back then. Nothing much changes. OK, so what you're suggesting is some kind of Shakespeare night?'

'Spot on.'

Crenshaw looked distinctly doubtful. 'Hang on, I know you're keen and all that love, but that lot out there can barely read. I can't see them lapping up Romeo and Juliet . . . unless Juliet's topless.'

'I don't think we'll have to go that far,' replied Mona, laughing as she perched her bottom on the table, next to the manager. ''Cause what I have in mind is a nice old-fashioned historical romp. A fancy-dress night. I thought we could call it Bards and Wenches. Lots of lusty maidens, plenty of cleavage, and some special Shakespeare Ale for the night. Maybe a few pies and call it a banquet. What do you reckon? Everybody loves dressing up.'

David Crenshaw pondered for a moment, scratched at his stubbly chin, and then declared: 'I reckon you're a very smart girl, Mona Starr.'

She decided it was time to play her trump card. 'You know, I might even be able to get my special friend Mad Dog McKindrick and his mates to come and play 'Rock Madrigal' if I ask them very nicely.'

'What – Afterlife? Live? That'd be brilliant,' murmured David. 'But why are you bothering to do all this?'

'Because I like this place, I really do. I know it's just a shitty old dive, but it's so . . . English.' She looked down at her feet, for once in her brazen life a touch embarrassed. 'And because I . . . I want to be good at something apart from pouting at a camera.'

'Which I'm sure you're great at doing. So, will you be wearing one of these lusty wench costumes then?'

'I might.'

'In that case you're on.'

Mona wore a smile of satisfaction. 'That's settled then; now all we need is a date. Oh, and just one other thing, David.'

'Yes?'

'If you put your hand on my knee again, I'll cut it off.'

Mona might have been congratulating herself on another upward step in her conquest of the Royal Shakespeare Tavern, but Gerry Craine wasn't far from her mind. He never was. And had she been at the vicarage when he arrived back home, she would have seen clearly that he wasn't congratulating himself about anything.

Belle was sitting with her mother at the kitchen table, sharing out the last of a bottle of red wine, when the front door clicked shut and Gerry's footsteps plodded down the stairs towards the kitchen.

There was something horribly leaden about the sound of those footsteps. Mother and daughter looked at each other, communicating all their fears, but didn't say anything. Maybe they were imagining too much.

Gerry stepped into the kitchen, flung his jacket over a chair and sat down on it, saying nothing. He looked completely shell-shocked.

Belle desperately wanted to say something, but she didn't know what. She was sure whatever it was would be the wrong thing. And how would he react if she gave him a hug? He looked so isolated, so withdrawn, as if he'd hardly even notice.

After what seemed like an age, but must only have been a minute or two, Brenda said brightly, 'Cup of tea, Gerry?'

'Thanks darling, that would be nice.' He still just went on sitting there, drooping, exuding infinite weariness. He watched his wife bustling around with the kettle, and finally declared with the ghost of a smile: 'Well, at least that's over with.'

Belle breathed a sigh of relief. It was obvious that her father had been given a hard time by the bishop, but he was back now and, like he said, it was over. He'd do whatever he had to do by way of punishment for all the bad publicity, and then he could begin again. Correction: they could. Because, after all, the events of the last couple of months had affected every single member of the Craine family.

Then, just when Belle was daring to relax a little, Gerry dropped the bombshell that was to blow the remnants of their peaceful existence into smithereens. 'I'm dreadfully sorry, but I'm afraid we have to leave St Jude's.'

Afterwards, Belle was sure that her heart had stopped beating for a moment. Her mother dropped the kettle heavily onto the worktop, and just gaped. 'Leave?' Brenda gasped. 'Oh Gerry, no – he sacked you! The bishop sacked you . . .'

Gerry went over to his trembling wife and put a steadying arm about her shoulders. 'No, no, it's not that; he didn't sack me. He just told me he'd take a very dim view if I didn't volunteer for a transfer to a different parish in Cheltenham.'

'Oh,' said Brenda, looking relieved. 'I hope you told him no, dim view or not.'

The faint smile returned, poised somewhere between humour and wistfulness. 'I'm afraid saying no wasn't an option, darling. So it's all settled; we'll definitely be moving.'

'Where to? When? Which parish?' Brenda's hands fluttered like agitated moths.

'Is it Prestbury?' wondered Belle. 'There's a vacancy there, isn't there?'

'Not Prestbury, no.'

'Where then?' demanded Brenda, half frantic with shock and shame and dreadful anticipation.

Gerry put on the bravest brave face Belle had ever seen, and replied: 'It's ... er ... St Mungo's.'

There was the most horrible silence that the vicarage had ever experienced; a silence so thick and cold and hard it seemed to freeze to the skin like icy rain.

'St Mungo's?' The words stabbed through Belle's brain like a five-thousand-volt electric shock. 'Isn't that the church in the middle of the—'

'Bluebell Estate? Yes love, I'm afraid it is,' confessed Gerry.

Brenda collapsed onto the nearest chair. 'The Bluebell Estate?' She wasn't normally given to swearing, but she let out a faint: 'Oh my God.'

'The Bluebell Estate,' echoed Belle, trying to make the words sink in. 'Oh dear.'

'Yes, I know it's not quite St Jude's,' conceded Gerry, ever the master of understatement, 'and it's earned itself a bit of a reputation. It'll be a big change for us, that's for sure. But look at it this way,' he added, as encouragingly as he could, 'it's going to be a challenge.'

Chapter 13

Jean Armitage was a woman of regular habits.

For instance today was Thursday, and on Thursday evenings she always took the ten-minute walk into town to take advantage of late-night shopping. It wasn't that she ever bought much, more the alluring possibility of bumping into someone with a juicy tale to tell.

Or – just maybe – catching sight of something intriguing . . .

She'd crossed the park and was heading for the High Street when someone, or rather something, attracted her attention because of its contrast with the surrounding twilight: a head of bright blonde, shoulder-length hair. Now, Jean knew there was no shortage of bottle blondes in Cheltenham, more was the pity, good taste and old-fashioned standards of propriety having long since departed, but few coiffures could rival this one in its honey-gold glory.

I'd know that hair anywhere, she thought with a flicker of curiosity. It belongs to that Mona girl, the nubile skeleton in Gerry Craine's closet.

There was no reason at all why Mona shouldn't have been taking an evening stroll, the same as anybody else, or simply walking back from work; but over her many years of dedicated snooping, Mrs Armitage had developed a sixth sense. That girl wasn't walking, she was lurking: glancing about her and rummaging in her handbag, and then taking out . . . what was that? Jean cursed her aged Varifocals and sneaked a little closer. Aha, a key. A door key by the look of it.

And now she was turning and walking briskly up the short driveway that led to Romilly House, the smart new block of flats that had sprung up on the site of the old primary school – the very block where young Annabelle Craine's fiancé lived. She distinctly remembered Brenda telling anyone who would listen what a lovely apartment her future son-in-law had bought, and what a wonderful investment it would be for the future. If only she could remember which number flat he lived in . . .

The fact that it was none of her business where Mona Starr went never even crossed Jean's mind. As far as she was concerned, everything was her business. And whatever Mona's business was, she was being distinctly furtive about it.

All those years of experience paid off as Jean managed to shadow Mona up the driveway by using the rhododendron bushes as cover, cursing just the once when one shoe came off in a patch of gluey mud, leaving her hopping around on one leg. It was worth a muddy sock though. She was close enough to see Mona push one of the buttons on the panel, taking a note of exactly which one it was. Oh for a pair of binoculars. And then, as though to confirm her suspicions, she distinctly heard Mona speaking into the entry phone: 'Anybody in? Kieran?'

Kieran! Well, well well . . .

Nobody answered, and after a final look around Mona unlocked the front door, slipped inside the lobby and disappeared from view.

After a couple of seconds, Jean Armitage sneaked up to the door and checked the panel. Sure enough, the button Mona had pressed was labelled 'Flat Six: Sawyer'.

She would have given anything for a chance to follow Mona inside.

The vicarage wasn't used to silence. It was accustomed to laughter and tears and arguments, but not to this awful, leaden absence of sound. Even the tick of the grandfather clock in the hall sounded muted, as if it knew, and was silencing itself out of respect.

At length, Gerry opened his mouth to speak. But it was Brenda's words that finally filled the void. 'Don't you dare,' she warned him. 'Don't you dare say it's all for the best.'

'Well . . . that's not impossible,' he ventured. 'This move might turn out to be a good thing – eventually I mean, when we all get used to it.'

'As if we ever could,' she retorted, with a savagery Belle had seldom seen her mother display. Years of gentrification and Christian forbearance might have smoothed over a lot of Brenda Craine's sharp edges, but Belle sensed that beneath the candy coating they were still there, raw as ever. 'But that's typical of you, Gerry. Bloody typical.'

'Brenda—' he began, but she hadn't finished.

'All these years we've lived here,' she went on bitterly, 'all the friends we've made – or I thought we'd made, everything I've worked for, for your benefit and the kids' . . . And now suddenly it's all gone up in smoke, and you're expecting us all just to "get used to it"?'

'It's bound to take time, I know that,' replied Gerry. 'But maybe this is something we're meant to do – you know, something that'll help to make us stronger as a family? After all, we've taken our comfortable life here for granted for a very long time.'

Brenda let out a gasp of exasperation. There was a glimmer of unnatural brightness in her eyes that looked to Belle like unshed tears. 'Comfortable? Have you forgotten how hard it was when we first came here? Because I haven't. The snobbery, the snide remarks ... "Oh, the vicar's wife's a bit common, isn't she? I wonder where he picked her up" ...'

'I'm sure they didn't—'

'Oh yes they did, Gerry. They hated me for months, and I hated them right back. Don't you remember that snotty woman who wrote to the bishop about how unsuitable I was for a "nice suburban parish"?' Gerry didn't answer, but it was plain that he did. 'It's taken me years of bloody raffles and coffee mornings to get them to accept me. I even thought some of them liked me. And now I'm supposed to give it all up without a fight? Smile and trot obediently back to the Bluebell Estate, like I never left it in the first place?'

'Oh Mum, I'm sure Dad didn't mean it like that,' said Belle.

'Your father can speak for himself, Annabelle.'

Gerry cleared his throat. 'Brenda love, I'd be nothing without you. Anything I've achieved, I've only achieved because I had you to help me. I know how hard this is, truly I do, but ... I need you to keep on helping me now, because otherwise I might just as well give up.'

It tore Belle apart to see what the bishop's decision was doing to her family. If she could, she'd have dragged him back to the vicarage with her own two hands and forced him to look at the consequences. Not that he'd have cared. People like him never did.

'Mum,' she said gently, 'it's not just Dad, we all need you. You're the one who keeps the whole family together.' And although the thought of leaving St Jude's was breaking her heart, she added, 'Does it really matter where the family's based if we've got each other?'

Brenda looked at her elder daughter and shook her head ruefully. 'Not an ounce of sense in you, just like your father. Of course it matters.' She heaved a sigh. 'But maybe not quite as much as I'm making out.'

'That's my girl.' Gerry took his wife in his arms. 'We'll be all right if we stick together,' he assured her. 'And if anybody can turn a parish around, it's you.'

She pulled a face at the very thought. 'You have to realise one thing, Gerry,' she told him. 'This is your crusade, not mine. I never really wanted to be a vicar's wife – just yours.'

'That's good enough for me.' He smiled.

Jax wasn't taking the news well.

She'd stomped into the house just in time to hear her father's bombshell announcement, and had promptly stomped right out again, without uttering a single word.

Half an hour later she returned, ashen-faced and smelling of lager. 'Is it true?' she demanded, confronting her parents and Belle as they sat round the kitchen table.

'Yes, I'm afraid so,' her father replied. 'But it's really not that bad. I've heard there's a really good community spirit around St Mungo's, and—'

'Not that bad? Not that bad!' Wide-eyed, Jax slid down the kitchen wall until she was sitting in a heap on the floor, school rucksack discarded at her feet. 'You're shipping us all off to St Mungo's and you reckon it's not that bad?'

'I know it's a bit of a shock,' began her father.

'But there's absolutely no point in overreacting,' cut in her mother firmly. 'It's not as if we're being thrown out on the street, or anything horrible like that. Lots of vicars have to move parishes.'

Jax wasn't quite so easily placated. 'But St Mungo's? St Mungo's? That's like the biggest dump in the whole of Cheltenham, everybody knows that.'

'I'm sure there are some very nice people living there,' Belle insisted gamely, though her own experiences of the place so far hadn't been too promising.

'Oh yeah? That's not what I've heard. Oh my God,' she agonised, 'what's everybody at school going to say when they find out about this?'

'Actually,' Gerry said gently, 'you'll probably have to move schools anyway.'

Jax shot bolt upright. 'What!'

'Well, you're there on a church scholarship because I'm the vicar of St Jude's,' he pointed out. 'And if I'm not any more . . .'

Jax made a noise that was somewhere between a groan and a roar. 'I can't take this! I won't!'

Belle cast her mind back to what it was like being sixteen, with more existential angst than a dozen Radiohead albums, and did her best to be sympathetic. 'Does it really matter what a bunch of kids at school say?' she asked. 'I mean, are they worth having as friends if that's the sort of thing they care about?'

Jax received this attempt at homespun philosophy with a look that said 'cretin'. 'Of course it matters, are you thick or what?' She sniffed. 'Not that you give a damn anyway.'

'Yes, I do,' Belle protested, though she was rapidly starting not to.

'Oh come on, why should you care? You've got it cushy, marrying lover-boy and buying a lovely new luxury apartment.'

'It's not going to be a luxury apartment,' Belle assured her with a laugh.

'Whatever.'

'Anyway,' Belle reminded her, 'only last week you said you'd rather be dead than ever get married!'

'Yeah, well, I would. But then I'm not you, am I?' Jax stuck her pert nose in the air. 'I'm talented and I'm going places.'

Belle bit her tongue. 'That's nice for you.'

'And you're nothing special, are you? All you do is work in a shop, but everything's all pink angels and fluffy kittens for you, isn't it? Do you call that fair? 'Cause I don't!'

Poor wee mite, thought Belle caustically. I wonder how many years you get for strangling your annoying little sister. Or maybe you get a knighthood or something. After all, it's not so much a crime as a public service.

'Fair doesn't come into it,' she said. 'Life's not fair. You'll realise that when you're older.'

Jax scowled. 'Don't come the age fascist with me, you smug bitch.'

That was it. The last frayed strand in Belle's mental elastic finally gave way. 'Oh grow up and stop feeling sorry for yourself, you selfish little cow!' she snapped.

Jax's mouth dropped open. 'What did you say?'

'I said, grow up! Don't you care about how Dad feels? And Mum? There's a whole world of bad people out there, but does all this bad stuff happen to them? No, it happens to Mum and Dad. Like I said, life's not fair and that's just the way it is.'

'But what about me?' protested Jax. 'How do you think I feel? Nobody thinks about my feelings, do they?'

Belle stared in disbelief. 'Your feelings?'

'Yes, my feelings,' Jax repeated. 'I mean, has anybody thought how traumatic this is for me? And do I get a say in what happens to me? Do I hell. As if it's not bad enough having a dad who's a vicar, now I've got one who's a vicar on the Bluebell Estate . . . Don't you realise?' Jax bristled with righteous fury. 'This is social death for me!'

At this point, Belle would have loved to floor her sister with something witty and venomous, but all she could come up with was 'Good!' This whole scene was in danger of turning into a kids' playground fight.

They stood up and scowled at each other. 'You really hate me, don't you?' Jax's mouth started to quiver with emotion. 'You all hate me.'

Belle had no patience left; not for any of this, not now. 'No, but if that's what you want to think, be my guest.'

The voice started to quaver. 'I've had enough of this, I'm going to my room!'

As the clomp, clomp, clomp of Jax's ubiquitous big boots died away up the stairs, the clock in St Jude's church tower, just across the road, struck a mournful half-hour.

'Don't you think you were a little hard on your sister?' asked Gerry quietly.

'I dunno.' Belle aimed a half-hearted kick at the skirting board. 'Maybe. Oh . . . damn. I hate today. Today sucks.'

Her gaze kept drifting to the gap in the kitchen curtains, hoping to catch a first glimpse of Kieran coming up the path. He was late – very late, in fact. What was he doing and where was he doing it? And with whom? Why wasn't he here, like he'd promised to be? And why had his mobile been switched off all afternoon?

'Jax is very upset,' observed Gerry, as the sounds of thrash metal began vibrating the timbers overhead.

'We're all upset,' his wife replied.

Gerry didn't move from the table; just kept sitting there, head resting in his hands. There was weariness in every curve of his body, every sagging muscle; every line in his face seemed twice-deepened by care and guilt. For the very first time in her life, Belle looked at him not with simple respect, admiration or love, but with pity and a surge of vengeful anger. How could anyone do this to her beloved dad?

With all the energy drained out of him, she glimpsed the old man he would one day be; and that wasn't right, because that shouldn't happen for years and years yet. This wasn't her dad. Her dad was strong and kind and clever and funny, and no matter how bad things might seem, they would always come out right in the end because everything was for the best.

'Everything's for the best.' She could hear him saying it again and again down the years, marking everything from failed exams to grazed knees. How often had he driven them all mad with that personal mantra of his? And how many times had they dusted themselves down and tried again, because they believed in him? Belle didn't class herself as overly religious, but she'd always believed in her dad.

She laid a hand on his shoulder, wishing with all her heart that she could make everything all right, the way Daddy had made things right when she was little; wanting to say the same words to him, but knowing that they just wouldn't sound the same coming from her lips. She'd lost count of the bumps and grazes, the hurts and insults and failures he and Mum had put right with nothing more than kisses and smiles.

She straightened up. 'Think I'll put the kettle on. Anybody else fancy another cup of tea?'

She'd hardly taken two steps towards the kettle when the front door banged shut and the sounds of laughter and matey insults filled the hall-way above.

'Well, if you hadn't been loping along like a three-legged dingo—'

'Oh come on, you were cheating that day!'

'Was not.'

'Yes you were, you elbowed me right into that ditch! You just wait till I can organise a rematch.'

Kieran and Mona came laughing down the stairs and into the vicarage kitchen like a couple of kids let out of school on the last day of term, Engelbert lolloping along behind them with the tatty remains of an umbrella proudly clamped in his jaws.

'Hi folks, hi Belle darling!' Kieran kissed her briefly. 'Look who I met as I was walking up the road.'

'Get a load of Engelbert,' laughed Mona. 'Did you ever see a dog like him for stealing stuff?'

'Hi,' said Belle quietly.

Maybe Kieran was especially unobservant that day, but he didn't seem to pick up on the mood at all. 'So, how did your meeting with the bishop go then, Gerry?' he asked, cheerily shrugging off his jacket and throwing it over a chair.

Nobody said anything. Surely even perpetually upbeat Mona couldn't be immune forever to the peculiar atmosphere of horrible stillness in the room.

Slowly something dawned, and she looked from Belle to Gerry and Brenda and then back again. 'Hey guys, is there something wrong?' she enquired, the smile freezing on her face. 'Is it me, or has something bad happened?'

The following morning, Belle's beaten-up Peugeot was bouncing over some of Cheltenham's premier potholes on its way to the Bluebell Estate. At least nobody could accuse the borough council of snobbery when it came to its road surfaces: be it uptown Montpellier or downtown Whaddon, they were all uniformly awful.

'You know, you really didn't have to take the morning off work to bring me,' said Gerry, just avoiding banging his head on the car roof as they went over a freestyle dollop of tarmac.

'Yes, I did, Dad,' replied Belle firmly. 'I wanted to. And besides, if some of the kids round here saw your nice car they'd probably have the wheels off the minute your back was turned.'

'Well . . . possibly,' he conceded. 'But I suppose we're going to have to get used to that sort of thing if we're living here.'

She looked at him in the rear view mirror. 'Good for the soul, eh Dad?'

He laughed. 'Maybe. But not for the no-claims bonus.'

Belle didn't give a damn about the hissy fit Waylon had thrown when she demanded half a day's leave. He spent half the week out of the store, and never bothered telling anybody when or whether he'd be in. One morning off was little enough reward for all the times she'd worked late or held the fort on his account. Besides, he owed her and Lily for the success of the new store layout they'd devised together. All in all, her conscience was clear.

Her only regret was that her mum had ducked out of the visit at the last moment, pleading a doctor's appointment that had mysteriously materialised out of thin air. Belle had wanted to try a bit harder to persuade her mum, but her father didn't want to put any pressure on Brenda: 'Give her time, I think she has to get used to the idea in her own way.'

Kieran of course was busy being a hot-shot local journalist, although Belle suspected he could have got the time off if he'd really tried. Funnily enough, she was almost glad he hadn't. The biggest surprise though was Mona. 'You won't want me there,' she'd said when Belle told her they were coming over to St Mungo's. 'I'd only be in the way.'

Mona? In the way? Mona had never let that stop her before. Normally she just merrily invited herself along to anything and everything, and if you wanted to get rid of her, you had to tell her so – in words of one syllable and no more than four letters. Why she should be any different this time round, wondered Belle. And why did her abrasive charm seem curiously muted? Maybe St Mungo's was just too downmarket for an international fashion model to be seen in.

There wasn't really time to ponder the mysterious ways of Mona Starr, because Belle's elderly runabout was bumping its way along Bluebell Boulevard towards the concrete eggbox that was St Mungo's Parish Church.

'Well, it's distinctive,' Belle remarked as she parked the car in the church car park, empty save for a skip filled with rubble and an up-ended supermarket trolley with only three wheels. 'You have to give it that.'

Gerry eased his lanky form out of the cramped interior and stretched his aching joints. 'Believe it or not, it won an award when it was built.'

'Who from?' puzzled Belle. 'The *Concrete Lovers' Gazette*?'

'Some architects' association in Sweden. The judges said it was a perfect fusion of form and function.' Gerry hrrmphed to himself. 'Just bears out what I've always thought about architects.'

St Mungo's church was nothing if not clearly visible. It had evidently been designed by an optimist, since it looked big enough to house the last night of the Proms, let alone the average Sunday service, and its high concrete walls – still glaringly white if you didn't count the graffiti – had dominated the local landscape for the best part of forty years, like a second-hand East German prison.

It was generally rectangular in shape, with a roof composed of two parallel rows of three miniature domes (hence its local nickname of 'the eggbox'), and a tall, needle-shaped spire at one corner, so thin that it looked more like a radio antenna. There had once been a cross on the top, but somebody had nicked it.

'You from the insurance then?' demanded an old man in a greasy tweed jacket, sagging jeans and plimsolls.

'Insurance?' enquired Belle.

The old man pointed with his walking stick at the distant roof of the church. 'You know, to see about the lead that got nicked the other night. Little buggers,' he added reflectively.

'Ah. Not exactly,' confessed Gerry, proffering a hand. 'My name's Gerry Craine, I'm the new vicar.'

The old bloke stared, scratched his head, stared a bit more, and finally chortled merrily. 'New vicar? Here? That's a good 'un.' He blew his nose on a grubby handkerchief. 'So who are you really, then?'

'You'll have to excuse old Albert, Vicar,' said Miss Edith Findlay, bustling about the church interior with a mop and a bucket of disinfectant. 'This has come as quite a shock to all of us, actually. A very nice shock,' she added hastily. 'You couldn't just lift your foot could you, Vicar? Only there's something nasty on the floor by the font.'

Belle shuddered and tried not to look as the sprightly churchwarden dealt with it. It wasn't the only nasty something inside St Mungo's; somebody had clearly been using the church as a doss-house, and worse. St Jude's this most definitely was not.

Miss Findlay wasn't slow in spotting the look on Belle's face. 'I'm afraid we do have a security problem here,' she confessed. 'We try hard to keep the vandals out, but they keep breaking in again. And the diocese just doesn't seem interested in helping us find the money to install proper metal shutters and gates. To be honest,' she went on, pausing to flick her greying chestnut fringe back off her face, 'we'd all pretty much assumed the bishop was planning to deconsecrate us altogether.' She giggled girlishly, belying her fifty-odd years. 'We certainly never dreamed he'd send us a lovely new full-time vicar out of the blue like this.'

Belle had been asking herself exactly the same question, and she knew her father must have been, too. Why practically abandon St Mungo's for three years and then suddenly have a complete change of heart? Just to humiliate one embarrassing priest? What a nasty, vindictive little man Thaddeus Grove was proving to be.

'Well, I'm very pleased to be here,' declared Gerry, rather to Belle's surprise, because if there was one thing her father never ever did, it was tell lies. After last night's utter despondency, today he seemed if not happy, then at least energised. 'And I promise I shall do my very best to fight St Mungo's cause.'

Miss Findlay beamed. 'You'll have the congregation's full support, of course. There may not be many of us, but we're all dedicated to our church.'

'So what sort of size congregation do you get, then?' asked Belle, eyeing up the cavernous interior of the church.

'You know, things aren't nearly as bad as they might be,' Miss Findlay replied proudly. 'At Sunday morning service, we sometimes get into double figures.' Belle couldn't bring herself to look her father in the eye. She knew he must be visualising the congregation he'd built up at St Jude's: the rows and rows of pews, packed with fat ladies in big hats and their pinstriped husbands. 'Anyhow, I'm sure things will improve no end once you've settled in here, Vicar.'

'I'll do my best,' replied Gerry. 'It's certainly going to be a stimulating challenge.'

Gazing into the distance, Belle caught sight of a furtive figure sneaking along behind the choir stalls, bowed beneath the weight of something large and heavy. His attempts to look unobtrusive weren't up to much: whoever he was, he might as well have been carrying a sign that read 'I'm up to no good'.

'Excuse me,' Belle said, cutting into the conversation, 'but I think somebody's stealing your keyboard.'

'What?' Miss Findlay swung round, spotted the figure, and waved at it. 'Oh that's only Jason, my nephew. Yoo-hoo Jason, see you at teatime!' She turned back. 'You don't need to worry about him, he's just taking it home for safe keeping. I'm afraid we have to after every service,' she explained, 'or it wouldn't be here next time.'

'I thought you had a pipe organ,' commented Gerry.

'We do,' replied the churchwarden apologetically, 'or rather, we did. But there was a big storm a couple of years ago, and the rain got in through the roof and damaged the pipework. Not to mention the rats chewing the bellows . . .' She sighed. 'We did ask for funding for the repairs, but I'm afraid the bishop wasn't very, how shall I put it, forthcoming.'

Surprise, surprise, thought Belle.

'He said our roof's not a priority.'

'Hm,' replied Gerry. 'Interesting. I wonder what is.'

Belle was tempted to say 'golf and fast cars', but she knew her dad was thinking it anyway. Seldom did a week go by without at least one colour photograph of Bishop Grove in the *Courant*'s 'Out and About' column, glass in hand and flanked by society bigwigs.

'At least Gladstone's more or less sorted out the rats,' said Miss Findlay, tipping the contents of the mop bucket down a nearby drain. 'Though he does tend to leave the bits all over the floor.'

'Who's Gladstone?' asked Belle. 'The verger?'

The churchwarden laughed. 'Sort of. That's him in there.'

Belle looked behind her and saw two ears and the tip of a ginger tail, just visible over the rim of the unspeakably ugly font. 'A church cat! That's really cute.'

'I'm not sure I'd call him cute exactly,' admitted Miss Findlay. 'Gladstone's certainly a character, but I wouldn't chance stroking him if I were you, not unless you've a few spare fingers you'd like to get rid of.'

She flicked her duster one last time over the lectern, and then popped it in the pocket of her apron. 'Right – that's the cleaning done. Now, if you'd like to follow me, Vicar, I'm sure you can't wait to see the vicarage.'

As her father got ready for Evensong at St Jude's, Belle sat on the sofa next to her mother, and showed her the pictures she'd taken that day on her digital camera. 'That's Miss Findlay, one of the churchwardens. You'll like her, she's lovely.' Then came the moment Belle had been dreading. 'Oh, and this is . . . er . . . St Mungo's vicarage.'

Brenda was silent for several shell-shocked seconds, then said faintly: 'It's . . . a council house.'

'Not any more,' Belle assured her. 'OK it used to be, but the church bought it years ago and converted it. It's quite . . . big, really.'

She longed desperately to be able to say something really positive, like, 'Wow, you should see the brand-new designer kitchen,' or 'It's really tastefully decorated,' but that was kind of problematic, since the kitchen still had its original Belfast sink and wooden draining board, and the previous occupants had favoured Seventies'-style lime green and purple wallpaper. 'Quite big' was about as close to a rave review as you could get – and that was pushing it.

'It's a council house,' Brenda insisted. 'I should know, we lived in one just like it when I was a kid. Dear God, this is a nightmare.' She gripped her daughter's arm. 'Tell me I'm going to wake up in a minute and find this was all a bad dream.'

Belle did the only thing she could: wrapped her arms round her mum and hugged her with all her strength. 'You know I can't say that, Mum, I wish I could. But everything's going to be all right, really it is.'

'How can you say that, Annabelle? It's about as far from all right as it could possibly be.'

She could feel her mother's petite frame trembling in her arms, and

145

knew that she must be utterly terrified of a future that seemed to promise nothing more than the very worst aspects of her own past. 'It'll be all right because you're not alone,' she said. 'You've got Dad, and me, and . . . um . . . Jax – and Kieran. You know Kieran adores you; he'd do anything to make things better.'

'I know.' The words caught in Brenda's throat, stifling a sob. 'I know how lucky I am to have you, but why? Why, Belle?'

'Why are the bad things happening to you and Dad? I don't know, Mum.'

'If only your father had never gone to Australia. He was just a boy. Just a silly boy who had one drink too many. Do we really all deserve to be punished like this for one idiotic mistake?'

'No Mum, of course not.'

Belle struggled to express an optimism she knew her mother didn't want to hear. It was either that or let her give in to gloom, and Belle wasn't ready to do that. 'You'll be happy and settled again soon, Mum. Going to St Mungo's doesn't mean you can't be happy.'

'Oh really?' Her mother looked her in the eye. 'Would you want to go there? Would you want to live on the Bluebell Estate?'

'No,' she admitted, recalling her disastrous morning's house-hunting with Kieran.

'Then please, please stop trying to tell me how great it is.'

'I'm not, I just—'

'It's OK Annabelle, I know what you're trying to do, and I love you for it, but you don't have to do it. I know I have to put up with this and make the best of it, because let's face it, what choice do I have? I'm a middle-aged mother with no education, and the only skill I've got is being a vicar's wife. So I'll stick at it and that's that.

'But that doesn't mean I've entirely forgiven your father. To be honest, I'm not sure if I ever can.'

Late that evening, Kieran turned up at Belle's flat just as she was going to bed.

'Why didn't you answer your phone? I've been waiting for you round at my place all evening,' he complained. 'Did you forget?'

'No,' she replied calmly. 'I just decided not to come.'

Kieran came in and closed the door behind him. 'I don't get it.'

'No,' observed Belle, 'you never do, do you?' Walking across to the coffee table, she picked up a copy of that day's *Cheltenham Courant* and thrust it in his face. 'Does this help?'

The headline on page three ran: LOVE-CHILD VICAR SENT TO INNER CITY HELL.

'Oh,' said Kieran. 'That. Look, I had nothing to do with it.'

'Yeah, right.'

'No, honestly. The news desk got a call from the bishop's press office first thing this morning, with the full story. I did suggest they might hold it for a day or two, but after all, it was bound to come out soon, wasn't it?'

'Nice of you to warn Mum and Dad they were going to be all over the paper again today.'

Kieran sighed irritably. 'Look, I've been working out of the office almost all day.'

'With Mona?'

'As it happens, yes.'

'Getting on terribly well with her, aren't you?'

Kieran looked distinctly weary. 'Yes, as a matter of fact I am. And I reckon she's really benefiting from the work experience. But what's that got to do with anything? I'm knackered, and telling you about the story just didn't seem that important, OK? For God's sake, Belle, it's only on page three.'

She flung aside the newspaper and sat down on the end of the bed. 'Page three? Oh, well, in that case it's perfectly fine! Don't know why you didn't phone up the vicarage and ask for a couple of nude photos to go with it.'

'Sarcasm doesn't suit you.'

'Really? Well self-righteousness doesn't look that great on you either, in case you were wondering.'

Kieran sat down next to her. 'What's the matter, Belle?'

She glared at him with eyes that couldn't decide whether to blaze or brim over with tears. 'I'm fed up, Kieran. I've had a horrible day and I'm fed up.'

He rubbed the back of his hand across his brow. 'Sometimes I just don't know what you want any more, Belle.'

'Sometimes I don't either,' she replied, turning her face away. 'But I do know one thing: this isn't it.'

Chapter 14

Easter was late that year, and as well as the usual showers April boasted giant chocolate bunnies, decorated eggs and a rash of bikinis in the ever-optimistic clothes shops of Cheltenham.

There was a definite Easter vibe at Green Goddess too, although Waylon had yet to persuade his staff into beachwear. The Spring Brides display had been redesigned to fit into one corner of the shop floor, next to the eco-friendly shaving products, leaving plenty of room for the special seasonal promotion. This year the product designers at head office had excelled themselves: there were rabbit-shaped soaps and cartons of egg-shaped bath bombs, decorated papier-mâché eggs that opened up to reveal shimmering bath pearls nestling on a bed of red velvet, gloriously chocolate-scented massage bars and a shampoo that smelt just like simnel cake. It was all so delicious that Belle and Lily had had to stop themselves – let alone the younger customers – eating the merchandise.

Spring fever must have touched Waylon too, for he had dug deep into the petty cash and hired a googly-eyed pink rabbit costume for Dan to wear as he patrolled the arcade, handing out leaflets and unwittingly terri-fying small children. Belle suspected that Waylon would have decked out all the female staff in *Playboy* bunny outfits and white stilettos if he thought he could get away with it. But even Waylon the unreconstructed male chauvinist had no desire to be hauled before a sexual harassment tri-bunal. Thank God, thought Belle. She had enough on, preventing cus-tomers from pinching the merchandise, never mind staff members' bottoms.

'You look exhausted,' remarked Lily, handing a gift-wrapped package to a customer with a cheery 'See you again soon!'. 'You really do, you know. Are you poorly?'

'No, just knackered.' Belle yawned and lowered her tired bottom onto a stool behind the counter. Lily was absolutely right; she was utterly worn out, not to mention demoralised. And it didn't help matters that, despite her protests, she seemed to be seeing less and less of Kieran. 'It's nothing,' she assured Lily, 'just all these late nights in the shop, doing Waylon's job for him. I'm sure I'd be fine if I could just have a couple of days off.'

Lily's bright eyes turned sceptical behind the cute little round glasses that made her look like a very wise, if very junior, owl. 'It's easy saying that, but if you had the time off you'd only spend it helping your folks shift more furniture, wouldn't you?'

'They do need all the help they can get,' reasoned Belle.

'That's what removal men are for.'

'No, removal men are for breaking priceless heirlooms and dropping pianos out of first-floor windows.'

'You've seen too many bad sitcoms. Look, what about Mona then? If she's so keen on being one of the family, shouldn't she be doing her share of furniture-shifting?'

'You're kidding,' retorted Belle. 'She's far too busy for anything as boring as that. She's got pub theme nights to organise, not to mention ageing rock stars' egos to polish.'

'Well, that's no reason to do everything yourself. It's not like your parents are ancient and incapable, is it?' Lily wagged an admonitory finger. 'For goodness' sake get some sleep; if you get any paler you'll turn into the Bride of Dracula. And then what will Kieran say?'

Belle grunted. 'Like he'd even notice.'

Lily's ears pricked up. 'Oh dear, what's this? All not well in love land?'

Who knows? thought Belle. Maybe they are, and maybe they aren't. Things had been so weird lately, even she wasn't sure any more. 'Put it this way,' she said. 'If you were thinking of jacking in your bloke for a new one any time soon, I'd leave it and get a goldfish instead. They're a lot less trouble and they don't leave the toilet seat up.'

'Actually,' replied Lily with unwonted coyness, 'I don't think I'd better jack him in at all. I think I might be pregnant.'

'Really?' Belle forgot her own troubles and enveloped Lily in a delighted hug. 'Oh Lily, that's brilliant!'

At that momentous juncture the doors to the shop glided open, letting in a brief cacophony of noisy kids and piped music, followed by a voluptuous strawberry blonde in a beautifully cut purple trouser suit.

'Hello people.' Clare's voice boomed jovially across the shop, completely drowning out the 'Waterfall Moods' CD tinkling prettily in the background. 'Belle, you'd better lead me to the men's section right away, it's emergency birthday present time.'

'Sorry?' Startled, Belle pointed to the far corner. 'Oh . . . over there, by the bridal make-up.'

Clare called after her: 'The shaving sets are nice. Why don't you come and help me choose, then I can drag all the latest gossip out of you at the same time.'

Belle didn't take too much persuading to abandon the drudgery of last week's sales totals to Lily's capable hands. She took a good, long look at the display. 'What about this?' she suggested, plucking a box off a rack.

'What is it?'

'The latest just-for-men pedicure kit, complete with essential skin-softening oils and a reflexology chart.' She sensed that Clare was building up to another bout of hilarity. 'O . . . K . . . maybe not. For your dad?'

'Yes, the old codger himself. I clean forgot it's his birthday tomorrow, and you must remember what he's like – he's one of those people with no hobbies that it's impossible to buy presents for.'

Belle cast her mind back all those years, to the days when she and Max were still an item, and recalled Levenshulme *père* as being a squat, slightly scary man who washed with carbolic soap and dismissed after-shave as 'scent for nancy-boys'. 'Let me guess . . . whatever it is, he's either got it already or he doesn't want it?' she ventured.

'That's my daddy. So in the end I thought "smellies", you can't go wrong with smellies, can you?'

'They're very popular,' agreed Belle with a smile. 'I think they're a sort of universal last resort.'

'Too right. The trouble is, they have to be macho smellies, if you know what I mean. Don't suppose you do anything with barbed wire and gravel?' She ran her eyes along the shelves. 'You're looking awfully pale, you know. All this business with your father's obviously getting to you.'

Belle rolled her eyes. 'I wish people would stop saying that! I'm fine.'

'You weren't last time I saw you,' Clare reminded her. 'You were a complete mess. And it must be pretty terrible, the whole family having to move out of St Jude's after all those years. And . . . I don't mean to be rude, but St Mungo's isn't exactly the nicest parish in Cheltenham, is it?'

'Be honest, it's a hole.'

'I didn't quite like to say.'

'Well, it is one anyway,' declared Belle. 'It stinks. And it's not just Mum and Dad who are having a bad time, either. Jax found out yesterday that she's going to have to leave St Jude's School and go to the compre-hensive on the Bluebell Estate.'

Clare looked stunned. 'Really – why?'

'Because Dad's not vicar of St Jude's church any more, and she only had a free place there because he was.'

Clare whistled. 'Hm, she's not going to like that.'

150

'You're telling me. I actually feel really sorry for her, and I haven't done that in a while. I mean, how callous can you get? The kid's got her AS exams coming up. But that's Thaddeus bloody Grove for you.'

'Thaddeus?' Clare giggled at the name. 'Who on earth has a name like Thaddeus?'

'The bishop. Fat, pompous bloke in a purple frock, with a face to match. Now, how about . . . one of these?' Belle reached up and took down a sturdy cardboard box, designed to look like a wooden sea-chest. She flipped it open. 'There you go – Dead Sea Mud soap, pumice body scrub, deodoriser for smelly feet – all kinds of manly stuff. What could be more macho than mud? And there's even one of those thingies for trimming the hair in his ears.'

Clare grabbed it from her. 'Sold.'

'I haven't told you the price yet!'

'On this occasion, it doesn't matter. This is a dad-friendly present and it's going to get me out of schtuck. You're a genius.' She headed briskly for the sales desk, handed Lily the exact amount in cash and even dropped a pound coin into the tips box. As Lily's hand moved towards the coloured tissue and sticky tape, Clare added: 'No need to gift-wrap it, Dad thinks fancy wrapping paper's for girlies.'

Dropping the package triumphantly into her capacious Mulberry bag, Clare turned back to Belle. 'Right, now that's over with, you can tell me all your news. And I do mean all.'

While her elder daughter was submitting to in-depth interrogation, over at St Jude's vicarage Brenda was standing in her bedroom amid the chaos of half-packed boxes, grimly trying on hats.

That was how Gerry found her when he came upstairs in search of his spare reading glasses. His eyes met his wife's in the dressing-table mirror, and without turning round she came out with: 'Well go on, which one – the blue one or the black and white?'

Since the vicar's thoughts were on his outgoing Easter sermon, this caught him somewhat on the hop. His mouth flapped open uselessly. 'Sorry?'

Brenda let out one of those short, irritated sounds that fall somewhere between a sigh and a gasp. 'This one?' she asked, jamming the blue feathery one on her head, 'or this one?' She switched it for the black and white flowerpot. 'Come on dear, it's a perfectly simple question.'

'They're both very nice,' he replied, hedging his bets.

But Brenda was in no mood for his diplomacy. 'Gerry!'

'Well, they are! Look love, if this is one of those awkward questions about what goes with what and what's in fashion, I think you'd better wait till Belle comes round and ask her. I'm bound to put my foot in it. I always do.'

Brenda shook her head obstinately. 'I want you to choose,' she insisted, and for that brief moment she sounded just like Jax in one of her sulky, unreasonable moods. 'All I want you to do is choose which hat I should wear for your last service at St Jude's. Is that so much to ask?'

'Oh,' said Gerry, beginning to understand why his wife was getting herself into such a state.

'It's not just the hat . . . it matters, you know. All of it.'

'I know.'

Brenda plonked herself down on the end of the old brass bedstead they'd rescued from a skip years ago and lovingly restored together. Back in those days there'd been so little money that Belle's first cradle was the drawer out of an old dressing table. But even then, Brenda had worked ceaselessly for the better times she craved and truly believed that they deserved. For a while she'd thought they'd made it. But where had it all got her today? Right back to where she came from in the first place.

Maybe it would be better if things didn't matter so much to her, if they'd never mattered at all.

'Well,' she said, 'maybe it's just silly pride, but I want to look my best for you. I want to show our snotty so-called friends and neighbours that we can go out in style.'

Gerry was an emotional man, though he could rarely afford to let those emotions show; and Brenda's fierce pride touched him deeply. 'You've always been a wonderful wife to me,' he said, sitting beside her and sliding his arm round her waist, 'but you know, we mustn't be angry or resentful about this.'

Her response startled him. 'No Gerry, you mustn't – you're the one who has to go through life being St Gerry, who never hates anybody or gets pissed off about anything. You're the one who's not allowed to have normal feelings. But I'm just an ordinary human being, and I'm going to be as angry and resentful as I damn well like. So there.'

For a moment Brenda thought she was going to get a sermon on forgiveness but, in spite of himself, Gerry laughed. 'That's my Brenda. Don't ever change, will you?'

She looked at him ruefully. 'Fat chance. I tried, remember? And look where it's got me – right back on the Bluebell Estate.' She plucked moodily at the feathers on her blue hat. 'It's like being in some giant game of snakes and ladders. You're throwing six after six and zooming up every ladder in sight, and then suddenly you land on the biggest snake you've ever seen and you're back at square one with nothing to show for all that effort.'

Gerry shook his head. 'You're wrong there, Brenda. You've come a long way since I first met you. And if we're being sent to St Mungo's it's for a reason, I'm sure of it.'

'I wish I was.'

He kissed her on the cheek. 'Just try not to be so pessimistic and full of anger. Negative emotions never really do us any good in the end, you know. We need to embrace change and move forward.'

Brenda grunted. 'Very eloquent Gerry, but I'm not your congregation so you can stop preaching at me. I'll deal with this in my own way. And it starts by looking good at that Easter service.'

There was right and there was wrong, and Clare was never in any doubt as to which was which.

'It's just not right,' she said firmly, as she and Belle stood by the window display in Green Goddess, watching damp shoppers troop by, gently steaming after the spring rain outside.

'I'm sure he doesn't mean it.' Belle knew her defence of Kieran sounded feeble; she wasn't even sure she quite believed it herself. 'He's only spending time with Mona because he likes her and he wants to help her.'

'Likes her?' There was a heavy accent of irony in Clare's voice. 'Yes, well, it certainly does sound that way, doesn't it? Seeing as he's spending more time with her than he is with his own fiancée.'

'It's not quite as bad as that . . .'

'But it's pretty bad, admit it. I can tell from the look on your face that you're not happy about it. Is this really what you want – sharing your bloke with this girl who's elbowed her way into your life? What if he keeps on behaving the same way after you're married?'

'Oh, I'm sure Kieran wouldn't do that. You've got him all wrong.'

The way Clare was talking made Belle feel distinctly uncomfortable; half of her wanted to be angry with Clare for directing ridiculous insinuations at Kieran, but the other half kept thinking, What if she's got a point, and you're just being stupid and naïve?

'I haven't really got time to talk about this,' she said, turning away. 'I should be helping Lily on the sales desk.'

Clare caught her by the arm. 'Helping her with what? I'm the only customer in here, Belle. Come on, stop avoiding the issue. Something's not quite right here, and you're trying to pretend it doesn't exist.'

Belle squirmed inwardly. It felt as though Clare had found an unbearably tender point on her body and was insistently jabbing her red-nailed finger into it. 'You've got completely the wrong idea about Kieran and Mona,' she insisted.

'Maybe I have.' Clare shrugged. 'But don't you think it makes sense to ask him a few questions? If it's all on the level he won't mind, will he?' Clare's expression softened and she put down her handbag and took both of Belle's hands in hers. 'You can be angry with me if you want, I don't mind. All I care about is protecting you – somebody has to.'

'I can protect myself!'

'Yes, well, maybe you can. But remember, I'm here if you need to talk.' She directed kisses at the air on either side of Belle's head. 'Got to go now, but I'll catch up with you later and that's a promise.'

As the door closed behind Clare's back, Belle tried to slam shut the door she had opened inside her mind. But it was too late, the thoughts just kept on flooding through. Kieran up to no good with Mona? An utterly ridiculous idea.

So why couldn't she stop thinking about it?

It was the following Saturday evening and the lights were coming on in St Jude's. Behind a discreetly twitching net curtain, Mrs Armitage surveyed developments at the vicarage with satisfaction. Everything was packed up, the removal vans were booked, and after three days and nights helping her mum and dad, Belle was finally able to close the door and go back home.

Wherever home was.

As she trudged back across town to her bedsit, she mentally wandered one last time through the rooms she'd known since childhood, remembering every inch of chipped paintwork, every stain on the carpet. The dent in the playroom ceiling, the legacy of Jax's childhood chemistry set. The snug den that Belle had made for herself up in the attic, amid the fusty-smelling trunks and boxes of old Christmas decorations. The old Victorian nursery with its barred windows; the massive kitchen fireplace, where the blackened range had stood; the ancient horse-chestnut tree in the garden, where Belle and her sister had swung from ropes in the summer and pelted each other with conkers every autumn.

All gone. The rooms emptied, the carpets rolled up, the rope long rotted from the tree. The truth was, by the time the vicarage had been emptied of everything save the odd bed and kettle, Belle couldn't wait to get away. There wasn't anything there for her any more. The vicarage she had grown up in now existed only in her memory, the building itself just a shell, waiting for the next occupants to lend it a new personality.

As she padded up the steps to her front door, she felt drained of energy. Too tired to eat, she could think only of hot chocolate and bed.

Pushing open the door, Belle heaved aside a mini-Everest of junk mail and free newspapers. It was truly amazing how much rubbish you could accumulate in just three days. She gathered up the whole lot and was about to throw it in the bin when a picture postcard fluttered free and landed at her feet.

Stooping, she picked it up. It showed shaven-headed monks in saffron robes, squatting outside a flower-covered pagoda. Somebody had drawn curly hair and glasses on one of the monks, and a ponytail on the other. They were labelled 'Belle' and 'Ros'.

About time too, thought Belle. I was beginning to think you'd vanished off the face of the earth.

Ros's mad handwriting careered all over the back of the card. 'Guess who's in Japan! Got bored with hamburgers and macho truckers, am now getting into sushi bigtime. Trying poisonous pufferfish tomorrow so if you don't hear from me again you know why! What's all this about you and Clare? Always thought she was a bit of a snotty cow, still you know best. Will email soon, love Ros xxx.'

Belle pulled down the bed and sank onto the end of it, dropping the card beside her. She rubbed a weary hand across her eyes, feeling Ros's absence and her own loneliness more keenly than ever. There was just the faintest suggestion of tears beneath her eyelids.

Was Clare a cow? Admittedly they hadn't exactly got on like a house on fire after the break-up with Max, to put it mildly, but that was years ago. And since they'd met up again, Clare couldn't have been more considerate. She can be a bit of a bitch when she wants to be, but at least she cares, thought Belle, which is more than you can say for some people.

And where are you anyway, Ros? Where are you when I need you to tell me what I should do about Kieran? You know I can't make these decisions on my own, I never have been able to. The thought just terrifies me.

Yeah, at least Clare's here when I need her. Not on the other side of the world, having the time of her life without me.

Easter Sunday arrived with a kind of momentous inevitability. Oddly, after all the gloomy anticipation and Brenda's dreadful certainty that it would be a horrible, humiliating experience, the big family service passed off with all the smooth perfection of a dream.

The bishop's excelled himself here, thought Belle as she watched the service from one of the rear pews. It was true. Somehow his office had stage-managed the whole event, complete with an appearance from the bishop himself, thanking Gerry from the pulpit for his 'invaluable service to the people of St Jude's' and praising him for 'selflessly volunteering' to take the helm at St Mungo's. It was all one big slick lie; but at least Belle didn't have to sit there watching her father being publicly castigated all over again. She supposed she had the wily bishop to thank for that. He's

155

still a bastard through and through though, she thought with un-Christian venom. *And I bet he's on the fiddle too.*

The pièce de résistance came at the very end of the service, in the form of a pink-faced and bespectacled young priest, fresh out of theological college and gleaming with well-scrubbed ardour. Even Jean Armitage looked utterly gobsmacked when he was introduced as 'Damian Gregory – the new vicar of St Jude's'; and it was obvious from Gerry's drained complexion that he'd known nothing about it. No doubt that was exactly the way Bishop Grove wanted it to be.

Afterwards, there was a sort of farewell tea party in the church hall, with fairy cakes and embarrassing speeches. Various members of the parochial church council got up and said how much they adored Gerry and his delightful family, and how much they were going to miss them; but most of them couldn't look him in the eye. They were, after all, the very same people who'd blanked Brenda in the supermarket and written nasty anonymous letters to the *Courant*.

As she listened to their insincere homilies and the sentimental poems they'd penned, Belle suddenly realised that she wasn't sad about leaving any more. In fact she couldn't wait to distance herself from these people. It wasn't pleasant to think that so many so-called friends were nothing of the sort, but her dad was right: there was no other way but forward.

She squeezed her mother's arm encouragingly. 'How's it going, Mum? You OK there?'

Brenda – positively queenly in a brand-new wine-coloured hat with gold trimmings – gave the sort of brief nod that said, 'Yes, but only just.' 'This tea's stewed,' she announced, putting down her cup with disdain. 'And the sandwiches fall apart when you pick them up. But then that Armitage woman has no idea how to run a kitchen.'

'It'd be much better if you were doing it,' agreed Belle, silently thinking that the cheapskates might at least have run to the odd bottle of wine. She guessed that Jax was thinking pretty much the same thing as she stood in the opposite corner of the hall with Razor, glaring at everything and everybody. For his part, Gerry seemed content to drift with the tide of conversation, smiling vaguely at people like a man whose spirit was already halfway to St Mungo's.

'Where's Kieran?' asked Brenda suddenly, as though she had only just realised he wasn't there. 'Not at work again, surely?'

Belle sighed. 'Yes, work again. Some big news story Sandra wanted him to cover because the news editor's off sick or something. And you know Kieran – he never says no to Sandra.'

'You know, I'm starting to think there's more to life than promotion prospects,' commented Brenda, much to Belle's surprise. Normally her mother was far more likely to harp on about how lucky her daughter was to have found a man with one eye on promotion and the other on his pension plan.

'Tell me about it.' You could have come, Kieran, she thought resentfully. You could have said no to work, just this once, on this one day when it really matters. And if you really had to go, did you have to take her with you?

Above the babble of conversation, Belle could hear Jean Armitage telling the new vicar what a wonderful asset he was going to be to the community, and how she'd be there at his side, ready to guide him every inch of the way. Poor bugger, thought Belle. Little does he know.

'Annabelle, darling!' gushed a woman she occasionally exchanged hellos with on her walk to work. She'd no idea at all what her name was.

'Er . . . hi. Nice you could come.'

'Such a tragedy,' lamented the woman. 'I just don't know how St Jude's is going to manage without your father.' She glanced round. 'Where's that lovely young man of yours? Out earning the deposit for your new flat?'

'Something like that.'

'Gosh, it must only be a few months now till you get married. You must be sooo excited! I know I was when it was my turn. I was so worked up about my big day that I couldn't sleep for weeks beforehand!'

Belle didn't reply. She wanted to say, 'Oh yes, it's really great,' but the words wouldn't come. Not that the woman minded; she just kept prattling on.

'That's a point,' she commented.

'What is?'

'Your wedding. Now that you're moving to St Mungo's, will you be moving it there? Or will you still be holding it here? St Jude's looks so lovely in wedding photos, I always think, but on the other hand . . .'

'Actually, I'm not sure,' confessed Belle. 'We haven't quite decided.' Which was stretching the truth somewhat, seeing as they hadn't even thought about it, let alone discussed it. In fact she could barely remember the last time she and Kieran had talked about any aspect of the wedding arrangements. It was as though the wedding had become something separate from the pair of them, weirdly detached, the way the two of them had started to become detached from each other.

And that surely couldn't be right.

She had no time to pursue that line of thought, because at that moment she saw Kieran push through the swing doors into the church hall, followed a couple of seconds later by the inevitable Spandex blonde. There was something a bit odd about Mona though; she wasn't smiling. In fact she was looking really glum.

Kieran waved and made his way through the throng. 'Sorry I'm late,' he said, giving his beloved the lightest of kisses on the cheek.

Something perverse and irritated made Belle snap back: 'Are you?'

'Am I what?'

'Sorry. Or are you just saying it because it's the thing to say?'

Kieran gave her a funny look. 'Sometimes I worry about you, Belle. Look, we'd have been here sooner, only the editor asked me to stop off and cover a big pile-up on the A419. And then,' he glanced sideways at his companion, 'Mona needed to . . . er . . . talk.'

'Mona needed to talk?' Belle didn't even bother concealing her hostility. 'Oh well, that's all right then. I mean, that's much more important than being here to support my dad on his last day! Thank God it wasn't something trivial.'

'What the hell's got into you, Belle?' demanded Kieran.

'Nothing. I'm just having a bit of a reality check, and I'm not sure I like what I see.'

They scowled at each other. It was Mona who intervened. 'Please, you two – don't argue about me, I'm not worth it. I'm sorry I took up Kieran's time, Belle, I just had a bit of a problem I wanted to talk through with him, that's all.'

'What kind of problem?' asked Belle, thinking it was probably nothing more than a shortage of performing dwarves for the Bards and Wenches night. All Mona's crises tended to be of miniature dimensions.

Mona looked at Kieran. 'Go on,' he said, 'you might as well tell Belle.'

'Tell me what?'

Kieran didn't answer. 'Come on, Mona, you're going to have to tell people some time.'

'I can't,' she protested.

Belle's interest quickened. 'What are you on about?'

'You tell her, Kieran,' begged Mona. 'I just can't say it.'

Kieran shrugged. 'OK. It's pretty straightforward anyhow,' he went on without embarrassment. 'Mona's pregnant.'

Chapter 15

'Pregnant?' Belle repeated as the information sank in. 'Oh.'

Mona hung her head. 'Yes. Oh.'

'So Mad Dog McKindrick's in for a bit of a surprise then, is he?'

'Er . . . not really,' replied Kieran. 'The baby's not his.'

'What?'

'Mad Dog's been completely infertile ever since he had that on-stage accident with the lighting rig in ninety-four,' Mona added by way of explanation. 'You should see the scars.'

A kind of miniature whirlwind passed through Belle's brain, leaving her dazed and confused and ever so slightly sick. 'Hold on,' she said slowly, 'if the baby's not Mad Dog's, then whose is it?'

Now, Belle Craine wasn't normally the sort of girl to leap to conclusions; but what was she supposed to think when her illegitimate half-sister and her fiancé – who had been practically inseparable for weeks – were looking at each other in that furtive way, both seemingly knowing something but unwilling to share it with anybody else?

'Well?' she said again, this time with greater insistence. When nobody answered, an icy trickle started making its way down her spine. 'Oh my God no,' she whispered. 'Not . . . Kieran?'

It took about half a second for the penny to drop, then Kieran flushed electric scarlet. 'What!' His involuntary shout made half the people in the hall turn round and stare at him. He dropped his voice to a whisper. 'Me? You think . . .?' Momentarily speechless, he managed something between laughter and a cough. 'I don't know where you get some of your ideas from, Belle, but I can assure you one hundred per cent that Mona's baby has absolutely nothing to do with me!'

She stared right into his face, daring him to flinch and give the game away. 'Oh really?'

'Yes, really! And thanks for the vote of confidence,' he added with a touch of bitterness.

Caught up in a maelstrom of uncertainty, Belle turned her attentions to Mona. 'All right then, if it's not Kieran's and it's not Mad Dog's, then whose is it?'

Mona glanced away, her cheeks reddening. 'I'd rather not say.'

'Well, I'd rather you did, if it's all the same to you!'

'We're in the middle of all these people,' she objected, 'and this is really embarrassing.'

'So whisper.'

'It's not you,' Mona assured her, 'I just don't want to tell anybody who the father is right now, OK?'

'No, it's not OK actually!'

'Lay off, Belle,' urged Kieran, 'if Mona doesn't want to say, she doesn't have to.'

No, Mona, thought Belle with a glare; you don't. But you can't stop me having my suspicions; and boy have I got plenty of those.

Five minutes later, Belle stood in front of the mirror in the Ladies', water dripping from her face. You need to cool down, she told herself. Right now, big time. You need to cool down and stop your imagination running riot, before it leads you into all kinds of stupid places. Not that it hasn't done that already.

What on earth got into you out there? she asked her reflection in the mirror. What on earth did you think you were saying?

Patting her face dry with paper towels, she reapplied her lipstick and mascara and felt just about ready to face the world again. And this time, she reminded herself, you're not going to make any silly assumptions, and you're not going to let your big mouth run away with you. This time you're going to try and blend into the background, the way you usually do. Be wallpaper woman. You've embarrassed yourself enough for one day.

As she re-emerged from the toilets into the passageway, a strong hand grabbed her by the arm, handed her her jacket, and whisked her towards the outside world.

'Kieran?' she managed to gasp.

'We need to talk.'

That at least was one thing they weren't about to disagree on. Meekly, Belle allowed herself to be towed through the sea of parishioners, through the double swing doors, and out into the car park, where a lone seagull was pecking at a squashed doughnut somebody had trodden into the tarmac.

The two of them stood there in the middle of the mosaic of cars, facing each other, both feeling a little silly. Belle realised for the first time that she was panting as if she'd been for a five-mile run.

'Can we get one thing straight, please?' asked Kieran finally. 'I am not, repeat not, the father of Mona's baby!'

Belle nodded limply. 'I know.'

'You didn't seem to know back there,' he pointed out, but not with any note of aggression in his voice.

'I'm sorry.'

He let out an impatient gasp. 'But why on earth would you think I was?'

'Can we go for a walk, please?' cut in Belle, shrugging on her jacket. 'I think I need to get away from this place.'

They walked away from the church hall and the church, away from Mrs Armitage's neatly net-curtained windows, and across a couple of streets into the lush green square that was Imperial Gardens, just starting to blush into colour with the first of the spring floral arrangements.

Belle didn't notice the flowers, but she was grateful for Kieran's hand as it curled around hers. For a moment at least, she didn't feel quite so alone.

'Shall we sit down for a bit?' suggested Kieran. Without waiting for an answer, he led her to one of the wooden benches that stood around the edge of the square. 'If you're cold you can have my jacket as well.'

She sat down on the hard wooden slats. 'I'm fine. Really.'

Kieran sat beside her – close, but not as close as he'd once have sat, all snuggled up against her with his arm around her waist and his face on her shoulder, breathing in the scent of her hair. She could have slid closer to him, but it felt awkward. It was as if somewhere along the way, the pair of them had forgotten how easy it was to be together: not doing or saying anything, just being.

He took her hand again. 'You're shaking. Are you sure you're not cold?'

She shook her head dumbly. The shaking had nothing to do with the temperature and everything to do with the strange way she felt all over. Maybe it was delayed shock from all the things that had happened to her family, culminating in today's big send-off. Or maybe it was more to do with the fact that she'd been half-expecting this conversation for a long time, and now that the time had come she was afraid of what they were both about to say.

'Belle,' he continued, 'did you really think . . . you know, about me and Mona?'

There seemed little point in lying. 'For a moment,' she admitted. 'It was a reflex, I guess.'

Kieran looked wounded, but not in an angry way. 'But how could you? How could you imagine I'd cheat on you with anyone? Let alone with your own sister?'

161

The word 'sister' still didn't quite ring true in Belle's mind when it was applied to Mona, but over time she'd grown a little more accustomed to it. 'What was I supposed to think?' she demanded, shifting the blame back to Kieran. 'You've been spending so much time with Mona, it's downright embarrassing! And then suddenly she's pregnant, and guess what – her boyfriend's not the father. God Kieran, you can hardly blame me for putting two and two together and making four!'

'That's ridiculous. We just get on really well, you know that! We share a lot of the same interests.'

'Yeah, quite,' Belle replied pointedly. 'What sort of interests, that's what I'm wondering.'

His expression darkened. 'That's a cheap shot, Belle.'

'Perhaps. But neglecting your fiancée to spend every spare minute with Mona is pretty cheap too.'

'I don't neglect you!'

'Says who? Mona?'

Kieran struggled to find an adequate reply. 'All right,' he said finally, 'exactly how have I been neglecting you?'

'Well, let's see ... you were at the Royal Shakespeare until closing time three nights last week—'

'You were working late on the stock-take,' he protested, 'and Mona was having some trouble from a bunch of yobs, so Oz and I went down to lend her a hand, that's all.'

Oz and Kieran. Belle couldn't suppress a smile. They were hardly Schwarzenegger and van Damme, more Spongebob Squarepants and Patrick. She threw him another challenge; there were plenty to choose from. 'All right then, what about Lily's birthday party last week? You say all along you're definitely coming, and then at the last minute you cry off because Mona wants you to drive her to Bassett Hall.'

Kieran made one of his 'why am I surrounded by idiots' faces. 'It wasn't like that at all! Mona rang me to say she'd finally persuaded Mad Dog to give me another exclusive, but only if I interviewed him that evening, and he wanted her there as well. I'm sorry I had to miss your mate's party,' he added, 'but it's not like it was anything really special.'

'Kieran, you knew damn' well it was a dinner party, and she'd been slaving over it all day. And when I got there I was the only person there without a partner. Lily was so upset, she got her husband to drag in her creepy next-door-neighbour so I'd have somebody to sit next to!'

'Ah,' recalled Kieran with a grimace. 'I'd forgotten that.'

'Like you forgot how important it was to me for you to be at Dad's last service today?' she enquired.

That was the killer punch, but Kieran wasn't going to just lie down and take it. 'Come on darling,' he pleaded, 'I got here as fast as I can, but this is work we're talking about! Sandra asked me specially—'

'Have you ever tried saying no to that woman?' asked Belle.

'No I bloody well haven't, and if I did, what do you reckon it'd do to my promotion prospects?' he snapped back.

Belle flopped back against the hard, cold bench. 'Oh God, Kieran, don't you ever think about anything but work?'

'Oh, so I think about more than one thing now, do I? A minute ago I was a one-track-minded sex maniac.'

'I never said that.'

'But you implied it. And now you're implying I'm some kind of ambitious career freak.'

'Well – aren't you?'

His eyebrows all but vanished into his hairline. 'Hark who's talking! Ever since you took on that bloody deputy manager's job, I've heard nothing from you but work, work, work! It's Waylon this, and head office that all the bloody time.'

'What? So it's OK for you to be ambitious, but if I want a decent job that's not on?'

'Don't be stupid.'

'You're the stupid one, if you think I'm going to sit here and put up with this crap.' Her heart racing, Belle made to stand up but Kieran held her back.

'Belle, don't go.' He raked the hair back off his face, and she saw the look of real concern in his eyes. 'Look darling, I'm sorry, I didn't mean to say that. Will you stay and listen? Please?'

After a moment's hesitation, Belle subsided onto the bench in a deflated, anticlimactic sort of way. There was a long silence, punctuated by the laughter of kids kicking a football around between the flower beds. 'You know, I think we got a bit carried away again,' she commented quietly.

'Yeah, we're making a habit of it.' Kieran tentatively slipped his arm round behind her, and she stiffened slightly but didn't push him away. 'Belle . . . please can we be nice to each other for a bit? It's so much pleasanter.'

Belle managed a half-smile. 'But I haven't slapped your face and called you a chauvinist pig yet!' she protested.

'Thank God for that.' Kieran's hand lightly stroked Belle's shoulder. It felt reassuring. 'It would be kind of nice if you didn't do that at all.'

Belle sat gazing down at her toes for a few seconds, mulling things over. 'Did you really mean all that?' she ventured. 'About me talking about nothing but work all the time?'

'Maybe . . . just a bit,' he admitted. 'But hey, I do it too, so who am I to complain?'

'But you did,' she pointed out.

He threw up his hands. 'So I'm Mr Unreasonable. And you were sort of right about me, you know,' he added. 'I have been neglecting you. I never meant to, you have to understand that. It's just . . . well, a lot's been happening, and I – I don't know, maybe I haven't been getting my priorities right.'

She laid a hand on his. 'An awful lot's been happening to everybody lately. I don't think any of us is quite the same any more.'

As she raised her head and turned it towards him, their eyes met.

'But we're the same, aren't we?' Kieran asked softly. 'You and me?'

A frisson of anguish shook Belle's body as she smiled and answered, 'Of course we are. All of this, it's just . . . circumstances. Things will be OK once the dust has settled, I'm sure they will.'

'But?'

'Who says there's a but?'

'There always is.'

'All right, I just wondered . . . maybe we've been trying to do too much and now the timing's all wrong.'

'For the wedding, you mean?'

She nodded, and felt a surge of relief at the admission. 'People keep asking me whether we're going to move it to St Mungo's or keep it here, and I just don't know, and then poor Mum's got her work cut out with the move, and I don't see how we can possibly ask her to organise our wedding this summer on top of all that. Do you?'

Kieran rubbed his chin, where the first hint of afternoon stubble was starting to sprout. 'I guess you've got a point there,' he conceded. 'I mean, if we postponed it, just for a little while of course . . .'

'It needn't be for long,' agreed Belle. 'Just a few months. Or whatever seems right.'

'Yeah. Until everyone's settled, and we know where we are.'

There was relief on his face too. She smiled back encouragingly. 'Exactly.'

'You wouldn't be upset? I mean . . . you do know I still love you and want to marry you and everything?'

'Of course I do!' she laughed. 'So why should I be upset?' She slipped her hand in his and felt the engagement ring press into her finger. 'And everybody else will understand, too. After all, it's not like we've fallen out or anything – this is the only sensible thing to do, isn't it?'

In truth it was; but behind her reassuring smile, Belle still felt like crying.

*

Alone in her almost-empty room at the vicarage that evening, Mona was packing up the last of her possessions for the move to St Mungo's.

I've done it, she told herself. I've actually done it. I've achieved everything I set out to do when I came over here, and more. I've destroyed Gerry Craine's career, wrecked his whole family's lives, messed up Kieran and Belle's romance ... even brought the world's smelliest and most objectionable hound into the house. She bent down and stroked Engelbert's head, and he rewarded her with a foul-smelling yawn. That man abandoned my mum and in return I've made him feel what it's like to be abandoned, hated, shunned. OK, so Mum doesn't actually know I've done it yet, but once she does she'll be pleased, I'm sure she will. And then we'll be as close as we used to be, before my stepdad passed away.

Mona and her mother hadn't been getting on so well since Rena moved her toyboy lover Chas into her house; in fact they'd parted with hardly a word. But things were going to get better, Mona knew it. She wondered what her mum would reckon to becoming a grandmother. Obviously pregnancy hadn't been on the agenda, but hey, maybe a baby was just the thing to bring her and her mum back together – even if the father wasn't going to be part of the happy family scene.

Absent-mindedly, Mona smoothed a hand over her still-flat stomach. Yes, she thought, I've achieved absolutely everything and accidentally got myself pregnant into the bargain, so by rights I should be packing up and heading back to Australia to make it up with Mum, not hanging around here working in a shitty pub and watching the vultures pick at Gerry Craine's carcase.

I should be happy. So why aren't I?

The truth of the matter was that all her triumphs felt like one huge anti-climax. Worst of all, no matter how hard she tried, Mona just couldn't force herself to hate the Craines; in fact she was in severe danger of growing to like them. Why else would she be moving to the God-awful Bluebell Estate with them?

And why else would she be feeling so horribly guilty?

Chapter 16

Jax might be smart, but there was no deceiving Razor. Quite apart from anything else, her grim face was even whiter than the make-up she meticulously plastered all over it on Goth music nights.

'Why won't you tell me what's wrong?' he repeated, trying not to slop any more lager onto the beer-soaked carpet as he pursued her across the public bar of the Hairy Newt. Razor was a lad of infinite patience; with Jax he needed to be. But when she was set on being stubborn, nothing short of dynamite could shift the truth from her.

She flung the answer back at him over her shoulder. 'Because there's nothing to tell, cloth-ears. Are you deaf, or what?'

'No,' he replied, without resentment. 'I just don't believe you.'

Jax scowled. 'Read my lips, Razor. There's nothing wrong. Why can't you just get the message and leave me alone?'

She nudged Snooker out of the way with an elbow so sharp that he winced, and hastily slid along the bench seat to make room for her. Every chain and buckle on her bondage trousers jingled angrily as she sat down.

'How was school?' ventured Demi.

Jax's scowl became a look of near-Satanic displeasure. 'Why?'

Demi was quite taken aback by this. 'Well, you know, with it being your first week at the new school and all that ... I just thought ... ' She faded out into hapless embarrassment. 'These crisps are nice – anybody want one?'

Jax banged her glass down on the sticky-ringed bar table. 'For the last time, school was fine, I'm fine, everything's bloody fine – OK? Now, can we talk about something else?'

Oh dear, thought Razor. It's worse than I thought.

St Mungo's vicarage smelt funny. That is to say, it didn't smell like home.

As Belle turned her newly cut key in one of several mortise locks, the front door clicked open and her nostrils picked up the mingled odours of fresh paint, old hymn books, thousand-year-old cat pee and just a hint of mould. It was a long way from the St Jude's cocktail of beeswax polish and old wood.

Nevertheless, the overall effect was considerably improved by the glorious, sweet scent of home-baked cakes. Belle breathed in deeply: mm, fruit loaf ... and wasn't that a lemon drizzle cake she could smell too? Maybe Mum's settling in after all, she thought. All this baking must surely be a good sign.

'Hi Mum – it's me!'

She walked the few steps down the hall and turned left into the kitchen. The vicarage was quite large for a former council house, but it still felt impossibly small after the mid-Victorian excesses of St Jude's.

'Mum?'

But Brenda wasn't in the kitchen; in fact nobody was there at all. The only real presence was a table laden with piles of still-warm cake.

Oh well, thought Belle, swiping a butterfly cake and peeling off the paper case, I expect they'll be back soon. I might as well go and watch some television while I'm waiting.

She headed straight for the living-room, still sporting its hideous salmon-pink Dutch blinds and matching fake dado rail – a real riot for the senses when you factored in the yellow wallpaper with the blue flowers on it. It was the only room Belle had ever seen where the wallpaper continued over the ceiling. Still, it would look a whole lot better once they'd got round to redecorating it.

A couple of steps from the living-room door, she passed the closed door of the downstairs cloakroom. If the house hadn't been so quiet and her ears less sensitive, she might not have heard it. But there was no doubt it was the sound of somebody sobbing. Who?

Belle stopped in her tracks, and knocked lightly on the door. 'Are you OK in there?' she asked, instantly realising what a daft thing it was to say to someone who was crying their eyes out.

There was a long silence, punctuated by sniffing and the gulping sound of somebody trying not to cry.

'Hello?' Belle ventured again.

At last a voice answered her from the other side of the door: 'Fuck off.'

Belle's eyebrows arched in surprise, not at the language, but at the distress. As far as she could recall, the only time she'd ever heard Jax cry before was when she turned on the waterworks to get something she wanted from Dad. But that was just play-acting. This was definitely for real, and a hundred times more upsetting.

'Jax? It's Belle. What's the matter?'

'Go.' Sniff. 'Away.'

'Come on Jax,' Belle said gently. 'Talk to me – maybe it's something I can help with.'

'It isn't, OK?'

Belle scratched her head, searching her mind for clues, and duly came up with the worst thing she could think of. 'You've not split up with Razor, have you?'

'No!'

Then Belle thought of something even worse. 'Oh God, you're not . . . pregnant, are you?'

'What!' Jax's reply was almost lost in a high-pitched, strangled squeak. 'D'you think I'm stupid like you or something? Like—' She clammed up suddenly.

'Like who? Mona?'

'Mona's not stupid,' Jax insisted, though with slightly less vehemence than usual. 'And neither am I. OK?'

It depends on how you define stupid, thought Belle, trying not to take the insult personally. After all, she'd had plenty of practice. 'Well you are if there's something upsetting you and you won't talk about it,' she replied, trying the door handle. It wouldn't turn. 'Why don't you unlock this door and we'll have some cake and talk about it?'

'Cake.' Jax sniffed contemptuously. 'Make it a litre of vodka and I might be interested. At least then I'll be so out of it I won't care what people call me.'

This gave Belle an inkling of what might be wrong. 'Are people being mean to you, then?' She thought for a moment. 'Wait a minute, this is all about your new school, isn't it?'

'Give that girl a prize,' Jax responded flatly.

'But it doesn't usually bother you what other people think,' observed Belle. 'I mean, dressing the way you do . . . it's not exactly inconspicuous, is it?'

'Yeah, well, that was before,' snapped Jax between blows of her nose. 'I didn't care then, because at St Jude's they respect the individual's right to be different.'

'You mean there were people there who looked even more outrageous than you?'

'Oh . . . shut up.'

Belle gave herself a mental slap on the wrist. 'I'm sorry, I couldn't resist it. So are they big on conformity at Winston Churchill Comprehensive, then?'

'Put it this way. If you don't wear Burberry and earrings the size of hula hoops, you can forget fitting in.'

'Surely it can't be that bad,' ventured Belle, although she was inclined to think that it might.

At this Jax burst into full-blown weeping again, great hacking sobs that must be shaking her apart. 'Yes it is. They call me ... they c-call me Freakoid,' she said bitterly. 'They said I should have a bolt through my neck. Stuff like that.'

'Oh Jax, that's a bit rough.' There was a small pause. Belle sensed that there was something worse, that Jax had to force herself to say. 'What is it, Jax? You can tell me.'

Jax gave a sort of shuddering sigh. 'They've started saying stuff about Dad. And I don't mean just the usual tedious crap about him being a vicar. When it began I couldn't believe it ... I thought all that was behind us, I thought people had forgotten.'

Belle's mouth was dry. 'What kind of stuff?'

'Mean stuff. Bad jokes, lies. Like ... how many other illegitimate kids has he got in Cheltenham? And hey, is he really the Freakoid's dad at all, or has her mum been playing around too?'

Belle found her eyes screwing themselves shut, as though this might take away the horrible mental images. It didn't. She imagined herself in Jax's place and felt for her, for her mum, for her dad. She felt just plain sick. 'Sounds like there are some people at your school with a really crap sense of humour,' she said quietly.

A flicker of Jax's old sarcasm returned. 'You think?'

'Once we've told Mum and Dad, they can have a chat with the head.' Belle did her best to sound encouraging. 'I'm sure if the teaching staff understand what's going on, they'll—'

Jax's voice cut in like surgical steel. 'Nobody's telling Mum and Dad. Nobody, you hear?'

'But if they don't know, how can they help?'

'I don't need them to help. I can help myself.'

'Yeah, right. Sounds like it,' retorted Belle. 'That's why you've been sobbing your heart out in the downstairs toilet.'

'Look, you may still need your parents to sort your problems out—'

Belle's jaw dropped. 'What?'

'But some of us are past that stage, OK? Some of us can handle our own lives.'

Belle was torn between a desire to help, and a strong urge to kick down the toilet door and give her sister a good thumping. 'Come on, see sense will you?' she shouted through the door. 'Listen to me, Jax: if you're being given a hard time at school, Mum and Dad need to know.'

Jax surprised her big sister with the vehemence of her reaction. 'No – you listen. What they don't need is another reminder of all this crap they've just been through. And I'm not going to tell them.'

There was the sound of a key turning in a lock, then the cloakroom door swung open and Jax stepped out, red-eyed but all guns blazing.

'And if you do,' Jax went on, emphasising the words with a jabbing forefinger, 'if you so much as breathe a word about this to anybody, I will fucking kill you. Got that?'

'Of course you've done the right thing,' soothed Clare, pouring herb tea into white porcelain mugs. 'Do stop worrying. Now drink that down, it's camomile. Very calming and relaxing.'

Belle tried not to wrinkle her nose in disgust as she caught a whiff of the aroma – half floral, half medicinal. It must be good for me, she mused as she took a sip; 'cause it tastes revolting. 'Thanks,' she said with a smile. 'Just what I need.'

'Add a spoonful of honey if you like.' Clare pushed the jar across her new reclaimed-oak kitchen table. 'It's local. Very good for strengthening the immune system, you know. And with all this stress you've been through lately, I should think yours is shot to bits by now.'

'Probably,' admitted Belle. She dropped a gloopy blob of honey into her mug and watched it sink to the bottom, slowly clouding and dissolving as it went. 'So you really, really think I was right, suggesting we should postpone the wedding for a few months?'

'Oh, absolutely. I mean, God, I'd have suggested it myself, only you don't like to overstep the mark, do you?'

Surprised, Belle looked at her across the table. 'You thought we should postpone the wedding?'

'Oh yes.'

'Why? Because of all the trouble with Mum and Dad, you mean?'

Clare sighed like some kindly adult faced with a child that's just been swindled out of its dinner money, and can't quite work out how. 'It was pretty obvious things weren't going too smoothly between you,' she said.

'Yes they were – I mean, are,' countered Belle defensively. 'There's nothing wrong between Kieran and me, well, nothing serious anyway.'

'Are you sure about that? Quite sure?' Clare's gaze was uncomfortably penetrating.

Belle fought the urge to squirm. 'We love each other!' she protested.

'But love isn't everything,' said Clare gravely. 'And besides, are you absolutely certain Kieran feels the same way about you as you do about him?'

The words hit Belle like a slamming door. 'What do you mean?'

'You know what I mean,' replied Clare. 'All this business with Mona – well, any fool can see there's something a bit iffy about it all. And you're no fool, Belle.'

Belle wondered if that was really true. Was she a justifiably loyal fiancée, or just a gullible idiot who'd believe Kieran was a Martian if he told her so? 'I've had a few . . . doubts,' she admitted quietly.

Clare sat back in her chair, triumphant. 'I knew it.'

'It's not been easy, watching him build up a close friendship with another girl, even if she is my half-sister. Mind you, it wouldn't be quite so difficult if Mona was a bit uglier.'

'It's not right, you know,' declared Clare. 'Running around all over Gloucestershire with some other woman and expecting you just to accept that he's "helping her with her homework" or some such crap. Who does he take you for – the village idiot?'

That stung. 'Oh, I don't think—' she protested.

But Clare cut her short. 'Well, I do. Face it Belle, he's been spending an awful lot of time with this Mona woman, and now she's pregnant and she won't tell anybody who the father is. And you've already told me Kieran's acting all protective towards her. What does that say to you?'

I don't want to think about what it says, thought Belle. I don't want it to say anything to me at all. 'Kieran absolutely swears the baby's nothing to do with him,' she said lamely.

'Yes, but then he would.' Clare sipped at her herbal tea. 'He's very keen on kids, your Kieran, isn't he?'

'Fairly,' hedged Belle, though 'fanatically' might have been more accurate. 'He wants to start a family straight after we're married.'

'And you don't?'

'I'd like to wait a while, that's all.'

Clare nodded sagely, as if all of this made perfect sense to her. 'So . . . just for argument's sake . . . he might be instinctively attracted to someone who, say, offered him the chance of a ready-made family? After all, he has no family of his own apart from his sister, does he? And from what you've said he hardly ever sees her.'

'A ready-made family?' Belle felt all the blood drain from her cheeks. 'You mean . . . Mona?'

Clare reached over and gave her hand a kindly squeeze. 'I'm probably completely wrong, of course. But I do think it's something you have to consider. Don't you?'

Kieran had some news for Belle. As he strode across from his flat to her tiny bedsit, he wondered how she'd take it. Maybe not that well to start off with, but Belle was reasonable; she'd come round in the end. At least, he hoped so.

He let himself in with his key and found Belle huddled on the pull-down bed in front of the TV, cuddling a cushion and drinking her way steadily through a bottle of some nasty pink liqueur somebody had brought back from a trip to the Czech Republic.

'Hi darling.' He kissed her and climbed up onto the bed next to her. She didn't fling her arms round him, but probably she was tired after work. 'What are you watching?'

'Nothing.' She jabbed the remote at the screen and it went blank.

'Oh. Well, I guess that's better really. Now we can have a proper talk.'

'What about?'

'Just a talk, darling. You know, like people do.' He leaned over and sniffed Belle's glass. 'Dear God, Belle, what the hell are you drinking?'

'Not sure,' she confessed. 'It was in the cupboard under the sink. I needed a drink.'

'You must have.' He dipped in a finger, licked it and wiped the rest off on his shirt. 'That stuff is truly nauseating. Tell you what, how's about I take you down the pub for a proper drink instead?'

Belle shook her head. 'I'm not really in the mood. Sorry.'

By now, Kieran was starting to get worried. 'Are you ill?'

'Not yet.' She eyed the liqueur bottle. 'But I may be tomorrow.'

'Have I . . . have I done something?'

This time she eyed him instead. 'I don't know, Kieran. Have you done something?' She drained her glass and topped it up again. 'How's the lovely Mona today?'

'Fine, I took her to . . .' Kieran gave a silent groan. 'This isn't all about Mona again, is it? I told you, she needed me to take her to the clinic while that old banger of hers is in the garage. I'm just being supportive.'

'Yes, you are aren't you? Regular white bloody knight, you are.' Belle burped, vaguely aware that she was on the edge of becoming very, very drunk.

'What's that supposed to mean?'

Her resistance was low, and the words just sort of forced themselves out. 'It means I'm fed up of it all,' she replied. 'It means if you're the father of Mona's baby, for God's sake say so because I couldn't be any more miserable than I am right now.'

Kieran stared at her. 'You're drunk.'

'Not yet, I'm not.'

'We've been through this, Belle! How many times have I told you? Mona is just a friend! We have a lot in common.'

Belle waved his protests away. 'Yeah, yeah, I know all that stuff.' She raised eyes that were sparkling with unshed tears. 'Look Kieran, if you want to be with her just do it, OK? I'm just tired of being lied to.'

'Oh for God's sake Belle!' Kieran sprang off the bed. 'Are you paranoid or something? Do I have to have a bloody DNA test?'

Belle didn't say anything.

'Don't you believe a word I say any more?'

'I want to. I really, really do.' The tears that Belle had striven so long to hold back suddenly spilled down her cheeks in fat, wet trails. 'And I'll never stop loving you. But I just don't know what I believe any more.'

Kieran couldn't remember ever feeling angrier – or more guilty.

As he slammed the front door of Belle's flat and strode away along the street, raincoat streaming out behind him, her cursed Belle, he cursed the world, and he cursed himself. Why did everything have to go so hideously wrong? It wasn't as if it was all his fault. First there was all the trouble with Gerry Craine, which hadn't exactly helped the course of true love to run smooth – not that he blamed Mona for that. If it was anybody's fault it was Belle's. If she hadn't got that stupid deputy manager's job and become work-obsessed, he was sure they'd have been looking forward to their first house and their first baby now, instead of barely speaking. Why in the name of sanity did a glorified shop assistant think it was worth going in at seven thirty every morning and bringing paperwork home with her every night, just for an extra pittance and a new job title? It didn't make any sense to him at all.

He thought about what Belle had said. Was there even a faint possibility that she was right, that Mona was the one he should be with, not her? He shook his head; the idea was ridiculous.

And yet he'd come away angry, without even telling Belle the news he'd come to break: that the editor of a major national newspaper had sounded him out about an upcoming feature writer's post; had practically offered it to him, there and then. It was a big decision to make. It would mean moving to London, for a start, and he'd been prepared with all his arguments, ready to persuade Belle that it was the right thing to do.

Instead of which, he'd lost his temper and not even told her.

Pulling up the collar of his coat against the evening drizzle, he lowered his head and breasted the cold northerly wind.

Perhaps he'd tell her tomorrow.

Chapter 17

A quiet day at work was the last thing Belle wanted; but the following morning, Green Goddess was as empty as a turkey shed on Boxing Day.

'Where've they all gone?' moaned Waylon, face pressed up against the front window. 'Where are all my lovely customers?'

'It's raining,' said Lily knowledgeably, 'and it's Tuesday. People don't buy soap on Tuesdays.'

Waylon turned and stared at her. 'You just made that up.'

'I didn't, honest,' she assured him. 'It was in one of those magazine surveys.'

Belle gave a long sigh and let her head drop onto her folded arms. 'Well, wake me up when it's not Tuesday any more,' she said glumly, the words somewhat muffled by the long sleeves of her T-shirt.

Waylon went back to pacing about the shop, fussing with the displays and needlessly moving things about. He was the kind of man who just couldn't stand still. If you forced him to stay in one place, he jiggled about on the spot as though he had mice in his trousers. Idleness was his idea of hell.

'What's the matter with you, anyway?' he asked Belle, swapping two bottles of Hairy Fairy shampoo for a basket of pink soap eggs. 'There's hardly been a sound out of you since you got here. You're not sickening for something germy, are you?' he added suspiciously. Next to idleness, Waylon despised the common cold. 'I've got enough to worry about with Lily getting herself pregnant.' He glared at her as though she'd done the deed expressly to annoy him. 'It takes time and money to train people, you know.'

Lily ignored him. 'What's up, Belle?'

Belle sat up, stretched and forced herself to reanimate. 'I'm OK, just having one of those days when you can't get going.'

'All my days are like that,' commented Lily cheerfully. 'And then there's the morning sickness. Fancy a coffee? Or do you want one of my herbal teas?'

'Oh go on then. One cup of coffee can't hurt. Ooh – hang on a minute, customer alert!' A woman walked right up to the front door of the shop, peered through the glass, hovered for a moment, then turned and walked back the way she'd come. 'Ah well, doesn't look like we're going to be rushed off our feet any time soon.'

While Lily was out making the coffee and Waylon was messing up the displays, Belle flicked idly through the latest issue of the newsletter that arrived every month from head office. Since head office was only up the road in Gloucester, there hardly seemed much point in sending it, but she supposed the people in the Inverness branch appreciated being remembered.

She turned from the colour photograph of a Z-list celebrity opening a new store in Penzance and hit the 'internal vacancies' page. Really and truly, she had no idea why she bothered scanning it every month, because there never seemed to be anything going between 'senior sales assistant' and 'regional manager'. All the interesting, middle-ranking jobs must be filled in-store . . . or by good old-fashioned nepotism. Not for nothing did Green Goddess style itself 'a traditional family firm'.

Hello though, what was this? Belle's attention was drawn by a box ad at the bottom of the page.

'Do you love our products?'

Belle nodded.

'And our customers?'

Well . . . some of them. She skipped over that bit.

'If your product knowledge is second to none, you have recent in-store supervisory experience and you love helping to solve our customers' problems, you could be the person we are looking for to head the new Customer Relations office at our Gloucester HQ . . .'

Nice job, thought Belle; for somebody else. Waylon maybe. They'd never look twice at me.

She was about to turn the page and dismiss the job from her mind when Lily bounced up behind her with the coffee. 'What's that you're reading? The sits vac? Anything good?'

'Not really. Just a—'

With uncanny accuracy, Lily promptly homed in on the very same advertisement. 'Customer Relations, eh? You could do that,' she remarked, stuffing a biscuit into her mouth.

'Me? Why me?'

'Because you like people. And you're so diplomatic. You never lose your temper – not like some people.' She nodded towards Waylon, who was swearing and straining at a cupboard door that had jammed shut.

'Of course I do!'

Lily shook her head firmly. 'Well I've never seen you do it. And some of the customers we get in here ... they don't need customer relations, they need a kick up the arse.'

'True,' agreed Belle, 'though I don't think kicking customers' arses is part of the job description.'

'Pity,' mused Lily wistfully. 'I'd be good at that.' She drew herself up. 'But I'm telling you, Belle, that job'd suit you down to the ground. And the pay's not bad, either. Mind you, the hours might be long ... I don't suppose Kieran would be too happy about that?'

No, thought Belle, he wouldn't. But so what? Did he ever think about her when he worked into the night without so much as a 'sorry darling, I may be a bit late'?

You know, she thought to herself, if it wasn't for the fact that I'm totally lacking in ambition and I wouldn't get it anyway, I just might consider applying for that job.

That evening, Ros came through on the webcam and Belle was able to have the first proper chat with her in weeks. It wasn't a very good webcam, and the picture was a bit flickery and fuzzy, but there was no mistaking the fact that Ros was looking great.

'The pufferfish didn't poison you then?'

Ros laughed. 'No, but the day after I got salmonella from a prawn sandwich! Ludicrous, isn't it?'

'Well, you're looking good on it.'

Ros wasn't one for beating about the bush. 'Wish I could say the same for you, kid,' she observed. 'You look like death.'

'It's just the crappy webcam picture,' insisted Belle.

'Is it bollocks! What's up – flu or something?'

'Come on Ros, you know me – I haven't had a cold since primary school.'

'Aha.'

'What do you mean, "aha"?'

'I mean, aha, so it's emotional stress then. More flak from your dad and Mona, is it? Or ... you've not had a fight with Kieran, have you?' Belle let out a low groan. 'Go on, spill the beans.'

Belle spilled them, in all their Technicolor glory.

'Bloody hell,' said Ros after a short pause. 'That's quite a mess. But you surely don't really think that Kieran and Mona ... you know? Do you?'

'No. I don't know. Maybe. Oh God.' Belle struggled against the tangled web of conflicting impulses and failed. 'Why did she have to come here in the first place?'

'I know, I know,' sympathised Ros. 'But she's here now and in a way she's not the problem. It's Kieran, isn't it? It all comes down to two questions.'

'What questions?' asked Belle dully.

'First, do you still love him?'

'Yes, of course I do.'

'Second, do you still trust him?'

There was a short silence which said it all.

'Can we change the subject?' asked Belle finally. Her heart felt as though it was pounding against her ribs, and her head was starting to spin.

'It's no good avoiding the issue,' warned Ros.

'Yes I know, and I won't.' Belle rubbed the back of her hand across her forehead. It came away cold and clammy. 'But just for now, can we talk about something else? I need time to sort all this out.'

'I wish I was there to help,' said Ros; and Belle very nearly burst into tears because that was exactly what she wished, too. Problems never got themselves this tangled up when Ros was around. Perhaps that was why Belle felt so at sea when she wasn't.

'I think I have to sort this one out my way,' confided Belle. She took a deep breath. 'I'd really appreciate your advice about Jax, though. She's going through hell at her new school, but she won't let me help. And if somebody doesn't, God knows what she'll end up doing.'

'To herself, you mean?'

'Yeah. Or somebody else.'

Things had been rather quiet in St Jude's since the Craine family left. Jean Armitage was reluctant to admit that she rather missed them, but she'd become accustomed to the daily buzz of imminent scandal, and without Gerry Craine to fuel it, the buzz had become more of an occasional strangled squeak. It just wasn't the same, going back to relying on Welsh Dave and his 'accidentally' torn parcels, or hanging around with the receptionist from the GP's surgery, in the hope of picking up the odd toothsome snippet. Quite simply, there was nothing like having a real-life soap opera on your doorstep.

Then again, there was not much point in possessing the gossip scoop of the decade if you had nobody to pass it on to, and Mrs Armitage had been carrying this one around for quite some time, waiting and longing for the right moment.

At last it came. She just happened to be out shopping in town one lunchtime at exactly the time when Belle Craine just happened to take her lunch break. That kind of coincidence took a fair bit of advance planning. Anyhow, she manoeuvred herself into position outside Seuss &

Goldmann's department store and waited for Belle to emerge from the Regent Arcade.

Almost before Belle's bottom had touched the bench, Jean Armitage was sitting there next to her. It came as quite a shock to Belle, who had been expecting a quiet quarter of an hour with a Sicilian meatball sub and the latest Fiona Walker.

Mrs Armitage launched instantly into an avalanche of greetings. 'Annabelle, my dear, it's been ages! How are you? How's your dear father? My, but you're looking thin, have you lost weight? I do hope you're not ill.'

As she paused for breath, Belle eased herself a little further along the bench. She'd never liked this nosy Armitage woman, and right now she was so uncomfortably close that Belle could actually smell her sour breath and cloying perfume.

'I'm fine thank you,' she said by way of an all-purpose answer. 'And how are you?'

'Most dreadfully saddened by your parents' departure from St Jude's,' Mrs Armitage assured her with a sincerity so perfect, it might almost have passed for genuine.

'Still, I'm sure you're enjoying having a new young vicar around the parish,' said Belle, wondering when the ghastly woman would stop tormenting her and go away.

'Damian is very willing and eager, of course,' conceded Mrs Armitage, making sure Belle noted that she and the new vicar were on first-name terms already. 'But there's really no substitute for experience, is there? And of course, being so young he doesn't have a family, so he can't really empathise with that aspect of our parochial life ... I do think having a family's so important, don't you?'

'Yes, I suppose.' Belle stole a look at her watch. 'My goodness, is that the time? I've got one or two things I need to do before I go back to work, and—'

As Mrs Armitage's gloved hand fell upon hers, Belle could almost hear the click of handcuffs. 'I did just want to have a little word with you, dear,' she smiled. For some reason her smile made Belle's stomach turn over. 'I couldn't help hearing that you and your fiancé had cancelled your wedding.'

'Postponed,' Belle corrected her firmly. 'Just until things are on a more even keel.'

'Ah, that's good to know. I mean, I wouldn't like to think that the rumours had been getting to you. Some of the gossip you hear is just downright malicious, don't you think?'

Belle stared at her. 'What rumours?'

Jean Armitage waved away her question. 'Oh, you don't want to know, I'm sure it's something and nothing. I wish I'd never mentioned it.'

'Tell me anyway.'

Mrs Armitage bent closer, delighting in her moment of absolute power. 'All I'll say is, you and Kieran must have a very trusting relationship, what with him being so close to that Mona girl.'

Oh God, not that again, thought Belle. 'They work together sometimes,' she said.

'Even at night?' Mrs Armitage enquired innocently.

That nasty, cold feeling crept back up Belle's spine. 'What do you mean, at night?'

'Well, I just happened to be passing your fiancé's flat quite late one evening – it must have been after eleven – and whom did I see but Mona Starr, letting herself in!'

Belle frowned. 'You mean Kieran answered the door and let her in?'

'Oh no,' replied Mrs Armitage sweetly. 'She was definitely letting herself in. With her own key. And between you and me she looked a little . . . well . . . furtive about it, if you know what I mean. Not that I'm suggesting anything, but well, there you have it.'

And there I have you too, thought Mrs Armitage, with a frisson of pure, sadistic excitement. Hook, line and sinker.

Kieran was either the last or the first person Belle wanted to see that evening, depending on her fluctuating mood. They'd previously agreed to meet up for a drink after work, but now she couldn't decide if she was dreading it or longing for an opportunity to ask him a few searching questions.

He looked serene enough as he came down the steps of the *Courant* offices, wriggling his arms into his leather jacket. Maybe he was just a really good actor? Belle dismissed that foolish thought from her mind. Jean Armitage was an evil old bitch.

Nevertheless, as they walked across to the bar on the corner, Belle couldn't help picturing the scene as Mona let herself in to Kieran's flat, with her own key. At the very least, he had some explaining to do.

'Are you OK, darling?' asked Kieran as he brought the drinks back to their table.

'Why shouldn't I be?' asked Belle.

He looked puzzled. 'No reason. You're just a bit quiet, that's all.'

'You'd be quiet if you'd spent the day shouting at a coachload of shoplifting kids.'

'I suppose I would, yeah.'

There was a pause.

'Now you've gone all quiet,' pointed out Belle. 'Are you sure you're all right?'

He reached across and clinked glasses. 'Cheers. I'm fine, I've just been saving up something to tell you. I should've told you the other day, only we had that argument and I thought you probably weren't in the right frame of mind to hear me out.'

He looks nervous, thought Belle. Her pulse quickened. Oh God, he's going to admit to something I don't want to hear. 'That sounds ominous,' she said, trying to make it sound like a joke.

Kieran smiled. 'Not really. Actually it's something pretty good – or at least, I think so. I'm hoping you will, too.'

'Well, if you tell me, maybe you'll find out.'

He took a deep breath. 'OK, here goes. I've been headhunted for a job as chief features writer on the *Daily Argus*. Me, just think! It'd be a big increase in salary, and the prospects are just brilliant. The job's not actually coming up for a few months yet, but hey, that just means longer to plan.'

She looked at his beaming, expectant face, and felt numb. 'The *London Daily Argus*?' she enquired, in the faint hope that it might not be.

'Absolutely. Nothing second-rate for me, eh?' He grasped Belle's hands and gazed into her eyes; she could feel him willing her to share his excitement. 'This is it, darling; the big break I've been waiting for. If I take this, the sky's the limit.' He paused. 'Of course, it all depends on how you feel about it, too.'

'Congratulations,' said Belle flatly. 'It sounds great.'

He gave her a searching look. 'But?'

'But I can't think about stuff like that when I'm not even sure you still love me.'

Kieran's eyes widened. 'What on earth are you going on about?'

'Jean Armitage saw Mona letting herself into your flat, late one night,' said Belle. 'Letting herself in, with her own key. I wonder where she got that from.'

'Her own key?' Kieran's brow furrowed. 'But I've never given her my key, let alone had one cut for her! You're the only person I'd do that for!'

'So I thought.'

'It's true! And why would I ask her round my flat at night, anyway?'

Belle moistened her dry lips with the tip of her tongue. 'You tell me.'

A look of ghastly realisation spread across Kieran's face. 'Oh no, you're not still obsessed with this idea that I'm having some sort of torrid affair with Mona, are you? You know damn well it's a heap of crap!'

Belle sighed, a bit too weary to be really, venomously mad at him. 'I'm not sure I do,' she replied quietly.

'Well, maybe you ought to stop listening to poisonous old hags like that Armitage woman.'

'Who else am I supposed to listen to?' retorted Belle. 'You never have any time for me any more. Whenever I want to discuss something serious, it's, "Sorry, I'm too busy, I've got an assignment," or "Sorry, I said I'd take Mona out to do an interview." And when somebody sees Mona going into your flat one night, you don't even come out and explain it, you just say it never happened! I'm sorry Kieran, I've just got this awful, nagging suspicion that I've been very, very stupid.'

'Stupid?' Kieran's voice rose to an angry growl. 'I'll tell you what's stupid: listening to meaningless gossip when you should be helping me to decide our future!'

Belle went on speaking softly. She didn't want to shout, didn't want to argue. She was so tired of confrontations. 'How come I get the feeling you'll decide it yourself, no matter what I think?'

'Because somebody's got to make decisions, and if it was left to you, you'd still be living in that God-awful bedsit when you're sixty!'

The suggestion of a tear prickled beneath Belle's eyelids. 'All I want to know is, why did you give Mona a key to your flat, and why did she come and see you so late at night?'

'I didn't and she didn't!' He virtually shouted out his answer, and everybody in the bar turned to stare, not that Kieran gave a damn. He pushed back his chair and stood up. 'You're supposed to love me, Belle!'

She looked up at him with brimming eyes. 'Don't you understand? I do love you! That's why it hurts so much when you lie to me.'

Kieran threw her a look of total exasperation. 'I'm sick of this, Belle. I'm sick of you doubting me all the time, questioning me about everything I do and everyone I see. If I want to be friends with Mona that's my business; why the hell shouldn't I be?'

'Friends as in staying the night together?' Belle didn't know how she managed to get the words out.

Kieran's anger turned cold as ice. 'What's the point of denying it? You won't believe me, will you?' He paused. 'For the last time, Belle, grow up.'

That was perhaps the very worst thing he could have said to her. Belle rose to her feet with as much dignity as she could, laid aside her drink and picked up her handbag and coat. 'Thanks for the advice, Kieran,' she said crisply. 'I'll bear it in mind.'

He swung round as she headed for the door. 'Where are you going?'

'Somewhere away from you.'

'Fine,' retorted Kieran. 'I might just do the same.'

'Good. Piss off and good riddance. I'm sure London will suit you down to the ground.'

She managed to get outside before the tears fell; then they mingled with the rain tumbling out of the grey-brown sky, and nobody walking past would have guessed that Belle Craine's world had just fallen apart.

Chapter 18

Belle's world might have fallen apart, but it didn't stay that way for very long.

One endless day elapsed in horrible, ominous silence; then Kieran's nerve broke and he phoned her at work. 'Are you OK?'

Belle's resolve to be cool and independent evaporated the moment she heard his voice. 'Not really,' she admitted.

'I'm really sorry,' he said.

'So am I.'

'Shall we have dinner together then?'

Relief washed over her. 'Yes please.'

They didn't go anywhere special, just the slightly pretentious pizza parlour on the corner of the Promenade; but it was familiar and comfortable, and frankly neither of them was much interested in the food.

At first it was awkward. As other couples at neighbouring tables clinked glasses and laughed, and Belle struggled through her salad, she could feel Kieran's eyes watching her every movement. At length she looked up and felt the full weight of his gaze. 'You're making me nervous,' she said, half jokingly. 'Have I got a zit on the end of my nose or something?'

'Sorry?'

'Only you haven't stopped staring at me ever since we walked in.'

'Oh God.' It was Kieran's turn to look embarrassed. 'I was just thinking how lovely you are, and how much I don't want to lose you.' He reached across the table and laid his hand upon hers. 'I haven't lost you, have I?'

She hesitated for just a moment. 'No, of course you haven't. It was just an argument. And everybody has arguments, don't they?' She wondered if she was trying to persuade him, or herself. But the thought of being without him, definitively detached from him, terrified her more than she could say. When all was said and done, she did love him.

'Does that mean you believe me now?' he asked, his eyes once again locking with hers.

Belle tried to wash the dryness from her throat with a gulp of wine. 'It wasn't exactly that I didn't believe you ... well, maybe it was, just for a while,' she conceded. 'It's just hard to get your head round something when people tell you all kinds of conflicting stuff.'

For a moment she thought Kieran was going to lose his temper again, but then he shrugged and said, 'Yeah, I know. And I haven't helped, have I? Spending so much time with Mona and refusing to justify it. I'm sorry for being a pompous git.'

Belle smiled properly for the first time. 'Me, I'm sorry for being paranoid. I should most probably stop listening to other people and start following my instincts.' Her fingers interlocked with his. 'After all, they've done OK for me so far.'

Kieran's eyes twinkled in the light from the tasteless chandeliers. 'You're so beautiful, Belle,' he whispered.

She blushed and giggled.

'No, really, you are.' He slipped a finger beneath her impish chin and tilted it up. 'Why the hell would I want to be with any other woman if I've got you?'

At that moment, the waitress came to take their plates away. 'These finished with, are they?' she demanded, whisking them away without waiting for a reply. 'Can I get you any desserts? Tiramisu, ice cream, chocolate cheesecake?'

'Not just now, thanks,' answered Belle, her eyes still gazing deep into Kieran's. How could she have doubted him? All right, so there were things that didn't quite make sense, but this was Kieran; the man she'd loved since the day she first set eyes on him. Kieran, who'd fallen in love with her even though the world was full of other women who were cleverer and more beautiful. Right now, the only thing she longed for was the feel of his body against hers, the intoxicating heat of his desire.

He seemed to feel the same way too. 'Nothing thank you, just the bill.' He flashed a brief smile at the waitress. 'Quick as you can please, there's somewhere we have to be in ten minutes' time.'

As they were walking out of the restaurant five minutes later, hand in hand, Belle turned to Kieran. 'Go on – you've really got me guessing. Where's this place we have to be so urgently?'

He bent to embrace her, pushing her lightly against the tiled wall of the porch as his lips kissed the breath from her body. Then he drew back and whispered one word in her ear:

'Bed.'

*

184

It was pretty obvious from the mile-wide smirk on Belle's face the next morning that she and Kieran had spent the night doing some serious making up. Clare didn't seem too thrilled about her decision to accept Kieran's version of events, but then Clare was just being a good friend: cautious and protective. And Lily was positively rapturous when she saw how much happier Belle looked. Clare would come around quickly enough once she realised that Kieran just wasn't the lying kind.

It wasn't until sometime after lunch that Belle realised her handbag was missing a few vital items. Her purse and keys were there, so she hadn't been robbed, but where were her favourite lipstick, her comb, her tube of sugar-free mints ... and the staff rota she'd spent an eternity drawing up the previous day? She rummaged frantically, half-convinced that if she did it often enough, the rota would eventually pop up from behind a postage stamp or a rogue five pence. Oh God, not the rota. The only bloody copy of the rota. The one time she hadn't bothered taking a photocopy, and she'd lost the flaming thing.

She sat down on the staff loo and pondered. This just didn't make sense. She was sure it had been in there the previous evening. In fact, she remembered noticing it when she touched up her make-up at the restaurant, just before they headed back to Kieran's flat for a night of unbridled passion.

Ah. Kieran's flat. A finger of memory prodded vaguely at her brain. Hadn't she flung her handbag and jacket onto his sofa as they came into the room, practically ripping each other's clothes off? And hadn't that selfsame handbag been sitting on the kitchen counter the following morning?

She called him up. 'Kieran darling?'

'Uh-huh?'

'Did you find my handbag on your sofa this morning?'

Kieran stifled a big yawn. 'Er ... yeah, I did. It was upside down and there was stuff all over the place so I crammed it all back in. Why? Have you lost something?'

'Yes, my staff rota! I don't suppose you remember seeing it? A sheet of A4 folded into four?'

Kieran deliberated. 'I did do a bit of clearing up this morning,' he admitted.

'And?'

'There's just a tiny possibility I might have thrown it out.'

Belle had a couple of hours owing, but she hadn't expected to have to spend them rooting around Kieran's apartment.

As bachelor flats went, his was one of the less squalid ones; and at least he kept it reasonably clean. But his living room still boasted a half-assembled racing bike, and inexplicably, one of the cupboards in his designer kitchen was full of socks.

Belle headed straight for the sofa and pulled off all the seat cushions. Sure enough, down the back she found the lipstick, the mints, the comb, not to mention two pounds fifty in assorted change and a sherbet lemon. But no tatty sheet of paper. It looked like Kieran was right – he'd thrown it in the bin.

She groaned as she upended every wastepaper basket and pedal bin, and grimaced as she tackled a kitchen swing bin full of yesterday's spaghetti Bolognese, all to no avail. Bugger. Belle flung her rubber gloves into the sink and slid limply down the wall. All this and she was still going to have to redo that rota. A whole month's worth.

Then a thought struck her: the recycling bin. That's where you'd throw a sheet of paper, wasn't it? She dragged it out from under the sink and removed the lid with a flourish. But the blasted thing was empty. Or almost empty.

Obviously something wet had got into it, because a thin mulch of wet newspaper adhered to the green plastic bottom of the box. When she peeled it off, right underneath it she found something that took her heart and squeezed it in her chest until it hurt so much, she was certain that nothing in the world could hurt more. It lay there, silently mocking her childish trust.

A flattened cardboard box, labelled 'Home Pregnancy Test'.

Belle burst through the door into the features department like a cyclone, the harassed receptionist from the front desk trailing in a couple of seconds behind her. 'I'm terribly sorry,' she panted, 'but you can't come in here without a visitor's badge.'

'Don't worry, I won't be staying long,' said Belle coldly. 'Just long enough to give Kieran a little present.'

Work ceased and everybody turned to enjoy the spectacle of one small but very angry-looking young woman, heading straight for Kieran like the proverbial bullet with his name on it. Even Sandra emerged from her editorial cubicle, ever on the alert for anything that might make good copy.

He got up slowly from his seat, an initial smile turning to a look of consternation. 'Belle?'

'What – no Mona today? I thought you two were inseparable.'

'I told you, she's working at the Royal Shakespeare today. Is something the matter? Only you're looking awfully flushed.'

'No, nothing's the matter,' replied Belle. 'Not now I've finally sorted out what's really been going on.' She upended a plastic carrier bag onto

186

Kieran's desk, and the pregnancy test box fell out. 'Congratulations, Daddy.'

'What's that?' demanded Kieran, frowning at the packet.

'What the hell does it look like?' Belle burned with humiliation, seethed with the agony of all the times he'd duped her and all the times she'd chosen to believe him, when all the time he and Mona had been laughing themselves witless behind her back. 'For God's sake Kieran, if you must get my own half-sister pregnant, at least admit it.'

'What!' Kieran's face turned chalk-white. Behind him, colleagues were starting to snigger. Sandra stood in the doorway to her cubicle, a look of slight amusement curving the crimson slash of her lips.

'Tut tut, Kieran,' remarked Sandra. 'Have we been a naughty boy?'

He ignored the jibe, but his eyes flamed. 'Whatever this is, Belle, it's got absolutely nothing to do with me! Nothing!'

All at once, Belle felt inexpressibly tired. Exhausted to the point where reality seemed like some distant and uninteresting hallucination. She felt her mind detach itself from the situation, her emotions switching off the way a circuit breaker does when an electrical surge is too strong. All of this was like one of those straight-to-video Hollywood movies, the ones you don't even need to see to be able to write the script.

'See you around, Kieran.' She turned and walked back towards the door, past the open-mouthed receptionist and out into the cool quiet of the lobby.

His footsteps thundered behind her until she felt his hand gripping her shoulder, swinging her round. 'You can't just . . . just storm in here, make a scene and then walk out again!'

Belle shook him off, like a dog ridding itself of fleas. 'Leave me alone, Kieran.'

'But we need to talk!'

'No, Kieran, you've had your say. You might need to talk but I don't need to listen, not any more. What I need is time to think.'

He stopped in his tracks and watched, white-faced, as she walked towards the outer door. 'Time? How much time?'

She didn't answer him. Just stepped out through the door and let it crash shut behind her, shuddering in its frame.

Chapter 19

A couple of days later, Sandra summoned Kieran to a meeting. She was wearing the sort of smile that he knew meant she wanted something.

'If it's more overtime,' he warned her before he'd even sat down at the table, 'I'm not interested. I've got a lot on my plate at the moment.'

Sandra's smile turned to one of sympathy. 'So I heard. I'm sorry to hear about your break-up with Annabelle.'

Kieran wilted on his chair. It was bad enough that it had happened; the last thing he wanted was to talk about it. 'I think everybody within a five-mile radius heard,' he said ruefully.

'Yes, she wasn't exactly subtle about it,' agreed Sandra, perching herself on the corner of the desk. 'But never mind, these things usually turn out to have been for the best, don't they?'

Kieran grunted, and Sandra took this as encouragement to continue.

'You've been through a lot, these last few months: the illegitimate Australian sister turning up, the arguments, the pregnancy, the accusations ... What I want to do, Kieran, is help you get over it in the best possible way.'

'Oh? And what would that be?' he enquired, instantly suspicious of this Mother Teresa moment.

'I want to give you the chance of working extra hours.'

'Uh?'

'Working hard is the best way to get over an emotional upset, ask anyone.' Sandra gave him a smile that reminded him of a snake. 'So as soon as these extra hours became available, naturally I thought of you.'

Only Sandra would try to make overtime sound like a privilege, thought Kieran. 'What you mean,' he corrected her, 'is that since Eva left you've been one journalist short, and you're desperate for somebody to do the work. Am I right?'

Sandra pouted. 'You must have a very low opinion of me, Kieran,' she complained.

Kieran surprised himself when he heard himself say: 'Sorry, not interested.'

'Come now,' she coaxed, 'think of all the Brownie points . . . and the extra cash.'

'Don't need either,' he replied, pushing back his chair and getting to his feet. 'And frankly I'm fed up with being dumped on.'

Sandra's smile hardened. 'I could put pressure on you to do it. Though I'd rather not, of course.'

'I wouldn't if I were you,' advised Kieran.

'Or what? You'll stamp your little feet and snap your pencil in my face?'

'I'll leave.'

His words were followed by a few seconds of absolute silence, not even disturbed by the ticking of a clock.

All expression seemed to slide off Sandra's face, leaving it blank and smooth. 'You wouldn't,' she said, but without conviction.

'I would, and you know it. You're not the only paper that wants to employ me. I'm the best bloody writer on this rag, and for the best part of the last year I've been keeping the features department going practically single-handed. If I leave now, you're stuffed.'

He turned back as he reached the door. 'It's your choice of course,' he said with an icy smile, and then he left, closing the door softly behind him.

So far, Belle felt she'd weathered the storm pretty well. She'd only cried twice, and since she was premenstrual anyway, that hardly counted. The overall feeling was one of numbness: the sort you get when you break your leg. For a short while it hurts like hell, then it swells up and goes dead, and it's almost like you don't have a leg there at all. Of course it hurts again later, when the swelling starts going down; but Belle didn't want to think about later. She just wanted to survive from one day to the next.

The worst part was telling her parents. She couldn't decide which was worse: her mother's anguished fussing, or her father's pious fatalism. Her mum and dad both cared deeply about her, and she was profoundly grateful for that; but at the moment she would have been happier with quiet acceptance and an understanding 'we'll say no more about it'. Not thinking about Kieran was the easiest way to get by, she'd found. And right now, a problem shared felt like a problem doubled, so – much as she'd have liked to point to Kieran as the cause of Mona's pregnancy – she'd kept the details of the break-up deliberately vague.

'At least it's happened now, and not after the wedding,' remarked her father encouragingly as Belle sat with them in the living-room. 'You wouldn't believe the number of couples who don't discover they're incompatible until they've been married a few months. That's when I get the fallout,' he confided. 'Not that there's much I can do to help them, not if they really are wrong for each other.'

Belle had a sudden urge to protest that she and Kieran hadn't been wrong for each other, at least not to begin with; but then reality kicked in and it seemed like a stupid thing to say. If you were right for each other, you didn't sleep with each other's half-sisters, did you?

'Yes Dad,' she said softly. 'This cake's nice, Mum,' she added, taking a brave stab at changing the subject.

Brenda eyed the monolithic coffee and walnut cake that occupied most of the sideboard. 'I made it for the church bring and buy sale,' she said darkly, 'but only three people turned up.'

'The parishioners are still getting used to having us here,' Gerry said, squeezing his wife's hand. 'Give it time.'

Brenda didn't argue, but Belle could see she wasn't at all convinced. Gerry didn't look that confident either, come to that. Everybody knew the Bluebell Estate was the ecclesiastical equivalent of the Wild West; taming it was going to take more than good intentions and cakes.

'Oh Annabelle,' sighed Brenda, 'Kieran seemed like such a lovely boy. He was like a son to me.'

'Yes, Mum.' Please, please stop talking about him, willed Belle. I don't think I can bear much more of this.

'Why couldn't you have split up before you decided to announce the wedding? First I had to send out all the invitations, then the letters about the postponement, and now I'll have to tell them there's not going to be a wedding at all.'

Belle prickled with annoyance. 'Mum! It's not as if I deliberately went out of my way to—'

'And what's the dress designer supposed to do with a half-made wedding dress? Then there's that outlandish outfit of your sister's . . .' Brenda adopted a martyred expression worthy of Joan of Arc. 'But I suppose I shall have to sort it out, just like I have to sort out everything else.'

This really did rub Belle up the wrong way. 'Look Mum, I'm sorry if this is all a bit inconvenient for you, and I know you've had a rough time over the last few months, but what do you think it's like for me? My whole life's fallen apart!'

Brenda shook her head in that irritatingly knowing way older people have. 'Don't be so melodramatic, dear. You're very young, there are plenty more men out there. Have another slice of cake.'

Her father reached out an arm and gave her a shoulder-hug. 'Things will sort themselves out,' he said. 'Everything sorts itself out in the end. We just have to have patience.'

Belle wasn't much enjoying her latest visit to St Mungo's vicarage, but then again she doubted her parents were much enjoying living there – let alone poor Jax. But at least there was one reason to be grateful: the appearance from Mona that she'd been so dreading hadn't materialised.

'Where's ... Mona?' She could hardly bring herself to spit out the name. 'Working?'

'Upstairs packing, dear,' replied her mother. 'She's moving out.'

This was music to Belle's ears. 'Moving out?' Then a nasty thought struck. 'She's not moving in with somebody, is she?' Please, please don't let it be Kieran, she silently pleaded.

'Not as far as I know, dear. No. Apparently she and the father "aren't together" at the moment.'

That at least was a relief. 'Why's she going, then? Have you thrown her out?' she asked hopefully.

'Don't be silly, dear. She's expecting a baby. Even if she is having it out of wedlock,' added Brenda with a touch of acid, just managing to prevent herself adding, 'Which is all this family needs right now.'

Yes, and don't I bloody well know it, thought Belle. 'So she's going back to Australia then?'

Her father helped himself to another cup of tea from the pot on the table. 'No, no, she's decided to have the baby over here.'

Belle's morale, which she'd been sure had reached rock-bottom, suddenly discovered a mine shaft and fell down it.

'Though you'd think a girl would want her mother around at a time like this,' interjected Brenda. 'I don't know,' she added with a meaningful look at her husband. 'Giving birth to an illegitimate child, just like her mother. Must be something bad in the genes.'

Gerry allowed the barbed remark to bounce off him. 'They've offered her a couple of rooms above the Royal Shakespeare, rent free,' he went on. 'She's moving over there in a week or two. It'll give her a bit of independence when the baby comes. Did you want a word with her?'

One word? thought Belle. Make that several dozen, most of them with four letters. But not right now. The last thing I want to do is break down and cry in front of that two-timing bitch who calls herself my sister.

That selfsame two-timing bitch was upstairs in her room, sorting through her meagre possessions ready for the forthcoming move. The voices coming from downstairs were muffled, but she could make out enough to know that Belle was there, and that she wasn't happy.

Once again, Mona waited for the satisfying buzz of *schadenfreude*, but it just didn't come. And she didn't dare dig too far below the surface of her feelings, because if she did, she might unearth that seam of guilt she'd recently discovered. I'm going soft, she told herself. Why should I care about her stupid wedding – or her stupid boyfriend for that matter?

Not soft enough to put more effort into persuading Belle that Kieran wasn't the father of her baby, though. If Belle wanted to believe that Kieran had done the dirty deed, then fine. As for Kieran, if he couldn't be bothered to work at winning back Belle's trust, well, maybe Belle was better off without him anyway.

What really mattered was what was best for Mona. The trouble was, revenge just wasn't half as satisfying as she'd expected. In fact, the only strong feeling she was experiencing at the moment was an overpowering urge to eat pilchards.

She laid a hand upon her stomach. Was there really a tiny heart beating inside there? It was still so hard to take in, still a shock to know that in a few months' time she – the girl who had never quite grown up – was going to become a mother herself. Not however quite as big a shock as it would be to her own mother, if and when she found out about her impending grandmotherhood.

Mona sat down on the window seat and gazed out at a couple of kids play-fighting in the churchyard. She hadn't allowed herself to speculate too much on what Rena's reaction would be, but she had a fair idea that it wouldn't be good. Like mother, like daughter . . .

She and her mother didn't talk much anyway these days. They'd been so close until a couple of years ago, when Rena got tired of mourning her dead husband and took up with a new boyfriend. Chas thought Mona was in the way, and the feeling was mutual; but as far as Rena was concerned, the sun shone out of his hairy backside. So Mona had avoided him and her mother for months, and finally left Australia altogether.

It still hurt. It felt like her mother was being taken away from her. First her dad, then her beloved stepdad, now her mum. Maybe that was the spur that had finally driven Mona to make this crazy trip to the other side of the world. Maybe it hadn't been entirely about revenge after all . . . but what did she know? She was pregnant, and pregnant women were packed so full of hormones, they could get sentimental over drying paint.

It was all pretty irrelevant anyway. Because, whatever her motivation and regardless of whether she derived any satisfaction from it or not, the vengeance juggernaut had taken on a life of its own, and was refusing to be stopped in its tracks. Mona no longer had to do anything at all except stand back and watch the whole Craine clan destroy itself from the inside.

Yet she wasn't at all sure that was what she wanted any more.

*

192

If Belle was intent on steering clear of Mona for the time being, Clare had other ideas.

'I reckon you need to get right out there and show your face,' she declared as the two sat in Clare's flat drinking Bailey's and watching *Brief Encounter*. 'Be wherever she is, show her you don't give a damn about her. It'll drive her absolutely crazy.'

'Maybe, but it'd drive me crazy too,' replied Belle.

'Rubbish.' Clare refilled Belle's glass with enough Bailey's to intoxicate half of Dublin. 'You're strong, you can take it. And you can start by going to the Bards and Wenches night.'

Belle coughed into her drink. 'What? At the Royal Shakespeare? The one Mona's organising? But that's tomorrow night. You're mad!'

'No, you're mad if you don't go,' replied Clare. 'She'll think you're hiding from her.'

'Clare, I am hiding from her.'

Clare tried a slightly different tack. 'She'll think she's won.'

That brought Belle up short. OK, so she was scared of what would happen if and when she and Mona came face to face again, but even if Mona had destroyed her life, there was no way Belle was about to let her know it. She swallowed hard. 'All right – but not on my own,' she warned. 'I just can't.'

Clare gave her a sisterly pat on the back. 'Of course not. I'm coming with you. Now, drink up and let's talk about what you're going to wear.'

'Are you sure this is a good idea?' asked Oz nervously as he and Kieran rolled up outside the Royal Shakespeare Tavern.

'We promised Mona we'd be here, remember?'

Oz shuffled his feet and pushed his not-very-medieval glasses up his nose. 'I really ought to be home by nine,' he said. 'I'm supposed to be dressing my mother's infected bunion.'

Kieran pulled a face. 'Good God man, are you a man or a mouse?'

Oz smiled feebly. 'I'm pretty fond of cheese.'

'That figures.' Kieran looked his hapless friend up and down. 'Oz, you're thirty-three years old, and your mother's got you pandering to her every whim! I wouldn't care, but there's nothing wrong with the woman! In fact she's fitter than you are. No wonder you can't keep a girlfriend for more than a week.'

Oz hung his head. 'Yes, all right. I know. But Mum gave up a lot to bring us kids up after Dad ran off with his secretary.'

'And she's been playing on it ever since,' Kieran reminded him. 'That's why your sister left home at sixteen. Actually, it's a pity you didn't go with her, if you ask me.'

Oz flushed. 'Well, I didn't. Actually. Look, can we go in and get this over with?'

'Suits me.' Kieran adjusted his doublet. He wasn't remotely in the mood for fancy dress, but a promise was a promise, and this was a big event for Mona: her first theme night. It had to be a success because she needed to keep her job if she and the baby were going to have any security. 'With a bit of luck, this might take my mind off . . . stuff.'

'I guess,' Oz conceded. He felt horribly conspicuous in his medieval minstrel outfit, particularly as it had been hastily converted from a costume last worn by Dopey in the last local production of *Snow White*. That was what happened when you dithered for too long and all the decent costumes had already been hired out. Trying to avoid his reflection in the bar window, he trailed behind Kieran as he walked into the pub.

Heads turned when Kieran entered. They always did – he was a tall, good-looking guy. But he looked even better than usual in his tight-fitting black and red velvet doublet and matching hose, complete with flowing cape. Most men would have looked ludicrous in bi-coloured tights; Kieran looked just plain virile.

There's no justice in the world, thought Oz gloomily, as his baggy, too-short trousers flapped around his calves. 'What are you drinking?' He nodded towards an old oak table someone had set up in the centre of the bar. D'you want to try some of that dodgy mead punch stuff? Or shall we play it safe and stick to beer?'

'Coward.'

'Guilty as charged.'

'I'll probably regret this, but let's try the mead.'

The Royal Shakespeare Tavern had undergone quite a transformation. Instead of looking like a bog-standard twenty-first-century dive, it now looked like a medieval dive, complete with two inches of straw on the floor and earthenware cups and pitchers instead of glasses. The wormy old roof-beams had been buffed up, and somebody had even hired a bunch of blokes with lutes and crumhorns to make atmospheric noises in the corner. You couldn't really call it medieval music; the minstrels had been drinking since five in the afternoon, and it was beginning to sound more like freeform jazz. But the thought was there. And there were rumours that Mad Dog McKindrick would be giving an impromptu performance of 'Rock Madrigal' later on in the evening.

Oz brightened a little as he caught sight of a fine figure of a woman in a low-cut, laced-up bodice. He nudged Kieran. 'Cor. Get a load of the wenches.'

'Yeah. Great.' Kieran tried to kick-start his enthusiasm, but it wasn't really there. Oz might not have the faintest inkling, but Kieran had had to force himself to come out this evening. Ever since the split a week ago, all he'd wanted to do was sit at home and kill people on his PlayStation. But he couldn't stay like that. He knew he had to make himself get out and get on with life, even though life didn't seem to get on with him at the moment.

Mona was standing behind the bar, looking statuesque and not at all pregnant in one of those off-the-shoulder peasant tops, with her golden hair all piled up underneath a lacy white mob cap. She waved and smiled as she caught sight of Kieran and Oz across the bar. 'You made it! Good on ya. Talk to you both later on.'

Kieran gave her a thumbs-up sign. Oz turned pink and shuffled his feet. 'I think I might have left the cooker on,' he ventured. 'Perhaps I should just go back and check?'

But Kieran wasn't listening. He was staring across the thronged bar, towards two girls crammed around a corner table. One, he dimly recognised as Clare, the spiky sister of Belle's obsessed ex-boyfriend. The other was totally gorgeous in a laced-up, plunging bodice, her dark hair falling loose about her bare shoulders.

The other one, of course, was Belle. It was almost more than he could bear, just looking at her.

Belle had tried dragging her feet, losing her costume, pleading a headache; but Clare was wise to all of it. Belle was going to the Bards and Wenches night, and that was all there was to it.

It turned out to be everything Belle had expected. The hordes of beery men included one wild-eyed Welsh bard, three William Shakespeares and two Merlin the Magicians, Batman and Robin, Bart Simpson and an astronaut, plus several in sweatshirts and jeans who really hadn't bothered to make an effort at all. The girls were uniformly squeezed into low-cut tops with push-up bras, which was probably why all the men looked so happy, and *Robin Hood, Prince of Thieves* was playing silently on the big-screen TV. As for Engelbert, he was moving systematically from table to table, hoovering up bits of 'medieval' meat pie and jingling the bells on his red and yellow jester's cap. And wherever Engelbert was, Mona couldn't be far away.

'There she is,' said Clare as she and Belle sat squeezed into a corner. 'At the far end of the bar. Cow.'

Belle was perfectly aware that Mona was behind the bar. She'd been aware of her every movement since they stepped through the door of the pub. It wasn't that she wanted to look at her, she just couldn't help it. It was as though Mona emitted some kind of signal that Belle was powerless to ignore.

She shifted uncomfortably on her seat. A bit of straw had got inside her sixteenth-century ankle-boot and was making her foot itch. What's more, the man opposite had developed an overt fascination with her enhanced cleavage, and frankly it was freaking her out. If all the women in Shakespeare's time walked round looking like this, Belle mused, it's a wonder he ever got any writing done.

After half an hour of acute discomfort, Belle made a decision. 'OK, he's not coming,' she said, draining her pot of mead and making to stand up. 'Let's go.'

Clare's hand reached out and gently but firmly pushed her back onto the bench. 'Not so fast, kid. It's not half-past yet, it's hardly got going.'

'But I just don't want to—'

'Just another ten minutes, eh? And then if he's still not here, we'll go. All right?'

Belle was about to say that no, it wasn't really all right at all; but then the door of the bar yawned open again and another group of punters tumbled in. She held her breath, then let it go. Just a bunch of kids.

No sooner had she said this to herself than she saw him. Kieran. He hadn't seen her though. He was looking back over his shoulder, arguing with Oz about something.

Clare elbowed her in the ribs. 'Over there.'

'Yes, I know.' Belle tracked Kieran and Oz as they jostled through the throng. Her heart ached with the nearness and the farness of it all. Kieran might be in the same room, but he could have been on the other side of the world and he still wouldn't have felt any further away.

She thought she might cry; but then a funny thing happened: the aching faded, and – just for a fleeting moment – a strange sensation rippled through her. A kind of weird excitement, a realisation – that she was not just alone, but free. Not the lesser half of a couple any more, not the unimportant adjunct to a much more interesting man. Just herself.

It only lasted a few seconds, then it was gone. And Belle felt the ache return as she watched Kieran walk up to the bar.

'Look,' said Clare. 'He's talking to Mona.'

'I can see that.'

'Now she's laughing, the bitch.'

'I can do without the running commentary, thanks.'

'Oh. Sorry. Didn't mean to upset you.' Clare took a sip from her glass. 'Why do some women just assume they can do whatever they like, no matter how much it hurts other people? It's not right.'

Belle didn't answer. She was watching Kieran and Mona, caught in helpless fascination. They looked happy together, easy in each other's company as if they'd known each other forever. If anyone looked uncomfortable it was Oz, pink-necked and perennially ill at ease with the female sex. Kieran looked anything but ill at ease; even his stupid costume flattered him.

Why am I here? Belle agonised silently. Why did I let Clare bully me into coming? The last thing I wanted to do was sit here, torturing myself and feeling like some kind of inferior species. Just don't turn round Kieran, she prayed; I'm not here, you haven't seen me. Please don't turn round and look in my direction.

But of course, he did. And as their eyes locked, the smile froze on his lips.

He looked shocked; but not guilty, or angry, or dismissive. And there was something sad about the look in his eyes; something that seemed just a little lost and afraid. For a moment, the tiniest fragment of doubt wormed its way into Belle's mind. Could she have been wrong? Was there the remotest possibility that she might have misjudged Kieran in any way?

She turned to Clare. 'Could Kieran and I ... do you think we could have found a way of staying together? You know, if I'd tried harder.'

Clare gave her a stern look and banged down a pitcher of mead punch in front of her. 'Don't be silly and sentimental, Belle. Kieran's a cheating bastard. Come on, have another drink. You know it'll make you feel better.'

Chapter 20

Retribution, as the saying goes, was swift and terrible. Belle's hangover was the kind that go down in legend; the kind where your eyeballs seem to have swollen hugely in their sockets, and some fiend has apparently poured paint-stripper down your throat in the night, while repeatedly hitting you over the head with something hard and knobbly.

It was a bad one.

She called in sick for the first time in ages, staggered back to bed and wondered how long it would take to feel vaguely human again. No more mead, she told herself. And no more mead punch ever.

The sound of the doorbell woke her and she fumbled for the bedside clock, squinting at it through bloodshot eyes in the sunlight that filtered through the bedroom curtains. Half-past one. She'd been asleep all morning.

The doorbell rang again, this time accompanied by a half-hearted rap on the door.

'OK, OK, hang on a minute, I'm coming.'

Rooting around for her dressing gown, Belle thrust her arms into it and raked the mess of hair back from her eyes. Her nostrils were still full of the smell of stale cigarette smoke and beer, and she had a shrewd suspicion she wasn't what you'd call presentable.

At last she shuffled to the door and wrenched it open, to find her younger sister standing outside. Jax didn't look exactly happy, but then Gothic gloom was par for the course where Jax was concerned. All the same, Belle doubted this was a social call. As a general rule, Jax made home visits only when she wanted to extort money, borrow stuff she never got round to returning, or set up an alibi for one of her all-night trysts with Razor.

'Hello stranger,' yawned Belle, surprised that she could actually produce any sound from her parched throat.

'You look crap,' observed Jax. 'And you smell. Can I come in?'

'If you put it so nicely, how can I refuse?' Belle let her sister in and followed Jax into the living-room.

'God, I don't know how you can stand living here,' said Jax, throwing her bag of school files onto the end of the bed. 'It's so poky.'

'You know, you're right,' agreed Belle. 'I must go out and rent myself a three-bedroom penthouse apartment straight away. I'm sure my enormous salary will run to it.'

Jax scowled. 'There's no need to be sarcastic.'

'And there's no need to be rude, but you always seem willing to make the effort.'

'Obviously it was a waste of time, my coming here,' snapped Jax. 'So I'll just piss off and let you get back to laughing at me behind my back.'

She turned to go, but Belle caught her, led her back to the sofa-bed, and sat her firmly down. 'Nobody's laughing at you,' she said.

'Oh yeah?'

'What's this all about?' It didn't take a great leap of the imagination to conclude: 'It's school again, isn't it?'

'Of course it's school.' Jax fiddled with the handle on her bag: a big, black effort bristling with spines like a rubberised hedgehog. 'Look – the other week. Did you mean what you said, about helping me?'

'Of course I did.'

Jax looked her straight in the eye. 'All right then, do it.'

Belle was somewhat taken aback by this. 'Oh. Well. I'm not sure it's quite as simple as that, but—'

'So you didn't mean it then?'

Belle let out a weary sigh and put an arm round her sister's shoulders. For once she didn't tense up or pull away, so that was a start. 'I meant it,' she promised. 'But you can't just expect me to come up with something at a moment's notice! I'm going to need to do some major thinking.'

Jax looked down at her big black boots. 'Please think fast,' she said, in the voice of a lost six-year-old. 'Because I've run out of ideas, and I just don't know how much more of this I can take.'

Jax might be habitually obnoxious, but Belle was still her sister, and she didn't have a heart of flint. So Jax's obvious desperation added another layer of misery to the way she was feeling, not to mention giving her plenty more practical problems to think about.

She'd been doing an awful lot of thinking in the week or so since she and Kieran had split up. It wasn't so much that she'd been moping about the disastrous end to their love affair, more that she was trying to find something positive to spur her on: something to fill the hole that her shattered illusions had left behind.

If the whole experience had taught her anything, it was that it was no good relying upon another person to bring her happiness, success, fulfilment. Maybe in time – a long, long time – she'd find those things again, with somebody else; but for now whatever she achieved would be down to her. She couldn't quite decide yet whether the prospect excited or intimidated her, but she had come to one major decision: in career terms at least, it was time to move on. Maybe she wasn't good enough to make the grade on her own, but she knew she had to try.

Belle hadn't intended telling anybody about the job application, but Lily spotted her dropping the envelope into the internal mail. 'Oh Belle!' Lily's eyes shone with excitement. 'Is that what I think it is?'

'It might be,' replied Belle. 'But if you so much as breathe a word to anybody, I'll have you minced up and turned into meatballs.'

Lily seemed unconcerned by this threat. 'Don't worry, my lips are sealed,' she declared in a dramatic stage whisper that would've drawn instant attention, had there been anybody else in the shop to hear. 'Is it that Customer Services job then? I just knew it was right for you.'

'Well, I did toy with this one.' Belle flicked through the pages of the latest in-house newsletter and pointed to one of the job ads. 'There, that one: area manager South-West Midlands, what do you reckon?'

Lily wrinkled her nose in horror. 'Ooh, scary! Rather you than me.'

Belle nodded. 'That's what I thought too.'

'All that telling people off, and being blamed when things go wrong . . . no thanks. I think I'd rather just be a humble minion.'

'It has its advantages,' Belle admitted. 'But with everything that's happened lately, I just feel it's now or never – if I don't get out there and find out what I can do, I probably never will.'

And maybe at long last I'll do something to make my family proud of me, instead of just basking in my fiancé's reflected glory, she mused. Maybe I really do have it in me to be someone, after all. If I turn out not to have, at least I can say I tried.

'And?' demanded Lily, puncturing Belle's reverie. 'What did you apply for in the end?'

'Shh!' pleaded Belle. 'The Customer Services job, what else?'

'Good for you! I'm sure you'll be brilliant,' Lily assured her, hopping up onto the step-stool to reach one of the top display shelves. 'Just like you always are.'

'Hang on, I haven't got it yet!' Belle reminded her. 'And I most probably won't.'

'You will.' Lily turned and gave her look of genuine sadness. 'Just make sure they get somebody nice to do your job here. It's going to be ever so lonely without you.'

Gerry was feeling pretty lonely too. He'd often wondered about the Creator's weird and wonderful ways, but never more so than now. Had he really been brought to the Bluebell Estate for some meaningful purpose? Or was that purpose just to bring him down to size after all the years he'd spent being comfortable and complacent at St Jude's?

He sat in his bosun's chair, swivelling slowly from side to side, trying to work it out and feeling ashamed that the move to St Mungo's had left him so shell-shocked. For all her prophecies of doom and gloom beforehand, Brenda had adapted to the new parish far better than he had. But then she had at least lived here once before, however she might wish to forget her impoverished childhood. By comparison, Gerry felt irremediably middle-class. No wonder nobody wanted to come to his services.

Passing quietly by, Mona paused and contemplated her father through the chink in the door as he sat there, looking utterly despondent. My father, she thought; and for the first time, the idea hit home and stuck. That sad man in there is my dad, and he's only sad because I made him that way.

Yeah, but he deserves it, doesn't he? argued the demon on her shoulder. For abandoning your mum, ignoring her letters when she was pregnant and needed his help. That was the argument she'd employed all along, believing it justified, but never before had it felt so flimsy or so vindictive. When all's said and done, she reminded herself, he's always insisted the story isn't true; and the guy's a priest.

Maybe that didn't count for much, but more importantly, Gerry Craine was a kind man who'd unquestioningly accepted her as his daughter. He hadn't asked any difficult questions about the new baby either, hadn't criticised her once, and steadfastly refused to take sides over Belle's split with Kieran. Even the normally outspoken Brenda had kept her own counsel and never suggested it might be better if Mona was to pack her bags and leave not just for a room above the pub, but for good.

As for Mona herself, she quite simply didn't have the taste for hurting Gerry Craine any more. Quite the reverse. She looked at him sitting there, and found that all she wanted to do was help.

On a whim, she pushed open the door of Gerry's boxroom-cum-office, and stuck her head round it. 'Hi there. You're looking a bit down in the dumps.'

He sat up straight and made a creditable attempt at a cheerful smile. 'Oh, I'm fine. Just thinking, you know.' He indicated his computer's blank screen. 'Trying to come up with a sermon for Sunday ... '

Mona came in, shutting the door quietly behind her. 'What you need are some new ideas for getting bums on seats – or should that be bums on pews? Anyhow, there's not much point writing sermons if there's hardly anybody to hear them, is there?'

Gerry nodded rather glumly. 'All suggestions gratefully received,' he said. 'I've tried all the usual bring and buy sales, church socials, that sort of thing.'

Mona laughed, but not unkindly. 'I'm not sure the people round here are your church social types,' she said. 'They'd rather have a few pints of lager than a cup of coffee. Pity you can't open a bar in the vestry.'

Gerry looked startled. 'Oh, I don't really think—'

'Joke,' she said hastily. 'Sorry, I have this talent for bad-taste humour, I just can't help it. Tell you what though, working at the Royal Shakespeare Tavern has given me a few ideas about what people like. And the ones we get in the pub aren't so different from the ones who live round here.'

'So what do you suggest?' he asked, his interest aroused.

'Well, what I've found at the pub is that there are two things that get people in – three actually, but I can't quite see you getting a troupe of strippers in at St Mungo's. Anyhow, these two things are cheap alcohol and free food. And bearing in mind that booze is pretty much out, I reckon you need to concentrate on the food.'

'We did hold a coffee morning,' Gerry reminded her, 'with lots of Brenda's home-made cakes. But hardly anybody turned up.'

'The thing is, Gerry, I'm not saying Brenda's cakes aren't great in the right place, 'cause they are, but what I'm talking about here is a full-scale meal. Offer people a real blow-out for free, and they're so damn' greedy they just won't be able to resist, you mark my words. Then once they're inside, you can hit them with the religion!'

Gerry looked at her and burst out laughing for the first time in weeks. It felt good.

'What's so funny?' puzzled Mona.

'Nothing,' he assured her. 'It's just, when you get all enthusiastic like that . . . you remind me of your mother. Rena was sparky exactly like you when I knew her.' He looked directly at his daughter. 'I did try to keep in touch with her, you know,' he said. 'I don't know what happened, but I promise you I would never have abandoned her.' He smiled wistfully. 'How could I? She was my first love.'

Mona was still pondering Gerry's words as she climbed the stairs to her soon-to-be-vacated room and collided with Jax, sending textbooks and notes tumbling all the way down to the hallway.

'Bloody hell, Mona!' raged Jax, in a most unecclesiastical manner, and

Mona half-expected to dodge a swinging fist. But to her surprise, Jax just flopped down onto the top step, hung her head and muttered, 'Oh, what's the fucking use?'

'Hey, it's OK. I'll have it all cleared up in a couple of minutes,' Mona assured her. 'It's no big deal. And if I've damaged anything I'll replace it.'

'I'm not talking about my stuff,' growled Jax. 'I'm talking about my life. It's a complete disaster. I might as well be dead.'

Jax put such feeling into the words that Mona sensed this was more than one of Jax's melodramatic moments. She made a space and sat down next to her. 'What's this all about?'

'You wouldn't be interested.'

'If I'm not interested, why am I asking?'

Jax hesitated for a long moment, visibly weighing up the pros and cons of opening her heart to Mona. 'I don't know if I trust you any more,' she said finally.

'You mean ... because of Kieran and Belle and my going to have a baby?'

'What do you think? I mean, if it's true what Belle says about you and Kieran ...'

Mona took a deep breath. Even though Belle hadn't told her parents about her suspicions, the burden of blame was starting to weigh very heavily on her shoulders. 'I didn't sleep with Kieran,' she said. 'I can't prove it and it's not something I want to talk about but I didn't, and it's up to you whether you believe it or not. And I won't push you to tell me anything if you don't want to, but you know where I am, any time.'

She was about to stand up, but Jax grabbed the tail of her shirt. 'All right. I'll tell you.'

Mona sat down again. 'OK. Fire away.'

And Jax told her about school, and the taunts about her father, and the pain of just not fitting in. 'You think I'm making a fuss about nothing,' she said when Mona didn't immediately react.

'Actually, I was thinking about how I felt when I was the only kid in my class with spots and braces on my teeth,' replied Mona. 'And don't look at me like that, it's true. When I was thirteen I was hideous – a cross between Hannibal Lecter and the surface of the moon. The other kids took the piss out of me twenty-four seven.'

'So what did you do about it?'

'I cried. I ate chocolate. Then I cried some more. Luckily my hormones sorted themselves out and by the time I was fifteen I had such big tits that nobody looked at my face any more.'

Jax subsided into gloom again. 'Great. Fine lot of help you are.'

'If I were you,' Mona said just as Jax was preparing to stalk off, 'I'd get a change of image. Stop doing this big Goth thing and pretty yourself up a bit. Remember all that talk about you coming to Oz and being a model?'

Jax coloured up. 'That was just me fantasising. I never really believed it. Underneath all this I'm just . . . really, really ordinary.'

'I'm sure you're not,' insisted Mona. 'I bet if you grew your hair a bit and dyed it . . . maybe a nice soft ash blonde, or chestnut . . . and then I could help you get some really feminine clothes to make the most of yourself, something fashionable and flattering . . . I bet they'd soon stop taking the mickey then.'

Jax struggled with the idea. 'But then I wouldn't be me any more, would I?' she said.

Mona laughed. 'Of course you would!'

Jax shook her head. 'No, this is me. That would be fake, like being in fancy dress or something. Thanks for the advice anyway,' she added as she got up and started retrieving her notes, 'but I think I have to find another way of handling this.'

Belle was still thinking about Jax, too. Scouring her brain for a solution that didn't amount to: 'Tell Mum and Dad and get yourself transferred to a different school.' She knew that would never be acceptable to Jax, and couldn't help respecting her for it.

Would I be so strong in that situation? she wondered as she got ready for work and grabbed her green apron from the chair where she'd thrown it the night before. No, not me, she concluded. I've always moved heaven and earth to fit in, blend in with the background. It takes guts to decide to be different, and then take the consequences single-handed. Either guts or plain, stubborn stupidity.

The doorbell rang and she threw down her last mouthful of coffee. The postmen round here have great timing, she thought. I'm already ten minutes behind schedule, and if it's a parcel you can bet it needs signing for.

She opened the door and gave a start. It wasn't the usual postman, but none other than Welsh Dave. He grinned wolfishly at her with his nicotine-stained teeth. 'Mornin', Miss Annabelle. Bet you didn't reckon on seeing me again so soon.'

'You could say,' she agreed. 'What a . . . nice surprise.'

'Stanley's in hospital with his ear,' Dave explained cheerfully, 'not that there's anything wrong with him, malingering git, so I'm doin' his round for him. I suppose you'll be wantin' your parcel then?' He shook it speculatively. 'Hm. Heavy, and it's from Swindon, so it's most likely from that book club of yours. Still enjoy a good historical romance, do you?'

'Er . . . yes, thank you.' She grabbed the package from his sweaty fingers and stashed it behind the hall table. It was all she could do not to wipe her hands on the seat of her trousers. 'Now if you'll just excuse me, I'm going to be late for work.'

'Hang on, there's a letter for you an' all.' Welsh Dave rummaged in his mailbag and extracted a crumpled brown envelope. 'Looks official,' he commented, craning his neck as she examined the postmark. 'You waitin' for any hospital appointments? Court summonses?'

He trailed behind her all the way to the bottom of the stairs, when thankfully the woman from Flat 2 accosted him about criminal damage to her letter box, and Belle made good her escape.

She was so late at work that it wasn't until she was sitting on the staff loo that she remembered the letter in her pocket. Gloucester postmark. Hm, that could be good or bad. First class though . . .

Holding her breath, she ripped the envelope open. The letters swam before her eyes; all she could make out was the phrase: 'We are pleased to invite you for interview at ten am on Tuesday . . .'

Oh my God, I've got an interview. She blinked and reread the letter, but it still said the same thing. Terror made her skin tingle all over. Thoughts fired back and forth across her brain like rounds from a scatter-gun. Why on earth did I apply? I was so sure I wouldn't get anywhere. I'm going to make a total idiot of myself. I could never do a job like this! They'll see right through me.

Maybe I should just phone up and cancel?

But two minutes later, Belle was on the phone calling Green Goddess HQ, and telling the sales director's silky-voiced PA that yes, of course she'd be absolutely delighted to attend for the interview.

Chapter 21

It had happened: the day Belle had never thought she'd ever see. Only a fortnight after she'd received the letter asking her to come for interview, Belle Craine was leaving the shop for pastures new.

Lily was a little sad but excited for her, the Saturday kids were surreptitiously drinking vodka and orange in the stockroom, and Waylon ... well, Waylon wasn't taking it at all well. In fact, Waylon was in tears.

'I'm sorry,' he snivelled as the last of the afternoon's customers drifted out of the shop and Belle locked the doors for the last time. 'It's just ...' He flung his arms about her in a melodramatic hug. 'It's just that I'm going to miss you so much.'

'Me too,' said Belle, in what she hoped was a consolatory way without being too friendly. 'You've all been wonderful friends to me, and you always will be. But you know how it is.'

'We all know how it is, and we're very proud of you. Come on, Waylon, you can have my share of the booze, seeing as I'm on the wagon.' Lily peeled off the sobbing Waylon and sat him down with a big glass of something that wasn't so much fruit cup as neat vodka with a slice of orange in it.

Waylon sniffed. 'Very, very proud. That's what we are.' Belle had the impression this wasn't his first drink of the day.

'It's going to be incredibly exciting for you,' Lily enthused.

Belle laughed dismissively. 'Oh, not nearly as exciting as you having your baby.'

'Oh come on – all those staff to boss around—'

'Well, only two,' cut in Belle, 'but it's a start.'

'And they're even fitting out a brand-new office for you. Bet you can't wait to play with all the new gadgets and gizmos.' Lily's eyes flicked around the store. 'As I recall, the last bit of new equipment we got here was a new stapler, and that was three years ago.'

'And we only got that because head office ordered it by mistake,' said Waylon, helping himself to more punch.

Belle gazed around her at the shelves she knew so well, the products whose ingredients she could recite blindfold and probably backwards as well. 'It's so hard to let go,' she said.

'I know,' sympathised Lily. 'It's bound to be, after all this time. And I know I'll find it difficult when I go off on maternity leave. But I'm sure Jerszy here will keep everything warm for you, just in case you decide you can't live without us and want to come back. Not that you'd be mad enough to do that,' she added sternly.

'No, of course I wouldn't,' agreed Belle with just a hint of doubt. Right now she was so scared, she'd have given anything just to stay here and not have to confront the big, bad world on her own.

Jerszy smiled at her in a bashful sort of way, and demonstrated a healthy dose of common sense by declining a second helping of punch. 'I very pleased to meet you,' he announced in English that might not be perfect, but was a lot better than Belle's Polish. 'I from a village near Cracow, is very nice here, yes?'

She accepted his handshake with a smile. What lovely blue eyes, she thought, realising with a shock that this was the first time she'd really noticed a good-looking bloke since she and Kieran broke up. Not that she saw Jerszy in that way of course. He might be in his twenties, but he looked exactly like a blond choirboy – not Belle's type at all.

'Cheltenham is a very nice town,' she agreed. 'You'll like it here. But why would anyone want to come here all the way from Poland to work in a shop?'

'I . . . I not know the words.' Floundering, Jerszy turned to Lily for a linguistic helping hand.

'Jerszy's girlfriend's mother needs an operation, and he's sending back money for it,' she explained.

'I save. Operation is very expensive, and wages here much higher than in Poland,' he agreed. 'Is nice here, but I miss my Masha.'

Waylon looked up, puzzled. 'His what?'

'Masha is Jerszy's girlfriend, he told you!' replied long-suffering Lily. 'She's training to be a dentist,' she added for Belle's benefit, 'so she'll be well off once she's qualified, but for now money's tight. So Jerszy's helping them both out – her and her mum. He hardly keeps anything for himself. Look how thin he is – I'm sure he doesn't eat properly.'

'I am fine, I eat well!' Jerszy turned pink to the tips of his ears. Gosh, thought Belle. A hero and modest with it. And there was I, thinking all men were cheating bastards. But no . . . it's probably just the ones I go out with.

Feeling a little bit down in the dumps, Belle walked slowly round the store, memorising every nook and cranny as if she'd never have a chance to visit the place again. Some things had stayed exactly the same ever since she arrived like the forged twenty-pound note sellotaped under the till for reference, and the cut-out plywood bride from the annual wedding promotion. Well, she wouldn't be too sorry to see the back of that.

Then there were other things that had changed a lot, some of them because of ideas that she'd had, and which Waylon had taken on board. My ideas, she thought; and they actually work! Perhaps it's not brains I'm short of after all, just belief . . .

As the others cleared up the debris of half-eaten mini-pretzels and swabbed spilled drink off the floor, Lily and Belle stood by the front window of the shop, eating the last of the chocolate finger biscuits and watching the last few stragglers taking a short cut home through the arcade.

'I'm really, really pleased for you, you know,' Lily said for the umpteenth time. 'You do know that, don't you?'

Belle bit the end off a chocolate finger. 'Of course I do. And I'd never even have applied for the job if it hadn't been for you.' She watched the shutters roll down for the night on the mobile phone store opposite and her stomach turned over. It felt as though the curtain was coming down on a whole era of her life. No more shop, no more Kieran. She turned to Lily. 'I'm scared,' she whispered.

Lily beamed back at her. 'Of course you are! All the best things in life are scary.'

'They are?'

'Well I'm scared stiff of labour,' she confided.

'Really?'

'Petrified. And it must take a lot of guts to travel round the world too. Just ask your friend Ros.'

Belle felt a twinge of sadness that Ros was so far away. But she laughed at the thought of her being scared. 'Ros is never frightened of anything,' she said.

'Everybody's afraid of something,' insisted Lily. 'Who was it said "feel the fear and do it anyway"?'

Belle shrugged. 'Some smart-arse.'

Lily shoved the last biscuit into Belle's open mouth. 'Well nobody's arse is smarter than yours, so get out there and conquer the universe.'

Early on Monday morning, Brenda took herself down to the local supermarket. She was feeling rather irritable and distracted, and it took an effort of will not to phone Belle on her mobile and find out how the first ten minutes of her new job were going.

The feeling was reminiscent of the day she'd taken Annabelle to school for the very first time, and had to leave her there despite her heart-rending pleas to come home. It was silly worrying, though. Annabelle was a big girl now, and if she'd taken it into her head that she was cut out for a career in management, well, Brenda would be behind her all the way, bursting with maternal pride but ready with the tissues in case it all went wrong. It was a good job Jacqueline never gave her any real cause for concern, though. Two problem daughters would be rather too much to cope with just now.

Cost-U-Less was the Bluebell Estate's one and only supermarket, and it wasn't very super. Unfortunately it was a far cry from the posh one Brenda used to patronise on the other side of town. But Gerry had decided that if they were going to integrate into local life, they must live like the locals. Brenda had demanded acidly if that meant they had to acquire a couple of rotting mattresses for the front garden, but Gerry was so brooding and introverted these days that he hadn't even noticed the jibe. At least they had no need to find themselves a semi-feral mutt or an unmarried daughter in the family way, Brenda had mused; not while Engelbert and Mona were regular visitors to the vicarage.

As she pushed her trolley round the store, Brenda's mood changed from moderately glum to maximally irritated. This place was absolutely useless! They barely had half the things she needed to cook the evening meal.

Eventually, she spotted a scrawny youth on Fruit and Veg, whose skinny neck emerged tortoise-like from a shirt collar at least three sizes too big. 'Excuse me, where can I find the fresh herbs and spices?' she asked.

'The what?'

'The fresh . . . look, these.' She showed him her list but he just looked blank.

'Dunno.' A small thought glimmered briefly in the air above the youth's head. 'I'll get the manager,' he announced, and scuttled for cover.

A couple of minutes later, a slightly older, slightly less scrawny youth in a suit emerged through the back door marked 'private'. 'Terry tells me you're looking for something,' he said. 'Can I help?'

'I'm looking for the fresh herbs and spices.'

'Sorry, we don't do them.'

'Well, what about sharon fruit?'

'You must be kidding.'

It was a desperate, last-ditch plea. 'Organic Brie?'

It was as much as the manager could do not to burst out laughing. 'Sorry madam, but I'm afraid we don't get much call for fancy foods around here.'

209

'Fancy?' All at once, Brenda realised how excruciatingly middle-class she had become: the living embodiment of all the things she'd despised as a teenager on this very estate. It wasn't a pleasant realisation.

'In fact,' the manager continued, 'off the record if we stopped selling fruit and veg altogether, I bet nobody would notice. It's too expensive and half of them don't know how to cook it anyway.'

'Really?'

'Believe me, madam, this is strictly a pie and chips neighbourhood. Of course, I didn't actually say that,' he added. 'Not officially.'

He reached over and whipped a gaily coloured plastic bag from one of the freezers. 'Don't suppose I can interest you in our two-for-one offer on chicken nuggets. They're our number one best-seller this week – well, every week actually.'

The sales director himself, Fraser Gillespie, was there to meet Belle at the end of her induction tour round the works. That in itself was an experience. A member of the Gillespie family which had controlled Green Goddess and its predecessor for over a century, he was a red-haired giant of a man with a giant voice to match, and fiery green eyes that could bore holes in steel plate.

Belle tried not to wince as he crushed her fingers in his welcoming grip. 'Did you enjoy your look round the factory?'

'Yes, thank you – it was very interesting. But I'm very keen to see my office and meet the people I'll be working with.'

'Excellent, excellent, of course you are,' Gillespie boomed. 'Property Services tell me it's all ready and waiting for you.' Sliding open the top drawer of his desk, he took out a key and dropped it into Belle's hand. 'There you go, the keys to your kingdom – or whatever they call it when you're a woman. Straight out of this door, down the stairs, out by reception, across the overspill car park and turn right at the incinerator. You can't miss it.'

Brenda hadn't done so much thinking in ages. Sitting on the only non-vandalised bench in the tatty apology for a park, she reflected on how much she'd changed since she left the estate, all those years ago.

It wasn't just that she'd put on a bit of weight here and there, despite an endless succession of diets and keep-fit classes; or the fact that she now had the odd extra chin. It was much more about the way her attitudes had been transformed, adapting so that she could fit in with the people who'd surrounded her. When all was said and done, St Jude's was a very different place to the Bluebell Estate. And if you happened to originate from that very estate, there were plenty of incentives to quietly forget the fact.

Brenda found herself feeling just a tad ashamed. Not ashamed of her origins, but of the convenient way in which she'd disposed of them, for the sake of harmony and Gerry's precious career. It was almost comical now, thinking how hard she'd striven to be a suitable consort to someone who played occasional golf with the bishop, only for the bishop to turn round and dispatch the pair of them back to the estate Brenda had escaped from in the first place. One pace forward and two back. That was what life consisted of, or so it seemed.

She thought back to the incident in the supermarket. Daft cow, she told herself. How on earth could I have breezed into a place like that, expecting to buy all the silly things that people on the posh side of the tracks like to think are indispensable? It was just plain embarrassing. Have I become an embarrassment too? Someone who doesn't quite fit into either world any more?

These gloomy thoughts lasted no more than a few minutes before others took their place. The manager's comments about the locals' eating habits had struck a chord with Brenda. She well remembered childhood suppers of bread and jam or chips, because there was no money for anything better; and she'd seen all those Jamie Oliver programmes about bad school dinners; but until now it hadn't really occurred to her that there were still people living in that selfsame way, just down the road.

Her organising instincts leapt into play. People round here needed good food and they weren't getting it. And she liked nothing better than a good old-fashioned crusade. If she, Brenda Craine, had been the brains behind the St Jude's Woodworm Appeal Fund, surely she could get vegetables to the needy masses.

As she marched towards the Bluebell community centre, her heart felt lighter already.

Belle's heart, on the other hand, was in her mouth.

Fraser Gillespie had been right: her new office was unmissable. Why? Because it was a Portakabin in the car park, ten yards from the incinerator: a squat prefab, painted grey, with a single dingy window and a ramp up to the door. You bastards, she fumed silently. So much for the 'commitment to prioritising unrivalled customer service'. I'm working in a bloody Portakabin!

She was standing there, staring at it and wondering if just possibly this might be some kind of bad joke, when the door opened and a matronly figure appeared. 'Excuse me, are you Ms Craine?' asked the fifty-something woman with the tight grey perm and Dame Edna glasses.

'Er . . . yes,' admitted Belle. 'Who are you?'

211

'Marilyn Grainger, I'm your PA. Could you come inside please? I want to hand you my resignation.'

Fired with enthusiasm, Brenda spent the next hour hogging the information point in the community centre, trying to find out about healthy eating initiatives in Gloucestershire. There were one or two small schemes, but nothing that seemed to target the Bluebell Estate. Already Brenda's mind was running over the possibilities: maybe divide up some of that field by the church as allotments? Get local farmers and retailers to donate fruit to schools? Or even . . . She snapped her fingers. How about a breakfast club for the kids at the church?

She was deep in thought, and almost jumped out of her skin when someone dealt her a hearty slap on the back.

'Bloody hell, little Brenda Morris!' A deep, masculine chuckle provoked a chorus of 'shhh's' all round the reading room. 'The minute I saw you bending over, I knew it was you!'

Brenda swung round and gave a little gasp of surprise. The man in front of her was fatter, balder and inevitably older than she remembered, but . . . 'Ken Tyler? Ken, it's never you is it?'

A quarter-century rolled away as those crinkly grey eyes twinkled at her. Of course it was Ken. Did she really need to ask? Her heart turned a little back-flip in her chest, and once again she was sixteen and madly in love with the lad whose dad drove the big bin wagon.

'Of course it's me,' he replied with a grin. 'My, but you're looking good, Brenda. Nice to see you with a bit of meat on you.'

Brenda pinked up with embarrassment, and drew him out of the reading room into the lobby, away from quite so many curious eyes. 'I thought you emigrated!'

'I came back. Missed the old stamping ground. Missed you too,' he added with a wink.

'Don't talk rubbish, the last I heard you were marrying that what's-her-name with the big bosoms.'

'Julie,' interjected Ken. 'It's been over twenty years now.'

'Congratulations. See?' Brenda pouted. 'You didn't give a damn about me.'

'Hey! You were all cosy with your holy man by then. What was the point in waiting?'

Brenda had to concede the point. 'I've often thought about you,' she admitted. 'You know, wondered what you were getting up to.'

'Well . . . let's just say I've always cherished a soft spot for you,' said Ken. 'And when I saw about you coming back here in the *Courant*, I was hoping I would run into you. Can I buy you a coffee?'

212

Brenda wondered if it was improper for a vicar's wife to be seen out and about with an old flame, even if that flame had been on the lowest of simmers for over two decades.

'Just for old times' sake?'

His smile was so warm that it melted right through Brenda's scruples. 'All right then, one cup of coffee. Just for old times' sake.'

As they were walking out of the centre, a woman remarked loudly to someone: 'Look, there's that new vicar's wife. Right stuck-up cow, so I heard. Mind you, they're all like that in St Jude's.'

Ken halted, turned round, and silenced her. 'Then you heard wrong, Tracey. This girl's one of us, always has been.' He gave Brenda's arm a squeeze. 'She's all right, is our Brenda.'

In the Portakabin of Doom, three other people were getting acquainted with each other.

'I'm very sorry,' said Marilyn, 'but in the circumstances I really can't accept being demoted like this.'

Zak, the affable nineteen-year-old in the wheelchair, glided across to Belle's desk with three mugs of coffee on a tray. 'You weren't demoted, Marilyn, you were moved sideways,' he reminded her. 'And look at me, I'm only here because I'm a token disabled employee, and they don't know what the hell to do with me 'cause they think if your legs don't work your brain doesn't either.'

Marilyn conceded the point. 'Yes, but I was PA to the managing direc- tor, Zak, John Gillespie himself! And now I'm relegated to this ... this hut, working for somebody who used to be a shop assistant!' She turned to Belle. 'I'm sorry to be impolite, but I had to say that.'

Belle shrugged. 'I've no problem with it,' she replied. 'After all, it's true. I was a shop assistant before I was a deputy manager, and I've never actually managed a store of my own. So I'm as surprised as you are that I've got this job. Mind you,' she continued, surveying the second-hand furniture inside the new Portakabin, 'I don't think anything could surprise me as much as this.'

'It was worse before,' Zak assured her, passing round the biscuit tin.

'Worse? How?' wondered Belle.

'Customer Services was just me and old John Bowers in a corner of the post room. People used to forget we existed until somebody complained about something, and then it was all our fault. At least we've got our own office now.'

Belle sat down in her 'executive' swivel chair. It looked good, but as she lowered her weight onto it, she felt the whole thing subside beneath her. 'I don't understand. If they didn't give a damn about Customer

Services before, why make an effort now?' Not that it's much of an effort, she mused.

'Ah well, that's all down to old Mr Gillespie – John senior,' explained Marilyn. 'He used to say that if the business was run properly, there should be no need for any sort of complaints department because there wouldn't be any complaints. And it wasn't much better after John junior took over. But then we had the incident with the dead rat last year, and after Health and Safety had been round, I think the board thought they'd better get their act together – or at least make some effort to look as if they were.'

Belle contemplated the murky depths of her coffee mug with a touch of unease. 'Dead rat?

'You don't want to know,' said Zak. 'Have another biscuit. Guaranteed rodent-free.'

'Of course,' Marilyn went on, 'the fat cats don't really care about this department at all. It's just a token.'

'All we do,' explained Zak, 'is send out money-off tokens or whatever to people who write in complaining about something, and then forward anything that mentions solicitors to the company secretary. And that's the last we hear of it.'

'That's it?' Belle was horror-stricken. So much for the fine spiel she'd been given at the interview, about rich and varied duties, expanding horizons, increased responsibilities ... Well done, Belle, she thought bitterly. From shop assistant to envelope-stuffer in one stupid move.

'So you see,' Marilyn continued apologetically, 'I really can't work here if that's the sort of low-level work I'd be expected to do.'

Belle nodded. She was thinking. 'What if it wasn't?'

'Sorry?'

'What if it wasn't low-level work? What if I really tried to get this department properly off the ground, expand its remit? I'm not saying I can do it, but I'm willing to give it a try. Of course, a lot depends on how much support the directors are prepared to give us. What do you think?'

Marilyn hesitated. 'I might be prepared to stay,' she replied slowly. 'For a trial period at least.'

'I'm going to need both your help,' Belle stressed. 'A lot of help.'

'Great,' said Zak, pouring the rest of his coffee down his throat. 'So when do we get started?'

Belle's first couple of weeks at Green Goddess HQ had been a baptism of fire. Never in her life had she imagined being so exhausted after achieving so little. Yet she was surprised by her own fighting spirit. She hadn't burst

214

into tears, or run back to Waylon, begging for her job back. And she didn't feel scared any more, just angry. God knows why I ever applied for the stupid job, she thought as she drove back to Cheltenham on Friday night. But now I've got it, what can I do but make the best of it? And I'm going to have a bloody good try. If nothing else, concentrating on work will help me forget about Kieran.

There was one more thing she had to do tonight, before crawling back to her bedsit to sleep the weekend away. And that was to have that long-postponed chat with Jax. She felt guilty that she'd left it so long, but somehow the time had just slipped her fingers. So no matter how knack-ered she felt tonight, this was one duty she wasn't going to put off any longer.

Jax was in her room, apathetically flicking through the insert from a Napalm Death album. 'Hi,' said Belle, hovering on the threshold. 'Can I come in?'

Jax looked her up and down coldly. 'Who are you?' she enquired. 'It's been so long I'm not sure I recognise you.'

Belle decided to take this as an invitation to come in and sit down. 'I'm really sorry it's been so long,' she said as she lowered her bottom onto one of her sister's beanbags.

'Huh,' replied Jax.

'No, really I am,' Belle insisted. 'And it's not as if I haven't been doing anything. I . . . um . . . hope you don't mind, but I phoned your head of year last week, just for a chat.'

Jax sat bolt upright. 'You did what!'

'It's OK, I told her not to breathe a word to Mum and Dad. She was very sympathetic actually, said she'd do her best to help – maybe have a discreet word with that Stacey girl who won't leave you alone.'

'You total prat!' seethed Jax. 'A discreet word? Oh great, now they all think I'm a wuss as well as a weirdo!'

Belle rubbed her aching temples. 'If it was the wrong thing to do, I'm sorry.'

'You keep saying that.'

'Yes, because I am!'

Jax looked daggers. 'Well maybe if you asked me before you did stupid things, you wouldn't have to be sorry!'

Belle wondered if leaving now might be the best solution. Whatever she said or did seemed to rub her sister up the wrong way. 'Look, I'm try-ing to help but obviously I'm going about it completely the wrong way. Shall I just bog off and let you sort it out yourself?'

The haunted look returned to Jax's eyes. 'No. Please don't do that, Belle. I'm . . . sorry.'

Things must be bad, thought Belle. Jax never, ever apologises for anything. 'I'd do anything to help you, you know,' she said softly, 'but when it comes down to it, I think mostly it's better if you do things yourself.' She raised a hand to silence her sister's sarcastic reaction. 'And yes, I know that sounds like a cop-out, but it isn't. Troublemakers like Stacey aren't going to take any notice of anything I do. But you might be able to make them see you differently.'

'Oh, right. So we're back to Mona's master-plan, are we? I put on a blonde wig, some stilettos and a pink velour tracksuit, and suddenly I'm one of the girls? Give me a break.'

The mental image of Jax glowering from underneath a long blonde wig was quite, quite hideous. Belle stifled a chuckle.

'Oh, so I'm funny now, as well as pathetic? Roll up everybody, come and take the piss out of Jax Craine.'

'You're not funny, it's just the idea of you all tarted up. Mind you, Mona does have a point. You could make a bit of an effort to fit in.'

'Why the hell should I want to?'

'They can't all be like Stacey. I bet some of them are really nice when you get to know them, but they're most probably scared stiff of you.'

'That's bollocks.'

'Have you looked at yourself in the mirror lately?'

'I'm not changing just to please a bunch of chavs.'

Belle sighed. 'Nobody's asking you to. I just thought maybe you should start going out a bit, instead of hiding away in your room or spending all your time at Razor's house. Perhaps one weekend the two of you could just happen to turn up at one of the clubs the others go to, then they could see you doing normal stuff, having a good time?'

'I don't do clubbing, you know that. The music sucks.'

Belle shrugged and got to her feet. 'It's your choice,' she said. 'But it must be bloody lonely, being you at the moment.' Then, without intending to, she blurted out: 'Almost as lonely as being me.'

Jax's eyes widened slightly. 'You're never lonely. You've always got stacks of friends, everybody loves nice normal Annabelle.'

'Now let's see. Ros is on the other side of the world, I've left the shop, Clare never seems to be in when I phone her, my half-sister's most likely pregnant by my ex-fiancé, and now I'm working in a prefabricated hut with two people who keep threatening to resign. Oh yes, and all of Kieran's friends are avoiding me, though that's hardly surprising, seeing as he is too.'

'Oh,' said Jax. 'I see what you mean.' She paused. 'Are you sure about Kieran and Mona though?'

'Of course I am.'

'Really, really sure? Only I hardly ever see them together, and Mona never talks about him. And when I asked her, she swore it wasn't true.'

'Maybe he's got bored and dumped her,' speculated Belle. The thought was vaguely comforting.

'Maybe,' conceded Jax, but Belle could see she didn't believe it. And whatever else she might be, Jax was no fool.

Is there just a chance I've got this all wrong? agonised Belle. Oh God I hope not; because if I have, it's far too late to do anything about it.

As Belle was on her way out, Jax piped up: 'About what you said. Fitting in and all that. I'll try if you do.'

'Me?'

Jax managed one of her rare smiles. 'Looks like I'm not the only one round here who could use a friend.'

Chapter 22

The members of the board of Green Goddess Ltd were shuffling their papers together and filing out after a long and tedious meeting.

In the good old days, there'd been virtually no need for formal meetings, since all the Board members were related and nobody ever disagreed with John Gillespie senior. But that was back when Green Goddess was plain old Gillespie's Hygienic Soap Company, and customers were an awful lot easier to please. Transforming the company into Green Goddess might have given it a new lease of life, but it had also sparked off countless boardroom arguments and family squabbles.

These days, there was no guarantee that one Gillespie would be on speaking terms with another, let alone voting the same way. And since the women of the family had started taking an active part in the business too, frankly you couldn't be sure of anything any more. At least, that was how Roderick, the late John senior's brother, saw it. Tricky things, women.

As the others disappeared left the boardroom, Roderick managed to buttonhole John junior in a corner.

'About this girl you've got running Customer Services.'

John folded his arms. 'Annabelle Craine? What about her?'

'I'm hearing the most alarming rumours. You do realise she's trying to turn the whole system inside out?'

John smiled. 'Is she indeed?'

'Don't tell me you didn't know. God knows what Fraser thought he was doing, taking someone like that on. I was expecting some nice little girlie who'd smile a lot and keep things ticking over, the way they always have done, not some harridan who keeps sending me bloody memos.'

At this, John Gillespie could not suppress a gust of laughter. 'Harridan? That's not quite how she struck me.'

Old Roderick was less than amused. 'It's no laughing matter,' he insisted, pulling a sheaf of papers from his briefcase. 'Look at these memos: re setting up of customer database, re logging of complaints, re upgrading of website, re expansion of Customer Service departmental remit – don't tell me you haven't been getting them too.'

John contemplated his uncle with a kind of affectionate scorn. 'You really are an old Luddite, aren't you, Uncle Roddy?'

Roderick puffed out his pigeon chest. 'This firm was founded on traditional lines, and that's the way it should stay. If you ask me, the rot set in when we voted to go "organic", whatever that's supposed to mean. All these changes . . . they're just not necessary.'

'If we'd left everything to you,' John pointed out, 'we'd still be making carbolic soap and pan scourers. Second thoughts, we wouldn't. Because we'd have gone out of business years ago.'

'Nonsense.' Stubborn to the last, Roderick jabbed a finger in his nephew's face. 'Somebody needs to put that girl in her place, before she gets any more bright ideas.'

'Actually, I happen to think she's in exactly the right place already.'

'But the girl's sticking her nose in everywhere, questioning the way we do things, she even wants to set up customer focus groups, for pity's sake! Frankly, she's a complete pain in the backside.'

John picked up his briefcase with a smile. 'Thanks for telling me,' he said. 'It's nice to know I picked exactly the right person for the job.'

What had started with a quick coffee in the local greasy spoon had become the renewal of an old friendship Brenda had thought she'd lost forever.

She and Ken Tyler couldn't ever be what they'd once been to each other, of course, but where was the harm in enjoying each other's company? Ken's wife Julie didn't seem interested in anything but TV soaps and breeding little yappy dogs, and as for Gerry . . .

Gerry had become so depressed by the minuscule Sunday congregations that he'd even persuaded himself that his pet project – the forthcoming Alpha course – was going to be a complete flop. Was the Bluebell Estate really interested in finding out about the fundamentals of Christianity? It seemed increasingly unlikely to Gerry, despite his initial optimism. These days he was so deeply absorbed in his own anxieties that he no longer bothered to ask what his wife did when she wasn't baking cakes for church functions that nobody bothered to attend.

Besides, thought Brenda as she and Ken printed off posters on the computer in the library, everything they were doing was designed to help Gerry rescue St Mungo's from terminal decline. So her conscience was completely clear, even if she did experience the occasional teenage frisson when her eyes met Ken's over the photocopier.

'These should do the trick,' said Ken confidently as he patted the posters into a neat pile.

'You don't think it's the wrong time of year to be recruiting then?' asked Brenda. 'I mean, we're getting towards the summer, and who plays football in the summer?'

'Ah, but if we're going to start a St Mungo's under-twelves' side, we need to have them signed up now,' explained Ken. 'That way, we can get them registered in the local boys' league ready for the new season. Don't worry,' he added with a grin, 'darts teams, rugby teams, even cheeserolling . . . I've done this kind of thing loads of times before. And you said it yourself, the vicar's really keen on getting these things up and running as soon as possible.'

Ken had indeed done a lot of things loads of times before; for Ken was the Mr Fixit of the Bluebell Estate. Even in her most optimistic mood, Brenda couldn't have hoped for a more useful local contact. With the exception of a few years abroad, he'd lived all his life round here. He knew everybody and everybody knew – and more importantly, liked – him. When Ken said something, people tended to listen. Quite simply, Ken was the one bit of good luck Brenda had had since she arrived at St Mungo's vicarage, and she intended making the most of him.

'So we've got the football team and the breakfast club planned out, and we're thinking about letting Golden Valley jazz club use the church on Mondays . . . What about starting a choir?' pondered Brenda. 'Every church needs a choir.'

'Steady on,' laughed Ken. 'I think St Mungo's needs a congregation first. But maybe you're right, a choir's a nice way of getting the kids involved. And you never know, maybe one or two of the football lads will turn out to have decent voices. Anyhow, I'll put the word around that there's a new football team looking for players. I'm sure there'll be some interest: there's not much else for kids to do round here.'

Brenda fiddled with one of her earrings. Just lately she'd taken to wearing them again, even treating herself to a couple of cheap new pairs; they made her feel like less of a drudge and more of a woman. Even if Gerry didn't ever notice them.

'They're nice, are those earrings,' commented Ken. 'The dangly ones always did suit you – they go with the shape of your face.' Brenda coloured up slightly, more from pleasure than embarrassment. 'Now, let's get out there and put some of these posters up.'

As they walked round the estate handing out flyers and putting up posters, they shared ideas for other things that might help the St Mungo's revival campaign. Brenda found herself surprisingly relaxed in Ken's company; more so in fact than when they were teenage sweethearts and raging adolescent hormones had got in the way of proper conversation.

'The church hall hardly ever gets used for anything,' remarked Ken. 'You could make a decent income from letting it out.'

'Except for the fact it's getting vandalised every five minutes,' pointed out Brenda.

'Ah, but the kids who are doing it are just bored. Give them something else to do at the church hall and maybe they'll stop trashing the place.'

'What, a youth club you mean?'

Ken wrinkled his nose. 'Maybe not that exactly. Youth clubs can be a bit patronising. But somewhere kids can meet up and play pool, maybe a few skateboard ramps in the car park . . . that sort of thing. I know a few big local lads who might be willing to supervise, make sure there was no fighting or drugs or anything.'

Brenda chuckled. 'You seem to know somebody for every possible circumstance!'

'Ah well, you meet a lot of interesting people when you're a bin man,' he replied. 'Not to mention the interesting stuff they chuck out.' He pondered for a moment. 'How about yoga?'

'Pardon?'

'Yoga. For the church hall. It's the big thing at the moment. They have it in the church hall in Whaddon, and it goes down a storm with the ladies. The oldies, too.'

'Yes, why not? And there's that church in Montpellier that lets its hall out for Scottish country dancing every Friday night.'

'Can't quite see that catching on round here,' laughed Ken. 'But you could try letting it out to some of the local bands who need somewhere to practise.'

Brenda nibbled a fingernail. 'It's not really church stuff though, is it? That's what Gerry might say. I mean, yoga's not exactly religious – unless you're a Hindu. All the same, it does get people involved . . .'

'That's it,' agreed Ken. 'And some of them might just decide to give one of Gerry's services a try. Anyway, which would he rather have, a hall full of people enjoying themselves, or nobody at all?'

There was really only one answer to that.

Brenda might have rediscovered an old friend, but Belle was feeling downright lonely.

Marilyn and Zak had turned out to be nice enough people to work with, but it was tiring and frustrating trying to change things without any support from her superiors. She knew she could have sat back, put her feet up and gone back to sending out money-off vouchers like her predecessor, and at least old fogies like Roderick Gillespie would be happy. But that would make the whole job-changing exercise completely pointless. She might just as well have stayed at the shop, where at least she'd have had some say in the way it was run. Besides, right now her life was in desperate need of a goal, and she bloody well wasn't going to give up the struggle to establish herself, just so that people could smirk and say 'I told you so.'

Even so, her new-found determination to make something of her career didn't ease the loneliness. She'd lost count of the number of times she'd phoned Clare lately, only to get her answering machine, which couldn't be recording her messages properly, because Clare hardly ever called back. When she occasionally did, her calls generally amounted to 'I'm really sorry but I can't chat now, I'm busy.'

As for the friends and acquaintances she'd made with Kieran, either they were deliberately keeping their distance, or Belle found it too painful to approach them. Just chatting to someone in the street could bring back a whole coach load of unwelcome memories. Belle had done with memories; all they did was hurt. From now on, all she was going to care about was the future. Her future.

What about Ros though? She was part of the past – and with any luck, the future. It was just the present that was the problem, because right now Ros wasn't even on the same continent. Belle would have given anything for one of their long girlie chats. Ros could make her see the funny side of anything.

But Ros wasn't available, which was why Belle kept gravitating back to the shop every time she had a day off or an excuse to drive to Cheltenham 'for business'. Lily was always pleased to see her, and to Belle's surprise, she'd quickly struck up a rapport with Jerszy, her replacement. She listened while he rhapsodised about his girlfriend in Cracow, and he seemed to empathise when Belle told him how alone she felt. It was an odd relationship, but it seemed to work rather well. Belle had started to look forward to their conversations.

On this particular morning, Jerszy greeted her with an excited smile and a badge that read 'Employee of the Month'.

'It was Waylon's idea,' explained Lily. 'He thought we all needed a bit of motivating, without you to boss us around. Jerszy's the teacher's pet, aren't you Jerszy?'

'Good for him.' Belle turned to Lily. 'I didn't really boss you all around, did I? Tell me that was a joke.'

'No can do,' replied Lily apologetically. 'You could be a real tyrant when you were in the mood! Never mind though, it's all good experience for what you're doing now, by the sound of it. Now you're in the Big Time.'

'Big Time?' Belle groaned. 'Now you really are joking. Unfortunately the people in my office don't need bossing about, and the others spend all their time bossing me.' She turned her attentions to Jerszy. 'You look like you're doing OK for yourself, though. I don't think I've ever seen anybody look so happy.'

He grinned even more broadly. 'It is a very good week. First Mr Waylon gives me this badge, then I have news from home. Masha's mother is much better, she maybe not need operation after all.'

Belle felt the sheer exhilaration and relief pouring out of him, and it seemed to lift her out of her own self-pity. 'Oh Jerszy, I'm so pleased for you. Really, really pleased.'

Then, quite without intending to, she hugged him; and he hugged right back. It was a bit like being hugged by a huge blond teddy-bear, comforting and warm. In her solitary frame of mind, she hadn't realised just how much she needed a really big, rib-crushing hug. It felt so good that she hugged Lily too, bump and all, until the two of them collapsed in giggles.

'What was that for?' gasped Lily, through her laughter.

'I don't know,' Belle giggled back, feeling lighter and airier than she had in ages. 'It just felt like the right thing to do.'

What it really felt like was coming home.

Kieran would have quite liked a chance to be alone for a while. The way he'd been feeling lately, the entire human race could fall off the edge of the planet and he wouldn't give a damn. He'd just have more peace and quiet to sit in his flat and mope along to a soundtrack of Morrissey and Leonard Cohen.

So he wasn't overjoyed when the girl from the reception desk at the *Courant* rang the features office to tell him he had a visitor.

'I'm not expecting anyone,' he objected. 'Who is it?'

'A Ms Levenshulme. She seems very keen to see you right away.'

Levenshulme? Kieran racked his brains. He didn't know any ... hang about though, wasn't that the surname of Belle's friend Clare, the one with the psychotic stalker brother? If it was her, why the hell would she want to see him? Come to that, he added, why the hell would I want to see her?

'Tell her I'm busy,' he said. 'Take her number and I'll get back to her.'

All done and dusted. So he was more than a little surprised a few minutes later, when the office door swung open and Clare Levenshulme herself sashayed in, looking particularly curvaceous in a well-cut, Forties-style suit and elegant heels. 'Kieran Sawyer?' She extended a hand. 'Yes, of course you are, I recognise you now. How could I forget such a handsome face? I'm Clare, by the way.'

'I know who you are,' replied Kieran, 'but I think there's been a mistake. I told the receptionist not to—'

Clare laid a delicate, well-manicured hand on his arm. 'Don't blame her Kieran, to be honest I sort of pushed my way in. I'm that kind of girl, I'm afraid. When I want something I just go for it.'

'Oh,' said Kieran, moderately amused by the woman's vampish style. She was a lot less scary than he'd expected her to be. Still, if she was who he thought she was, the possession of a slightly nutty brother didn't necessarily make her strange too. 'So do I assume you want something from me?'

She beamed. 'I certainly do. You see, I'm in charge of my company's advertising and PR, and I'm looking at the possibility of having an advertorial written about the company and published in the *Courant*. Maybe even a full-colour pull-out supplement,' she added enticingly.

'Ah well, that's not my department I'm afraid,' Kieran replied. 'You want Advertising Services, on the ground floor. Shall I phone down for you?'

Clare's hand was on his arm again, only this time the grip was tighter and the nails were digging in. 'Like I said,' she went on, 'I want something from you. I want to talk to you about it – you and nobody else, is that quite clear?'

He shrugged. 'I suppose so, but—'

'You can take the details and pass them on to whoever you like.'

'Well . . . OK, whatever.'

Clare's face relaxed once again into a smile. 'Excellent. Anyway, what I'd like to do is take you out for dinner tomorrow night, so we can discuss it properly. At our leisure.' The tip of her tongue ran along the bottom of her upper lip. 'I take it you don't have any objections to a little tête-à-tête?'

Razor took hold of Jax's hand, and for once she didn't pull it away. 'You look great,' he enthused. 'Absolutely blinding. My gorgeous Goth princess, that's what you are.'

'Empress,' Jax corrected him.

'Yes, of course. Don't know what I was thinking of.' He gave her hand a reassuring squeeze. 'You'll knock 'em dead.'

'Yeah? Well, someone's going to die if those bitches don't stop blanking me,' she retorted with a confidence she didn't feel.

'Maybe I could—' began Razor, but Jax stopped him.

'Don't start offering to beat them up again. It's kind of sweet that you want to, but you can't even swat flies without worrying if you hurt them. Face it, Razor, violence just isn't your bag.' She grinned ferociously. 'It's mine.'

She stood in front of her bedroom mirror and appraised her clubbing finery. The hair was still predominantly blue, but she'd combed some wash-out silver dye through it for a bit of extra drama. Her top was a black, bell-sleeved T-shirt with BLOOD written across the front in wobbly crimson letters, and she was wearing her favourite red PVC trousers with a black net skirt over the top. As an enormous concession for the occasion, she'd replaced her beloved big boots with a pair of beaded Moroccan slippers. If she did – as her mother said – look like a dog's dinner, then it was a dinner for a very superior kind of dog.

As for Razor, he had gone for a vaguely nineteenth-century look, somewhere between Heathcliff and Mr Hyde, only a lot bigger and burlier. He looked like the kind of bloke who might draw a swordstick and skewer your vitals, or snap your neck with a flick of the wrist. So it was rather ironic that he was about as hard as a strawberry marshmallow. Bless you, thought Jax in a moment of tenderness; you're just a sheep in wolf's clothing – and a pretty soft sheep at that.

'If you're nervous we don't have to go,' ventured Razor. 'I mean, they're only a bunch of stupid kids. We could go round to my house instead and meet up with some of the gang from St Jude's.'

The forbidden word made Jax's eyes flash with rage. 'I am NOT nervous,' she snapped. 'Have you got that?'

'Er . . . yes. Loud and clear.'

'Well what are you waiting for? Hurry up, you big daft lump, we've got a club to go to.'

Jax and Razor weren't the only people with places to go. While they were taking a taxi to Club Casablanca, Kieran was sitting at a table in a posh Italian restaurant, waiting for Clare Levenshulme.

Not for the first time, he wondered what the bloody hell he was doing here. Like he'd told her, arranging and writing advertorials for outside companies had absolutely nothing to do with him. The sales department handled all that kind of thing. But Clare Levenshulme was a pushy sort of girl, and he knew that unless he played this her way, the *Courant* wasn't going to get the business at all.

There was more to it than that, though. Kieran was intrigued by her. Why was she so dead set on dealing with him? Why wouldn't somebody else do? Misgivings niggled away at him. Clare was friendly with Belle: he hoped this wasn't some ploy to deliver a tirade about how badly he'd treated her friend, or fling a custard pie in his face or something.

He didn't have much longer to wonder, because as he glanced towards the door of the restaurant it opened and she glided in, wafting a sweet aura of Poison before her.

Her glossy red lips curved into a delighted smile as she caught sight of Kieran and headed for the table. 'Hi, Kieran, hope you don't mind eating here. It's always been one of my favourite restaurants.'

Kieran shrugged. 'Fine by me. I don't often get taken out for a free dinner.'

Clare ordered a bottle of red wine. 'Really? That's terrible. A sexy guy like you should be out every night.'

'That's ... um ... very flattering,' said Kieran, feeling rather uncomfortable.

She leaned over, giving him a better view of her impressive cleavage. 'Oh no, it's not flattery – it's perfectly true. Besides,' she added breathily, 'they say flattery gets you nowhere. And nowhere's definitely not where I'm aiming to get.'

Alarms went off in Kieran's mind. Is this woman hitting on me? No, she can't be, she's just messing around. Yes, she is, she's hitting on you!

He eased his collar away from his overheated neck. 'Shall we get on to this advertorial you'd like us to do?' he suggested, hastily changing the subject.

'No thanks,' she replied. 'We can talk about that later. Much later. What I want to talk about right now is you.' She was practically purring at him. 'And me.'

Chapter 23

While Kieran and Clare were furthering their acquaintance, Jax and Razor were having slight problems dancing the night away.

The doorman at the Casablanca looked them up and down. 'Sorry, no weirdos.'

'We're not weirdos!' protested Razor. A little way behind them in the queue to get in, Jax's nemesis Stacey was giggling unpleasantly.

'You look like it to me,' insisted the doorman. 'Talk about "Dracula is risen from the grave". You need to get some serious fashion advice, mate.'

'And a life,' sniggered Stacey. She's already pissed, thought Jax disdainfully. I can smell her breath from here.

Jax was all for lunging at Stacey, but Razor held her back. 'Oh go on, please let us in,' he pleaded. And he took the lone twenty-pound note from his wallet and flashed it at the doorman. 'Please?'

'Well ...' The doorman pocketed the twenty. 'All right.' He jabbed a podgy finger at Jax. 'She can come in 'cause I like the look of 'er, but you're staying out. You look like the sort what cause trouble.'

'You can't do that!'

'Oh yes I can. So what's it to be, one in or both out?'

Razor was all set to turn and leave, with Jax on his arm, but unexpectedly she pulled away. 'OK,' she said. 'I'm going in.'

Razor was horrified. 'In there? Without me?'

'I'll be fine.'

'But ... you can't!'

'Don't you tell me what I can and can't do!'

'How will you get back?'

She tossed her haughty blue and silver head. 'In a taxi. I'm not completely helpless you know. Go home, Razor. Looks like this is one battle I'm going to have to fight on my own.'

*

227

God I hate this place, thought Jax a split second after walking into the Club Casablanca. The decor was supposed to look richly exotic in a North African sort of way, but really it just looked like someone had gone mad with a fretsaw and a lot of painted plywood, plus a few of those crappy square lanterns, pre-rusted to give them that authentic sand-blasted look.

It was bargain basement kitsch, and it was obvious that Stacey and her squealing posse loved it. Mind you, thought Jax, even I might learn to love it if I had that much drink inside me. She wondered how many pubs Stacey's crowd had visited on their way to the club . . . and whether her advanced state of inebriation might make her any friendlier.

She forced herself to push through the crowds to where they were standing, giggling over the available talent and awarding marks out of ten. Stacey herself was pointing an unsteady finger into the mass of dancers. 'That one,' she said, stifling a belch. 'Anyone want to bet me I can't get into his pants before the end of tonight?'

The idea was greeted with gales of laughter. Stacey's reputation was pretty awesome.

More laughter accompanied Jax's arrival. 'Oh look.' Stacey's mate Tray nudged her in the ribs. 'It's the Freakoid.'

'Hi,' said Jax, trying her very, very hardest not to lose her temper and smack somebody into the middle of next week. 'Having a good time?'

Stacey blinked slightly unfocused eyes. 'You. Freakoid.' The eyes narrowed. 'What're you doing here?'

'Just having a night out, like you.'

'The Freakoid, in a nightclub?' goaded Tray. 'Shouldn't you be out raiding the blood bank or something?'

Jax's teeth clenched with the painful effort of being civil to this bunch of creeps. 'Oh, you know. Thought I'd try lager instead.'

'Well piss off back to your coffin,' snapped Stacey. 'You're making the place stink.'

It was around eleven, and Jax was bored out of her skull. She'd spent the last hour propping up the bar, trying to filter out any interesting bits of the barman's conversation and discovering that there weren't any. Was it Sartre who'd said that hell was other people? It was certainly true if the other people were the patrons of the Club Casablanca.

A hand tapped her on the shoulder. 'Wanna dance?'

Without even turning round, she growled, 'No.'

'Oh go on.'

This time she gave him the full five-thousand-volt glare, and the small, inoffensive-looking youth in the Star Trek shirt shrank like a slug in a salt cellar. 'I said no!'

She glanced across to where the girls from the comprehensive were dancing. Well, more shuffling than dancing; they were all half-cut. Should she go over and make another attempt at being sociable? Oh fuck it. Why the hell should she humiliate herself in some feeble attempt to be accepted by a bunch of obnoxious harpies? Maybe it was time to take Stacey's advice and piss off.

As she tossed the last of her lager down her throat, she noticed that Stacey and Tray were heading for the bar. If they saw her, they gave no indication of it.

'Two more vodkas. Doubles,' ordered Stacey.

'Trebles,' giggled Tray. 'Your round.'

'Fuck.' Stacey rummaged in her little silver purse, turned it upside down and found just a single solitary pound coin. 'Out of dosh.'

'I can—' began Tray. But Stacey already had the problem in hand.

'Cash machine round the corner,' she declared. 'Back in five.'

Jax watched her as she moved slowly and with excessive care across the floor of the club to the front door, had a quick word with the doorman and disappeared outside. Let's see, thought Jax. Either I can hang around until my nemesis comes back and insults me some more, or I can bugger off home.

Right now, home sounded really good.

At about the time Jax was heading for home, Clare was driving aimlessly around the darkened streets.

Home held no attraction for Clare. Nothing attracted her any more; nothing filled her with excitement, or warmth, or desire. The only emotions that inhabited her body now were fury and resentment.

Tonight was supposed to be her crowning glory, the moment when she finally got her revenge on that callous bitch Annabelle, for what she'd done to poor Max. He'd had a dazzling future ahead of him when he first met Belle, but she'd put a stop to that. No way would he ever have left medical school and moved to a squat to work with junkies, if she hadn't dumped him like that and broken his spirit. He'd have been well on the way to being a top London consultant by now. All that rubbish about him being obsessive was precisely that. And what he'd told his sister, about 'developing a social conscience' and 'reassessing what he really wanted out of life' was just his way of protecting Belle.

All he'd ever wanted was love. Belle's love.

Clare had been working her way up to this moment for months, glorying in the gradual disintegration of her pretend friend's life. Little by little she'd helped to dismantle the relationship between Belle and Kieran, and tonight she had planned to take things that one essential step further.

There was no possibility that it could go wrong. Clare was after all irresistible. She'd treated the men in Paris like dogs, and still had them cringing at her feet, begging her to love them. She was quite sure Kieran would be the same as all the rest.

Instead of which, he had spent the entire evening talking about nothing but Belle. Belle, Belle, that bloody bitch Belle and nothing else. The moment he'd realised that Clare was interested in him, he'd made his excuses and fled like a rat back to its sewer.

She was still trembling with the humiliation of being left alone in that restaurant, a failure for all to see.

She wasn't done for yet though. She still had fight in her, and if she had to she'd walk barefoot across hot coals to make Belle Craine suffer.

She was doing it for the only man she'd ever truly cared about: her beloved brother, Max.

Jax finished her drink, collected her jacket from the cloakroom and headed for the exit. The doorman caught her by the arm as she passed. 'You can't get back in without a pass.' He rubbed his fingers together under her nose. 'Ten quid to you.'

'I don't think so, thanks.' She extricated her arm with dignity. 'I wouldn't come back in here if you paid me.'

As she stepped from the smoky-blue fug of the nightclub into the fresh May evening, Jax took a long, deep breath. So much for Belle and her ever-optimistic advice. Her trouble was, Belle always made the mistake of thinking that human beings were nice. But you couldn't make friends with people who thought you were scum ... especially if you thought they were scum too. Looked like she'd have to take the other route Belle had outlined, the coward's way out: tell Mum and Dad and get them to transfer her to a different school. That made her angry and sad. Jax Craine hated to be on the losing side.

She shrugged on her jacket and was about to turn right and head for the taxi rank when a horrible sound tore through the night air.

A girl's scream.

There it was again, louder and more hysterical now, and very close at hand. Shouldn't something be happening? Shouldn't policemen be arriving in droves? But nothing did. Instinctively, Jax headed for the source of the sound and as she rounded the corner into Mafeking Street, she saw.

Stacey and a man were struggling by the cash machine. She was kicking out and screaming, but he was far stronger, more purposeful, and less drunk. As she hesitated, Jax saw the man seize what he'd wanted and fling Stacey away from him. She hit her head on the wall and slid down into an inert heap of flesh.

Then the man turned and as he did he saw Jax staring right back at him. As their eyes met, Jax started running.

Chapter 24

Stacey awoke with the biggest, fattest, most violent headache she'd ever had in her life. She'd had plenty of hangovers in the last couple of years, but never one that could compare with this.

Her eyes squinted painfully in the light reflected off the pale green ceiling. Pale green? Not her own bedroom then. Maybe she'd got lucky and gone home with that guy in the—

She turned over in bed, and was violently sick.

'There, there, never mind, better out than in,' said the staff nurse, wiping her mouth and popping a paper cover over the bowl of vomit. 'You'll feel better now.' She patted the pillows around Stacey's head. 'You're in the General, dear. Your mum and dad have just popped out for a breath of fresh air. You had a bit of an accident last night.'

'An ... accident?' Her fuzzy memories slowly coming back into focus, she struggled to sit up in. That was when she saw the other person, sitting on a chair beside her, looking about as comfortable as Dracula on a sunbed.

Stacey started and winced as her head filled with pain. 'You! What the hell are you doing here?'

The nurse smiled and answered the question herself. 'Jacqueline's been sitting here with you all night,' she revealed. 'You're a very lucky girl, you know. She saved your life.'

'What? Her?' Stacey strained to remember. Then it all came back to her in a rush: the dance, the drink, the man at the cash machine ... and Jax. 'Oh God no,' she groaned.

And promptly passed out again.

Marilyn and Zak were full of sympathy, but there wasn't much they could do to help Belle.

'It was bound to happen,' mused Zak. 'You have been rattling a lot of people's cages, haven't you? Not that that's a bad thing,' he added. 'I mean, I've been having the time of my life since you arrived.'

'Yes, well, I must say my job's been a whole lot more stimulating since you've been sending us out there, following up complaints,' nodded Marilyn, a touch wistfully. 'But it does rather look like the party's over. A summons to John junior's office is no laughing matter.'

'It could have been worse,' Zak pointed out. 'It could've been Roderick. Then you could be certain you were getting the sack.'

Belle felt curiously blasé about it all. She'd enjoyed working with Zak and Marilyn, savoured the Dunkirk spirit they'd built up together. But she knew perfectly well that in her relatively lowly position, she couldn't go on annoying important people – however legitimately – forever and get away with it. Besides, she'd known almost from the start that this job wasn't right for her. She wondered if she'd have been so recklessly gung-ho if she'd been desperate to keep it.

She shrugged. 'Like you said, it had to happen. I've been expecting a summons to the top floor for ages.' She got up from her desk and slowly put on her jacket. 'I ... er ...'

'Never say die,' commanded Zak, brandishing his lunchtime baguette like a sword of justice.

'Right on.' Belle smiled. 'I'll see you later,' she promised.

'Yes,' sighed Marilyn as the Portakabin door closed behind Belle. 'When she comes back to clear her desk.'

JOHN GILLESPIE, JUNIOR: MANAGING DIRECTOR, read the nameplate on the door.

'You can go in,' his PA reminded her, with one of those 'I know what's in store for you' smiles. 'He's expecting you.'

There was nothing for it. Belle took a deep breath, knocked and entered without waiting for a response.

John Gillespie was standing with his back to her, gazing out of the window over the Green Goddess factory.

'Do you realise how long we've been doing things a certain way at Green Goddess?'

'A long time?' ventured Belle, hovering near the door.

'Years and bloody years.' The MD swung round to confront her. 'And then you come along out of nowhere, and in the space of a few weeks you've turned everything upside down. You've had my ex-PA firing off memos every five minutes, and that boy in the wheelchair's been terrorising the production department about customer complaints. Some of the directors are baying for your head on a plate, I can tell you.'

'I'm not surprised.'

'So – do you have anything more to say for yourself?' he demanded.

233

'I'm ... um ... very sorry?' ventured Belle, wondering if he'd spot the insincerity in her eyes.

'Hm,' grunted Gillespie. 'Well, you shouldn't be. You're the best thing to happen to Green Goddess in years.'

'What?' said Belle faintly.

'Unsafe practices, inadequate customer support, outdated technology, unofficial use of non-organic ingredients ... The very fact that my old fogey of an uncle Roderick thinks you're the spawn of the Devil shows that you're doing everything right.' His ferocious face softened and he stuck out a hand. 'Congratulations on an impressive debut, Annabelle.'

'Er ... thanks.'

'Hope you weren't worried when you got called up to my office. I just wanted to say thanks, you're doing great, and if you carry on the way you are doing, you've got a great future in store at Green Goddess.

'Between you and me, I'm planning a management buyout of this rotting heap of a company, and there's definitely a place for you in my plan. If things go right, Green Goddess will be going global.'

Belle swallowed hard. 'That's really kind of you,' she said with an embarrassed smile, extricating her squashed fingers from his enthusiastic handshake. 'But the thing is ...' She rummaged in her jacket pocket and withdrew a long white envelope. 'I've come to hand in my resignation.'

That evening Belle drove home in her comfy old car, relieved to have done the right thing but wondering just what was going to happen next.

She knew everybody would think she was mad, giving up the job just when she was starting to do it really well. Maybe she was. But being able to do something and wanting to do it weren't necessarily the same thing. And as she'd settled into the job, Belle had become more and more acutely aware that this person she was pretending to be, this role she was playing, just wasn't her.

Proving she could be a career success had seemed like a good idea for a while; both a distraction and a way of getting back at Kieran. But nothing was worth that horrible feeling of being like a bicycle caught in a tramline, inexorably directed towards a place she didn't want to go. Yes, relief; that was all she felt. Maybe the regrets would come later, but she seriously doubted it.

All things considered, Mr Gillespie had been very understanding, and inclined to agree that Marilyn would make a competent successor to Belle in Customer Services. But that didn't solve the problem of what to do with Belle. All she wanted was to get back into frontline store management, preferably with Green Goddess, but that depended on vacancies. And what if the only ones that turned up were in Inverness? Or Norwich? She'd never been further than a day trip to London, if you didn't count package holidays. She just wasn't the adventurous kind – or at least, she never had been in the past.

Was this going to be an adventure too far?

She wasn't alone with her thoughts for long, because just as she was parking outside her flat, her mobile rang: it was her mum. Great timing, she thought. I'm really not quite ready to tell you that I've just torpedoed my own career.

'Annabelle? Annabelle, you have to come round right now. It's Jacqueline.'

'Jax? What's wrong with her?'

'That's what I want you to find out. She didn't come home all night, just phoned me up at two in the morning to tell me she was "fine", and then when she finally crawls in with Razor in tow, she has a black eye and a split lip!'

Belle raised an eyebrow. 'Really? Well what does she have to say for herself?'

'Nothing,' replied Brenda in frustration. 'Absolutely not one word. And Razor's just as bad.'

Possibly the last person Belle would have wanted to see was Mona; but after all was said and done, even if she was renting rooms above the Royal Shakespeare now, she was still ... sort of ... a member of the family.

When Belle arrived, Mona was up in Jax's room, trying to coax some sort of information, however scanty, from her. But Jax and Razor were putting up a united front.

Jax looked up in annoyance at Belle's arrival. 'Oh no, not you as well. Has Mum been phoning round the whole of Gloucestershire?'

'No, just the bit that's related to you,' replied Belle. 'So what have you been up to this time then? That's a very impressive black eye you've got, by the way.'

Jax fingered it gingerly. 'You should see the other guy,' she replied with grim pleasure.

'What other guy?' demanded Mona.

'Nobody. Look, I told you – everything's sorted.'

'Like she said.' Razor nodded. 'Everything's sorted now, so can you please leave her alone?'

Belle and Mona repaired to the lounge. 'Well?' demanded Brenda.

'Nothing,' replied Belle with an apologetic shrug. 'I expect she'll talk when she's ready.'

'Daughters!' exclaimed Brenda and bustled off upstairs. 'Listen to me Jacqueline, I'm your mother and I'm not going anywhere until you tell me where you got yourself in that mess.'

'Good luck,' commented Mona with a half-smile. 'That kid's not going to talk for anybody till she's good and ready.'

'What do you know?' grunted Belle, uncomfortable about being alone in a room with her half-sister – and even more uncomfortable at finding herself in agreement with her.

'Enough,' replied Mona.

Belle seethed. 'What's that supposed to mean?'

Mona sighed. 'Nothing – I just meant, I've been here a while and by now I know a bit about the whole family. Even you.'

Belle scowled. 'Oh yeah? I suppose you got all that from your cosy little tête-à-têtes with Kieran, did you?'

'Oh for God's sake!' groaned Mona. 'Look, I'm not going to try to tell you again what really happened, because I know you won't believe me. All I'm going to say is, why won't you phone Kieran?'

Belle stared back at her, wondering if this was some sneaky form of torture. 'Phone Kieran? Why the hell would I want to do that? So he can humiliate me again? No thanks.'

'Look – I know you don't like me—'

'Oh, so you do know something then?'

'But for my sins it just so happens that I quite like you, so will you shut up just for five seconds?' Belle gaped. 'Thanks. Listen to me, Belle, Kieran's totally miserable without you. He talks about you all the time. He'd be so pleased if you'd just pick up the phone and give him a call.'

At last, Belle found her voice. 'That's a very touching picture you're painting there, Mona,' she said, 'but it doesn't really fit what other people are telling me. Other people I trust,' she added.

'Meaning?'

'Well, Clare among others.'

Mona shook her head slowly. 'Maybe you don't know Clare as well as you think you do,' she suggested. 'Maybe she's not as—'

'Bloody hell, Mona, why do people keep trying to make me think bad thoughts about Clare?' Belle felt the sting of tears under her eyelids. 'She's the only true friend I've got.'

'If you say so,' said Mona quietly.

'I do. And why should I listen to you anyway? You've done nothing but lie to me since you got here.'

*

236

That evening, as Belle sat fiddling around on her PC and pondering her future, the phone rang. It was Clare.

'Hi, Belle darling. How are you feeling?'

'Oh . . . you know.'

'You handed your resignation in today, didn't you? Ah well, I'm sure it's for the best.' Clare sounded positively pleased. 'I mean, concentrating on your career's never been your thing really, has it?'

'No. You're right.' She didn't feel much like talking about it, though – or about anything much. Solitary brooding was much more in keeping with her mood, especially after her conversation with Mona. Was there any chance that what she'd said about Kieran was true?

'I'm really sorry to make things worse,' Clare went on in her gentle, sweet voice, 'but there's something I really think you should know.'

'Go on,' said Belle. It can't make me feel much worse, she thought to herself.

'Well . . . I was passing that really posh Italian restaurant in town the other night – you know, the one on Suffolk Parade? – and I'm afraid . . . oh no, I can't say it.'

'Say it.'

Clare took a deep breath. 'I happened to glance through the window and I . . . I saw Kieran inside. Having dinner with a girl.'

A slight shiver ran across Belle's body, but after all, dinner was only dinner. 'Maybe it was a client from work?' she suggested.

'I don't think so,' replied Clare. 'Not the way he was kissing her over dessert. I'm afraid you're going to have to face facts, Belle; Kieran's got himself a new girlfriend. And from what I saw, it looks pretty serious.'

Belle didn't cry. She didn't lose her temper. She didn't feel an awful lot at all, really; just a dull ache that had been there before, but which seemed to have grown a little deeper, a fraction darker.

So Kieran had a new girl in his life; so what? He was a free agent, and either Mona was being malicious, or she'd seriously got the wrong end of the stick. Either way, Belle had to try and put him out of her mind.

A little after ten, Ros came through on the PC, eager for an online chat. 'How's it going, kid?'

'Pants. Don't start telling me how fantastic it is out there, or I'll pull the plug on you.'

'Oh dear, sounds pretty bad. Looks like I need to get back to Blighty asap.'

Belle started. 'Come home? Really? When?'

237

'Oh . . . soon. As soon as I've done Australia, I'm getting bored with all this gallivanting. And I miss you. Anyhow,' she went on, 'it's next stop Oz and you'll never guess what: I've blagged an invitation to visit the *Neighbours* studios in Melbourne!

'Anybody you'd like me to look up while I'm there?'

Chapter 25

As it happened, Australia was also on the minds of patrons at the Royal Shakespeare Tavern. Big Bob had just come back from a holiday with his daughter, and was threatening to bore everybody with snaps of his new baby granddaughter.

Mona felt quite nostalgic as the photos were passed round. It wasn't the clichéd things that made you homesick, she mused – not photos of the Great Barrier Reef, or kangaroos and stuff. It was the little ones: the Tam Tam biscuits you could only buy in Australia, the mouth-watering memory of piping-hot barramundi and chips on the seafront in Sydney.

Yet she had no real desire to go home, not even to have her baby, because in a funny way it felt as if she was already there. Cheltenham had become home; she'd acquired far more family here than she'd ever had in Australia, and moreover she'd become fonder of them too, what with Ma having taken up with her new boyfriend and to all intents and purposes more or less forgotten about Mona. Ironic really, since she'd come over here expressly to mess up the Craine family's lives. And had succeeded.

Down the other end of the bar, Big Bob was doling out presents to his mates: a plastic crocodile here, a hat with corks on it there, not to mention a fluffy koala for Mona 'because it's so cute it reminds me of you'.

Bob's mate Larry was overcome with emotion as he received his gift: a genuine Australian girlie mag, entitled *Outback Babes*. 'Hey, good on yer mate as they say over there! This is bloody great!'

'Yeah, well, I know you've got a collection of that crap from all over the world, you old perv. Should've seen me sweating when I came through customs.'

Larry and his mates were already busy flicking through the colour pages. 'Cor, Bob mate, you really want to see this one.'

'No thanks.' Bob took a swig of beer. 'Rather watch *Top Gear* any day – that's what gets my juices flowing.'

The laughter came to a very abrupt halt. 'Oh my God,' said Larry. The man next to him whistled, stuck his head on one side and said, 'Blimey.'

'Is it?'

'Who else could it be?'

'Nah, can't be.'

'It bloody well is!'

'Er miss? Mona?' With trembling hands, Larry lifted up the magazine and handed it with the utmost care to Mona. 'Could you settle an argument?'

'What about?'

'This picture of "Sexy Sheila ropin' 'em in on the ranch" – it is you, isn't it?'

All eyes in the bar turned expectantly to focus on Mona, who turned as white as a newly bleached sheet.

It was Friday evening, and Belle found her father at St Mungo's, getting the church ready for a wedding the next day.

The moment she stepped inside, the transformation hit her. There was still waterproof sheeting all over the organ pipes, but the grey concrete walls had been enlivened with colourful hangings from the local primary school, the graffiti had been scrubbed off or painted over, and everywhere was filled with the scents of floor polish and flowers. The vast, empty barn was starting to feel like a real church again.

'First one we've had here in ages,' said Miss Findlay, putting some elbow grease into polishing the big brass eagle lectern. 'Jason and his mates are going to sleep here overnight, to make sure nobody gets in and spoils the lovely flower arrangements.'

'They're going to camp out in the church!' marvelled Belle, thinking how much dedication it must take to cope with all that darkness, discomfort and general creepiness. 'Won't they be cold and uncomfortable?'

'Ah well, needs must,' replied Miss Findlay. 'They're good boys, especially now they've got the new football team to keep them occupied. Pity they haven't got any equipment, but no doubt the Lord will provide.' She leaned towards Belle. 'He's a lovely man, is your father,' she said.

'I know.'

'And as for your mother – well! She's just what we've been needing round here, a real dose of salts. She's even got people organising events for the church roof fund, and believe me, I never thought we'd see that.'

Belle smiled. 'That's my mum. If she sees something, she has to organise it.'

Miss Findlay laughed. 'Well, obviously you take after her then.'

'Me?'

'From what I've heard, you're quite an organiser yourself – something important in customer services, isn't it?'

'It's nothing special, really; my sister's the ambitious one,' protested Belle, her heart sinking. Dad had evidently been broadcasting her achievements to the parish. What was he going to say when she told him the latest development? Whatever he said, she was pretty sure it wouldn't be her mother's inevitable 'I told you so', and that was precisely why she was taking the cowardly option and telling him first.

'Well your father's very proud of you,' Miss Findlay replied. 'Gerry,' she trilled across the nave, 'come and tell your daughter she's far too modest!'

Gerry appeared in the door of the vestry, a sheaf of papers in hand. His face brightened at the sight of his elder daughter. 'Ah, Belle!' He welcomed her with a warm hug. 'I knew it couldn't be Jax,' he said with a twinkle in his eye, 'not when the word "modest" came up. Come and have a sit down and tell me all the exciting things you've been up to.'

He cleared a pile of purple and orange robes off a chair to make room for her. 'They're for the choir,' he explained, in answer to her perplexed expression. 'Cast-offs from that big gospel choir in Gloucester. Your mother's friend Ken what's-his-name got them for a song. Useful chap to know.'

Belle blinked. 'Aren't they a bit . . . bright?'

Gerry chuckled. 'Between you and me,' he confessed, 'I'm sort of hoping the congregation will be so dazzled that they won't notice most of the kids can't actually sing. Still, they're very keen,' he added. 'Ever since they found out they're going to get paid for weddings and funerals.'

'I'm not surprised,' commented Belle. 'Can I sign up too? I might sort of be at a bit of a loose end in a few weeks' time.'

'A loose end?' Gerry frowned. 'I'd have thought you were quite busy enough shaking everybody up at Green Goddess.' Belle looked away to avoid eye contact. 'Belle? Is there something wrong?'

'Not really,' she admitted after a moment's silence. And she forced herself to look at her dad. 'It's just . . . um . . . you know I had all those misgivings about taking the job in the first place?'

He nodded. 'You thought you might not be up to it. But I knew you were. I've always known you had hidden depths, you know.'

'Yeah, so well hidden they're hardly there at all.'

'Don't run yourself down, Belle. You've got a lot going for you, if only you can start believing in yourself instead of leaving it to me to do it for you!'

Belle breathed deeply and the familiar scent of old cassocks and musty hymn books enveloped her like a cradling arm. 'Well anyway, you were right – I am up to the job. The MD called me in the other day to tell me I was doing well.'

'But?' he enquired.

All of Belle's tension escaped in a rush. 'Oh Dad, I hate every minute of it. I miss the shop and the customers, and the creativity, and I'm just not cut out for all that office politics. I guess I can do it, but I just don't want to. That's why I handed in my resignation.' She looked sheepishly up at him, waiting for his reaction.

He sat back in his chair, scratched his ear, folded his hands in his lap. 'Oh,' he said. 'Fair enough.'

Belle could hardly believe her ears. 'Dad, did you not hear me? I just jacked in the job of a lifetime!'

'Somebody's lifetime, maybe,' he nodded, 'but not yours. You did the right thing for you. Do you want me to criticise you? Because I'm not going to.' His kindly face radiated an understanding Belle wasn't sure she deserved. 'Look love, the only thing that really matters is doing what you believe is right. I've always admired you, you know.'

'Me! Why me?'

'Because even when you were a little girl, you always had these really strong principles. You wouldn't do anything if you knew it would hurt somebody else. You hated practical jokes. And do you remember when you were six, and you punched that boy for pulling the legs off a beetle? And the head teacher tried to get you to apologise in front of the whole class, and you wouldn't?'

Belle nodded ruefully. 'I was a bit of a pain in the bottom, wasn't I?'

Gerry threw back his head and laughed. 'Belle, you were a ray of sunshine! Sometimes I'd have a bad day and I'd start wondering about all kinds of things . . . having doubts . . .'

'You?'

'Yes, Belle, me. This dog collar doesn't make me immune, you know. There have been times, believe me . . . But you've always been different. As a child, you never had any doubts about what was right and wrong. It wasn't a religious thing, just some kind of instinct. You knew yourself so well, like no other child I've met. And I don't see that anything much has changed.'

'Oh Dad,' groaned Belle, 'you don't know how wrong you are. I don't think I know myself at all any more. One minute I'm getting married, I'm planning to settle down and have a family and I couldn't care less about work; the next, Kieran's gone and I'm playing at being a high-flyer . . . and it's all wrong. Everything's wrong, and I don't think I know who I am any more.

'What am I going to do, Dad?'

242

'Oh Tadpole.' He held out his arms and wrapped them round her, the way he'd done when she was a little girl and there were monsters under the bed. 'You're going to do what you've always done,' he said softly. 'Just follow your heart. And in the end, things will turn out right. Just you wait and see.'

'All right, all right,' shouted Mona, silencing the uproar in the Royal Shakespeare's public bar. 'You've had your laugh, but now I've got something to say so you can all shut up and listen.'

It was the night after Larry's landmark unmasking of Sexy Sheila the Outback Babe, and the hilarity still hadn't died down, although nobody seriously believed that the woman in the girlie shots really was Mona Starr, startling resemblance or not. Mona was, after all, a former fashion model, strictly legit: hadn't she said so herself?

So it came as a bit of a surprise when Mona reached down under the bar and slapped a bundle of paper and card on the counter. 'There you go, boys: New South Wales Plumbers' Federation calendar, half a dozen girlie mags, couple of ads for head-lice remover, and a pack of saucy playing cards.'

'What's all this?' enquired Big Bob.

Mona fixed the bar-room throng with a steady, sweeping gaze. 'My modelling career,' she replied.

A gasp ran round the assembled drinkers.

Mona held her head high. 'That's right, I am Sexy Sheila . . . and I think you'll find I'm also Bouncy Bunty and Risqué Rita, as well as Miss July and Miss October in the Plumbers' Federation calendar.'

For a moment there wasn't a sound in the bar. Everyone was too shocked to do anything but stare in open-mouthed amazement. Finally Big Bob broke the silence. 'But what about all the fashion modelling?'

Mona gave a weary sigh. 'There was no fashion modelling!' She pointed to her well-rounded bosom. 'Have you ever seen a catwalk model this shape?' Her audience had to admit that, now they came to think of it, Mona didn't look much like Kate Moss – and was all the better for it. 'Look,' she went on, 'if you made a living flashing your boobs in men's mags, and your new dad was a vicar, wouldn't you pretty things up a little?'

'Oh,' said Big Bob. 'Right.'

'Blimey,' said Larry.

'Two pints and a packet of pork scratchings, please,' piped up a man at the back, pushing forward with a ten-pound note.

God knows why I did that, thought Mona as she served the thirsty hordes; it'll be round Cheltenham in five minutes and Gerry and Brenda

243

will probably disown me. But somehow it felt better, for all that. At least she felt closer to being her true self again.

A little later, when the furore had died down and Mona's pictures had been well thumbed by the Royal Shakespeare's patrons, Big Bob sidled up to her at the end of the bar. 'Could I have a quiet word? Only I've got an idea.'

'I bet you have,' she replied coolly, as she polished away at a beer glass. Engelbert, who was lounging on the bar top in defiance of sixty-seven different health and safety regulations, raised his tatty head and growled, as if to make a point.

'Not that sort of idea,' said Bob, mollifying Engelbert with the last of his crisps. 'A business proposition. You see, I've got this mate who's a photographer—'

'Oh yeah?' There was a world of scepticism in Mona's voice.

'No really, a professional photographer. He's done *Gloucestershire Life* and a couple of Sunday supplements, and he did that "Brickies in the Buff" calendar last year for the Cotswolds Building Federation.'

'And?' enquired Mona.

'I thought maybe the three of us could get together and do a Mona Starr calendar. Very tasteful of course.'

'The three of us? Exactly what sort of proposition is this?'

'An honest one.' Big Bob grinned cheesily. 'Well, you'll need a man-ager, won't you? To make sure you're not ripped off.'

Mona was on the point of retorting that she wouldn't be ripped off because she wasn't doing it, when a thought occurred to her. She'd been wanting to do something to assuage her conscience, something that would be of practical help . . . well, here was her chance.

'But I'm pregnant,' she pointed out.

'Only a bit. You're so slim you hardly show at all. If we start shooting right away, nobody will notice. Besides, my mate's a whiz with his artistic poses.'

She put down the glass and the towel. 'OK,' she said, 'if your mate's on the level, I'll do it.'

Big Bob nearly toppled backwards into the jukebox. 'What?' he said faintly.

'I said, I'll do it. But only on one condition.'

'What's that then?'

'All the proceeds go to charity. And that charity is the St Mungo's Church Restoration Fund.'

So Mona wasn't a fashion model after all.

The news didn't come as much of a surprise to Belle; hadn't she sensed from the start that there was something phoney about her new half-sister? No wonder nobody could ever recall seeing her face on the cover of *Vogue*. She'd been far too busy twanging her thong for the Plumbers' Federation. A couple of emails to and from Australia, and Ros had dug up a whole load more incriminating photos to confirm the awful truth. Part of Belle was turning cartwheels and laughing its socks off at Mona's humiliation. But at the same time, in her heart of hearts she could sympathise with the deception. It took guts to tell a town like Cheltenham that you were not only a vicar's illegitimate daughter, but a topless model as well.

More guts than I've got, that's for sure, mused Belle as she sat outside the pavement café in the summer sunshine with her rapidly-cooling macchiato and an untouched crossword. It was her day off. She ought to be doing something interesting: but what? Clare wasn't just unavailable; for some reason, she'd become positively distant in their infrequent phone conversations. The gym reminded her of the big buff wedding that never was. Shopping inevitably took her past her old stamping ground, and made her feel more stupid then ever.

Besides, anything she did would just be a diversion from the decision she had to make. John Gillespie had asked the question simply and clearly; all she had to do was give him an equally unambiguous answer. Was she prepared to take the first store management vacancy that arose, no matter where it might be? Or was she dead set on taking the safe course of action, remaining close to home? If she chose the latter, she could be waiting for a long time. Besides, now that Kieran was no longer a part of her life, did she really want to keep on hanging around, knowing that from time to time she was bound to bump into him with his new girlfriend? Whoever she might be. Frankly, Belle didn't want to know.

Her mobile rang as she took a sip of coffee. 'Belle Craine?'

'John Gillespie here. Listen, I promised I'd let you know if anything came up and it looks like there may be a couple of suitable vacancies in the offing. There's just one thing: I need a quick decision.'

Chapter 26

Belle hardly slept that night, and before breakfast the following morning she was on the road to the Bluebell Estate. She really needed to talk this over with Dad ... or Mum at a pinch, if she'd got over lecturing her about square pegs and round holes.

At least she didn't have to worry about parking in the street. Her beloved old heap was so uncool that not even the local nine year-olds would have been seen dead joyriding in it.

Turning her key in the front door, Belle gave a breezy 'Mum, Dad, it's me!'

The only reply she received was a good licking from Engelbert, who had been amusing himself with an old lamb-bone he must have thieved from somebody's dustbin. He looked up at her lovingly, rotting lamb-scented drool dripping from his jaws onto the carpet.

'Nice Engelbert.' Belle patted him warily. 'What are you doing here? Why aren't you at the Royal Shakespeare with Mona?'

A voice answered from the top of the stairs. 'Because Mona's here.'

Surprised, Belle looked up. Mona was standing on the landing in her pyjamas and fluffy mules, unusually pale without any make-up and with her blonde hair all over the place. She yawned. 'They'll be back on Monday – they've gone away for a couple of days,' she announced, coming slowly down the stairs.

'What – Mum and Dad?'

'And Jax. They've gone to your Auntie June's in Norfolk,' she said. 'To sort of make up for not having a holiday. Didn't they tell you?'

Belle pouted. She did vaguely remember her mother having muttered something about Auntie June, but she hadn't been listening properly. 'Yes, of course they did,' she retorted. 'It just sort of slipped my mind. So you're house-sitting then?'

'Me and Engelbert, that's right.' Mona eased one of Brenda's ornaments out of the dog's jaws, buffed it on the seat of her pyjamas and replaced it on the shelf above the hall radiator. 'Engelbert's a great guard dog, aren't you boy?'

'Well, he's a deterrent,' conceded Belle. She felt profoundly uncomfortable, but somehow couldn't bring herself just to leg it with a quick 'see you around'. 'Er . . . how's things?'

Mona shrugged as she led the way towards the kitchen. 'Oh, I'm OK. Bit queasy. S'pose you heard about Sexy Sheila the Outback Babe?'

'I did sort of hear a few things on the grapevine.' She didn't mention the fact that if Big Bob hadn't put the cat among the kookaburras, Ros's researches soon would. She swallowed, feeling ever so slightly guilty for some inexplicable reason. 'Must've been a bit embarrassing for you, that.'

Mona looked back at her with a smile. 'Really I was just worried about how Gerry was going to take it, but he's been great. Especially when I told him about the charity calendar.'

'What charity calendar?' demanded Belle as Mona put the kettle on and got two mugs out of the cupboard. Mona explained. Belle's eyes widened. 'You? In the nude? In aid of St Mungo's?'

'All in very good taste, I promise,' laughed Mona. 'Of course, they'll have to get a move on taking the pics – I'm just starting to show a bit.' She patted her stomach, which was scarcely much more rounded than Belle's was on a normal day.

'And Dad's behind this?' Belle felt as though she had just wandered into an alternate reality, where things looked the same but nothing made sense. 'He actually thinks it's a good idea?'

'I haven't exactly gone into all the details yet,' admitted Mona, 'but no worries. The actual format will be a surprise for him.'

No shit, thought Belle.

'Besides, it's not an official St Mungo's calendar or anything. Once it's printed up, we'll just sell it and give all the proceeds to the church.'

Belle flopped onto a kitchen chair. 'Well, you've got guts,' she admitted reluctantly, not for the first time.

'But you don't approve, right?'

'Does it matter what I think?'

'Of course it does. You're my sister.' Mona emptied cornflakes into a bowl and sloshed milk over them. 'Had your breakfast?'

'Not yet, but—'

Mona put the bowl in front of her and handed her a spoon. 'Here, you have these, I'll get myself another bowl.' She eyed Belle up and down. 'Jeez, I thought I looked bad but you're really looking peaky. You crook or something?'

Belle jabbed her spoon into the cornflakes. 'I'm not ill, I'm just tired. And . . . a bit worried,' she added.

'What about?'

'A lot of things.' She hadn't meant to say a word about her problems to Mona – why tell her when she'd only gloat? – but now she was here, the words just seemed to say themselves. 'But right at this minute, work.'

Mona drew up a chair and sat down. 'Look, you don't have to tell me and seeing as you hate my guts, you probably won't. But I'm the only one here and you look like you could use a listener.'

Damn you for being right, thought Belle. In fact, damn you for existing. And then she opened her mouth and it all came spilling out.

Mona chewed reflectively. 'Liverpool?'

Belle nodded glumly. 'That's the choice John Gillespie's giving me. There's a store manager's job going up there, and it's mine if I want it.'

'Or?'

'Or I can go back to my own store but only as assistant manager. And that's only available because Lily's pregnant and they're going to need somebody to cover for maternity leave. It might not even be permanent.'

'Not much of a choice on the face of it, is it?' commented Mona.

'Nope. I'd be mad if I didn't take the Liverpool job.'

'And that's what you're going to do?'

A wave of utter misery swept over Belle. She looked up at Mona with real despair in her eyes. 'What's the point of my staying in Cheltenham? What is there here for me any more? At least Liverpool will give me a chance to make a clean break. If I stick around here ... maybe I never will.'

Mona drew circles in her coffee with the teaspoon. 'At the end of the day this is all about Kieran, isn't it?'

Belle looked her straight in the eye, too sad to be really angry any more. 'You should know,' she replied quietly.

Mona looked across the table at her half-sister. Belle was the picture of misery. Six months ago, she thought to herself, I'd have been celebrating if I thought I could make her that miserable.

But time had moved on, and the reasons that had brought her across the oceans like an avenging demon just didn't seem important any more. Maybe, deep down, they weren't even the real reasons why she'd come. She wondered fleetingly if it had all been more about her jealousy of her mother's obnoxious new boyfriend than it was about some biological father she'd never really thought about until the day her stepfather died.

In any event, that was just all so much psychobabble. The only things that really seemed to matter now were feelings, and the ones inhabiting the vicarage kitchen at that moment were all bad. Yes, Belle Craine could be an infuriating, smug little goody-two-shoes sometimes, but did she deserve to feel like this? And did Mona want to go through the rest of her

248

life sick to her stomach with guilt because of all the people's happiness she'd destroyed?

'Do you know how long it is since I've seen Kieran?' Mona demanded. 'Not since this whole stupid business got out.'

Belle shrugged. 'It's your own fault if you choose a bloke who abandons you the minute he gets you pregnant.'

Mona let out a long, low groan of frustration and surrender. 'Listen, kid,' she said. 'There's something I have to tell you.'

'Who says I have to listen?' replied Belle.

'Nobody. But if you don't, you'll never know the truth.'

Belle listened in stunned silence as Mona told her the whole sorry tale. She knew she ought to be angry, but all she felt was numb.

'Revenge,' she said softly.

Mona nodded. 'Revenge. That's the only reason I came to Cheltenham.' She gave a twisted smile. 'Not that Ma realised. I told her I was going backpacking, and she might not hear from me for a while. Not that she'd care. Since she took up with that creep Chas, we've not been close.'

'But you still went ahead?'

'It was just something I had to do, I couldn't get it out of my head. I was so sure Gerry had deliberately abandoned my mother when he knew she was pregnant, refused to answer her letters, deprived me of a proper dad and a proper childhood ... And maybe deep down, I thought it'd make Ma proud of me. Trouble is, once I got to know Gerry, I wasn't so sure. I couldn't make myself believe he was the sort of guy who'd do that kind of thing and then lie about it.'

'My father would never do a thing like that,' said Belle, finding a grain of anger in her love for her father.

'Our father,' Mona reminded her. 'Yes, I know that now. The thing is, I believe my mother too. And she swore she wrote to him and never got an answer. Someone's been lying. The question is, who's the liar?'

Belle thought for a moment, curiously cool and detached. 'Maybe it's neither of them,' she replied. 'Maybe somebody else wanted them both to suffer.'

Mona considered this. 'Maybe. But I'll tell you one thing for sure: you may drive me nuts sometimes, but you're still my sister and I don't want you to suffer any more because of my stupid pride. Which is why I'm going to tell you who the father of my baby really is.'

'You don't need to tell me,' snapped Belle, her temper quickening. 'I already know – everybody knows. There's no need to make it feel worse than it already is.'

'Will you shut your big mouth for one minute?' demanded Mona. And

Belle was so surprised that she did. 'Kieran Sawyer is not the father of my baby. Got that? Give me something to swear on – the Bible, my baby's life, anything – and I'll swear it.' She stroked her stomach. 'This little one in here is nothing to do with him. And what's more, I have never even kissed the bloke, let alone slept with him.'

Why is she doing this to me? wondered Belle. Why can't she just admit it, then we can get on with our lives? 'You really expect me to believe that?' she demanded.

'Whether you believe it or not isn't my responsibility,' Mona replied. 'I'm just telling you the truth. It's up to you whether you accept it or not.'

Belle fiddled with the handle on her mug. There was something about Mona's directness that made this impossible to simply dismiss, whatever the evidence might say. 'All right, let's just say I suspend disbelief for a moment. If Kieran's not the father of your baby, who is?'

She stared into Mona's face, and to her surprise it turned bright crimson with embarrassment. There was a long, uncomfortable silence, and then . . .

'Oz,' Mona whispered, looking for all the world like she wanted the floor to open up and swallow her.

'Oz!' Belle choked on the indigestible idea. 'Is this your idea of a very bad joke?'

Mona wilted visibly beneath her laser gaze. 'For God's sake Belle, do you really think I'd say it was Oz if it wasn't? I mean, have you any idea how embarrassing this is for me?'

Belle was stunned. 'We are talking about the same Oz? The Oz who's Kieran's nerdy mate with the big insect fetish? The one who's thirty-three and still lives with his mum?'

Mona nodded in dumb agony.

'But it doesn't make any sense! It's ridiculous! Why would someone like you even notice a guy whose favourite hobby is breeding termites?'

'You tell me,' replied Mona. 'It's a mystery to me, too. We just clicked, that's all I can tell you. There was something there – a spark of magnetism, I don't know. Plus he seemed like a nice, regular kind of guy and there aren't that many of those around.'

Belle had to admit that this at least was true. But the words 'magnetism' and 'Oz' just didn't go together in her head at all. 'No,' she said, pushing away her cereal bowl, 'I'm not buying this, you're having me on. Besides, what about the pregnancy test box I found in Kieran's flat?'

Mona fiddled with the tie-belt on her robe. 'You know how Kieran sometimes lent out his key to Oz so he could meet his girlfriends there?' Belle nodded. 'Well, the girl he was meeting was me. And when I realised

I might be pregnant, I needed somewhere private to do the test – I hardly wanted one of you finding it. So I got the key off Oz and slipped in when nobody was around.' She sighed. ''Course, I didn't bargain on you searching through the garbage like that.'

'I didn't!' protested Belle, 'I just accidentally ... So you're saying Kieran knew nothing about it?'

'Nothing at all, at least not from me. And Oz is so terrified of his mother finding out he's seeing girls that you'd probably have to torture him to get any kind of admission out of him.'

Belle considered the idea and found it vaguely appealing. If Mona was telling the truth, she desperately needed someone to blame for this unholy mess, and Oz would fit the bill nicely. 'If his mother's as bad as I think she is,' she mused, 'I should think she's giving him one hell of a time as it is.'

'She probably would be,' replied Mona, 'if she knew.'

This brought Belle up short. 'You're telling me his mother doesn't know about the baby?'

'She doesn't even know about me. But then again, Oz doesn't actually know I'm pregnant either. The thing is, we stopped seeing each other a while back ... it got too difficult, dodging his mother and all that. I blew him out, told him he was pathetic.'

Belle flopped back in her chair, utterly flabbergasted. 'I don't believe this! You're carrying his baby and you haven't told him?'

'There's no point,' insisted Mona. 'He made it quite clear he's not ready for any kind of commitment. You know what he's like. At the start, I guess I thought maybe I could change him, but I was just deceiving myself. Why bother involving a guy who'll just freak out and then run a mile?'

'He might not,' reasoned Belle.

'You reckon?'

'OK, maybe he would. But doesn't he have a right to know? Come to that, doesn't the baby have a right to know who its father is? I'd have thought you of all people ...'

This cut like a blade; Belle saw the pain on Mona's face. 'You make it sound so easy,' she said with an edge of bitterness.

They sat there for a few moments in silence. Belle was caught between confusion, elation and a horrible nauseous feeling. If what Mona said was true ...

Just supposing it was true, then Belle had blamed Kieran for something he hadn't done, and worse – thrown away what might very well have been the love of her life. She looked up at Mona. 'So how do you feel about Oz now?'

Mona looked even more discomfited. 'About the same way you feel about Kieran,' she replied.

Belle's heart missed a beat. 'What's that supposed to mean?'

'That I'm still in love with a middle-aged nerd, and you're still in love with Kieran. Don't bother saying you're not,' she added wearily, 'because it's bloody obvious that you are.'

The protective cocoon of indifference Belle had been so carefully constructing around her crumbled away like so much parched earth. Mona was right, there was little point in denying it. Her love for Kieran might have changed, been battered and beleaguered, but it was still there. 'Maybe that's why I have to take the job in Liverpool,' she said after a moment.

'Why? You love him, I've told you there was never anything between him and me . . . why on earth would you want to get away from him?'

The words took an awful lot of saying. 'Because he doesn't love me,' Belle replied.

Mona blinked at her. 'But that's . . . crap!'

'Oh really? So why has he got himself a new girlfriend then?'

Mona looked genuinely startled. 'He hasn't – has he?'

Belle told her what Clare had revealed, describing the passionate kiss in the restaurant in all its agonising detail. 'So you see, I may as well just bugger off and leave him to it.'

Mona cocked her head on one side. 'Do you believe everything people tell you?'

'Of course not! I didn't believe you until just now, did I?'

'That's true. But what about other people? What about Clare?'

'Clare's my friend.'

'So she says. When's the last time she called you?'

'It's been a few weeks,' Belle admitted. 'But—'

'But nothing,' cut in Mona. 'Look, I get the feeling I've been had somewhere along the way – about Ma and Gerry and the non-existent letters. Someone, somewhere, has been playing games with the truth. All I'm going to say is, believe whatever you choose to believe, just don't let the same thing happen to you.'

Chapter 27

As Belle settled back into her old branch of Green Goddess, the crazy interlude in Gloucester began to seem more and more like a peculiar dream, from which she had finally returned to reality.

Yet things weren't quite the same as before. With a pregnant Lily (who'd replaced her) headed for maternity leave and Waylon now in charge of several branches, Belle had a little more day-to-day responsibility than when she'd worked at the shop before, but there was still no guarantee that her job would be made permanent. Lily swore she wouldn't want to come back full-time after she'd had the baby, but if she changed her mind, Belle would be either back as a humble shop assistant or out of a job completely: the irony being that she'd be worse off than her protégé Jerszy, who'd recently landed himself a senior sales adviser's job at the shiny new Cardiff store.

Or maybe she'd be on her way to whatever far-flung branch head office might pluck out of the hat for her. Still, that was the price you paid for taking a wrong turn on the career highway. How stupid could you get? Not much stupider than me, thought Belle ruefully. If I'd hung on at the Cheltenham store, instead of playing silly power games at Head Office, I could have been store manager by now.

After all, when it came to her career, that was the sum total of everything she'd ever wanted.

Every day, she wondered if she'd done the right thing this time around. All logic decreed that she ought to have accepted the Liverpool job and made a fresh start for herself, instead of hanging around Cheltenham like one of those dead spirits that couldn't quite bring themselves to leave the mortal plane. After all, it wasn't as if she'd exchanged more than a few words with Kieran all summer – and then only when they'd bumped into each other accidentally in the street.

If she saw him heading towards her, she bolted round the nearest corner or dived into a shop. She was quite sure that he was doing the same. In her case, it wasn't because she didn't want to talk to him, but because she did want to, much too much; and she couldn't have coped with the unbearable awkwardness as the two of them stood there tongue-tied in the middle of the pavement, while the rest of humanity surged unfeelingly past and got on with its life.

She asked herself: should I let Mona talk to Kieran for me? The offer had been made. But Mona had enough to cope with, preparing for the birth of her child; anyhow, it wasn't as if she and Kieran were bosom buddies any more. Besides, Belle still had a few shreds of pride left. She knew in her heart of hearts that if anything was ever going to be salvaged from the wrecked relationship, she would have to do the salvaging herself: if she ever got enough courage together. Courage had never been Belle's strong point.

Even then, was it worth it? She'd made such an awful mess of her own life and Kieran's. Wouldn't it be better just to leave him be; let him go and start over again with somebody who really trusted him?

And yet ... Belle slipped a hand into her jacket pocket, and fingered the key to his apartment that Kieran had never asked her to give back, and which she had never got round to giving him. Was it time for one final try, or had she left it far too late?

At last, Jax had the whole world at her feet. Or if not the world, then at least a goodly portion of Bluebell Comprehensive.

Things had certainly changed a bit since that night at the Club Casablanca. For a start Stacey and her mates had become – however grudgingly – almost civil, overnight. Then one or two of the other students had noticed a useful thing about Jax: she was extremely clever. Name any subject you liked, and she'd be good at it. Mind you, her valuable expertise didn't come for free. It was amazing what a flourishing essay-writing and coursework business an enterprising girl could develop when, basically, she knew all the answers.

'How did that last exam go then?' asked Demi, as Jax and the gang arrived for Heavy Rock Nite at the Hairy Newt.

Jax breathed on her sparkly-blue varnished nails and polished them on her black cobweb top. 'Peachy. Anyway, it was only worth twenty per cent of the marks, and I'd already got a starred A on the coursework.'

Snooker sighed. 'You jammy cow. I worked my rocks off and what did I get? A D. If I get a pass overall I'll be happy, I'm telling you.'

Proud as anything, Razor slid an arm about Jax's shoulders. 'Ah well, that's because my lady here is smarter than all the rest of Cheltenham put together,' he declared in his public school tones, which clashed a bit with his new red and green Mohawk and PVC bondage trousers.

'Too damn' right I am,' agreed Jax, who'd never been one for false – or genuine – modesty. 'And now Stacey and I aren't trying to kill each other any more, I'm actually quite pleased I moved schools.'

Demi gave her a puzzled look. 'Have you gone nuts or something? Who'd want to swap St Jude's for a grotty comprehensive on the Bluebell Estate? It was in "special measures" till last September – they were threatening to close it down!'

'Ah, but that's the whole point, don't you see?' Jax looked distinctly smug. 'Nowadays, all the universities are giving preference to pupils from schools in deprived areas, aren't they? There's all kinds of sponsorships and bursaries and stuff around if you live somewhere really horrible. And I'm going to play the system right to the hilt. I'm heading for one of the top universities .' She tossed the rest of her pint down her throat and wiped a hand across her mouth. 'Play my cards right, and I might even make Oxbridge!'

'Told you she was smart,' said Razor. 'I may be as thick as pigs' droppings myself, and indeed I am, but I do have the most excellent taste in girlfriends, don't I, my sexy little Goth princess?'

'Empress!' She threw him a long-suffering look as he kissed her on the end of her nose, but underneath the vampish white make-up her cheeks were pink with pleasure. 'For God's sake! Stop fannying about and get them in, Razor,' she scolded him. 'It's your round.'

'You old romantic,' quipped Demi as Razor lumbered off happily to the bar. 'You two are just like a pair of turtle doves.'

Jax laughed, but not without affection. 'Yeah, right.'

'Speaking of lovebirds,' piped up Snooker, 'wasn't your sister's wedding supposed to be about now?'

'God, yes.' Jax let the realisation sink in. 'Next Saturday. You know, I'd forgotten all about it, what with them splitting up and my exams and all that business with Stacey. Poor Belle,' she said quietly.

Looks of amazement were exchanged. 'Excuse me,' said Demi, 'but did I just hear you say "poor Belle"? Sympathy for your sister? That's a first.'

Jax pulled a face. 'All right, I know I haven't always been that sympathetic – but you can see my point of view, can't you? I mean, she is a drippy prat most of the time. Never has a clue what she wants, or how to go about getting it. But she did try to help me, and it's a shame about her and Kieran. I thought they were really right for each other.'

'You mean they were both drippy prats?' enquired Demi.

'Yeah, a proper matching pair. But what with all that crap about Kieran and Mona ... I mean, the whole idea of him knocking her up is ludicrous, and I do believe Mona when she says it's all a big misunderstanding, but I can still see where Belle's coming from. If I'd found that pregnancy test ... Well, I'd kill somebody first and think later, that's all I can say.'

'And you don't think they'll get together again, then?'

'After all this time?' Jax stuffed her face with crisps. 'Nah. There's more chance of Razor winning Miss World.'

St Mungo's was fast becoming a family affair.

It wasn't just that one kid would join the football team or the choir, and then half his or her family would start turning up at the church in dribs and drabs, just to get a glimpse of the 'sex-scandal' new vicar and see what all the fuss was about. All the Craines had become thoroughly involved, too.

I never thought I'd be doing this, thought Belle as she sat side by side with Mona in her mum's sitting room, folding the leaflets Brenda and Ken had produced for the upcoming Alpha course. With anybody else, maybe; but not with Mona. Things were certainly changing, in ways she would never have predicted. Maybe if I'm patient, she told herself, eventually I'll stop pining after what I can't have, and my life will finally find some kind of direction.

At least Brenda was looking happy after months of misery, bustling about and ordering people around, the way she always had before the bad stuff happened. As for Belle's dad, he never looked more content than when his wife was organising his life for him, so Belle guessed he must be in clover. He was the spiritual one; she was the born administrator. Now that Brenda was back at the helm, he had been liberated from the daily grind of trying to remember what he had to do next – and the relief showed on his face.

'Tell me again, dear,' he said, as he sat on the sofa reading over the sermon for next Sunday. 'Where am I supposed to be on Tuesday evening?'

Brenda peered at him over the top of her half-moon reading glasses. 'Holy Trinity, Nailsworth,' she reminded him patiently. 'For the diocesan ecumenical service. The bishop might be there, so you'll have to wear your best surplice and have a proper haircut.'

Belle giggled, and Engelbert – who was lying across her feet – raised his head in interest. 'Mum, you make it sound like speech day at school!'

'I thought we were giving two fingers to Bishop Grove anyway,' added Mona. 'He certainly deserves it – miserable old bastard.'

'Mona!' Brenda looked quite shocked. 'You can't call the bishop a bastard!' And then she burst out laughing, and Engelbert joined in with some wild tail-thrashing and a bit of off-key howling.

'Do shut that dog up, dear,' said Brenda reprovingly. 'The people next door will think we're having an exorcism.'

'I couldn't care less what my vestments look like,' declared Gerry, examining a hole in his favourite comfy sweater. 'And I'm definitely not dressing up for Thaddeus Grove.' He thought for a moment as something niggled at the back of his mind. 'What was it you said about trifle?'

Brenda offered up a silent prayer. 'That was for the Alpha course, dear. Don't you remember? I want you to ask the churchwardens whether they'd prefer chocolate mousse or sherry trifle after the shepherd's pie.'

'You'd better make it mousse, Mum,' counselled Belle, folding another leaflet with inky fingers. 'I've heard the whole Armstrong family's coming, and you know what they're like when they come within fifty yards of alcohol! Even Great-Grandma Armstrong has an ASBO, and she's seventy-six.'

Brenda paled slightly. 'The Armstrong family? As in, the source of ninety-nine per cent of all crime in Cheltenham?'

'Allegedly,' cut in Mona, with a smile. 'Well, them and the Sullivans.'

'Isn't Ricky Armstrong still in jail for ram-raiding Sainsbury's?' mused Belle, recalling the Bluebell Estate's answer to Don Corleone.

'Not any more,' replied Mona. 'I heard he got out on licence a couple of weeks ago.'

This snippet of news didn't go down too well. Brenda mopped her brow with a crisp, clean handkerchief. 'Ah well, these things come to try us. Let's just hope the Sullivans don't turn up as well . . .'

Mona shook her head confidently. 'They won't. They can't stand to be in the same room together. Anyway, St Mungo's is on the Armstrongs' patch. If any of the Sullivans turned up, they'd be ripped apart.'

'Good grief,' commented Belle, 'it's like living in one of those East-End thrillers. I'm half expecting Vinnie Jones to turn up any minute.'

'If he does,' said Brenda sternly, 'he won't be getting any sherry trifle.'

At that moment the doorbell rang. Belle was already on her way to answer it when her mother briskly interposed herself between Belle and the door. 'I'll get it, dear. I'm expecting someone.'

'Oh?' said Belle. 'Who?'

'Just someone who's coming to help with the leaflets. You'll see.'

Belle went and sat down. 'I bet it's Ken,' she whispered to Mona. 'These days it always is.'

Mona nodded. 'I know what you mean.' She lowered her voice so that

257

Gerry wouldn't hear. 'You don't think he and your mother are ... you know? Bouncy-bouncy?'

Belle's face creased up in horror. 'Ugh! You have to be kidding!'

'Actually yes, I am,' Mona admitted with a laugh. 'But you have to admit it's an entertaining thought.'

Entertaining or not, it was about to be totally banished; because just then there were voices in the hall, and the sitting-room door opened.

At first Belle didn't look up, but Mona's jaw dropped and she let out a startled 'Oh my God!', clapped her hand over her mouth and muttered, 'I mean ... sorry Gerry.'

When Belle did look up, she nearly fainted. Mind you, the new arrival appeared equally stunned.

'Kieran?'

Kieran stared back at Belle, and for a couple of seconds he was speechless. Then he turned to Brenda, and said accusingly, 'You might have told me Belle was going to be here.'

'Yes,' agreed Brenda with a knowing smile. 'But then you wouldn't have come, would you?' She snapped her fingers. 'Gerry, Mona – come with me, there's something I want to show you upstairs.'

The stratagem was lost on Gerry. 'But—'

Brenda sighed and shook her head. 'Upstairs, Gerry. Now. I think these two young people want to say a few things to each other in private.'

The silent staring continued for several long moments after the door had closed behind Brenda.

He hates me, thought Belle as she looked straight into those blank and steely eyes, remembering with anguish how they'd once been full of warmth and smiles. He hates me, and how can I blame him? I'm probably just about the last person on earth he wants to be stuck in a room with. She wondered if she could get away with running upstairs and hiding in the bathroom until she was certain he'd gone. But she had a nasty feeling her mother would drag her back down again to face the music.

After an eternity of mutual discomfort, Kieran blurted out: 'I'm sorry I gave you a shock, Belle, your mother told me you weren't going to be here. She said she just wanted me to pick up some leaflets to deliver.'

Most jilted fiancés would probably have run a mile from any contact with their former intended's parents, but not Kieran. He didn't want to upset Belle by being around all the time, but neither could he divorce himself from the only proper family he'd ever had. Silently, he willed her to understand.

'My mother is the Mata Hari of St Mungo's,' said Belle drily. 'You should know that after all this time.'

'That's true,' he admitted ruefully. 'But just being acquainted with somebody for a long time doesn't necessarily mean you really, well, know them, does it?'

She bore the pain of his too-searching gaze. 'It certainly doesn't.'

He hovered near the door. 'Should I go then?'

Belle shrugged, feigning indifference although it was the diametrical opposite of what she was feeling. She couldn't let him detect the maelstrom inside her, she just couldn't. 'That's up to you. Don't go on my account.'

'What if I wanted to stay – on your account?' he asked softly. 'What if I wanted to apologise for being an arrogant idiot?'

The look in his eyes seemed softer, too. But how could she know what he was really thinking and feeling? God, she thought, I hate this game, even though I still go on playing it. She decided to play a straight bat. 'Then I'd have to apologise too,' she replied, 'seeing as some of this mess is my fault.' She paused. 'Look, don't go just yet. I need to tell you something.'

'Oh yes?'

'Would you mind sitting down? Only you're making me feel really uncomfortable, sort of looming over me like that.'

Kieran looked surprised, but sat down in one of the armchairs by the fire. 'Looming? That's one thing I've not been accused of before,' he commented. He observed Belle as she paced backwards and forwards across the beaten-up old hearthrug her father had made when her mum was in labour with Jax. 'Aren't you going to sit down? You're starting to make me feel a bit weird, too.'

'What? Oh. Yes, all right.' She forced herself to relax sufficiently to perch on the edge of the sofa, and sat there staring down at the toes of her shoes. How often had she rehearsed this little speech in front of her bedroom mirror? The words ought to come easily to her, but they didn't. 'I know everything now,' she announced in a sudden rush. 'Well, I think I do. At least, I know you didn't get Mona pregnant.'

He blinked. 'You do?'

She nodded in shame.

'So . . . what changed?'

'I did.'

'Oh. You mean, you just had a rethink?'

'Sort of.' She took a deep breath. 'And I finally had that long chat with Mona, and realised how stupid I've been.'

'No stupider than I have,' replied Kieran.

But this unexpected interjection didn't stop Belle's confessional flow. 'And I'm really, truly sorry I didn't believe you before,' she continued, her eyes begging him to believe her. 'I know that doesn't make it all right, or change what's happened between us . . . but for the record, I am sorry. What's done is done, I guess. I think I'm just a bit crap at relationships.' She floundered, all out of words. 'I can't think of anything else to say. Only "sorry".'

'You don't have to say anything.'

'You mean I'd best shut up before I dig myself an even deeper hole?' ventured Belle.

Kieran laughed, but not cruelly. 'You haven't changed as much as all that,' he commented. 'You still assume the worst about everything. No,' he went on, 'I meant if you're feeling stupid, how do you think I've been feeling? All that avoiding you because I was too arrogant or too scared or I don't know what to face you.'

Belle raised an eyebrow. 'Scared? You?'

'Oh yes. And pissed-off because you didn't believe me. Silly sod that I am, I just thought "stuff you", instead of making an effort to get you to believe me.'

Belle considered this. 'I've been avoiding you, too,' she confessed. 'There was this one time . . .' She coloured up.

'Go on.'

'I was walking round that big garden centre in Bourton looking for Mum, and I spotted you out of the corner of my eye.'

'And?' coaxed Kieran.

Belle winced. 'And I was so determined not to meet you that I hid inside one of the garden sheds.'

'That's nothing. I was in the North Place car park and the only free space was next to your car. So I went and parked on the street and got a ticket instead.'

She looked up at Kieran and there was silence for a brief moment, before the pair of them started giggling and couldn't stop until the bone-cracking tension between them had been laughed away.

'Pathetic, or what?' said Belle when she'd wiped her eyes on her sleeve.

'There's got to be a lesson in this somewhere,' observed Kieran. 'But I don't suppose we'll learn it.'

'We could always try,' suggested Belle after a moment's hesitation. 'To be friends, I mean,' she added hastily, in case he'd got the wrong impression. 'After all, we have been a part of each other's lives for the best part of five years.'

Kieran rubbed his stubbly chin. 'You're right,' he said. 'And besides, it's not as if we've ever stopped . . . well, caring about each other, is it? I don't imagine we ever will do.'

Kieran's words hurt. There's caring and there's caring, thought Belle. And he's talking about the kind of caring you share with your gay mate, or your girl friends; the kind where you exchange supportive hugs and are on hand for each other's weddings, christenings and divorces. The sort of caring that's safe and secure, and never turns into a love affair.

'Of course we won't,' she said, forcing a smile. 'But I'm sure you care a little bit more about this new girlfriend of yours,' she added, making it sound like she was half joking rather than deadly serious and resentful as hell.

Kieran looked puzzled, which Belle found irritating. 'What new girl-friend?' he demanded.

Belle's temper quickened. 'Come on Kieran, don't play games with me.'

'I'm not,' he insisted. 'I don't have a girlfriend. If you really must know, I haven't been out with anybody since we split up.'

'Oh really?' Belle folded her arms across her chest, hugging in her annoyance and hurt. 'What about the blonde with the big boobs you were snogging the other week, in that swanky Italian place on North Street?'

Kieran looked even more baffled. 'What – La Primavera? You're kid-ding, I can't afford those prices ... And what blonde? I haven't been snogging anyone—'

'Since we split up, yeah, yeah, I know.' Belle's anger was turning to weariness. 'You were seen, Kieran, why bother denying it? It's not like you were cheating on me or something.'

'Exactly!' retorted Kieran. 'So why would I bother denying it – unless it wasn't true?' His eyes narrowed. 'And who told you, anyway?'

Belle shuffled her feet on the carpet. 'Does it matter?'

'Yes, as a matter of fact it does! If someone's been telling lies about me, I'd quite like to know who it was.'

After a moment's hesitation, Belle said, 'Clare.'

'Clare!' Kieran's startled expression somehow didn't square with a man who'd just been caught out. He looked genuinely surprised.

'She phoned me late one evening. Said she was passing the restaurant, looked in through the window and saw you eating the face off this glam-orous blonde. She said she thought I ought to know.'

'Well, well.' Kieran whistled. 'I bet she did.'

'What's that supposed to mean?'

He flung back his head and stared up at the ceiling. 'It means I've only ever been to La Primavera once – and that was with your so-called friend Clare.' Belle opened her mouth to interject, but Kieran raised a hand. 'And before you fly off the handle, it was a business meeting, not a date.' He turned to look at Belle. 'Or at least it was supposed to be.'

All kinds of warring thoughts were seething around inside Belle's head. 'Would you care to explain that? Only you're not making much sense.'

'Nothing about that evening made sense,' replied Kieran. He explained about the phone call from Clare, her insistence on meeting up over dinner to discuss the proposed advertorial ... and her sudden loss of interest when she discovered he didn't share her concept of 'business'.

Belle couldn't believe her ears. 'So you're telling me Clare came on to you, you told her you weren't interested and then you just left? You really expect me to believe that?' Kieran answered with an affirmative shrug. 'But ... she wouldn't. She's supposed to be my friend!'

Supposed to be. The words echoed ominously inside Belle's head, and she found herself thinking: is anybody, anywhere, ever exactly what they say they are? She shook her head, but couldn't rid herself of the conviction that somebody was lying and the chances were it wasn't Kieran.

'I'm sorry,' said Kieran, 'but whatever you might think, I'd never lie to you. And I wasn't imagining it either. The woman practically poured herself all over me.'

'Why would she want to do that?' Belle repeated over and over. 'Why would someone who says she's my friend want to do that to me, and then make it worse by lying to me as well?'

'I don't know,' replied Kieran, though he looked as though he might have one or two ideas. 'And there's only one person who can give you the answer. It looks like you're going to be having a quiet word with Clare.'

The following afternoon was hot and oppressive, and Mona felt distinctly pregnant as she wiped down the beer pumps and draped them with towels. Five months of pregnancy still to come, and already she was starting to feel like a weary, swollen-ankled blimp.

As if in answer to her silent prayers, just as she was walking across to bolt the door of the Royal Shakespeare it opened and a head popped through.

'Excuse me.' The head belonged to a thin-faced woman with dark circles under her eyes and her home-highlighted hair scraped back in a rubber band. 'I've come about the advert in the post office. For an early-morning cleaner.'

Mona brightened. This was the first response after a week. She'd started to wonder if there was anybody in the whole of Cheltenham desperate enough to scrub toilets and polish pub tables pock-marked with cigarette burns.

'That's great.' She wiped a hand and proffered it. 'Hi. Mona, I'm the manager.'

'Cindy. Can you let me have an application form, and I'll drop it in tomorrow when I pick the kids up from school?'

'No need – come in and we can talk about it now.' I'm not letting this one get away, thought Mona. She might be the only applicant. 'Tell you what, I'll take you round first and show you what needs doing, and then we can have a nice cup of tea and talk about it.'

Cindy glanced nervously at her watch. 'I'll need to be away by half-past, 'cause I have to get my youngest from his dad's. Chas gets really pissed off if I don't pick the kids up on time.'

'How many kids have you got?' enquired Mona.

'Four. All under six.'

Four ankle-biters! Mona's imagination reeled at the very thought of it. 'That's . . . nice,' she ventured.

'No, it isn't,' Cindy replied firmly. 'It's shite.'

'Oh,' said Mona, for once lost for a snappy reply.

'It wouldn't be so bad if their dads weren't such total losers. Still, I guess it's my own fault for being so bloody stupid,' sighed Cindy. 'Had my first at fifteen and I've never stopped.'

'Really? So how old are you now . . . if you don't mind me asking?'

Cindy looked her straight in the eye. 'Twenty-two.' She must have seen the look of horrified disbelief on Mona's face, because she went on: 'Yeah I know, don't tell me, I look more like thirty-two going on fifty. Still, that's what motherhood does to you.'

A ghastly, cold feeling ran down Mona's spine. 'It's worth it though, isn't it? Being a mum I mean. You know, the smiles on their little faces and all that?'

Cindy let out a short burst of laughter. 'It's obvious you've got no kids! Look,' she continued, more softly, 'don't get me wrong, I love the little buggers to bits, and it's probably great being a mother when you've got a husband with a good job and a 4x4 and all that shit. But if you're trying to go it alone . . . Can't say I recommend it, that's for sure.'

Mona swallowed, her throat dry and constricted. 'You don't?'

'Which would you rather do? Take on three jobs scrubbing stinking toilets to make ends meet, or sit at home while your bloke puts up shelves?' She poked a finger at Mona's rounded belly. 'Don't know why I'm going on at you, mind. I'm sure you found a decent bloke before you got yourself up the duff,' she said with a laugh. 'You look far too sensible to get yourself into trouble.'

About half an hour after Cindy left the pub, Mona was still sitting at one of the tables by the door, staring at an undrunk half of non-alcoholic lager

263

as the Guinness clock on the wall behind the bar counted out the seconds in noisy clunks.

Suddenly, without a word or a sound, Mona pushed away the glass, took out her mobile from her handbag and dialled.

'Oz? Is that you? Yes, of course it's me, you pillock. Look, do you think we could meet up somewhere? Only I've got something important to tell you.'

Chapter 28

Just as she was climbing the steps of Excalibur House, the building where Clare worked, Belle's mobile rang somewhere in the depths of her handbag. She reached inside and turned it off without looking.

Now that she'd decided to do this, nothing was going to get in her way.

The smartly suited receptionist looked up politely as Belle strode into the lobby, exuding a confidence she didn't feel. 'Can I help you?' she enquired.

'Annabelle Craine, I have an appointment with Clare Levenshulme in Marketing.' The lie popped out with unexpected ease.

The receptionist reached for her handset. 'If you'd just like to wait there a moment, I'll phone up and tell her you're here.'

'Don't bother,' replied Belle, already halfway to the lift. 'I want this to be a surprise.'

The receptionist's protests faded to nothing as the lift doors slid shut and the cage began its upward glide to the fifth floor. Belle was terrified, her palms slick with sweat, but extremely focused and just a tiny bit excited too. It occurred to her that she didn't really care what the consequences might be, or what might happen in the end – just as long as she got to say what had to be said. That was all that mattered.

The lift pinged to a halt on the fifth floor and Belle stepped out and turned right. She'd only been in the building once before, but she remembered the way to Clare's office. It was one of those glass-walled capsules, arranged around the edges of a big open-plan affair like display cases in a museum.

Nobody challenged her as she strode across the nasty blue monogrammed carpet; in fact hardly anybody even glanced at her. Dressed in her charcoal grey interview suit, she looked every bit as anonymous as everybody else. This is what it must be like to be an ant, she thought as she spotted Clare's strawberry-blonde hair through the transparent wall of her office. Best of all, there was somebody else in the office with her.

The more the merrier, thought Belle with grim humour as she got within two yards of the office door and suddenly Clare looked up from the notes on her desk ... and saw her. It was worth the trip up to the fifth floor, just to see the expression on Clare's face.

But at that selfsame moment, somebody came up behind Belle and touched her on the arm. 'Excuse me?'

Belle swung round.

'I'm sorry,' said a girl with orange lipstick and a fringe that half-obscured her eyes, 'Ms Levenshulme's in a meeting. You can't go in there.'

'That's where you're wrong,' declared Belle, and with a single sweep of her arm she dragged open the sliding door, revealing a semicircle of startled faces. 'Hello Clare, long time, no see.'

'Who is this?' demanded a middle-aged man at Clare's right elbow.

'Nobody.' Clare got slowly to her feet. 'Belle, what are you doing here?' she hissed. 'Can't you see this is a bad time?'

'Actually it's a really good one for me,' replied Belle. 'And you haven't exactly been making yourself accessible lately, have you?' She leaned against the doorframe, arms folded, to all appearances completely at ease – even if her heart was dancing flamenco in her chest. 'I have one or two things to say to you, and I'm not going until they've been said.'

The middle-aged man reached for the phone. 'Shall I call security?'

Clare shook her head and waved him away. 'No need. Look, would you people mind just waiting for a moment while this ... person and I go somewhere for a private chat?'

Without waiting for a reply, she pushed her way out of the office, sliding the door shut behind her with a crash. 'What the hell do you think you're doing?' she snapped.

'Making your life difficult,' replied Belle, 'just like you've been doing with mine.' She smiled sweetly at Clare's expression. 'Or are you going to tell me I'm imagining it?'

Clare glanced around the office. Several people had stopped work and were eyeing the pair with interest. Behind her, her colleagues were watching too. Her face and neck started to turn pink. 'Come with me,' she said, stalking across to the coffee room and evicting the two junior clerks who were necking over the espresso machine. Belle followed in silence, not afraid any more, just quietly angry.

Clare slammed the door shut behind them. 'What's all this crap about?'

'Nice to see you, too,' commented Belle. 'How many weeks is it since you returned one of my calls?'

'I told you, I've been busy.'

'Yes you have, haven't you?' Belle took a deep breath and fixed Clare with an unflinching gaze. 'You've been lying to me, Clare. That much is pretty bloody obvious. And I want to know why.'

There was a short hiatus. Then, much to Belle's surprise, Clare started to laugh. 'My God, Belle, you're even thicker than I thought you were! Has it really taken you this long to work out that I've been telling you porkies?' She wiped a tear of mirth from her eye. 'It'd be almost tragic . . . if I gave a shit.'

This was a whole new Clare, and Belle wondered why she hadn't glimpsed it before, lurking beneath the veneer of camaraderie. Maybe I really am stupid, she thought; or maybe it's just easy to be duped when you're desperate for a friend. Determined not to let the hurt of rejection deflate her anger, she cut into Clare's mocking laughter.

'I don't care about any of that. All I want to know is why. Why work your guts out to destroy the only relationship I've ever had that ever meant anything to me?'

'Don't you see?' Clare gave her a slightly pitying smile. 'That's exactly why I had to destroy it. Because it meant something to you. An eye for an eye, Belle.'

'I don't understand!' protested Belle in exasperation. 'What have I ever done to you?'

Any vestiges of mirth slipped from Clare's face, leaving it a cold, white mask of pure hatred. 'How can you say that? You ruined my brother's life.'

Belle's jaw dropped. 'Max's life? You're talking about Max? All those years ago?'

'He loved you, and you used him. You just cast him aside, and it broke him. Do you know where he is now? No, of course you don't, because you didn't even care enough to ask. And after all that you did to him.'

'What did I do?' Belle's head was starting to spin, but she wasn't going to let Clare get to her. She and Max had had fun for a while but ultimately it hadn't worked out. He hadn't taken their break-up well but that had been years ago. 'Look, Claire, Max and I were together for a while and I'm sorry he took it so badly when we split up but that's ancient history now.'

Clare just glared stonily back at her. 'He loved you. All you had to do was love him back.'

'And you really think it's that simple?'

'If you'd given him what he needed, he'd be happy, not. . .not where he is now.'

From Clare's melodramatic delivery, anyone would have thought

267

Max was in jail, or locked up in some maximum-security mental institution, thought Belle, suddenly registering the unpalatable fact that if
anyone in the Levenshulme family was unhinged, it wasn't Max but his
sister.

'What are you on about?' she demanded. 'He's in London isn't he? And
what the hell is wrong with Max doing social work? You should be
pleased he's found something he likes – something that makes a difference to people.'

Clare returned her gaze with a look of unmitigated loathing. 'Pleased?
Are you crazy? Max was going to be one of the top doctors in this country, he was the most brilliant student in his year. Then you came along,
and now his friends are all stinking junkies. And you want me to be
pleased!'

'My God, Clare,' said Belle quietly. 'All this trouble you've caused,
just because basically you're a snob.'

Somebody knocked at the coffee-room door and the girl with the fringe
poked her head inside. 'Mr Carter says he has to leave for London in ten
minutes.'

Clare replied without turning to look at her. 'Tell him I'll be there in a
moment.'

The door closed again, but the tension of the moment was broken.

'I'm going to have to choose my friends a bit more carefully from now
on,' commented Belle. At the door, she turned back. 'Oh, and by the way,
I know all about you trying to seduce Kieran – and failing. You know, for
a while I was actually scared of you, but I was wrong. You're a little bit
sad really, aren't you?'

'Excuse me. Miss! I need to have a word—'

Belle sped through the lobby without even pausing to acknowledge the
receptionist's existence. All she could think about was getting out of this
place and into the fresh air.

As she punched through the swing doors and out onto the pavement,
she half expected to turn round and see a squad of security men on her
tail; but the only thing behind her was a lone pigeon, pecking at a scatter-
ing of sandwich crumbs.

She stood there for several minutes, motionless as a rock in a stream, as
the two-way tide of humanity flooded by her. Congratulations, said a
voice inside her head. You did it. You fought your corner and made a
complete exhibition of yourself, and now you're glad you did, aren't you?
Really glad.

'Really glad,' she echoed. But even as she mouthed the words, tears
flooded her eyes and drenched her cheeks. Why, she didn't entirely know.

Maybe it was just shock, or relief, or the brutal sadness of being betrayed by a friend who never was.

Either way, she wept silently until a passing businessman asked her if she was all right; and as she nodded and blew hard into a borrowed hanky, she realised that all of a sudden, she was.

I could go to him now, she thought to herself. Go to Kieran and tell him what's been going on, tell him I know I was wrong. Tell him I love him. Maybe even ask if we could start again ...

But she knew that was impossible now. Everything they'd had together was ruined, not just through Clare's fault. It was hers, too: for not having had enough faith in Kieran's love to believe him.

Hideously nervous, Mona checked her watch for the fifteenth time. It was still only almost ten to, and she wasn't due to meet Oz until eleven. What now: another walk round the block?

She shuffled from one foot to the other, and hoped she didn't look too much as though she was soliciting for passing trade as she loitered around the fringes of the bus station. Killing time was no joke when the only distractions on offer were a couple of bus timetables and a display window advertising the local council's pest control service.

Oh sod it, she thought, hitching the strap of her handbag back onto her shoulder; what's wrong with being a few minutes early anyway? The sooner Oz knows what's going on, the better. Head down, hands in pockets, she trudged off determinedly in the direction of their rendezvous.

The Churchill Tea Room nestled in a quiet corner of 'select' Montpellier, and numbered pupils from the Ladies' College and their super-affluent parents among its regulars, as well as a steady stream of tourists and tweedy locals with thick ankles. Basically it was a shrine to every British cliché in the book: a plaster bulldog in a Union Jack waistcoat and top hat stood guard at the door, the waitresses wore black dresses, frilly aprons and broderie anglaise caps, and a portrait of Winston Churchill munching on a cigar glared down from the wall above the massive marble fireplace, as though daring anyone to drop jam on the white damask tablecloths.

Frankly, Mona had been rather surprised when Oz texted her to suggest they meet up for afternoon tea at the Churchill. Burger King was more his style, or the local kebab house, where there was always the thrilling possibility that he might find a bit of fried bug in amongst his shredded lettuce.

The moment she stepped through the door, Mona felt uncomfortable. The moment after that, she realised why. Oz was already sitting at a table by the window ... and it didn't take a genius IQ to work out why he was looking so down in the mouth.

'Oh shit,' said Mona under her breath as she clocked the small, sour, pinch-faced woman sitting next to Oz, and recollected the family snapshot he'd once shown her. 'The daft dingo's only gone and brought his mother with him.'

Dolores Hepplewhite knew a gold-digger when she saw one. Not that her son Oswald actually had much in the way of gold to dig, but with a first-class brain like his it was only a matter of time. And until the glorious day when he dazzled the scientific world with his brilliant entomological discoveries, Dolores regarded it as her sacred duty to protect him from anything – or anyone – who might distract him from his glorious destiny. So far, she'd had a one hundred per cent success rate in snuffing out all of Oz's embryonic relationships, and she wasn't planning on letting that record slip.

She'd had her suspicions for months about Oz's 'late nights at the lab'. A few judicious phone calls and just a hint of Gestapo-style interrogation had finally prised the truth out of him: as Dolores had feared, there was another female behind the whole thing. And a colonial one at that. Now, just when the whole thing looked to have been safely scuppered and the pair split up, here she was again, the Jezebel, inviting her son to a clandestine rendezvous behind his mother's back.

Hmph. They'd see about that.

It had been the work of but a moment to get Oswald to switch the venue from that ghastly burger bar to Dolores's own home turf: the tearoom owned by her friend Anthea from the bowls club. And now she had the home advantage, Dolores was darned if she was going to give this cheap Australian doxy any room to manoeuvre.

'Hi,' said Mona. (Dolores shuddered. Why couldn't these Antipodeans speak proper English? Doubtless it was the result of being descended from criminals.)

'Hello,' said Oswald, with a pained smile and roll of the eyes that said, 'Sorry, I couldn't stop her coming.'

His mother glared at him, and he wilted like lettuce on a gas ring. 'Hm,' she said, eyeing Mona regally down the steep gradient of her long, thin nose. 'I suppose you must be Mona Starr.' She managed to squeeze a whole world of disdain into those seven innocent words. 'I must say, you're exactly what I'd expected.'

To her disappointment, Mona didn't crumple or flinch. There wasn't a hint of wobble about her lower lip. She just drew up a chair, bold as you please, sat herself down at the table and ordered another pot of tea. 'I guess you must be Oz's mum, then.'

'I prefer "Mrs Hepplewhite", thank you,' replied the matriarch with acid precision.

'Fair enough, Mrs H.' Mona stuck out a hand. 'Oz has told me a lot about you.'

'Oh he has, has he?' Dolores directed a withering look at her son. She declined the handshake and cut straight to the chase. 'Tell me, Miss Starr. Is it true that you have been . . . consorting with my son?'

'Mo-ther, please!' Oz gave a little groan and hid his face in his hands.

'Well, I don't think I've ever heard it called that before,' commented Mona with a flicker of amusement. 'But whatever you want to call it, we stopped doing it a couple of months back.'

This came as a considerable relief to Dolores. 'I must say I'm very glad to hear that. My Oswald is far too busy with his research to involve himself in dalliances with frivolous young women.'

Mona returned Dolores's bad-smell-under-the-nose look with the sweetest and most infuriating of smiles. 'It was inevitable, I'm afraid. A girl can't have a meaningful relationship with a bloke who has his mother on speed dial, can she, Oz?'

Oz looked even more uncomfortable, if such a thing were humanly possible. Taking in the pathetic spectacle, Mona found herself wondering what she'd ever seen in the hapless little twerp . . . though a small and unrealistic part of her still hoped he might undergo a miracle transformation: gag his mother with a rock cake, sweep Mona up in his arms and carry her off to a secret love nest.

Yeah, right, she thought. Clearly it was true what all those magazines said: pregnancy really did turn your brain to sentimental mush.

'We could've talked things through,' Oz protested, albeit not very robustly. 'Maybe worked something out.'

'Don't be silly Oswald,' snapped his mother. 'Of course you couldn't.' She turned back to Mona, her eyes narrowing suspiciously as they lighted on her belly, swelling modestly beneath her loose-fitting linen shirt. 'So if this fleeting liaison between you and my son is over, Miss Starr, why this sudden desire to see him again?'

Mona had met some interfering mothers before, but never quite on the scale of Dolores Hepplewhite. You had to hand it to the old trout, she had a certain style. If the situation hadn't been so dire, Mona might even have enjoyed a verbal joust with her.

As it was, she was perilously close to braining her with the cake stand.

'If you must know,' she said, her jaw aching with the effort of not clenching her teeth, 'I have something to tell Oz. Something private.'

'Oswald has no secrets from me.'

'No, I can see that,' commented Mona, adding 'poor bastard' under her breath. 'But I've a feeling he might like to break with tradition and keep this one to himself.'

Oz's expression altered subtly, from abject to anxious, and he hauled himself up straight in his seat. 'Keep what to myself – why? What's going on?'

Mona opened her mouth to answer, but to her surprise Dolores got there first. 'Oswald Hepplewhite,' she said wearily, 'I cannot believe that I brought you up to be so naïve.'

Oz wrinkled his nose. 'Sorry?'

His mother rolled her eyes. 'Are you blind? The girl is blatantly pregnant, and now she's about to try and make you believe that you're the father so that you'll marry her and bail her out of the trouble she's got herself into.'

'Pregnant?' gulped Oz. 'Is this some kind of joke?'

'Keep your voice down!' hissed Dolores. 'Do you want the whole of Cheltenham knowing our business? Why you couldn't have arranged this meeting somewhere more discreet, I shall never know.'

'Pregnant,' echoed Oz. It was scarcely more than a strangled croak.

His mother snorted. 'It's the oldest trick in the book.' Dolores leaned back in her chair, pleased to see that she'd finally dented the Australian girl's composure. 'I am right, aren't I Miss Starr?'

At this climactic moment, the waitress returned with a platter of cream cakes. 'I'm afraid we're out of home-made banoffee éclairs,' she prattled brightly, 'but Chef highly recommends the strawberry millefeuilles, or there's the coconut and cherry . . .'

She suddenly realised that none of the people at the table was taking the slightest bit of notice of her. She might just as well not have been there. The skinny young bloke was staring, round-eyed, at the statuesque blonde; the statuesque blonde was looking ruffled and a bit pissed off; and the old witch with the hurricane-proof perm was sneering for Britain. Nobody moved an inch. It was like blundering into a tableau at Madame Tussaud's.

'Er . . . cream cakes? Would anybody like to choose a cream cake?' The waitress waited in vain for a reply and hovered miserably, stumped for what to do. Still nobody said anything – and the girl's nerve finally broke. 'Tell you what, you have a think about it and I'll pop back later.'

Dumping the laden cake stand on the table, she beat a swift retreat through the swing doors to the safety of the kitchen, muttering something about loonies.

'Well?' enquired Dolores after an extremely expectant pause.

'Pregnant?' whimpered Oz. 'You're not are you, Mona? What, like – really pregnant? No, you can't be.'

Mona's exasperation boiled over. 'Oh for God's sake, Oz! I'm only expecting a baby, it's hardly the eighth wonder of the world!'

All at once, this meeting seemed like the stupidest of all stupid ideas, and Mona wished heartily that she'd never suggested it. At least then she'd have been spared the spectacle of his complete uselessness – not to mention his bloody psychic mother. She could have sent him a nice, safe letter, scarpered off back to Australia and never set eyes on him again. Or even better, kept her mouth shut about the whole baby thing and left him in blissful ignorance. How could she ever have imagined, even for a single second, that Oz might make a half-decent, hands-on father, given that he had all the maturity of a day-old fruit fly?

'That's right,' she repeated, 'I'm pregnant. Yes, Oz, it's yours. And no, I'm not trying to get you to marry me.' Mona warmed to her subject. 'Because believe me, I wouldn't marry you if you were a bucket of water and my arse was on fire.'

Oz looked like he was about to burst into tears. Dolores's face drained of colour, and all the hairs on her chin bristled with rage. 'How dare you say such things about my Oswald!'

Mona ignored her, picked up her handbag and got to her feet. 'Now, if you'll both excuse me, I have a pub to open.'

Dolores wasn't brushed off quite as easily as that. She pursued Mona all the way to the lace-curtained door, quite forgetting about discretion in her desire to put the Australian harlot in her place. 'I don't know what your game is, my girl, but I am quite certain that my son is not the father of your . . .' Dolores's lip curled into a sneer. 'Your illegitimate brat.'

'Oh really? I can assure you that he is,' retorted Mona. 'And it's not a brat, it's an innocent baby.' She glanced back towards the table and saw that Oz was still sitting there, motionless and shell-shocked. For a split second she almost felt sorry for him. Dolores Hepplewhite wasn't the sort of mother you'd wish on your worst enemy, and whatever else he might be, Oz had never been and never would be her enemy. In her madder moments, she'd even started to believe that she might be falling in love with him. She looked at Dolores and thought: lucky escape.

'My Oswald is far too sensible to get himself involved in those sort of sordid antics,' Dolores asserted piously. 'He's an academic – his mind is on higher things.'

Mona chuckled drily. 'Actually, I think you'll find his brain's in his underpants, just like every other bloke.'

At this, a woman at a neighbouring table choked on a slice of bara brith and had to be patted on the back to dislodge it.

'You won't get a penny out of him without a DNA test!' spat Mrs Hepplewhite, fortissimo.

'Fine,' Mona replied. 'I don't want his money anyway. Money's something I can earn for myself.'

Dolores looked back at her, puzzled and wary. 'Then what do you want?' she demanded.

Mona shrugged. 'Oh you know, everything and nothing. I just had this crazy idea that a kid and its dad have a right to know each other, that's all. Insane, isn't it? I must need my head examining.'

For a moment, Dolores Hepplewhite's expression almost softened; then it set into a triumphal sneer. 'Well you won't be able to get your claws into him anyway, because as of next week he's not going to be here any more!'

Mona frowned. 'Why's that?'

Mrs Hepplewhite threw a possessive look in the direction of her son. 'My Oswald has been selected to take part in a research exchange with a laboratory in San Diego,' she announced proudly. 'Isn't that right, Oswald?'

Oz cringed behind her, like a small fluffy mammal sheltering behind a rock in a sandstorm. He nodded, his face white as a sheet. 'San Diego.'

Something fell, stone-like, into the bottomless pit of Mona's stomach. This shouldn't matter to her, shouldn't matter one bit. But she felt a cold hollow open up inside her. 'America? How long will he be away for?'

Oz opened his mouth to answer, but Dolores got there first, smirking all the way. 'Perhaps weeks, perhaps months ... perhaps longer. Who can say?' She spun it out, really enjoying herself. 'You never know, if it goes really well he might decide to stay over there and not come back to Cheltenham at all.'

A couple of evenings later, Belle found herself up to her elbows in dust and cobwebs in the prefabricated hut that had served St Mungo's as a church hall for the last thirty-odd years. Once again, her mother had suckered her into helping out with the church functions – and this time, Mona hadn't escaped either.

They'd both found themselves 'volunteering' to start clearing out the hall, ready for the following week's first Alpha course supper, where everyone would get together over a meal, listen to a talk about God, and then split into groups to thrash out how much they did – or didn't – believe. Assuming anybody turned up, of course. Tidying up was proving to be a long and tedious task. With hindsight, mused Belle, it might have been easier to have burned the hall to the ground and then started all over again. She'd never seen so much muck and rubbish in all her life.

'Are you sure you're OK?' Belle called down to Mona, who was scrabbling about in the storage area underneath the creaky old stage. 'I'm a bit worried about you – I mean, shouldn't I be doing that instead of you?'

A head popped up out of the hatch in the stage. 'If you say "in your condition", I swear I'll brain you,' warned Mona, wiping desiccated blue-bottles out of her eyebrows. 'Just 'cause I'm pregnant, it doesn't mean I'm disabled!'

'True, but if you go into labour down there, we'll never find the baby among all the junk!' Belle stooped and reached down to grasp Mona's hand. 'Come on out of there, it's time we both had a rest. I've got some juice and a bar of chocolate in my bag.'

'Oh go on then, you've persuaded me.' Mona squeezed herself back up through the trapdoor, and slung something big, black and hairy at Belle's feet.

Startled, Belle jumped back. 'Eww! What on earth is that? It looks like a squashed toupee!'

Mona nudged it with her toe, and Belle half expected it to scuttle off across the floor. 'I think it's meant to be a giant cuddly spider, but it's only got six legs.'

'Must be left over from an old panto or something.' Belle picked it up by one hairy appendage and waggled it in Mona's face. They both sneezed violently.

'You wouldn't believe all the crap down there,' said Mona, sitting down on the edge of the stage with her legs dangling free. 'Chairs with missing legs, boxes of mouldy old books, a rusty old fridge-freezer – I reckon people round here have been dumping their rubbish under the stage for the last thirty years.'

'Perhaps there's something down there we could raffle off at the summer fair,' suggested Belle rather optimistically. 'We're really short of prizes, and it can't all be rubbish.' Mona guffawed. 'Can it?'

'Well, if you've always wanted thirty years' worth of discarded news-paper, you've come to the right place.'

'Ah. Oh well, never mind. Looks like we'll have to rely on Auntie Maureen's knitted knick-knacks and Mum's home-made cake stall to bring in the dosh.'

'Don't forget Jax's fortune-telling routine,' Mona reminded her.

Belle groaned. 'As if I could. You do realise it's only an excuse for her to dress up like Morticia?'

'And there's your "Guess the Weight of the Cake" stall, and that sit-on steam train Gerry's borrowed from the model railway club. That should be fun.'

'True,' agreed Belle, 'but somehow I don't think five minutes round the field can compete with your raunchy calendar.'

'Not raunchy,' Mona corrected her, 'artistic. There's not a single naked nipple in there, you know, and it's amazing what you can hide with a couple of really big grapefruit. Not that you'd be able to hide it now,' she mused, smoothing a hand over the swell of her belly. 'Good job we got the pics taken in double-quick time.' She yawned. 'Oh, and that Ken bloke of your mum's has persuaded me to sell kisses as well, though I can't imagine why anybody'd want to be kissed by me, especially in my current state.'

'They will,' Belle reassured her. 'Take it from me, there's going to be a riot.'

She joined Mona sitting on the edge of the stage and they passed the bottle of juice between each other as they munched through the chocolate. 'You're a bit quiet tonight,' remarked Belle. 'Are you feeling all right?'

'Stop worrying! I'm fine.' Mona swung her legs listlessly, and let her heels thud back against the wooden stage with a hollow, ominous sound.

'But?' persisted Belle.

'Who says there's a but?'

'I do. Come on, it's obvious.'

Mona gave her a look of mock annoyance. 'God, but you're a nosy little bint. Never leave anything alone, do you?'

'I'm my mother's daughter,' replied Belle. 'So what's up?'

'Nothing much really,' replied Mona. 'It's just ... well, I finally decided to tell Oz he was going to be a dad.'

'Right. But I thought—'

'Yes, so did I. I wasn't going to say a word to him about the baby. But then I went and changed my mind, didn't I? Thought he had a right to know, and all that PC stuff, so I fixed up this meeting with him in a café. Must've taken leave of my senses.'

'He didn't take it well, then?'

Mona let out a short laugh. 'His bloody mother only found out we were meeting up and invited herself along! And while she's blazing away about me being a cheap slut and her precious son not being the baby's father at all, Oz is sitting there looking like a retarded bloody sheep with an electric cattle prod up its arse.'

'Oh dear,' said Belle. It wasn't the most adequate of responses, but what could you say? It was the sort of mental image that killed conversation stone dead. 'So not a big success then?'

'Let's just say I'm not expecting any bouquets and choccies when the baby's born. Not unless it's a venus fly trap and the choccies are poisoned ones from Oz's mother.' Mona hung her head. 'Guess I'm not as shit-hot at people skills as I thought I was.'

Belle contemplated the two last squares of chocolate and handed them both to Mona. She needed them. 'You can't help it if Oz is a coward and his mother's a bully. I'm sure he does care about you though,' she added.

'Oz? Care about me?' Mona grunted. 'In that case he's got a funny way of showing it. And I reckon I'm past the stage where I give a damn one way or the other.' She patted her stomach. 'From here on in it's just me and Junior. You know, even my own mother hasn't bothered to try and contact me in all these months I've been away from home.'

'Really?'

'Really.' Mona shook away the self-pity. 'Mind you, I haven't exactly made that much effort to contact her either. Anyhow, if this is going to be a lonely road I might as well get used to it.'

'You're not alone,' objected Belle. 'You've got us: me, Jax, Dad – even Mum wants to help.'

For the first time that evening, Mona smiled. 'I know, I'm just being a bit of a drama queen. You guys have been great. And when I think of the mean things I was trying to do to you when I first came over here, it's a lot more than I deserve.'

Belle turned the empty juice bottle round in her hands, picking at the paper label. 'Maybe, maybe not,' she replied. 'In any case it doesn't matter. You're family now.' She laughed. 'And when you're family you can get away with anything. How do you think Jax has got away with being a pain in the arse for so long?'

'Well,' said Mona, 'I guess that's how come I made my decision the way I did.'

Belle looked up. 'What decision?'

'About having the baby. I was going to pack up and head back to Australia, then I thought, why? It's not like there's anybody back there who really gives a flying toss about me. That's when I made my mind up: I'm having this baby right here, in Cheltenham.'

She turned to look at Belle. 'There's, um, something I wanted to ask you. A favour. But it's OK, you can say no if you don't want to and I won't mind.'

'What sort of favour?' wondered Belle.

'About the baby.' Mona's manner was awkward, almost shy. 'I was just wondering ... if I asked you very nicely, would you consider being my birthing partner?'

Belle was still staring back at her half-sister in open-mouthed surprise when the door at the far end of the church hall swung open, and a familiar figure walked in.

'Hi,' said Kieran, setting down a six-foot length of plastic drainpipe, contorted into a fantastical corkscrew shape and attached to a wooden frame. 'Where's everybody else? Brenda said everybody was meeting up to clear the hall tonight.'

Belle and Mona exchanged looks. 'We're all there is,' replied Belle, hopping down off the stage. 'I think you've been conned again.'

'What on earth is that?' Mona indicated the curious plastic corkscrew.

Kieran's chest swelled with pride. 'This is my contribution to the summer fair,' he revealed, carefully leaning the rickety apparatus against the wall. 'It's for my Whack-A-Rat stall.'

'Wow,' said Mona. 'What's Whack-A-Rat when it's at home?'

'You know,' said Belle. 'You drop the rat in at the top and the other person has a cricket bat and they have to try and whack it when it shoots out of the other end of the tube.'

'Only one problem,' said Kieran. 'My rat's gone missing.'

'How on earth can a stuffed rat go missing?' wondered Belle.

'Between you and me,' confessed Kieran, 'I think your mum threw it out when she dropped in to see me the other day.'

Typical Mum, thought Belle. She can't let go of Kieran, and more than he can let go of us. And she was glad. Because although it hurt to have become Kieran's surrogate sister, it still hurt a lot less than if he'd walked away and out of their lives.

'Yeah, she was over at the weekend. The rat was a bit disgusting after it fell in that cowpat last year at the St Jude's fete,' Kieran went on, 'and I did hear her mention something about MRSA.' His eyes met Belle's. 'She reckons my standards of hygiene have been slipping since you and I ... oh, you know what I'm talking about.'

Belle did, and she felt her cheeks burn. She wanted to look away, but she couldn't drag her eyes from Kieran's face. 'Yeah, well ... you know.'

Mona rescued her with a brisk, 'You'll just have to improvise then, won't you?'

'Don't suppose either of you have got an old teddy bear or something you could spare?' asked Kieran. 'Nothing too precious though – it's going to end up getting squashed flat.'

'It just so happens ... Here, we found this under the stage.' Belle lobbed him the six-legged arachnid with the body hair problem. 'Catch!'

He caught it one-handed, with that effortless, athletic ease that Belle had always found so mesmerising, back in the days before they were Just Friends. Kieran beamed. 'Fab. This'll really scare the pants off the little kiddies. What is it, by the way?'

'Mona insists it's a spider,' replied Belle, 'but I'm convinced it's a mutant toupee.'

Kieran balanced it experimentally on top of his head. 'Yes, definitely.

Very comfy. Your dad could wear this in the pulpit, it'd keep the draught off his bald spot.'

Belle giggled. 'Ah, but what if it's a killer mutant toupee and it ate its last owner?'

'Hm, good point. Better handle it with care then.' Kieran glanced at the hall clock as he stuffed the black furry thing into the top of the drainpipe. 'Well, if nobody else is coming tonight, maybe I should go?'

Mona had him by the elbow before he'd moved an inch. 'You're not getting away that easily. There's lots of work still to do, and I've got just the job for you.'

'Oh yes?' he enquired with a look of suspicion.

'Oh yes. You and Belle can clear out the rest of the rubbish from under the stage.'

'But I thought you were going to—' piped up Belle. Mona threw her a surreptitious wink.

'All that clambering about in confined spaces? And it's sooo dark down there ... I couldn't possibly do that, not in my condition.' Mona even managed a jaw-cracking yawn for good measure. 'In fact, if you two don't mind, I think I might just get on home for a nice warm bath, and leave you to it.'

Before Kieran and Belle had time to voice a single word of protest, her coat was on and she was halfway out of the door.

'See you in the morning – 'bye!'

There was a long silence after the door had closed. The two of them stood there just looking at each other.

'Well,' said Kieran, shifting from one foot to the other.

Belle's heart was in her mouth. 'Yes.'

'Have you been, you know, all right.'

She shrugged. 'You know. All right. Ish. You?'

'Er ... yeah. I guess.'

Kieran looked her in the eyes, and for a moment Belle was certain he was going to say something deep and meaningful. Her heart turned a back-flip in her ribcage.

And then the alarm went off on Kieran's watch, and he started. 'Oh. Wow. Is that the time? Really sorry, but I have to rush off; I sort of promised I'd take Oz out for a bon voyage drink.'

'Oh. Right. See you around then.'

He took her hand and gave it a brief squeeze. 'See you around. For sure.'

Then he was gone. And Belle couldn't decide whether she was disappointed or relieved.

*

279

It had been a long time coming, but Friday night was Alpha night.

There had been posters up all over the Bluebell Estate for weeks. Even Chelt FM, the local radio station, had given the course a plug. There couldn't be anyone in the parish who didn't know it was on. The big question was, would anybody bother to turn up?

'Of course they will,' declared Belle as she helped her mother count out paper plates and plastic cups in the vicarage kitchen. 'There's home-made shepherd's pie and fresh-cream chocolate mousse: what's not to come for?'

'I do appreciate your optimism dear,' replied her mother with an audible sigh, 'but you and I both know the Bluebell Estate isn't the most, well, religiously-minded place in the world.'

'Maybe not, but there's a lot of decent people around who enjoy a good debate. And maybe some of them will get a bit more than that from the course.' Belle folded disposable napkins into triangles and popped them into a box. 'Your friend Ken seems to think he knows a lot of people who are planning to come.'

'Yes, he does, doesn't he?'

Brenda's expression became ever so slightly dreamy. Not for the first time, Belle found herself wondering if Mona was right. Could her mother possibly fancy a man who wore Adidas jogging pants to church, could play the National Anthem on his teeth, and seemed to live on Pot Noodles? Surely not, thought Belle, shaking some sense into herself. Brenda was no candidate for a torrid roll in the hay. This was, after all, a woman who firmly believed that public toilet seats ought not to be sat on, and even socks ought to be thoroughly ironed and stored in colour-coded drawers.

'He's not usually wrong,' Belle pointed out.

'No, I suppose not.' Brenda snapped back into efficiency mode, all hints of girlish daydreams melting from her eyes.. 'I just wish there weren't all these rumours going round about the Armstrongs and the Sullivans turning up, just to cause trouble.'

Belle patted her hand. 'I'm sure that's all they are, Mum. Just rumours. If one lot turn up, the others are sure to stay away.'

'I sincerely hope so, dear. I do wonder if I ought to notify the local police though, just in case . . .'

There was a distant knock at the front door, and a few seconds later Jax appeared at the top of the kitchen stairs. 'Anybody seen Mona?'

'I think she's taken Engelbert for a walk, dear.'

'Oh. Only there's a huge man at the door with a big metal bar through his nose, and he insists on talking to Mona. All he'll say is it's something to do with security, whatever that means.'

*

Mickey 'The Teeth' Sullivan was getting ready for a night out.

He liked a nice night on the tiles, only this time he wasn't heading downtown to get bladdered and trash a nightclub or down to Whaddon Road to put the boot in on some visiting football fans. This was a special occasion, and one which had caused ripples right across the estate. Mickey Sullivan was going to church.

He grinned at himself in the bathroom mirror and a row of gold teeth glinted back at him. They were his trademark and his fortune, those teeth. When he got the real ones knocked out in a brawl with the Armstrongs, he'd had a whole new set put in: reinforced titanium, clad with twenty-two carat gold. You could really cause damage with a set of gnashers like those, and Mickey had bitten a good few people in his time. In fact he'd not long been released from jail after getting eighteen months for swallowing half a policeman's ear.

Prison was boring. Mickey was in the mood for a really good night out. Or rather, he was in the mood for a really good ruck. And he reckoned this Alpha rubbish down at the eggbox would provide him with just what he was looking for. Him and all the other Sullivans, in fact; because everybody on the estate knew that the Sullivans and the Armstrongs and all their massive broods had been limbering up for weeks in preparation for this latest round of their never-ending feud.

'I'm off to church, Gran,' he called out as he jogged downstairs, a merry whistle on his lips.

'You're such a good boy,' his doting grandmother called back.

'Don't wait up. Oh – and if the filth call tell 'em I've been home all night.'

Sorted, he thought with satisfaction as he adjusted the lapels of his one decent jacket: the one he'd bought all those years back, for his very first court appearance. He only kept it for nostalgia value really. It was a bit tight across the shoulders now, but he wasn't planning on keeping it on for long.

You couldn't fight with a jacket on. It just got in the way.

By six-thirty that evening, St Mungo's church hall was a hive of activity. Gerry was rushing about trying to 'coordinate' and getting in the way, while Miss Findlay and Albert and the other old-stagers followed on behind, putting right all the things he'd messed up. Meanwhile, Brenda was overseeing catering arrangements from the tiny kitchenette, and Belle was doing her best to direct people to their seats.

'You needn't have worried about nobody turning up, Dad,' pointed out Belle as he dashed past. 'Many more, and we'll have to put up a "house full" sign.'

Gerry paused in his nervous flitting, to survey the packed seats. 'Gosh,' he said. 'You don't think they're all going to be horribly disappointed, do you?'

'Not with this shepherd's pie anyway,' cut in Mona, bustling past with a tray of steaming plates. 'Greedy beggars can't eat it fast enough.'

Belle had to admit that things were going very nicely so far. First the supper, then the 'getting to know you' talk, then the discussion in groups over coffee and biscuits. Even if they found the religious stuff hard going (and frankly it wasn't really Belle's cup of tea, come to that), at least they could head home knowing they'd had a decent meal and it hadn't cost them a penny.

It was just as she was thinking about telling Albert to close the doors that she saw him: a tall, broad-shouldered man whose teeth glinted like razors in the lights.

Oh no. Belle gripped Mona's arm as she went by with an empty tray. 'Look. Over there. Look at his teeth! That's Mickey Sullivan.'

Mona reacted with surprising calm. 'So it is,' she commented. 'I hope he likes shepherd's pie.'

'But . . . oh shit, look, he's brought his brothers with him too!'

'The more the merrier.'

'You're surely not suggesting they've actually come here for the good of their souls?' Belle threw Mona a funny look. 'Do you know something I don't?'

She winked. 'Loads of things. Now, why don't you get yourself a plate before it's all gone?'

The last thing Belle was thinking about was food; because only seconds after Mickey and his thuggish brothers had shouldered their way into the church hall, the doors sprang wide open again, and half the Armstrong clan strolled in.

This is it, thought Belle. This is the bit where all hell's let loose. Come tomorrow, it'll be all over the front page of the *Courant*: Mayhem at St Mungo's. Oh please God, she prayed silently as the Armstrongs eyeballed the Sullivans, I know I haven't spoken to You for an awfully long time, but if You could possibly see Your way clear to a bit of divine intervention, I'd be really, really grateful.

Just as everybody was holding their breath and wondering who would land the first punch, something strange and rather wonderful happened. As if from nowhere, a dozen truly enormous young men in studded black leather materialised out of the shadows, calmly surrounding the two families and effectively blocking their exit. Belle caught sight of the back of one of their jackets. It read: GOTH BIKERS FOR JESUS.

The very largest of all removed his bike helmet and loomed over Mickey Sullivan. 'Evening,' he said with a smile so scary that even the terrifying Mickey let out an involuntary whimper. 'Nice that you could come. There are free seats over there.'

He pointed with a huge, leather-gloved finger to the front row of the audience.

Mickey demurred. 'Actually, we were just thinking of leaving, weren't we?'

The Sullivans nodded eagerly. The Armstrongs edged nearer to the exit, but the doors were shut and blocked off.

The huge biker cracked his finger joints. 'Oh no, that would be such a pity. We can't have you leaving so soon. Can we lads?'

His comrades shook their helmeted heads silently.

'So.' The finger pointed again. 'Do sit down. Just there.' He paused, then followed up with a menacing grin. 'If you'd be so kind.'

Belle watched in open-mouthed amazement as the Bluebell Estate's baddest boys filed obediently to their seats and sat in uncomfortable silence. She turned to a smirking Mona. 'You knew . . . You're behind all this, aren't you?'

Mona shrugged. 'Oh, I'm just a big fan of networking, that's all. Didn't I tell you Big Bob sometimes does security for Mad Dog? That big one there with the silver skull helmet, that's Bob's brother, Knuckles. Very religious fellow, Knuckles. I'm sure he and his mates are going to enjoy leading the group discussions.'

She stuck two fingers in the corners of her mouth and let out a piercing whistle.

It had the intended shock effect; all chatter ceased, and absolute silence filled the hall.

'Right then.' Mona rubbed her hands together. 'Some of you are a right bunch of heathens and that's OK 'cause I am too, but we're all going to sit nice and quiet now, and listen to the Reverend while he gives his talk. Aren't we, folks?'

A murmur of nervous assent ran round the hall.

She gave Gerry the thumbs-up. 'Right you are, Gerry. Off you go. Hope there's plenty of fire and brimstone.'

It wasn't the most orthodox start to an Alpha course, but it worked. There wasn't a wriggle or a peep out of the Armstrongs or the Sullivans until the end of the talk, thanks to the Goth bikers none of the discussions turned into brawls, and even when it came to coffee there was no pushing and shoving in the queue.

'You're bloody amazing, Mona,' whispered Belle as they queued for their drinks, goggling at the spectacle of an Armstrong helping a Sullivan to the sugar. Mona laughed, but Belle was serious. 'I mean it, you know,' Belle said. And then she spoke words she'd never have dreamed of uttering only a few months ago.

'I'm really proud to have you for a sister.'

Chapter 29

Lily shook her head firmly. 'It's no good, I just don't believe it,' she declared. 'Nobody does that to the Armstrongs and lives. Or the Sullivans. They're like the Krays of the Bluebell Estate.'

'Ah yes, that's what they'd like you to think, but I'm telling you, they were a total bunch of wimps that night.' Belle went on stacking tins of talc-free dusting powder. 'It's true!' she insisted in the face of Lily's sceptical expression. 'I wish you'd seen it for yourself. Those Goth bikers were something else – but Mona . . . she was truly awesome.'

'Something tells me you're starting to enjoy having a big sister,' remarked Lily, her baby bump resplendent in a swathe of paisley-print eco-jersey that made her look like an extra from *Free Willy*. 'Am I right? Have you stopped sticking pins in that wax effigy?'

'Ha, ha.' Belle stuck out her tongue. 'You're always right, little Miss Smarty-Pants. Especially since you got pregnant. You're developing that . . . matriarchal look. It's quite scary actually.'

Lily looked horrified. 'Matriarchal? Oh my God, you make me sound like I'm a thousand years old and the size of a bus!'

'Well, a VW camper van at least . . .' Belle eyed the magnificent swell of Lily's stomach. 'Are you sure you haven't got quads in there? You're twice the size of Mona, and she's a dead ringer for a Teletubby.'

Lily's riposte was a swipe on the bottom with a long-handled back brush. 'Cheeky cow – just you wait till it's your turn!' she threatened. 'It'll all catch up with you one day. One minute it's all career dressing and fun, the next it's buns in the oven and your big end's gone. Mark my words – once a bloke gets you under his spell, gets you right where he wants you, you're never the same again.'

The smile faded from Belle's face. 'No,' she said softly. 'You're not.'

It took a couple of seconds for Lily to twig what was up. 'Oh Belle, you're not still moping about Kieran are you? I thought you were well over him by now.'

'Oh, I am,' insisted Belle, getting up off her knees and patting the white, scented dusting powder from her skirt. 'We're getting used to being just good mates. But after all we went through together, I don't think I'm the same person any more. In fact we both reckon we've changed. Do you think I'm different now?'

Head on one side, Lily contemplated Belle for a few moments. 'Maybe,' she conceded, 'but there's nothing about you I can see that's not a change for the better.'

'Really?' Belle brightened.

'Really. And remember: I'm always right. You said so yourself.' Lily glanced past a huddle of giggling teenage browsers to the big, round clock over the door. 'Hey, didn't you say you needed to get off an hour early today?'

'If you're sure it's still OK.'

'Fine by me,' Lily replied with a shrug. 'We're hardly rushed off our feet and it's not as if I'm on my own in the shop. What're you planning, anyway? Romantic assignation, or is it just a dentist's appointment?'

'Nothing very interesting, I'm afraid. I got my arm twisted to help get stuff ready for the church summer fair tomorrow.'

Lily shook her head reprovingly. 'Belle Craine, do you really think you're ever going to meet the man of your dreams when your social life consists entirely of church fêtes and consorting with the local lowlife?'

'Probably not,' admitted Belle with a smile. 'Still, you never know, do you?'

She didn't admit to Lily that the main reason she'd agreed to help out that evening was because she knew Kieran had promised to be there too. And why ever not? Kieran was her friend, and she liked spending time with her friends – all her friends. But if she told Lily, Lily would wilfully get the wrong idea, and that would never do.

After all, Belle told herself firmly, romance was the very last thing on her mind.

Saturday dawned promisingly warm, with only the tiniest skeins of white cotton cloud arranged here and there in the sky, as if to relieve its too-rich blue. It was going to be one of those perfect, sunny August days when it seemed that summer was going to go on and on forever and autumn was just a rumour.

Belle lay in bed for a little while with the curtains open and the windows wide, luxuriating in the summer warmth and thinking about the previous evening, when she, her mother and Kieran had wrapped up silly little presents for the bran tub, and Jax had moaned all evening, the way she always did, yet still managed to do more than the rest of them put together, because they'd spent all their time laughing and behaving like five-year-olds.

It had been just like old times, the way it was when Belle and Kieran were an item, and it had seemed certain that this was how it would always be. Just like the summer: perfect and cloudless and with no hint of an end in sight.

Part of Belle knew that seeking out Kieran's company like this wasn't necessarily a good thing. She could persuade herself as much as she liked that she was just continuing their friendship, but in her heart of hearts she knew that what she was really doing was torturing herself with images and imaginings of what she could no longer have. Like a broken mirror, their relationship might be glued back together in some semblance of its former shape, but it could never be the same as when it was whole. It had become a fragmented thing, artificially held together by Belle's desperate desire not to lose Kieran completely.

But was it really better to have Kieran as a friend than not to have him around at all? Wouldn't it be less painful just to relax and let go? For several years their lives had touched and intertwined, but the bond of romance had been broken and now they were drifting quite naturally apart, with only her stubborn will – or so it seemed to Belle – holding them together. Why not just admit defeat and move on? Maybe that was what he wanted her to do.

They'd had plenty of opportunity to talk about it. But every time they found themselves alone together, all they seemed to do was chat about trivia, sidestepping everything that might have any bearing at all on emotions. Maybe it was cowardice; maybe it was just a mutual, unspoken determination not to risk damaging the fragile new way they'd found of being together without actually *being* together. All Belle knew was that the way things were now, couldn't last forever.

She rolled onto her side and gazed out of the window of her bedsit into the little communal garden. It was flooded with sunlight, and in the birdbath two sparrows were flapping and fluttering in a haze of water droplets. You couldn't feel defeatist or sad or maudlin on a day like this. Biological optimism was far more powerful than common sense. Bloody hormones, she thought. Why can't we all be robots? Life would be so much simpler.

Anyhow, she reasoned as she slipped out of bed, she had to go to the summer fair because she'd promised Mum and Dad that she would. Who was going to take the gate money and help with the donkey rides if she didn't? She couldn't possibly let Mum and Dad down.

All of this was quite true. But Belle couldn't deceive herself completely.

287

There was one, overriding reason why she was going to the St Mungo's church summer fair; and that reason was Kieran Sawyer.

The horrible patch of waste ground that had festered for years opposite St Mungo's was completely unrecognisable.

Anyone who'd seen it six months ago, half-obliterated by rubble, rubbish and the odd upturned shopping trolley, would have laughed themselves silly at the notion of anyone turning it into a half-decent football pitch. It wouldn't even have made the grade as a second-rate swamp. But – thanks to Ken, Brenda and a handful of determined parents – the miracle had happened. And now St Mungo's church field was hosting its very first summer fair.

It wasn't one of those posh fêtes you got in la-di-dah Gloucestershire villages, complete with media personalities, the odd minor royal and an exhibition match by the local polo team. This was much more fun. Brenda's army of volunteer cooks had produced enough food to sink the Bluebell Estate through the earth's crust under its own weight, Mona's pub was running a cracking beer tent, and for sheer entertainment, what could beat the pleasure of throwing wet sponges at the local headmaster?

By two pm, the field was absolutely packed. Belle finished her stint on the gate, where the Goth bikers were keeping an eye on the cash box, and strolled over to the beer tent, where she had to breathe in and squeeze through the jostling crowds to get anywhere near the bar. Mona greeted her with a cheery 'G'day' and a pint on the house.

'This is good,' commented Belle, sipping from her glass.

'Specially brewed by that new micro-brewery in Bishop's Cleeve. We've got St Mungo's mead too, if you fancy something exotic.'

'Thanks, but I think I'll stick to this for now. I'm steering clear of mead after Bards and Wenches Night.' She felt in the pocket of her jeans for some cash. 'I'll have a pint for Kieran too, please. He must be thirsty by now.' While Mona pulled the pint, Belle stood on tiptoe to look around her. 'Where's Dad?'

'Flitting about like a bluebottle with its arse on fire, last time I saw him,' replied Mona. 'All 'cause of that bastard bishop. I mean, why invite Grove of all people to do the official opening? Nasty little slimeball.'

'Dunno,' admitted Belle. 'Perhaps Dad wants to show the bishop how much has been achieved here since he took over. It is pretty impressive, after all.'

Mona nodded slowly as she considered this angle. 'Rub his nose in it, you mean? Hm, I like that.' She handed over Kieran's pint. 'Maybe our dad's not quite the newborn lamb I thought he was.'

*

Meanwhile, Brenda and Ken were manning the tombola stall. It wasn't as easy as it sounded, as Ken had to keep a weather eye on the prizes to make sure they didn't grow legs and disappear before they were won, while Brenda had to keep popping over to the refreshment tent to check if they'd run out of fairy cakes and sandwiches. Then there was the ever-present problem of Engelbert, who had loudly refused to be tethered outside the tea tent and was currently marauding around the fair in search of abandoned burgers and ice-cream-toting children to mug. Basically, you needed eyes in the back of your head.

'Look, mister, I won!' A boy held out a pink tombola ticket and waited expectantly. 'Sixty-five, see? I'll have that bottle of whisky.'

Ken reached across the table and gently moved the boy's thumb, revealing an extra number seven. 'Nice try,' he said, 'but I wasn't born yesterday.'

The boy muttered something with 'old git' at the end, then shuffled off with his hood up and his hands in his pockets.

'Wasn't that Shane Armstrong?' asked Brenda as the boy disappeared into the crowd and the stall was left deserted. 'You do realise he's probably off to complain to his big brothers – all seven of them?'

'He can complain all he likes,' Ken replied robustly. 'He's not fiddling my tombola and that's flat.'

Brenda smiled up at him. 'That's my hero.'

'Really?' he asked with pleased surprise.

'Oh, absolutely.'

Ken wondered if it was only a joke, or whether she might be just a tiny bit serious. She looked really young and pretty with her golden hair up like that, he thought. Even more beautiful than she usually looked. It took years off her.

'Julie never called me a hero,' he recollected soberly. He couldn't quite suppress a quiver as he felt Brenda's hand on his arm.

'I'm really sorry about you and Julie splitting up,' said Brenda.

He looked down at the bare, knobbly toes sticking out of his sandals. 'I'm no prize,' he replied, rather stating the obvious, 'and Julie found somebody better.'

'Not better,' objected Brenda. 'I'm sure he's not better, just … well, maybe he and Julie are just better suited.' She paused. 'Is there a chance you might get back together?'

He looked directly into her eyes and hoped that the truth was what she wanted to hear. 'Nope. We had a decent innings, but basically we were never that great together. Not that it was anybody's fault,' he added quickly, 'and Julie's a nice lady, but … but she was never, well, you.'

He knew from the way Brenda changed the subject, lightning-fast, that he'd just uttered the verbal equivalent of nitro-glycerine. He hadn't meant to, it was just that he had always had this really strong impulse to tell the truth.

Brenda took convenient advantage of a couple of passers-by to flog them a whole strip of tickets. 'Oh look, you've got a winning ticket!' She dropped it into the box. 'That's ... the tin of assorted biscuits. There you are, enjoy them!'

Business might be quiet at the moment, but that was mainly because so many tickets had been sold that most of the good prizes had already gone. 'The way things are going,' she remarked, pushing a straggle of hair off her perspiring forehead, 'there'll be nothing left by the time the bishop gets here – except maybe that revolting mooning garden gnome.'

Ken grunted. 'Just make sure you hide that bottle of whisky. Last time he visited St Mungo's, the treasurer swears blind he made off with a whole case of communion wine.'

Brenda's hand flew to her mouth, turning a giggle into a cough. 'He never did!'

'As I live and breathe. Thaddeus Grove likes a drink, and that's the plain truth.' He said it loudly enough for several heads to turn.

'Shh!' Brenda appealed, going a touch pink at the edges. 'He'll be arriving any moment ... and somebody might tell him.'

Ken was distinctly unconcerned. 'Oh really? And what's he going to do about it? Sue me? He's welcome to try. Send you and Gerry to Devil's Island? Face it Bren, there aren't any worse parishes he could send you to – as far as Gloucestershire's concerned, St Mungo's is as bad as it gets.'

'Oh I don't know,' said Brenda, returning his gaze with a smile. 'It's turned out to have some compensations.'

He couldn't quite believe she'd said that. 'Pardon?'

The smile was still there – a little shy perhaps, but very definitely there. 'You heard,' she replied. 'Do you really need me to explain?'

He didn't, and she knew it. Somehow, neither of them was quite sure exactly how, their fingers edged closer together, not quite touching but neither drew away. And then their eyes locked, and somewhere in Ken's heart fountains gushed and fireworks exploded into coloured sparks.

'I'm so glad I met you again, you know,' said Ken. 'All those years ... I never stopped thinking about you.'

Brenda swallowed. Her lips felt unnaturally dry. 'If only I'd known twenty-five years ago, I'd have—'

A man's voice broke into their joint reverie. 'Ken mate, are you going to snog the vicar's wife or sell me a ticket?'

Brenda froze in mortal embarrassment. Ken turned to face the speaker. It was Geordie, one of the fathers from the under-thirteens' football squad. Geordie Collins, he of the big wallet and even bigger mouth. He was sporting a lascivious grin, and holding out a ten-pound note. ''Course, if you want to snog her first and then sell me a ticket, I can wait. I like a nice romance, I do.' He winked. 'Not sure what the vicar'd say about it, mind.'

'Geordie, what the hell are you on about?' spat Ken.

'You two, staring into each other's eyes like a pair of lovesick sheep.'

'You're sick, you are.' Ken gave him a long, hard look. 'And you've got a very dirty mind.'

'Me? But it's you two who were . . .' Geordie looked from Ken's stern face to Brenda's embarrassed one, and then back again. He struggled to grasp what was really going on, gave a shrug, and finally capitulated. 'Only having a laugh, mate. You know me.'

'Well go and do it at somebody else's expense.'

More might have been said, but just then a sleek, metallic-blue Mercedes slid through the gates onto the field, completely ignored the parking marshals and the big yellow arrows, scattered the crowd with a parp of its horn, and halted ostentatiously right beside the dais where prizes were being awarded for the dog with the waggiest tail.

The bishop had arrived, and he wanted everybody to know it.

It was all go at Kieran's Whack the Rat stall – or Splat the Spider, as he had had to rename it after the disappearance of the rat.

Belle was laughing so much that she was spilling more of her beer than she was drinking. But that was hardly surprising. It wasn't every day that you saw a man in the back end of a pantomime cow suit (who'd just shared first prize in the adult fancy dress section) hit a giant six-legged spider over the church hall roof with a cricket bat. When the applause had died down, a search party was despatched to retrieve the said spider from the upper branches of a neighbouring tree while Kieran and Belle took a much-needed break on a couple of upturned plastic crates outside the beer tent.

'Just look what you've done,' Belle scolded as she blew her nose and mopped beer off the front of her T-shirt. 'Look at the state of me!'

'It's not often I make a woman wet herself,' agreed Kieran. Belle cuffed him round the ear. 'Ow! What did I say?'

'If you don't behave, I'll tell my dad you weighted that spider to cheat the punters,' she threatened him, still breathless with laughter.

'You wouldn't!'

'Oh yes I would! It was going all over the place back there – every which way but straight! Heavens knows how that bloke in the cow suit ever managed to hit it.'

291

'But I was only trying to make the game more challenging and stimulating,' Kieran protested, the very model of feigned innocence.

'And avoid giving out any prizes,' Belle pointed out.

'Yes, that too; you got me there. But who'd want to part with these adorable plastic trolls your mum got for nothing from that shop that went bankrupt?' He waggled one of the most grotesque ones in Belle's face. 'Look – it's wearing little orange polyester trousers, and its eyes go all googly when you turn it upside down.'

'Don't!' she giggled. 'Put it away!'

'Ah,' sighed Kieran wistfully, 'that's what all the girls say.'

She caught his gaze and his eyes were laughing back at her. He seemed so free from care that it almost hurt to see him that way, the way he used to be before she played her part in messing everything up. 'I never used to say it though,' she blurted out. 'Did I?'

'Say what?' Kieran stopped laughing and looked at her. 'Oh. Yes. I see what you're getting at.' He cleared his throat awkwardly. 'No, you didn't, did you? Well, not while we were . . . er, no.'

'Did I just say something stupid?' she wondered.

'No.'

'Yes, I did, we were having a laugh and then I said that, and now you look like . . . oh I don't know, like a little boy with a punctured balloon.'

'Do I?' He smiled. 'Well, you're pouting.'

She reacted with indignation. 'I don't pout!'

'Yes you do – and you are now, I could land a helicopter on that bottom lip of yours.'

She giggled. 'I'd rather you didn't.'

'Me too. I'd much rather look at your face without a helicopter in front of it. That'd really spoil the view.'

Belle felt warmth spread over her cheeks, making her feel more self-conscious than ever. 'Why would you want to look at my face?'

'Why wouldn't I?'

They were looking at each other, and the warmth and the laughter and the alcohol seemed to be wrapping them up, drawing them in closer. Just for a split second Belle found herself thinking, maybe something could happen. Maybe even now. If I try not to want it too much.

It was a moment of perfectly balanced suspense. Then, as quickly as it had come, that moment was gone. Kieran was up on his feet and gazing across the field, one hand shading his screwed-up eyes. 'Bloody hell – who's that lunatic in the blue Merc? And what's he trying to do, mow down half of Cheltenham?'

Belle snapped back to reality and followed his gaze. She recognised the car instantly, and her heart sank into her boots at the thought of Gerry

Craine's nemesis. 'It's Thaddeus Grove,' she groaned, dragging herself to her feet. 'Better go and tell Dad his favourite bishop's arrived.'

It wasn't a marriage made in heaven, but all things considered, it was going rather well. Belle breathed a sigh of relief and Mona held on tight to Engelbert's lead. Nobody was going to foul this up, and that included a renegade mutt with a lust for chaos.

Gerry and Bishop Grove clearly loathed each other: that much was obvious to anyone with eyes to see. But nevertheless they were managing to do it with impeccably good manners. Thaddeus Grove strolled round the fair making all the right noises about 'encouraging developments in St Mungo's outreach initiatives', and even managed not to swear when he was forced into having a go at unseating the headmaster and splashed his stylish ecclesiastical threads with cold baked beans.

As for Gerry, he was trying very hard not to smirk as he pointed out the new football team (complete with a brace of juvenile Sullivans fresh from the young offenders' institution), the new choir (in its 'adventurous' gospel robes), the St Mungo's Majorettes, and the all-new over-sixties' yoga display team, which boasted a combined age of nine hundred and seventy-six.

'I'm so pleased things are working out for you here, Gerry,' lied the bishop through a smile so thin it could have modelled for Dior, as he favoured the vicar of St Mungo's with a limp and disdainful handshake. 'Obviously your vocation always lay in the more deprived parishes. I really should have recognised that earlier in your career.'

'Oh, so you mean by removing me from St Jude's you were doing me a favour?' enquired Gerry.

The heavy irony went right over Thaddeus Grove's head. 'Yes,' he nodded. 'I do believe I was.' He rubbed his podgy hands together with evident self-satisfaction. 'Now, shall we give out those prizes to the jam-makers and what have you? Not that I'm not having a ... er ... fabulous time here, but I have to be in Circencester in half an hour, you know – important Church business.'

In the watching crowd, Belle leaned over and whispered loudly in Kieran's ear: 'Golf tournament.'

'That figures.'

Large as life and twice as pompous, Bishop Grove joined Gerry and both halves of the pantomime cow (now joined together and wearing a winner's rosette) on the wooden dais. The cow did a little tap-dance and got more applause than the bishop.

'What is that?' demanded the bishop, with his hand over the microphone.

293

'It's a cow.'

'I can see that, Craine, why is it here?'

Gerry sighed. The spirit of old-fashioned knockabout fun seemed to have passed the bishop by. 'It's the winner of the fancy dress competition, Bishop, and it's holding the names of the winners in its mouth,' he explained, indicating a sheaf of envelopes. 'I pick one and read it out, and then you award the prize. Simple, see?'

'Cretinous,' replied the Bishop, checking his watch. 'Can we get on with this? I have to be at the club house – I mean conference centre – by three.'

One by one, the winners climbed up to accept their prizes for everything from Best Face Paint (Darth Vader) to Fattest Pet (a thirty-two-pound rabbit) and Top Church Fundraiser (a very embarrassed Ken). For the most part they were modest prizes, except in the category everybody was waiting for: Guess the Weight of the Cake.

It was one of the most impressive cakes Belle had ever seen, crafted with loving care, a ton of dried fruit and gallons of royal icing in Brenda's very own magic kitchen. Then there were all the sugar roses and silver dragées that made it positively shimmer in the afternoon sunshine. If you were a cake connoisseur, this was your Mona Lisa. Even if you weren't, it represented a good few weeks of solid cake consumption. Everybody wanted to be in with a shot of winning it.

'And now for the moment we've all been waiting for. In just a moment, I'll be asking Bishop Grove to present this magnificent cake to the person who has come nearest to guessing its correct weight.' Gerry indicated the cake, sitting on its plinth flanked by two burly minders.

'Get on with it, Craine,' muttered the bishop, unaware that his hand wasn't quite covering his microphone. 'It's only a bloody fruit cake.'

A murmur ran around the crowd. Engelbert whined and strained at his leash at the sight of so much lovely food, so near and yet so far away.

'Stop it, Engelbert,' hissed Mona.

Gerry turned to the cow. 'Daisy – can I have the winning envelope please?' The pantomime cow rubbed its head against the vicar's shoulder and dropped the gold envelope daintily into his hand.

'Your dad isn't half making a meal of this,' Mona commented to Belle. 'If you ask me, he's enjoying pissing the bishop off.'

Kieran chuckled. Belle gave Mona the thumbs-up. 'Good – I can't think of a more deserving case.'

Brenda looked on despairingly. 'I do hope your father isn't going to make an exhibition of himself in front of the bishop.'

In the event, what happened wasn't Gerry's fault at all. If you were being charitable, you might even say it wasn't Engelbert's either; after all, a dog can only take so much. Perhaps it was the unbearable proximity of the cake that did it, or perhaps it was the sight of the Dog with the Waggiest Tail, sniffing around the podium; but all at once, with a deft flick of his scruffy neck, he slipped his collar and made a lunge for the dais just as Gerry held the winning card aloft.

'And the winner is . . .' Gerry nudged the bishop with his elbow. 'Bishop Grove, if you would – the cake?'

'What? Oh. Very well.' The bishop reluctantly heaved the cake waist-high, grimacing under the weight.

'The winner is . . .'

Before he'd even spoken the name on the card, a woman pushed her way to the front of the crowd and stepped forward. 'Hello, Gerry; long time no see. Remember me?'

'Oh, my . . . No . . . no, it can't be!' His mouth fell open like a trapdoor, his eyes bulging as if they couldn't quite come to terms with what they were seeing. 'Rena? Rena Starr?'

Suddenly, all the colour drained out of Gerry's face and he staggered sideways. If he'd staggered to the right, the pantomime cow would have borne the brunt with no damage done. Stumble forwards, and Engelbert would at least have stood a fighting chance of getting out of the way. But unfortunately he staggered to his left – right into Thaddeus Grove, who lost his footing and, in a valiant attempt to avoid falling off the dais, did the only thing he could. He let go of the cake.

And the crowd went 'Ooooh' as it made its short journey from the bishop's hands to the ground.

Via Engelbert's head.

Chapter 30

Rena Starr. First Gerry's eldest daughter and now his first love, ruining a day when Brenda had almost dropped her guard and started to feel happy again. Suddenly that woman had appeared from nowhere, taking all Brenda's humiliation and thrusting it in her face. It was all too much to bear.

As chaos reigned around her, she felt peculiarly detached from all of it. So much had happened to her since the previous autumn that she no longer felt surprised when bad things happened. But what had she and Gerry done to deserve all this?

What have I done? she demanded, as people argued, a photographer from the *Courant* appeared from nowhere, and a slightly concussed Engelbert consoled himself by gobbling up bits of atomised cake. What have I done that's so very bad? I've always been a dutiful vicar's wife, even when the whole idea of another jumble sale or another interminable coffee morning bored me to the verge of tears. I've endured everything that's been asked of me, and all I've ever asked in return is to be respectable.

The one thing the Bluebell Estate never gave me, and which it now wants to take away from me again.

It was all just too monstrously unfair.

She was dimly aware of voices calling to her, but she'd had it with everyone and everything, and she just kept on walking in the opposite direction. This time, they could all just damn well sort themselves out. Without her.

In a cordoned-off corner of the empty tea tent, Rena Starr and her daughter were getting upfront and personal.

'What the hell did you think you were playing at, Mum?' fumed Mona. 'Swanning out in front of the bishop like that? And what the fuck are you doing in England anyway? I thought you weren't speaking to me.'

'Me? What about you? You're the one who said she wouldn't set foot in my house again until I gave Chas his marching orders, and then buggered off to England for months without so much as a postcard.'

Ah, thought Belle with a wave of unease. *Something tells me this might be my fault.* What were the chances that Rena's sudden appearance didn't have something to do with a certain email she'd sent to Ros? Pretty remote, she had to admit. What was it she'd said? 'Seeing as you're going to be in Melbourne anyway, why don't you see if you can find out anything about Mona's mother? Maybe even track her down ...' *Well done Belle,* she told herself, trying not to look too horribly guilty. *You should've known Ros never gives up. If somebody gets murdered in St Mungo's tonight by a mad Australian, it'll be all down to you, kid.*

The woman with the straw-textured hair and skin that had seen far too much sun in its near half-century wasn't taking any cheek off her daughter. 'I'll have you know I was making a big entrance. Scared the shit out of that wimp Gerry, didn't I?' She threw a disparaging look at Belle and Kieran. 'And I'd have had my say, too, if these two hadn't dragged me off like a sack of bloody potatoes. Who the hell are they, anyway?'

'I'm Kieran Sawyer,' he said. 'And this here is Belle Craine. Gerry's daughter.'

'And Mona's half-sister,' added Belle.

Rena at last displayed interest. 'You never are, you're too short and your arse is too big.' She looked closer. 'Blimey, Gerry's eyes.'

At least Bishop Grove must be halfway down the M5 by now, mused Belle gratefully, and still picking shards of royal icing out of his mitre. No doubt he was still wondering who that crazy-woman heckler was, and why he'd been suddenly bundled into his Merc with all the formal courtesy of a rugby scrum. *Good riddance,* she thought; *I hate to think what he'd have made of all this.*

Belle had always had trouble keeping quiet when she was nervous. 'It's ... um ... nice to meet you anyhow,' she blurted out during the first lull in hostilities. 'Mona's told me so much about you.'

Rena snorted like a camel with sinusitis. 'Has she now? That's a novelty. 'Cause believe me, she never let on a word to me about any of this.' Rena fixed Mona with a penetrating stare. 'Did you?'

Mona bristled defensively. 'You never asked! All these months I've been away, and you've never bothered getting in touch once! Not one letter, not one email, not one phone call – zip!'

'Yeah right.' Rena swept away the accusation. 'Well if we're talking lack of communication, what about that?' Rena's scarlet fingernail pointed the way to her daughter's belly, ever-so-gently swelling out beneath her tight crop-top. 'That's definitely something you kept quiet about! What happened – did it just slip your memory, or what?'

Mona folded her arms across her chest and glowered. 'I didn't ask you to come here and create a scene,' she growled. 'Come to think of it, I never asked you to come here at all.'

'No,' agreed her mother. 'A little bird had to come and whisper in my ear that my stupid bloody daughter had got herself up the stick.'

'What "little bird"?' demanded Mona. 'What bastard dobbed me in?'

Belle wished the ground would swallow her up. Later on she would just have to confess, even if her half-sister did knock her into the middle of next week. But for now, she was keeping the lowest of low profiles.

It was Rena who saved her bacon, by ploughing on regardless. 'Go on,' she dared Mona, 'tell me that's just a bit of extra weight you've put on through eating too much English food.'

Mona drew herself up to her full, dignified height. 'No, Mum,' she replied. 'Actually I'm pregnant, and it's due in December. There: satisfied?'

'Satisfied? Satisfied! You have to be kidding me, my girl. I mean, one minute I'm waving you off on some once-in-a-lifetime backpacking trip to the Himalayas – "Don't bother trying to get in touch, Mum, I'll be halfway up a mountain" – and the next I find out you're in bloody England, getting yourself pregnant—'

'Hardly a first for the Starr family, is it?' cut in Mona sarcastically.

Her mother chose to ignore the jibe. 'Not to mention digging up the family skeletons without so much as a by your leave from me.'

'I'm not the one who caused the skeletons,' Mona retorted. 'And I don't need permission from you to find my family.'

'I'm your family. Chas is your family now, too.'

Mona's lip curled. 'Your useless boyfriend Chas is a no-good letch who's playing you for every dollar you've got. By the way, did I mention the time he tried to grope me in the cellar?' Rena's planned expletive turned into a fit of coughing. 'No? Well I am now. Anyhow, I'd have thought you'd be pleased your daughter wanted to track down the man who got you pregnant and find out what really happened, all those years ago.'

Instead of letting fly at her daughter again, Rena collapsed, speechless, into one of the folding plastic chairs Brenda had begged and borrowed from the local garden centre.

'Mum?' ventured Mona after a few seconds of silence.

Rena looked up at her. 'You came all this way to do that? To sort out some stupid mess I got into the best part of thirty years ago?'

Mona looked taken aback. 'Stupid mess? I thought what happened with Gerry Craine ruined your entire life. I wanted to sort it all out . . .'

Her mother gave her an odd look. 'Did I drop you on your head when you were a baby, or what? Or maybe it's the English genes that made you turn out so weird. Listen Mona, it may have been a bit inconvenient, getting put in the club when I was only a kid myself—'

'Inconvenient!'

'But after all's said and done, me and your stepdad Eddie were already courting. I admit I was a bit upset about Gerry not returning my letters, but it's not like we were Romeo and Juliet or anything.'

'You weren't?' Belle tried to imagine them romantically entwined all those years ago, this rough-round-the-edges woman and her softly spoken, almost-apologetic dad. Admittedly it was a hard thing to do. 'But I sort of got this impression—'

'So did I,' cut in Mona.

'That Dad was, well, the love of your life. Or something.'

'Gerry?' Rena snorted. 'The love of my life? Typical bloody Pom more like. Quick drunken fumble, then too much of a coward to write back once he knew I was pregnant. That's why I couldn't resist giving him a little bit of a fright out there. Call it my little bit of revenge, if you like.'

'Excuse me.'

Gerry Craine's soft, melodious voice made everybody turn round. He was hovering in the entrance to the deserted tea tent, almost apologetic to be disturbing other people when they were busy running him down.

'Dad,' said Belle. 'Did you find Mum?'

He shook his head. 'No sign of her, I can't think where she's gone.' His gaze was fixed on Rena. 'You haven't changed,' he said, walking towards her across the grassy floor of the tent.

'I thought vicars weren't supposed to tell lies,' retorted Rena.

'It's no lie. I recognised you the instant I saw you. It's the eyes you see – that same, sparkly blue. Mona has it too, that's how I was so sure she was your daughter the day she came to the vicarage.'

Rena shook her head. 'Still the same old smooth talk, Gerry Craine? Shouldn't you be hanging your head in shame?'

He frowned. 'Shame?'

'For what you did. All those letters I wrote, telling you about the baby coming, and you never answered any of them. Not one.'

Gerry was standing beside her now. Belle looked at the two of them, half-expecting to feel some magical spark of erotic energy pass between them, even after all this time. After all, they had been lovers. First lovers – and wasn't first love supposed to be the most powerful of all? Maybe not, she thought, reflecting on the way she felt about Max. But as they contemplated each other, all Belle sensed was a kind of weary curiosity. It's true, she thought; and a tingle of relief ran down her spine. They never were Romeo and Juliet, or Abelard and Heloise. They were just two hormonally charged kids, a very long time ago. In that moment she wished her mum was there to see it, to feel it, because she knew it would make a world of difference to the way Brenda felt.

'I never answered your letters because I never received them,' replied Gerry.

'You can drop the lies now, Gerry.'

'I've never lied to you, Rena, and I'm not going to now. The fact is, I wrote to you every day for weeks. I was besotted with you, you know, and when I never received a single reply … well, it broke my heart for a long time – I thought you must have decided I was just a stupid kid or something, and didn't want anything to do with me any more. Of course, Mother thought it was for the best … but that's mothers for you.'

'Yeah,' said Rena quietly. 'Mine was the same. "Forget about him, he's not the one for you, plenty of other fish in the sea." She was made up when I married Mona's stepdad.' She looked Gerry in the eye. 'If you're lying to me, I'll have your balls for earrings.'

'I'm sure he isn't,' said Kieran, wincing.

Belle cut in. 'He isn't. He couldn't, you see. Dad just doesn't lie.'

Rena looked her up and down. 'You seem awfully sure of what's right and wrong and the way things are.'

'That's because she's her father's daughter,' cut in Mona; and she slid her arm through Belle's. 'We both are.'

Ken finally caught up with Brenda by the tatty bike sheds behind the comprehensive. Somehow he'd known instinctively where he'd find her. She was all huddled up in her pink cardigan, alternately crying and pulling on a cigarette, and she looked about fourteen and utterly lost.

'Smoking, Brenda? I thought you gave it up years ago.'

'It seemed like a good time to start again.' She looked up as he came into view, sniffed and wiped a trail of mascara off her cheek. Her hand was shaking as she dropped the cigarette butt and ground it into the asphalt with her heel. 'You guessed,' she said.

'Of course I guessed. This was our special place. I've lost count of the number of times we bunked off lessons to come here.'

She looked around her grim surroundings and laughed humourlessly. 'Not that it's all that special when you come to look at it. Bit like my whole life, really. That was her back there, you know, causing all that trouble,' she added after a pause. 'Mona's mother. Gerry's boyhood bit on the side.'

'Ah. I thought it might be something like that.'

'All the way from bloody Australia, just to cause a scene and make my life a misery.' She ran a hand through a fringe that was wet with perspiration. 'I thought I was coping with everything OK you know, I really did. And then she turns up.' She sniffed back a tear. 'Do you think he still loves her?'

'Gerry? I don't know. I suppose it's possible,' Ken admitted, 'but he didn't look that pleased to see her.'

'No, that's true.' Brenda let out a long sigh. 'But then again, even if she was the love of his life he'd never say so. He'd never let me down however much he wanted to, you see, 'cause I'm his wife for better or worse, and what matters to Gerry more than anything else is doing the right thing.' There was an edge of bitterness in her voice as she added, 'I guess some people are just born holy or something.'

There was a short, uncomfortable silence. Then Ken cleared his throat.

'Brenda . . . what you said about your life, and not being special and all that. If you don't mind my saying so, that's a load of old bollocks.'

'It is?'

'You'll always be special to me, Brenda, more special than anything: I thought you'd realise that by now. You're the most special thing that ever happened to me, and if I'd had half a brain when I was seventeen I'd never have let you go.' He took a couple of steps towards her, then stopped. 'There's something I want to do,' he said, 'only I don't know if I should.'

Brenda looked at him questioningly. 'What?'

'This,' he said, and by way of explanation he took her face in his hands and kissed her, ever so gently.

'Oh Ken, we shouldn't,' she said. But she kissed him back anyway.

'No,' he agreed, 'we shouldn't.'

They stood looking at each other for a long time, neither of them able to turn and leave, yet both silently aware that sooner or later they must.

'I can't ever leave Gerry,' whispered Brenda, on the verge of tears again. 'I just couldn't, he'd never cope without me. And besides—'

Ken cut in before she could finish. 'You love him.' He was glad she couldn't see the profound sadness in his eyes; it would only have made things harder. 'That much is obvious, even to a clod like me.'

'It doesn't mean I don't love you too.'

Ken buried his face in the soft fragrance of her hair. 'It's OK, Brenda, I know when I'm in a fight I can't win. Just promise me one thing.'

She drew back a little and gave him a questioning look. 'What?'

301

'If you ever, ever change your mind about Gerry, you'll remember there's somebody around who'd give anything for a second chance.'

Brenda smiled through her tears. 'Of course I'll remember.'

'That's OK then.' Ken straightened himself up, took out his rumpled handkerchief and handed it to Brenda. 'Well, we'd best get you sorted out and find that pesky husband of yours,' he remarked with a joviality he didn't quite feel. 'I reckon he's got a bit of explaining to do.'

Chapter 31

A few weeks later, as summer was sliding seamlessly into autumn, Oswald Hepplewhite crept back into Cheltenham.

He didn't actually resort to wearing a wig and false ears, but if invisibility paint had been on offer at the airport shop, Oz would have invested in a couple of gallons on the spot. As it was, instead of heading straight home he took an unscheduled turn off the motorway, and holed up at the nearest Travelodge. This would have come as news to his mother, not to mention Mona, neither of whom had any idea he was even back in the country.

Not that Mona gave a damn about her erstwhile beau, or his mother, or at least, not if she was to be believed. She was more bothered about her own mother, who had moved into a guest house in town and was showing no sign at all of going home. On the contrary, she seemed to be enormously enjoying the looks she got whenever she walked through the Bluebell Estate, not to mention the atmosphere each time she called in at the vicarage for a gargantuan pot of tea and one of her 'little family chats'.

'You know, I really couldn't care less if I never see Oz again,' declared Mona, as Belle helped her collect up the glasses at the pub one evening, just after closing time. 'In fact, if the miserable little tick came to me on bended knee and begged me to take him back, I'd ... I'd tell him to go boil his head!'

Belle really did want to believe that it was true; it was just that she couldn't quite manage it. After all, she'd told herself often enough that she was over Kieran, and that clearly wasn't true either. Still, at least she and Kieran had managed to forge a new kind of friendship out of the mess of the break-up; and friendship had to be better than nothing.

Or was she even better at deluding herself than Mona was?

Over at the offices of the *Cheltenham Courant*, the following Saturday morning, there was a definite gleam in Sandra the features editor's eye.

'Hang on,' protested Kieran as she whipped the scrawled notes off his desk. 'I took the call, it should be my story.'

She looked at him pityingly. 'Kieran, sweetie – didn't anyone ever tell you that all's fair in love and journalism? I'm the boss round here, so it's my story.' She stuffed the paper into her pocket and headed for the door. 'I'm not missing out on this, it could be my passport out of this pathetic little town.'

Kieran watched the door slam behind her back. He was not the happiest of bunnies. First someone rings up with a great story, about 'reformed' Mad Dog McKindrick being photographed at some kind of cocaine-fuelled orgy; then just as he's on his way to follow it up, Sandra steals it from him. And now, he mused darkly, he was going to have to take the assignment he'd desperately hoped he wouldn't have time for: covering the Beautiful Brides show at a local hotel.

Oh joy, he thought as he plodded out to his car. This is all I need: a day surrounded by starry-eyed lovers – as if I didn't feel a big enough roman-tic failure already. There must be at least a thousand more entertaining ways to spend a Saturday.

He gave the ghastly event a couple of hours to get underway, and showed up at the hotel around noon. With any luck there'd be free canapés or a buckshee glass of Buck's Fizz on offer to ease the monotony, and plenty of garrulous punters just dying to be interviewed. An hour should do it, he decided as models pranced past him on their way to the catwalk, encased in varying sizes of meringue. Then ten minutes with the photographer and back to the office for a quick write-up. If I get a move on, there might even be time to get down to Whaddon Road for the match.

There were a variety of display stands in the hotel lobby, and Kieran decided to start there. He was just heading towards a huge mass of heart-shaped balloons when something – or rather someone – caught the corner of his eye. Funny how some people remind you of others, he thought, glancing to the right. That guy over there, for instance . . . he's a dead ringer for . . . Kieran took a few steps further.

'Oz?'

The guy jumped six inches and swung round. 'Kieran? Oh, thank God, it's only you. I thought it might be somebody, you know, important.'

'Charming,' remarked Kieran. 'So who are all these important people? And what are you doing at a wedding fair? Why aren't you in America?'

Oz grabbed him by the sleeve and dragged him off into the relative quiet of the residents' bar. 'I'm not at a wedding fair,' he insisted.

'You are, you know.'

'No I'm not! I just happened to be passing through – if you really want to know, I'm staying here. But for God's sake don't tell anyone, or they're bound to open their big mouths and then my mother will find out I'm not in San Diego.'

Kieran coughed into his fruit juice. 'Your mother doesn't know you're back in England? Bloody hell.'

Oz shifted uncomfortably on his bar stool. 'I need some space,' he said. 'Without people bothering me.'

'People like Mona?' Kieran enquired.

A wave of anxiety passed across Oz's already hunted-looking face. 'You won't tell her, will you?' he begged. 'You won't let on to her that I'm back?'

Kieran shrugged. 'If that's what you want. But you do realise you can't hide out here forever? I mean, she's going to find out sooner or later.'

'I know,' moaned Oz, gazing forlornly into the depths of his glass. 'And what am I do then, Kieran?'

Around the time that Kieran was telling Oz to pull himself together, Belle was paying a visit to the vicarage, only to discover that her mum was very far from her usual calm and collected self.

'What on earth am I supposed to do?' demanded Brenda, standing amid the chaos of her normally tidy kitchen. 'Talk about short notice – why doesn't anybody ever think to tell me anything until the last minute?'

Belle put her shopping down on the counter. 'What's wrong, Mum? What's happened?'

'Your father's only invited his blessed mother over for a "nice family get-together and a bit of a party".'

'Oh yes of course,' said Belle. 'It's Nanna Craine's eighty-fifth birthday on Tuesday. I posted her present yesterday.'

'Well, she won't get it,' snapped Brenda, 'because she's flying in from the Isle of Man first thing tomorrow morning, and apparently I'm driving over to Birmingham, to pick her up from the airport. Not that I knew that until breakfast time this morning,' she added resentfully. 'Apparently it slipped your father's mind.'

'Oh dear, that's a bit much,' Belle sympathised. 'But you know how absent-minded he is when he's got a lot on his mind. Would you like me to take half a day's leave and go and fetch her for you?'

Brenda shook her head. 'Don't get me wrong dear, I do appreciate the offer, but you've got more important things to do with your day.' She broke eggs disconsolately into a pudding basin. 'And after all – cooking, errands, loaves and fishes, it's all par for the course when you're a vicar's wife, isn't it?'

'I'm sure Dad wouldn't want you thinking like that,' Belle insisted.

'It's wrong of him to take you for granted, but he loves you to bits, you know that.'

Brenda sighed and nodded. 'I know.'

For the first time in quite a while, she was seriously worried about her mum. First the trauma of the move, and all the publicity about Mona, and now Mona's mother settled indefinitely at a guest house in town. She was sure the split from Kieran hadn't helped either. Little by little, these humiliations had been chipping away at Brenda's armour and, while Gerry had begun to find his feet in his new parish, Belle had never seen her mother looking so fed up.

'I wouldn't mind so much,' Brenda went on, mechanically mixing up cake mixture, 'but it's like I'm totally insignificant until there's a crisis, then it's, "Oh, Brenda will cope, Brenda always copes."' She looked across the kitchen table at her daughter. 'Only sometimes, I don't feel as if I can.'

'Then the rest of us will help you. Oh Mum.' Belle put her arms round the bits of her mother that weren't coated in flour. 'You're the best. The best mum and the best cook and the best organiser ever.'

Brenda hrmphed. 'You make me sound like some kind of domestic goddess.'

'So you are!' Belle helped herself to a fingerful of cake batter. 'You're far sexier than Nigella though. And I bet she couldn't run a pensioners' yoga class to save her life.'

This at least provoked a laugh. 'Neither can I! I'm only doing it till we can find someone who actually knows their lotus from their sun salutation.'

'Stop running yourself down, Mum!' ordered Belle. 'Face it, the only person who thinks you're not totally great is you.'

Brenda would probably have come back with some kind of scathing remark, but Jax came clattering down the stairs into the kitchen, dragging her rucksack behind her.

'Mum, where's my shirt?'

'Which shirt, dear?'

'You know, my shirt!' Jax flapped her arms impatiently. 'Razor's taking me to the Coven of Blood gig in Pittville Park, and I absolutely have to wear it!'

'Why's that then?' enquired Belle, as much to irritate her younger sister as anything. She clearly remembered the time she'd refused to go out for a week because the washing machine had chewed holes in her beloved Jasper Conran jeans.

Jax pursed her lips, forming a crimson rosebud beneath geisha eyebrows and panda eyes. 'Because it's my favourite shirt!' she replied in exasperation. 'Mum, where is it? I put it out for washing last night and I haven't got it back yet.'

Brenda poured cake mixture into baking tins. 'That'll be because it's still in the laundry basket,' she replied.

'You haven't washed it?' Jax's face registered horror. 'But Mum!'

'Jax,' cut in Belle, 'what colour's this shirt of yours?'

'Black.'

'What colour are all your shirts?'

'Black – why?'

'Why don't you wear another one, and leave Mum alone? Can't you see she's rushed off her feet?'

'But I can't!' protested Jax. And to Belle's surprise, her lower lip began to wobble. 'This is all to do with him, isn't it? Mum's fed up with Dad and she's going to move in with him and leave us!'

'What on earth are you on about?' demanded Belle. She stole a glance at her mother, but Brenda's eyes were firmly fixed on her baking tins so she turned back to Jax. 'What do you mean, "him"?'

Jax's eyes were very bright, almost staring. 'I'm right, aren't I? It's that bloke Ken she's been carrying on with. Isn't it, Mum?'

'Jax – shh!' Horrified, Belle shut her sister up, but the cat was already well out of the bag.

'Don't you shush me, Belle, we've all heard the rumours.'

'Rumours!' Brenda clapped a trembling hand to her mouth.

'Don't take any notice, Mum,' Belle said, a trifle feebly. 'Jax is just talking a load of rubbish – as usual. There aren't any rumours. Are there, Jax?'

There was a long, taut silence. And then Jax emitted a sound that might have been 'No.'

One by one, and without saying a word, Brenda carried the cake tins across to the oven and slid them inside. Once the door was closed on them, she turned round, wiping her hands methodically on her apron.

'For your information,' she announced with quiet dignity, 'Ken has been a very good friend to me; a very good friend, but nothing more, do you hear? Anyway, he's going away. He's got a job up North, running a youth project.' Her voice wavered ever so slightly. 'It's for the best.'

Then she turned and walked silently out of the kitchen, closing the door behind her with a click of finality.

When the phone rang that evening, Mona was expecting it to be Belle, phoning her with details of Nanna Craine's big birthday do. Not normally known for her liberal attitude to family life, Nanna Craine had regally condescended to talk to to Mona on the phone, and subsequently announced that she and her mother were to be invited to the party so that they could be 'given the once-over'. People were not in the habit of saying 'no' to Nanna, dowager duchess of the Craines. Besides, Brenda and Gerry were still trying to make it up to her for the cancelled wedding she'd been so looking forward to.

All keyed up for strict instructions on what she should wear to the party, Mona was tongue-tied with shock when she heard Oz's voice on the other end of the line.

'Hello, Mona. I . . . um . . . wanted to check to see if you're all right.' Pause. 'Mona? Mona, are you still there?'

She shook herself back to reality. 'You've not bothered with me for the last two months,' she pointed out acerbically. 'Why the sudden interest in me now?'

'Don't be like that, Mona,' pleaded Oz. 'I've been thinking about you a lot while I was . . . I mean while I'm here. In America,' he added, just in case she'd forgotten where his firm had sent him.

'Well, isn't that nice to know?' Mona's head was reeling. Half of her wanted to tell him to get lost, while the other – hormonal – half was urging her to if not kiss then at least make up with him. After all, whether she liked it or not he was the father of the swiftly developing blob in her belly.

'Er . . . so how are you?' asked Oz.

'Still pregnant. For the next three months or so, anyhow.'

There really was no answer to that. Silence fell for several leaden seconds, then mainly to fill the silence Mona remarked: 'This is an awfully good line. You sound really close, like you're just up the road or something.'

Oz gave a nervous laugh that turned into a sort of cough. 'Yes. Great, isn't it? Technology I mean. Would you . . . I mean when I get back . . . like to sort of . . . meet up or something?'

'I'll think about it,' replied Mona. Then she relented a little. Maybe it was just the hormonal havoc of being pregnant, but she couldn't help being just a little bit fond of Oz, even if he was totally useless and the world's biggest wimp. 'All right, why not? If nothing else, we can discuss whether being a snob and a cow runs in your family.'

'Oh,' said Oz, rather taken aback. 'OK.'

'Just one thing though.'

'Yes?'

'Leave your mother at home this time.'

Wherever Rena was, she was in the habit of making herself at home. She was busy brewing tea in Mona's kitchenette when the phone rang. Like every other mother on the planet, she had long since developed bat-like hearing, so sensitive that it could pick up the sound of a bra strap being undone in the next street. It wasn't much of a challenge to work out who was on the phone in the next room.

Aha. So, the randy little worm had finally dared to poke his nose above ground level. Once Mona had ended the call and gone downstairs to check on the bar, Rena crept into the sitting room and picked up the phone. Call it a hunch – it was no more than that – but she couldn't lose anything by acting on it.

Swiftly she dialled 1471, waited, and then a big, sly smile crept right across her face. Well, well, who'd have guessed? A local number.

Gotcha.

Nanna Craine arrived the following morning, with a crate of Manx kippers and enough warm vests to last her for six months.

A small, rounded widow with a generous bosom and an accent people found difficult to pin down, Hettie Craine was English but had married young, to a man who was comfortably off, Manx right back to the Vikings and proud of it. She had spent the last half-century on the Island and made only the rarest of forays to the mainland, to stock up on cardigans and tell her relatives how fat they were getting.

Although she was tiny and plump and he was tall and spare, it was easy to see the resemblance between her and her only son, Gerry. They both had the same large, dark eyes, almost magnetic in the way they dominated the face and drew others' attention. There though the resemblance ended, for whereas Gerry was easygoing and affable, sometimes to the point of naivety, Hettie had a soul of pure granite.

In Hettie's world, there was right, wrong and nothing in between. She had been sternly brought up by her ex-Indian Army father, and it showed. Good manners were essential, a woman who couldn't knit wasn't worth the time of day, and if she had her way, mobile phones would be consigned to the dustbin of history, along with sliced bread, the Common Market (she refused to call it the European Union), decimalisation, thongs and supermarket ready meals.

For all that though, people liked her. Belle had many happy memories of sitting on Nanna and Grandpa's bed in the dark, listening to terrifying tales of bugganes and the moiddhey dhoo, and all manner of nasty beasts from Manx folklore; and sunny afternoons on the beach at Port St Mary, looking for sea anemones and crabs in the little rock pools. And nobody insulted people like Nanna Craine. Do her wrong and you did so at your peril. Wherever she shopped, she left a trail of sobbing salesman in her wake. Whenever anyone came to stay with her, she would greet them at the door with a breezy: 'Hello, when are you going back?'

She was quite a woman, and it was good to have her around, if only for a few days. And anyway, what possible trouble could one small, eighty-five-year-old woman cause?

After a discreet word with her dad, Belle prompted him to move the family party to Treakles, a Cotswolds restaurant that specialised in the kind of all-English fare Nanna Craine favoured. In this way her mother's job was made a little easier: cooking a four-course roast dinner with all the trimmings for an assortment of relatives from all over the place surely couldn't be anybody's idea of fun. And Gerry's sister, Belle's Auntie Rose, had all kinds of allergies, which caused no end of culinary problems, not to mention much huffing and puffing from Nanna, who firmly believed all allergies to be a figment of the imagination.

Despite the new catering arrangements, Belle was concerned. She could sense a tension in her mother that maybe wasn't entirely connected to her grandmother's visit. But every time she got near enough to ask how she was, Brenda brushed her aside with a brusque 'Not now dear, I'm busy.'

It wasn't until half an hour before the party, when some of the guests had already left for the restaurant, that Belle finally managed to trap her mother into a conversation.

Brenda was sitting at her dressing table, putting the finishing touches to her make-up.

'You look lovely, Mum,' said Belle, closing the door behind her. 'That green dress really suits you.'

Her mother smiled back at her in the mirror. 'Thank you, Annabelle, your gran says it makes me look like a vegetable marrow.'

'Oh, you know Nanna. She loves causing mischief. Fill her full of Bristol Cream and she's no trouble at all.'

'That's true,' agreed Brenda, applying a slick of lip gloss. 'A couple of sweet sherries, and she's even polite to Cousin Trixie, "chavette" or not.'

Belle smiled. Trixie – Aunt Rose's daughter – was loud, colourful and totally unrepentant. 'Poor Trixie – Nanna's never forgiven her for getting hair extensions.' Belle watched the smile fade from her mother's lips. 'Mum, something's wrong, isn't it? Have you and Dad been rowing?'

'No! No, it's nothing like that. Nothing you should worry about at all.'

'But Mum, I am worried. I can see something's bothering you.'

After a moment's hesitation, Brenda swung round on her stool. 'All right, I'll tell you. But you're not to say a word to anyone else. Do you promise me that?'

Belle sat down on the end of the bed. 'Of course I do, Mum. What is it?'

Brenda hung her head. 'It's really nothing at all, I don't know why I'm so down in the mouth about it. I should just pull myself together. It's Ken.' She looked up. 'He left Cheltenham today. And he won't be coming back.'

'Oh.' Belle didn't quite know what to say. What were you supposed to say when you weren't sure if your mother had been having an affair or not, and if so, you weren't quite sure how you felt about it either? 'Did you . . . I mean, did you think about . . .'

Brenda seemed to read her thoughts. 'Going with him? Of course I did.' An electric shock of fear ran through Belle. 'For about thirty seconds. Then reality kicked in.'

'You mean – Dad?'

Brenda reached across and took Belle's hands in hers. It was a gesture more intimate than Belle had come to expect from her light, airy, ever-breezy mother. 'I love your father very much,' she said, looking earnestly into her daughter's eyes. 'I want you to understand that. I love him and respect him, and I would never ever do anything to hurt him.'

'Even if you wanted to?'

'Even if – just for a moment – I wanted to. The thing is, Belle, what Ken and I had belongs to the past, when we were just a couple of kids. We could never be more than friends now; we still love each other in our own way, but it's not a grown-up kind of love, not like I have with your dad.'

A kind of ripple of relief ran across Belle's skin. 'Only friends? You mean you and Ken – you weren't actually . . . .' Belle flushed scarlet. 'You know?'

'Lovers?' Brenda's eyebrows arched and Belle felt utterly mortified. How had she dared ask her mother such a question? 'Excuse me Annabelle, but when did you become my mother?'

'I'm sorry. I shouldn't have asked.'

'It's OK.' Brenda squeezed her daughter's hand. 'I would've asked if I were you. And the answer's no, we weren't lovers. But we could have been . . .'

She was gazing into the middle distance as Belle crept away to finish getting ready.

When they arrived at the restaurant, half an hour late, everyone else was already seated at the table and Nanna Craine was on her second sherry. 'Where on earth have you been, Brenda?' she scolded.

Gerry smiled up at his wife and made a place for her next to him. 'You know, for a moment there,' he joked, 'I thought you'd left me.'

And for a split second, Belle thought that maybe, just maybe, her father wasn't joking.

*

311

Belle had lost count of how much Nanna Craine had drunk, but it was enough to fell a sumo wrestler. Hettie showed no signs of slowing up however; in fact she had fallen into a sort of drinking competition with Rena, who to everyone's surprise seemed to have struck up a rapport with her. As Hettie put it, midway through the dessert course: 'I can hold my own with the colonials, any day of the week!'

Maybe it was the drink, maybe it was Hettie's instinct for devilment. Or perhaps it was a mixture of both. But either way, she turned the conversation to Rena and Gerry, and what had happened between them all those years ago.

'Don't you think it would be better if—' began Gerry, but he was silenced from all sides.

'Come on Gerry,' urged his sister Rose. I'm sure we'd all like to know what *really* happened, wouldn't we?'

A murmur of agreement ran round the table.

That was Rena's cue to drone on about how she'd written to Gerry but he'd never written back, and then Gerry's cue to protest that yes, he had written to her, every day for weeks, but that he'd never heard a single word back from Australia.

'Ah well,' said Mona in the ensuing silence, 'I don't suppose we'll ever know the true story, eh Belle?'

Everyone might have settled for that – if the sherry hadn't loosened Hettie's tongue. She looked round the table, drained her glass and started laughing. 'Look at the lot of you, not a brain between you! Did it never occur to you two that you weren't the only people involved?'

Rena and Gerry looked at each other, then at Hettie. 'What do you mean?' demanded Rena.

Hettie shook her head and sighed. 'Even back then we had telephones, you know, Rena. It wasn't the Stone Age. The minute she knew what was up, your mother was on the phone to me.'

'What!' said Rena. 'She never said.'

'Of course she didn't! You weren't supposed to know. Anyhow,' Hettie went on, waving her glass and accidentally spilling sherry into the fat salesman's lap, 'she and I, we cooked up this little plan. She'd intercept Gerry's letters before Rena got them, and I'd intercept Rena's. Then we'd destroy them, and bingo!'

Gerry stared at his mother in dismay. 'Bingo? Mother, are you saying you deliberately prevented us contacting each other and stopped me finding out I'd fathered a child?'

Hettie blinked at him unconcernedly. 'Yes, of course I am. Haven't you been listening to a word I said?' She leaned back in her chair. 'We both agreed, it just wasn't suitable. You weren't right for each other.'

'How dare you!' exploded Rena. 'Are you saying I wasn't good enough for your precious son?'

'Well, if the cap fits,' replied Hettie with a shrug. 'Anyhow, your mother was none too keen on the romance anyway, she wanted you to marry some fellow you were supposed to be getting engaged to. There you are, it all worked out in the end, didn't it?'

Everyone looked at everyone else. Speechless. It was Belle who finally broke the silence. 'So it was you, Nanna? All this time it was you?'

'It was for the best,' insisted Nanna Craine, full to the brim with righteous conviction and sherry. She held out her glass for a refill. 'Come on everybody, this is supposed to be a celebration.'

Chapter 32

'And then she says, right in the middle of dinner: "Oh by the way, Rena's mother and I fixed the whole thing. The reason you never got any letters is because we destroyed them all"!'

Lily listened to Belle with rapt attention. 'No!'

'Yes!' Belle plugged in the kettle in the Green Goddess staff room, and rummaged in the tatty overhead cupboard for the jar of instant coffee. 'They both decided the whole romance thing was totally unsuitable, baby or no baby, and that was that.'

Lily whistled. 'There was I, thinking your granny was just a nice little white-haired old lady. And all the time she's a ruthless schemer.' She struggled to get comfortable on the bucket-shaped chair they'd rescued from a skip behind the Italian coffee bar. She'd miss Belle while she was on maternity leave, but she certainly wouldn't miss these chairs. 'So what happened then?'

'Everything went horribly quiet, and for a minute I thought there was going to be a riot. I mean, you've seen Rena – and I bet she packs one hell of a punch. Then all of a sudden, she starts laughing and tells Nanna Craine she did them both a favour, 'cause if they'd got married they'd probably have ended up killing each other!'

'Hm. Well, it's one way of looking at it I suppose.' Lily rubbed her back and grimaced. 'I don't know if it's the chair or the baby, but I just can't shift this horrible backache.'

Belle brought the coffees over and sat down on the other chair: a rickety refugee from a clear-out at the bric-a-brac shop round the corner. Unfortunately, Green Goddess's commitment to staff wellbeing had never extended as far as providing them with something decent to sit on when they were having their breaks. Belle suspected it was all an underhanded incentive not to take their breaks at all.

'There's only one thing for it,' she declared. 'You'll have to buy yourself a giant Mars Bar – best painkiller I know.'

'Ah, chocolate ... I feel better already.' Lily sank into her chair with half-closed eyes and a blissful expression on her face. 'You know, there's only one good thing about pregnancy,' she remarked.

Belle searched around for a biscuit to munch. 'You mean the fact that at the end of it all you get a cute little baby?'

'What?' Lily opened one cynical eye. 'No.'

'Maternity leave then?' hazarded Belle, musing that at the end of Lily's, she might be out of a job.

'No! I'm talking about having permission to be fat! Think about it, when else in her lifetime is a woman praised for looking like Mr Blobby?'

'Until she's had the baby and still can't shift the weight,' pointed out Belle. 'And her boobs droop so they're like tennis balls in a sock.'

Lily stuck out her tongue. 'Gee thanks! And I'd almost convinced myself it was worth all those years of sleepless nights and smelly nappies. Just you wait till it's your turn and even your feet are so fat that you spend your life in flip-flops.'

'With my total absence of sex life?' The end of Belle's bourbon biscuit fell off into her coffee, and she tried unsuccessfully to take it out with her finger.

'Come on kid, Kieran wasn't the only fish in the sea, not by a long chalk.'

'No. I know that,' said Belle, aware she didn't sound all that convinced.

'And you're just not sure you fancy any of the other fish?'

'Something like that, yeah.' Belle shook off her attack of the blues. 'Anyhow, you can forget about getting me into maternity dungarees. There's not much chance of that, m'dear.'

'Not much chance of what?' Waylon stuck his head round the door.

'Belle's got no bloke,' said Lily. 'She's looking for a Mr Right to come along and whisk her away from all this.'

'I am not!' spluttered Belle.

'Ah well, I'd marry you myself love,' lamented Waylon, 'only I've got girlfriends all over Gloucestershire, and I wouldn't want them to get jealous.' He winked. 'By the way,' he added, 'I don't want to worry you, but a coachload of Japanese tourists has just come into the shop, and you've only got Millie and Dan out there to stem the hordes.'

'We're on our break!' pleaded Lily. 'Belle's only just made the coffee.'

'That's all right.' Waylon beamed as he relieved Belle of her mug. 'You two go and sort out the shop, and I'll stay here and finish this coffee. Waste not, want not.' He raised his mug in an ironic toast. 'Cheers, girls.'

'Bastard,' Lily flung back over her shoulder – just as Waylon sat down in the wonky bucket chair and it toppled sideways, taking him with it in a tangle of legs, arms and curses.

*

Oz was finding his clandestine life somewhat difficult to manage, since the only person who knew he was in Cheltenham was Kieran. Or at least, he hoped he was.

Oz's ever-loving mama was under the impression that he was still in America because of 'last-minute developments'. As far as the lab was concerned, he had taken two weeks' leave and was probably hacking his way through some rainforest in search of undiscovered bugs, or up to his ankles in Sri Lankan hissing cockroaches. Everyone knew that a holiday simply wasn't a holiday for Oz if it didn't include insects. Big ones. His colleagues would never have believed the truth: that he was holed up in a budget-priced hotel on the outskirts of Cheltenham, trying to work out what the hell to do about Mona.

And the baby. Oh God, the baby. He came out in gooseflesh just thinking the word. At least in his state of chronic uncertainty, Oz was certain about one thing: he and fatherhood just weren't ready to make each other's intimate acquaintance. Far from it.

With a shudder of sheer panic, he turned up the TV, lay on his bed and closed his eyes, praying that when he reopened them it would all have been just a scary dream.

Round about thirty seconds later, somebody knocked at the door of his room. The 'do not disturb' sign was hanging on the handle outside, so he ignored whoever it was; but a minute or so later the knocking started again. Irritated, Oz got up and plodded to the door. Couldn't the chamber-maids in this place read or something? Was a bit of peace and quiet so much to ask?

He'd barely opened the door an inch when a human whirlwind swept in past him, slamming the door behind it and leaving him standing there, gaping like a complete idiot.

Slowly he turned to give the intruder a piece of his mind. But the middle-aged, hard-faced woman who had barged past him was sitting calmly on the end of his bed, arms folded and staring at him as though he was the one who ought not to be there.

'Excuse me, madam,' began Oz, 'but you're in my room.'

The woman looked him up and down with a critical eye. 'Well, at least you're observant,' she commented in a strident Antipodean accent, 'if nothing else. You're a puny one though,' she went on. 'Hardly more than a rasher of wind. God only knows what Mona saw in you.'

'Mona?' Oz reacted as though he had just stuck his finger into a plug socket.

'Yes, Mona,' the woman replied irritably. 'My daughter. I'm Rena Starr, and unless I'm very much mistaken you're the bastard who got her pregnant and then ran off to America.'

Oz swallowed hard, took a couple of steps and collapsed into an armchair. 'Oh my God, you're Mona's mother.'

'Yes, we've been through that bit already.'

A thought struck him. 'How did you know I was here? Kieran didn't tell you.'

'Nobody told me anything. I worked it all out for myself. You see, Oswald – Jeez, your parents must've really hated you – not all women are as stupid or as gullible as my Mona.'

'Why are you here?' asked Oz faintly, the words 'to beat the crap out of me' insinuating themselves scarily into his brain. Rena was, after all, considerably brawnier than he was and looked as hard as triple-reinforced concrete.

Rena fixed him with a bowel-loosening stare. 'I'm here to tell you to keep the hell away from Mona,' she replied.

This was not at all what he'd expected. 'But – why?'

'Because it's pretty bloody obvious that you've had your fun, you're not interested in facing up to your responsibilities and I don't want you messing up her life even more than you already have done. Got that?'

'Yes . . . I mean, no!' Oz protested. 'What if I don't want to stay away from her?'

Rena raised a cynical eyebrow. 'It's a bit bloody late, don't you think?'

'I didn't go to America because I wanted to,' he said. 'The firm sent me.'

'And they stopped you phoning her more than twice the whole time you were there?'

Oz reddened with discomfort. 'It's been difficult. I've been . . . confused. And there's my mother . . . she sometimes doesn't take things very, er, calmly.'

'Confused. Right.' Rena made it sound like the most pathetic thing to be in the whole universe. And perhaps, Oz mused, she was right.

'That's why I'm staying here,' he went on, for some reason desperate to convince this terrifying woman that he wasn't as weak and reprehensible as all that. 'I decided to take a bit of time out to work things through. You know, decide what I ought to do.'

Rena got to her feet. She was a full head taller than Oz, with muscles to match. 'That settles it.'

'Settles what?'

'If you need time to work out what you ought to do, you're even less of a man than I thought you were. So like I said, keep away from Mona. And the baby, when it's born.'

Oz pursued her to the door. 'What if I don't want to keep away?' he said again. 'What if—' He cut himself short.

317

'What if you what?'

Oz stared down at the toes of his tartan slippers, embarrassed beyond belief. 'What if I love her?' he mumbled, almost inaudibly.

'I can't hear you,' said Rena. 'You'll have to speak up.'

He coughed painfully. 'I said, what if I . . . I love Mona? What if I'm in love with her?'

'That might make a difference,' replied Rena, her hand on the door latch, 'and then again it might not. It's not whether you love her or not, is it? It's what you intend doing about it.'

The following evening, Kieran phoned Belle to ask her if she'd like to come out for a pizza 'you know, just as mates'. And she answered that 'just as mates' she'd love to. She didn't let on that she'd have been even happier to come out with him as something more than mates; that kind of pointless wishful thinking could only lead to trouble.

Over a Piquant Pepperoni Passion, Kieran related the panicky phone call he'd had from Oz. 'And then she gave him an ultimatum,' he went on, licking spicy tomato sauce from his fingers. 'Get his act together or stay away from Mona for good. Unless he fancies having his head ripped off by a mad Australian, that is.'

Belle winced. Despite his tendency to haplessness she was very fond of Oz, and had no desire to see his head ripped off by Rena – or by his mother, come to that. But on the other hand, she'd grown very fond of Mona too . . . 'What do you think he'll do?' she asked.

Kieran shrugged. 'You know Oz. Present him with a do-or-die situation and he's like a bunny caught in the headlights. Probably nothing.'

'So he'll lose Mona and the baby.'

'I guess so, yes.'

'But you said he told you he's in love with her.'

'He did.' Kieran called over the waitress and asked for another Peroni and a glass of house white. 'And I'm sure it's true. The trouble is, he's also terrified – not just of his mum, it's the whole responsibility thing.'

Belle fingered the stem of her wine glass. 'I suppose he's not the only one,' she remarked.

Kieran spoke through a mouthful of pizza. 'It honestly never bothered me,' he said. 'You know, when we were . . . taking the plunge.'

'I know. I guess it was me really. Being all unsettled and stuff, and wondering what it must be like to be a success.' She looked up at him. 'But I tried that when I was running the Customer Services office, and it was crap. Not me at all.'

'You did the job well though,' Kieran pointed out. 'They tried to get you to stay.'

318

'But I hated it – and you hated me doing it,' Belle reminded him.

He was quiet for a few seconds, then admitted, 'I did come over a bit caveman, didn't I?'

She smiled at his downcast expression. 'Only a little bit. And face it: I look silly in a power suit.'

They went on eating for a while. On the other side of the dining area, a violinist in gypsy costume was serenading a pink-cheeked woman and her beau. Outside the windows of the restaurant, autumn rain started to fall, turning into golden rods in the light from the street lamps.

'Lily's going off on maternity leave, isn't she? What are you going to do when she comes back?' asked Kieran.

Belle paused. 'I don't know. Either I'll stay where I am and be an ordinary shop assistant again, or ... or maybe I'll do something else. Head office did offer me a job up in Liverpool last time,' she pointed out.

'Oh,' said Kieran.

'Is there something wrong?'

'No, of course not. I'm having a great time – how about you?'

'Great,' she echoed. 'Mind you I was a bit surprised when you chose this particular restaurant, seeing as it's where we came on our very first date.'

She expected him to clap a hand over his mouth, exclaim, 'Oh shit, I forgot,' or something of the kind. But he didn't. He looked her straight in the eye and said, 'I know. That's why I picked it. You don't mind, do you?'

Belle wanted to tell him how very much she didn't mind, but somehow she couldn't get the words out, and she ended up just saying 'No. No, I like it here.'

'There's something I should tell you,' Kieran added. The words sounded so ominous that they sent a cold shiver running down Belle's back. Oh God no, he's got a new girlfriend, she thought. And she's moving in with him. Or worse, they're buying a place together and they're getting married. Or she's pregnant ...

'What?' she asked, in the most timid of whispers imaginable.

'I went up to London the other week, to talk to the editor on that national newspaper who's been talking about taking me on as a feature writer.'

Belle held her breath and prepared herself for the worst. This is it, she told herself; he's leaving and it's too late to do anything about it. 'Go on,' she said, trying to keep the tremor out of her voice.

'I had a look round, chatted to him about stuff, but to be honest I hated the whole atmosphere of the place.'

'You did?' Belle's eyes opened wide.

'All the bitching, the crap hours, the feeling you're on a knife-edge all the bloody time. I thought hard about it, but in the end I turned him down.'

'But—'

'There'll be other jobs, Belle.'

She struggled to get her head round what Kieran was saying. 'What other jobs? Surely this was the big one, the one you've been going on about for years?'

'Maybe I only thought I wanted it. And between you and me, there may be a suitable vacancy at the *Courant* in the not-too-distant future. Nothing official yet, but it could just happen. And you know, I do like living in Cheltenham. Apart from anything else, you live here.'

'Unless I suddenly get offered a job in Liverpool,' Belle reminded him.

'And if you did, would you go?'

He was hanging on her words. But she owed it to him to be honest. 'I don't know, Kieran. I just don't know. I might.'

'Well, whatever else may happen, I know I still made the right decision,' declared Kieran firmly. 'I told the London editor there were other things that mattered to me besides more money and my byline in the *Argos*.'

'Things?'

He was looking at her again, in that terribly, uncomfortably intense way. 'Things like getting to know you all over again, bringing the romance back into our relationship. Loving you until I die. The kinds of things that you deserve.'

'But what if . . . what if I had to go somewhere else to work?'

He smiled back at her, imperturbable. 'Oh I wouldn't let a little thing like that put me off, even if I was in Cheltenham and you were on Mars. All it takes is a little motivation.'

She tried to fight down the sudden rush of elation, tell herself that this was some silly romantic impulse that Kieran would regret in the morning, but somewhere inside Belle's heart a big red rose blossomed. 'But you and me,' she stammered. 'Romantically speaking, I mean . . . I thought . . . well, it's all over, isn't it?'

Kieran's hand reached tentatively across the tablecloth and his finger-tips touched hers. 'That kind of depends,' he replied. 'Do you want it to be?'

That autumn was the strangest ever for Belle. Being courted all over again by Kieran made her feel as though she was embarking on an entirely new romance, yet this was a man she'd already loved, lost and practically lived with. Could love really be completely different the second time around? she asked herself. Hadn't they travelled along this path once already and ended up hopelessly lost?

Nobody could predict the future, but Belle had made a resolution and Kieran knew she was going to stick to it: wherever else romance might take them, there was one place it definitely wasn't going to lead – the altar. Having – almost – been there, done that and bought the wedding dress, Belle was in no hurry to sign herself up for the whole ghastly pantomime again, no matter how often Nanna Craine might ring up from her Island home to ask if she should buy a new hat.

Before she could even think about being attached to anybody else, first of all she wanted to concentrate on being happy in her own skin; finding out how to be the sort of person who'd never be overburdened with regrets. Perhaps she couldn't be a real adventurer like Ros, but that didn't mean she had to settle for being like Oz, either. Or like her mum, who'd harboured teenage dreams of opening a glamorous boutique in the West End, but had ended up as a bored vicar's wife instead.

After all, thought Belle, I'm not even twenty-five until November, and what have I done? Not that much.

Life still had an awful lot left to throw at her. The difficult part was going to be deciding when to catch, and when to dodge swiftly away.

She had a notion it was going to be fun trying.

'Good heavens!' Gerry Craine peered over the top of his half-moon reading glasses at the enormous pyramid of tins stacked in the vicarage hallway. 'What on earth is this?'

Jax poked her head out of the living-room door. 'Stewed steak in gravy, carrots, peas and a few cases of fruit salad.'

'I can see that, love, but how on earth did it get here?'

'A man brought it round in a van this morning, while you were down the police station, bailing out the Sullivans,' she replied blithely. During the months the Craines had been living on the Bluebell Estate, such events had become routine. And since the Sullivans had been arrested for beating up a thug from a neighbouring estate who'd been vandalising the church, Gerry Craine was the natural first port of call when they needed bailing out. 'He said it's a present from the Armstrongs, for the harvest festival on Sunday.'

Gerry scratched his head and scrutinised the tins. 'These labels are all in Polish,' he commented.

Jax came out to join him in the hall. 'Yes, that's right. Don't worry, the man said they're not nicked and the sell-by dates are fine, just don't ask any questions about the import duties.'

'Ah,' said Gerry. 'So I'm in possession of a big pile of dodgy food, am I?'

'Not that dodgy, Dad,' pointed out Jax. 'You're not going to send it back, are you?'

Gerry laughed. Back in the St Jude's days, the slightest hint of fiscal iffiness would have had him calling the police. But then St Jude's was the sort of parish where people donated kumquats and jars of organic pesto to the harvest festival, and fed tinned stewed steak to their dogs.

'What, look a gift horse in the mouth? Not likely! I'm not turning my nose up at perfectly good stew, and I bet the homeless people at the shelter won't either.' He chuckled to himself. 'Who knows – if news of the Armstrongs' generosity gets round the parish fast enough, perhaps the Sullivans will donate some pudding and custard to go with it.'

Sunday morning dawned misty, mellow and fruitful, with a church full of fruit and flowers and a vestry filled with not-quite-legitimate stew.

After events at the St Mungo's summer fair, nobody was too surprised when the bishop didn't turn up for the Harvest Festival, or even write a letter congratulating the parish on raising enough money to start work on replacing the leaky church roof. With the church full to bursting for the first time in well over thirty years nobody missed him much either, though there might have been a few sniggers if they'd known exactly what was keeping him so preoccupied.

Bishop Thaddeus Grove was standing by the magnificent carved fireplace in his office and roaring at the quivering archdeacon.

'The vicar of St Jude's said WHAT?'

The archdeacon flinched. 'He said his conscience won't allow him to remain silent any longer, my lord. Apparently he has determined to – ah – as it were, make his big announcement at Sunday morning service.'

'When?'

'Today.'

The bishop's face turned the colour of pickled red cabbage. 'Then he must be stopped! I will not have it!' he spluttered.

The archdeacon sighed. 'Unfortunately that would be quite pointless, my lord. It appears that he has already given certain – ah – interviews to a variety of newspapers and specialist periodicals. Along with – um – photographs.

'And after morning service today, he wants everybody to see him as he – ah – really is. As it were. In a ... er ... dress.'

Momentarily speechless with rage, the bishop turned away and thumped the solid marble mantelpiece, bruising his fist in the process. 'First I have a vicar who fathers illegitimate children in the colonies and subsequently turns into a simpering, smarmy do-gooder,' he seethed, sucking blood from his knuckles. 'And now I have one who insists on dressing up in frocks and calling himself Elsie.'

'That's not strictly true, my lord, he merely—'

'Shut up, Atkins. The fact remains that once again, this office has been insulted. The Church has been insulted. Once again, I find myself afflicted with a clergyman of abnormal appetites. He must go. Now.'

'But my lord, there is nothing actually in the Church's statutes about transves—'

Bishop Grove fixed the archdeacon with a stony glare. 'Then we shall have to write something,' he replied, running a hand across his perspiring forehead. 'I tell you, that parish is cursed. Cursed!'

And he sank into his opulent leather armchair with a deep groan as he pondered on what St Jude's parishioners would have to say about their cross-dressing vicar.

If he closed his eyes, he could almost hear Jean Armitage screaming for his blood.

On that same Sunday morning, at about the time that the people of the Bluebell Estate were wending their way to St Mungo's, and the bishop was bawling out the archdeacon, Sandra the features editor was sitting up in bed, receiving a phone call from the editor of the *Cheltenham Courant*.

'But,' she protested, shushing the naked hunk lying in the bed beside her. 'I only—'

The voice on the other end blasted back at her before she'd got more than a few words out. It mentioned Mad Dog McKindrick, a certain feature article Sandra had penned in the *Courant*, and then the words 'sue', 'lawsuit' and 'libel'.

By the end of the phone call Sandra was not smiling.

Nor, for that matter, did she have a job any more.

Belle and Kieran were standing at the back of St Mungo's church – not from choice but necessity. The eggbox was officially full to bursting, for the very first time since it had been thrown up in a fit of post-war optimism.

'Do you think everybody on the estate has suddenly come over all holy?' whispered Kieran.

'I doubt it,' replied Belle with a stifled giggle. 'I think it's got more to do with the free food and the cider-tasting afterwards.'

As she spoke the choir burst into song, resplendent in their borrowed orange kaftans, and Kieran pulled a face. 'Well, I don't think they've come for the music.'

Belle had to admit that Kieran had a point. If you weren't into gospel

323

standards bellowed so raucously that they sounded like football chants, or the world's worst-ever Christian skiffle band, St Mungo's Harvest Festival was not the place for you. The music was noisy, under-rehearsed and raw around the edges. On the other hand, it was delivered with such gusto that as Belle glanced around her, she even saw her opera-loving mother tapping her feet, and Jax actually smiling at Razor.

There was energy in St Mungo's that day. The kind of positive energy it hadn't seen in an awfully long time, if ever. The old graffiti was still visible under two fresh coats of emulsion, but nobody was looking. There was still plastic sheeting draped over the organ pipes, and the stained glass windows were mostly obscured by their thick metal grilles. But who cared? Even Belle found herself carried along on the rhythm of sheer celebration.

Maybe nobody was quite sure what they were celebrating, but they were enjoying themselves doing it. And in the middle of it all stood Gerry, looking brighter-eyed than Belle could ever remember him being; somehow rejuvenated by this self-confessed lawless bunch of heathens who had improbably decided that he was one of theirs.

'Dad's really happy,' said Belle.

She felt Kieran's hand curl about hers. 'He's not the only one,' he said.

After the service, there was a general stampede for the dilapidated scout-hut across the road that liked to call itself St Mungo's church hall. It wasn't just the lure of free sandwiches and locally brewed cider: free tickets were being given away for that night's harvest supper. There weren't many locals who hadn't either sampled or heard rave reviews about Brenda Craine's cooking.

Mona decided against joining the mob of people queuing up to say complimentary things to the vicar and his wife, and bag a free supper ticket in the process. It wasn't that she didn't think Gerry was doing a great job, just the fact that lately she wasn't really in a party frame of mind.

She was standing alone in a corner, wondering whether she could slip out unnoticed, when her mother loomed up out of the crowd and made a beeline for her.

'Not drinking?' Rena eyed Mona's half-sandwich and glass of watery orange squash.

'I don't think the bump would reckon much to home-made cider,' replied Mona. 'Besides, I see so much booze at work, I'm sick of the sight of the stuff.'

Rena downed a slug of scrumpy. 'It's an old wives' tale if you ask me,' she said. 'I drank like a bloody fish when I was pregnant with you, and I

324

don't care what the doctors said, I'm sure it did me a power of good. God, who'd want to go through nine months of hell without the occasional stiff drink?'

'Hm,' said Mona, gazing vacantly ahead of her.

'You're not listening to me, are you?' Rena peered into her daughter's face. 'What's the matter?'

Mona started. 'What? Nothing, Ma, nothing's wrong.'

Rena's lips pursed. 'I know that look. You're mooning over that wimp Oswald again, aren't you?'

'It's Oz, Ma,' Mona corrected her. 'And I'm not mooning, I'm just . . . thinking.'

Mona had been doing quite a bit of thinking since Belle's conscience had prompted her to let slip that 'she'd heard' Oz was in Cheltenham. Belle wouldn't be drawn on how she knew, but that didn't matter to Mona. What did matter was that Oz hadn't come near her, hadn't even phoned since that last time when he'd pretended he was still in America.

It was a pretty unambiguous message – which was why Mona hadn't even tried to find out exactly where he was. Face the facts, she told herself; it was just a fling and you were an idiot to think that it was something more. Deep down, you never even liked him that much, did you? So stop acting like the sky's fallen in, and get a grip on your life. You've got your English family, you've got Ma, and you've got the Bump. What more do you need?

Reading her thoughts, as mothers have a tendency to do, Rena laid a hand on her daughter's arm. 'Listen Mo, I can book us on a flight back to Australia first thing tomorrow – what d'you say? Forget the little squirt, after all he's forgotten about you.'

Although it hurt her more than she could say, Mona was dangerously close to admitting that, for once, her mother was right.

As he laughed and chatted with Belle and Jax, Kieran's eyes kept straying back across the hall to where Mona was standing. Although her mother was next to her, she looked tired, fraught and alone.

With hindsight, it was probably just as well that Belle had cracked and told Mona about Oz. But what neither of them knew was that, only a few days ago, Oz had been on the phone to Kieran, asking if he had any idea how much it cost to fly to Mexico.

Oh Mona, he thought, almost guilty in his own newfound happiness with Belle; it's been bad for you already, but I've got an awful feeling things are going to get even worse.

Brenda was taking a back seat, letting Gerry enjoy being praised for the first time in what seemed like an eternity. He deserved it; nobody could have worked harder than he had to bring life to St Mungo's – except Brenda, and that was just the way things were when you'd chosen to be a vicar's wife. You toiled on behind the scenes, and nobody ever noticed.

For a little while she'd resented it, and cast around desperately for something, anything that might make things better. It was natural enough, she supposed. Lots of middle-aged women turned to other men to relieve the tedium of their married lives. She didn't feel particularly guilty about the comfort she and Ken had given each other. Besides, that was all in the past.

Nevertheless, it came as a shock when she looked across the hall and spotted Ken Tyler chatting with a group of people from the Alpha course. She'd had no idea he was planning to travel down for the special service. When he turned to look in her direction, she fully expected to feel like a lovesick schoolgirl all over again.

Only curiously, she didn't. The spell was broken; the edge had gone.

He smiled at her; she smiled politely back at him. Then she turned away.

'Isn't that Ken over there?' asked Gerry.

'Who? Oh, yes, I think it probably is.'

'Don't you want to go over and talk to him? You two used to be such great friends.'

Brenda looked into her husband's honest, trusting, handsome face. There wasn't a hint of suspicion or blame in his voice, yet in that instant she saw something in his eyes that told her he knew.

'I don't think so, I doubt we'd have anything much to talk about,' she replied truthfully. 'I'd much rather stay here with you.'

Loving him all over again, she slipped an arm through his. Maybe there was still something missing from her life, but now she understood how mistaken she'd been: that elusive something had nothing to do with her marriage.

Her hand firmly clasped in his, Belle gazed up at Kieran and wondered when the fairy tale would end.

It surely must, because over the past year the Craines had been well and truly jinxed. It was just a question of when. When would Kieran start being irritated by her again? When would he realise that he'd made a big mistake in turning down his dream job in London for her sake, and start looking for a way out?

At the moment, she felt so happy that it almost hurt. If she could only have been certain that it would last . . . Instead of which, she found herself constantly expecting the worst.

What happened next might not have been the worst, but she certainly wasn't expecting it. A burly, bearded man with a very loud voice, dressed in a town crier's costume, entered the hall, parting the crowds with shouts of 'Oyez' and much ringing of his handbell.

'What's this pantomime?' wondered Mona, instinctively turning suspicious eyes on her mother.

'Don't look at me! I expect it's one of those quaint old English customs you're so fond of these days.'

The town crier unfurled a parchment scroll, and made his big announcement: 'Oyez, oyez! Mr Oswald Hepplewhite wishes it to be known that he has recently been behaving like a complete coward, an utter scoundrel and prat of the worst order, and that he is thoroughly ashamed of himself.

'He wishes to apologise most sincerely to Miss Mona Starr, but is too scared to do it himself, not in case she punches him, which he deserves, but because he is hopeless at everything, especially putting words together so that they make proper sense.'

Mona looked at her mother. The granite expression was not softening one iota. 'He's a complete and utter no-good wimp, Mona,' she hissed.

'Yes, I know, but—'

'No buts.'

The town crier cleared his throat and went on. 'Mr Hepplewhite would be eternally grateful if Miss Starr would step outside the hall straight away, as he has something he'd like to show her.'

A titter ran round the hall.

'I bet he has,' growled Rena. 'Don't you dare go outside, you're only encouraging him!'

She spoke to no avail. Because not just Mona, but everyone was pushing towards the door of the hall, eager to find out exactly what was going on outside.

Standing in the field outside, Oz agonised over each passing second, unable to take his eyes off his watch. 'It's not going to work, she's going to be too late! Oh, I do hope she hurries up ... Do I look all right? Oh God, I wish I'd let Kieran in on this ...'

Just as he was about to give up hope, people started pouring out of the hall and he saw Mona among them, her mother vainly attempting to hold her back. Her eyes met his and widened at the sight of him.

She came across to him, her beautiful mouth agape. 'Oz, what's all this about? Smart tuxedo, bow tie, new haircut – my God Oz, you look really ... sexy!' She spoke the word as though it were the most incredible one imaginable, which perhaps it was. 'And then there was that scroll thing. What the hell are you up to?'

'I . . . um . . . oh dear . . .' Oz flailed for the right words like an inept juggler. 'I'm no good at this, you see, and—'

A distant, mechanical rumble made him offer up a prayer of gratitude as, over the horizon, came a little biplane, black-and-yellow-striped like an oversized wasp, and trailing something in the air behind it.

'Oh look!' said someone in the crowd, pointing up at the sky. 'There's a banner or something.'

A banner? Mona looked questioningly at Oz, his face contorted with nerves.

'Please read it,' he begged. 'It says it so much better than I ever could.'

And she looked up at the sky, and as the banner fluttered past, these words were written across the heavens for all the world to see:

I LOVE YOU MONA. PLEASE MARRY ME.

When she looked back down, with tears welling up in her eyes, she saw that Oz was on one knee before her, holding out a diamond ring that nestled in crimson velvet. 'Will you?' he pleaded.

'Of course she won't!' exclaimed Rena, marching up behind her daughter. 'She's got far too much sense for that.'

'Shut up, Ma.' Mona looked into Oz's eyes. 'Did you mean all that? Do you really love me?'

'With all my heart.'

'Even more than . . . than bugs?'

'A hundred times more.'

'You lied to me.'

Oz hung his head. 'I'm so sorry, it was wrong and I swear I'll never lie to you again. I guess I was just afraid. The biggest responsibility I've had so far is choosing which socks to put on.'

'That's going to change if you marry me,' Mona pointed out.

'Good. It's about time I grew up, don't you think?'

'Your mother hates me' Mona reminded him.

'That's OK,' he replied cheerfully. 'She hates me too. When she found out I'd been in hiding at the Travelodge, she told me I'd couldn't come home at all.'

'Then where are you staying now?'

'At the lab, mostly. I've got a sleeping bag. Till I can work something out about a flat or something.'

Rena refused to be silenced any longer. 'You are coming straight back to Australia with me, young lady,' she said firmly. 'Chas and I will take good care of you and the little one. If you marry this . . . this drongo, you'll do it over my dead body!'

'She's right,' sighed Oz. 'You'd be much better off in Australia. Both of you. I'm not much of a catch.'

There was a moment of awkward silence. Oz wobbled as he struggled to keep his balance on one knee. Then Mona held out her hand to him. 'For goodness' sake, get up Oz.'

'Why? Why bother?'

'Because I can't bend down in my condition, and if you don't stand up how can you kiss me? It is traditional to kiss your fiancée in England, isn't it?'

For a few seconds, Oz just knelt there looking shell-shocked. Then he leapt to his feet, flung his arms round Mona and kissed her as though he was afraid that at any moment she might disappear.

Outside in the car park later on, Kieran and Belle could still scarcely believe what had happened.

'That was brave of Oz,' commented Belle. 'Did you see how much he was shaking?'

'I bet he'll be shaking even more on his wedding day.' Kieran shook his head in disbelief. 'And there was I, thinking he'd be living in his mum's spare room for the next thirty years.'

'Instead of which he's going to be a dad, and he's whisking Mona and the baby off on a late honeymoon, to see the butterfly migrations in Mexico. Isn't that sweet?'

'Well, well,' sighed Kieran. 'Way things are going, pretty soon I'll be the only boring bachelor left in Cheltenham.' He switched his mobile back on. 'Uh-oh, text message from work. Something's going on with Sandra, they want me to come in.' He saw Belle's face fall. 'Of course, I could always lie and tell them I'm ill in bed with a beautiful woman, and it'd be almost true. After all, you are beautiful, and I do feel like taking you back to bed.'

He caressed her cheek and she caught his hand and kissed it softly. 'I'd like that,' she admitted. 'In fact, I'd love it.'

Kieran prepared to phone in sick.

'But I really think you should go. I know you gave up London, but your work's still really important to you and I don't intend to get in the way of it.'

'Is that your way of telling me that I mustn't get in the way of yours?' he enquired.

I wonder if it is, thought Belle. 'No, not really . . . well perhaps. I don't know,' she confessed. 'I mean, I'm never going to be Anita Roddick, but that doesn't mean I'm ready for a life of washing nappies either.'

'So I can't persuade you to marry me then?'

A little shiver, half fear, half excitement, ran up Belle's spine. Almost inconsequentially, he had spoken the words she'd feared she might never hear again. How often had she dreamed of that? 'Not right now,' she replied, and it was one of the hardest things she'd ever had to say. 'But one day maybe. Yeah, definitely maybe.'

They walked hand in hand to Kieran's car. As Belle watched him get in and drive away, she wondered how she could ever bear not to be in the same place, not to see him every morning and curl up with him every night.

But deep inside she knew that she had nothing to fear. Because even if she and Kieran ever found themselves at opposite ends of the world, their lives were so in tune that they could never really be more than a heartbeat apart.

Chapter 33

It was the week before Christmas when Oz and Mona walked up the aisle at St Mungo's. Whilst the church itself might possess all the allure of a wartime concrete pillbox, everything else was picture postcard perfect for a winter wedding: even the weather obliged with a light dusting of early snow, as fine and powdery as icing sugar.

Oz looked remarkably composed for a man who'd woken up, the day after his stag night, stark naked in the insect house at the Animal Experience. His colleagues from the lab swore they'd had nothing to do with it, but best man Kieran had had his beady eye on them ever since, and had tipped off Big Bob and Sean the cellarman to check the wedding reception buffet for anything with more than two legs. What with that, and protecting Oz from his irate estranged mother, he probably ought to have asked for danger money.

As for Mona, she was just plain beautiful. Admittedly she was just about as fat as a pregnant woman could get, but in her little fur-trimmed minidress that made her look like an oversized but irresistibly cute baby bird.

It wasn't the most conventional of white weddings. The marriage was conducted by the bride's own father, the male guests' buttonholes were made from a rare South American insectivorous orchid, the bride wore Ugg boots because her feet were so swollen up, and one of the brides-maids was a dog.

After a bath and a flea treatment, Engelbert looked presentable if embarrassed in his pink ruffled collar. The other bridesmaid – Belle – stood right beside him, one hand on her bouquet, the other firmly gripping his lead, ready to rugby tackle him if he slipped his collar and made a break for it. Jax sat on the front row of the congregation in her big boots, congratulating herself on a lucky escape.

It felt so strange to be standing here, at the altar, with Kieran just a couple of feet away and her father right in front of them, intoning the words of the marriage service. Just a few months ago, she recalled, she and Kieran should have been standing where Mona and Oz were today. Instead of which they were here, sort of together and yet not together, if that made any kind of sense.

As Mona and Oz prepared to take their vows, Kieran half-turned to look at Belle and mouthed 'I love you.' Belle felt her heart glow with happiness. It didn't matter whether or not they were married to each other; all that mattered was that they were here, and that they loved each other. 'Me too,' she mouthed back, with the silliest of grins all over her face. As she turned, she caught the eye of a smiling Ros, who'd arrived back only a few weeks before and was sitting in a nearby pew, sandwiched between Nanna Craine and Ros's brand-new Swedish boyfriend, Lars. 'That's the thing about adventures,' Ros had told her with a wink. 'You never know what you'll pick up along the way.'

Not everybody was smiling. Rena Starr was fully occupied eyeballing Oz with a ferocious stare. If stares came in varying degrees of hardness, this one was definitely diamond-edged titanium. It seemed to say, 'One false move and I'll rip your heart out,' but the one person it was lost on was Oz. He was far too busy mixing his words up, fumbling the ring, gazing at his bride and generally being happier than any geek had a right to be.

The happy couple were ablaze with smiles as they walked out of the church, flanked by an honour guard of leather-clad Goth bikers, and made their way to the 'wedding car' – one of the brewery's old-fashioned drays, pulled by a brace of Clydesdale horses. It took Oz several attempts to hoist his new wife up beside the driver, but with a helping hand from Kieran they managed it, and the wedding party set off at a leisurely amble for the reception.

'What do you reckon to this marriage lark then?' called out Kieran as the dray pulled away.

Oz gave him the thumbs-up. 'Flipping marvellous, mate. You should give it a try.'

'Just give me a chance and I will,' murmured Kieran to himself. But there was only one potential candidate for the post of Mrs Kieran Sawyer, and if she kept saying no, well, he'd just have to stay a bachelor for ever.

The venerable rafters of the Royal Shakespeare Tavern hadn't been shaken so much since the Bard himself was a lad. In fact the function room upstairs was so jam-packed with wedding guests that Belle was convinced the floorboards would give way at any moment, sending them all crashing down into the public bar.

'Ee, but I do love a wedding,' enthused Nanna Craine over her third

332

glass of sherry. 'And she's not a bad granddaughter – for an illegitimate Australian.' Nanna found it hard not to warm to a girl who could both domesticate a hopeless case like Oz *and* rustle up a mean kipper pâté.

'You like weddings then? You mean all the nice dresses and having a good cry and that stuff?' asked Ros.

Nanna Craine guffawed. 'Good heavens no! I'm talking about all the bitching and the drunken brawling, and trying to guess which bridesmaid the best man's going to get off with before the night's up.'

'It had better be me,' declared Belle, 'or I'm really going to get a self-image problem.' Engelbert looked up at her adoringly, yawned and enveloped her in his own distinctive aroma of halitosis mixed with cheese and onion crisps. 'You're right Engelbert,' Belle agreed ruefully. 'How could Kieran possibly resist you? Looks like I'm history.'

Suddenly the background music stopped, which was a relief for everyone, seeing as it was being provided by a tone-deaf string quartet Big Bob's mate Larry had picked up cheap through a friend of a friend.

'Oh look!' Belle grabbed Ros's arm. 'Oz is going to make his speech.'

Oz sidled up to the microphone, looking much more like his usual awkward self. He blew into it, deafening everyone in the room, and tapped it a few times with his finger. 'Is this on?' He was rewarded by a shrill whine of feedback. 'Oh, it is. Right. Well, I'm ... er ... that is to say we ... that's me and my lovely new wife Mona ... Oh bugger, what was I going to say... I'm not very good at this.'

Mona gave him a look of loving desperation, kissed him on the cheek and took the microphone from his hand. 'What he's trying to say,' she said, smiling at her bashful bridegroom, 'is that—' Suddenly, Mona's expression was transformed, and she doubled up, grabbing at her stomach and gasping into the microphone: 'Oh shit, Oz. I think I'm in labour.'

The midwives at Cotswold General were very understanding, but equally firm. The delivery suite was strictly for ladies delivering babies and their partners – and definitely not for wedding receptions, with or without a string quartet.

'But Mona's missing out on her own wedding do,' protested Sean the cellarman, who had brightened up considerably since Mona had let him showcase his DJ set at the Tavern every Friday night.

'Yeah,' agreed Big Bob's mate Larry. 'Can't we take her in a bottle of bubbly and a few Twiglets? Have a bit of a sing-song and that, cheer her up?'

'Sorry love,' the midwife replied firmly. 'But you'll have to wait downstairs in the waiting room. That's all of you,' she emphasised.

'Miserable sods,' grumbled Larry as about thirty wedding guests muttered among themselves and trooped back down the stairs, taking their champagne with them. 'S'pose we might as well go home then.'

It was Ros who saved the day. 'Why don't we have the reception here, in the waiting room?' she suggested.

Belle was aghast. 'You can't do that!'

'Why not? A couple of shandies and a few vol-au-vents never harmed anybody. I'm sure if we don't make too much row they won't chuck us out. What about it? Who's going to fetch the food?'

While the hard-core revellers were eating canapés in the waiting room, Gerry Craine was pacing agitatedly up and down the corridor outside.

Brenda caught up with him and tried to make him sit down, but he just couldn't keep still. 'What's wrong, love?'

He could hardly look at her. 'Oh Brenda, I know you'll think I'm stupid.'

She gently turned his face towards hers. 'Stupid? Why?'

'I'm afraid.'

'For Mona and the baby?'

He nodded. 'I know she's young and healthy, and she's getting all the best care and all of that, but somehow ... well, it all feels different when it's,' he looked away, 'your own child.'

'I know.'

'You can't keep your mind off the thousand and one things that could go wrong.'

'That's not stupid,' Brenda said softly. 'Remember how we both felt when I was pregnant with Annabelle and the doctors told us about the detached placenta? Everything happened in such a rush that I hardly had time to agonise about it, but I can remember looking at your face, just as they were taking me down to the operating theatre. You were white as a ghost.' She squeezed his hand. 'You see, you mustn't feel stupid, it's only natural.'

'I know I can't expect you to feel the same way about Mona,' Gerry went on, 'I mean, why should you? It's a miracle you don't hate her – and me too, for that matter. You've been wonderful to me, Brenda. Through all of this, just wonderful. Nobody in the world could ever replace you.'

'I'm your wife,' she said simply.

'But that doesn't mean—'

She took his face in her hands and kissed it. 'Yes it does, Gerry, it means more than you'll ever know. And you're wrong about Mona. In spite of everything, I do understand. Mona may not be my flesh and blood, but she's a part of our family now, and she's a part of me too. We can't choose who we love, can we?' She laughed to herself. 'Heavens, I've even grown quite fond of that disgusting smelly dog.'

334

He looked at her thoughtfully. 'If you could choose, would you still choose me?'

She kissed him. 'Every time. Now, come with me and sit down. We could have a long wait ahead of us.'

They didn't.

With her gift for the unexpected, Mona gave birth in record time, and without an epidural in sight. 'Apparently it's because I'm really fit and my abs are so strong,' she said, beaming as she and Oz showed off the new addition to the Craine and Hepplewhite dynasties.

With Gerry and Brenda, Belle and Kieran, Razor and Jax, Rena and Nanna Craine, there were so many people gathered round Mona's bed that Belle fully expected some Hattie Jacques-style matron to burst in and chase them all away.

'What are you going to call her?' asked Belle, hardly daring to touch the tiny, fragile-looking creature who was her new niece.

Oz and Mona exchanged looks. 'Well, we thought about Annabelle and Jacqueline . . . and Brenda and Rena of course,' began Oz.

'But then we thought hey, Geraldine's a nice name,' Mona continued. 'Gerry for short. What do you reckon, Gramps?'

Gerry didn't answer immediately. Taking his tiny granddaughter into his arms, as delicately as if she were made of antique porcelain, he felt her tiny hand curl about his finger and pressed it to his lips. 'Hello Geraldine,' he whispered. 'I'm your granddad. And this lovely lady here is Grandma Brenda. And you're going to have the most wonderful life.' When he looked up, his eyes were very bright and his smile crinkly. 'I think Mum had better take you now, little one,' he said, his voice quavering. 'I might just blub all over you.'

Over in the corner, Nanna Craine was in no danger of crying; nor was Rena. They were old hands at this baby-producing thing, though it did still hold a certain genealogical interest.

'She's got her mother's eyes,' remarked Rena.

'And Gerry's hair,' countered Nanna Craine, not wishing to be outdone.

Rena glanced around, lowered her voice and whispered in Nanna Craine's ear: 'Actually, I think he's got my Eddie's nose.'

It took just a split second for Nanna Craine to get the drift of what Rena was saying. 'Your late husband? Surely you're not saying . . .'

'I'm *pretty* sure Mona's Gerry's child, but you know, I can't be one *hundred* per cent certain . . . I mean, Eddie and I were already courting when I had my little, er, encounter with Gerry. We were practically engaged. And even in those days, you couldn't expect a couple to do nothing but hold hands, could you?'

Nanna Craine contemplated Rena with a sniff. 'Your mother was right about you,' she commented.

'Right? Why, what did she say?'

'You don't want to know, dear. Something about bitches in heat, as I recall.'

'Well really!'

Gerry's mother shrugged. 'The question is, what do you intend to do about it? Gerry looks so happy about being a grandfather, doesn't he?'

Rena had the decency to look guilty. 'He does rather. So, do you think I ought to tell him? About Mona?'

'If I were you,' replied Nanna Craine, 'I'd turn over a new leaf and keep my big Aussie mouth shut. Your family's caused enough shenanigans as it is. Now dear, shall we go and introduce ourselves to *our* new great-granddaughter? I'm sure she has a look of me, you know . . .'

After a while, Belle left the postnatal ward and went down to the terrace outside for a breath of fresh air. It had been a long day, and it was beginning to tell on her. But before she could slope off for a proper rest, she'd promised her mum she'd phone a whole host of geographically-scattered Craines to let them know about the new arrival.

As she switched on her mobile, a little envelope appeared on the screen. New text message. Ah well, she might as well take a look at it.

Unexpectedly, it was from John Gillespie at Green Goddess HQ. 'Please phone asap, got interesting proposition for you, JG.'

A tingly feeling made the hairs stand up on the back of her neck, and yet she almost didn't bother phoning. There was a part of Belle that really didn't want to know about interesting propositions, that just wanted to go on and on and on in the same way, being ordinary and uninteresting and being with Kieran.

And yet . . .

She phoned, exchanged pleasantries for a few moments, then listened to what he had to say. He was right, it was interesting. Not just interesting, adventurous. Maybe too adventurous for her . . . It wouldn't just mean being away from Cheltenham for a while, it would mean travelling abroad. Me! she thought. Abroad!

'So what do you reckon?' John Gillespie repeated. 'I do need an answer quickly. Are you up for an adventure, yes or no?'

Before she'd had the time to think and be afraid, Belle heard herself answer: 'Yes.'

Epilogue

One year later ...

A year was a long time, and yet to Belle it seemed as though the last twelve months had passed in a blur of frantic activity.

Never in her wildest dreams had she ever imagined that she'd be working for Green Goddess halfway across the world, helping to set up all the new stores the company was opening since John Gillespie organised a management buyout. She'd started with the easy stuff: France, Belgium, Ireland – the places where things were familiar and she never felt too far from home. Or from Kieran. It was a lot easier to bear the separation when she knew he was only a quick budget flight and a long weekend away.

But her confidence had grown with her skills. Before she knew it, she was being sent to places she couldn't even pinpoint on a map. Krakow – where she helped Jerszy to set up his own store; Prague, and even Estonia.

And now she was in Hong Kong. As she stood at the window of her small but neat apartment, gazing down into the teeming streets, she thought of Kieran, thousands of miles away. She was happy doing the things she was good at: setting up stores, training and motivating people. But with Kieran so far away, there was a big hole where her heart should be. She loved him so much, and yet she couldn't just throw away this chance of a lifetime; this opportunity to be something more than just 'ordinary little Belle Craine'.

Should she let him go? Should she take a deep breath and set him free, the way you might set free a beautiful bird when you knew it could have a happier life elsewhere, with some other mate? Should she?

Could she?

It was very early in the morning when Belle's phone rang. She glanced at the alarm clock with blurry eyes, made out '4.03 am', groaned and then, very reluctantly, lifted the receiver.

'Yes?'

'Belle, is that you?'

She sat bolt upright in bed, suddenly awake. 'Kieran! It's the middle of the night here.'

'Oh God, is it? I keep getting these time differences all mixed up. The thing is, I'm really excited and I just had to tell you.'

'Tell me what?'

'I've resigned from my job at the *Courant*. Isn't it great?'

'Resigned? But Kieran, what are you going to do?'

'Travel with you! I've booked a flight over to Hong Kong on Tuesday.'

There was a short, stunned silence.

'B-but . . . what about your work?' stammered Belle.

'Don't worry, I'll find something.' Then he said something Belle had never dreamed he would ever say. 'Besides, work isn't everything, is it?'

'Hey! That's my line.'

Kieran paused. 'Oh hell, have I done something stupid? Are you going to tell me you've gone off me and you don't want me to come out at all?'

Belle didn't know whether to laugh or cry. In the end she settled for doing both. 'Kieran, you idiot! Of course I want you to come! You've got no idea how much I want you to!'

And the moment she'd put the phone down, Belle sobbed for sheer joy.

Two years later . . .

The Dubai sunshine beat down upon the pure, pale sand of a flawless beach, its intensity magnified again and again as it reflected off the shining glass and white facades of the bright new towers on the man-made archipelago.

At the base of one of those luxurious, air-conditioned towers was the Dubai branch of Green Goddess; in its very first week of trading, and currently under the guiding hand of its temporary manager, Belle Craine. On the other side of the island, just over halfway up an equally luxurious and air-conditioned tower, was the head office of *International Running Monthly*, where a certain journalist called Kieran Sawyer was currently making a name – and a nice, tax-free salary – as a top feature writer.

And in a third tower, on the neighbouring island, stood the beautiful white-walled apartment where Belle and Kieran lived, waking every morning to the sound of the surf and the promise of another day together.

Oz clumped up the beach in his flip-flops, rubbing factor 60 sunblock into his bright-red nose. 'I don't think this climate quite agrees with my complexion,' he commented. 'Still, Mona's loving it, aren't you darling?'

'Sure am, sweetie.' A heavily pregnant Mona skipped towards them with the lightness of a gazelle, seemingly unhindered by her bump or by the lusty toddler bawling under her arm. 'Could you just take Gerry for me for a mo, Ozzie? Only I left her potty in the car.'

Mona went back to the car for the potty, Oz watching her with the gaze of a man who still couldn't believe his luck.

Kieran patted Oz's stomach. 'What's this Oz? Sympathetic pregnancy?'

'Too much good food, more like,' Oz lamented.

'You want to go running with Kieran.' Belle gave Kieran's biceps a squeeze.

'No fear. And I bet you don't, either.'

'Me, go running?' Belle fell about laughing. 'What do you think I am, mad?'

Mona returned, plus potty, and all was returned to relative calm and tranquillity.

'Well Gerry,' said Oz to the toddler, who was busy filling one of her shoes with sand, 'I reckon we'd better get that webcam sorted out, otherwise Granny and Grandad and Auntie Jax, and all the other people back home won't be able to see Auntie Belle and Uncle Kieran getting married.'

Belle and Kieran were married by the local registrar on the beach that very afternoon, with Mona as bridesmaid, Oz as best man and little Geraldine as Belle's flower-girl. Jax skilfully managed to escape being bridesmaid yet again by being up at Oxford, where Razor had wangled himself a trainee manager's job in his uncle's Bentley dealership because Jax had flatly refused to go to university without him.

It was a quiet, low-key wedding, but it didn't mean any less because of that. If anything, Belle's feelings were intensified by being almost alone on that beach with the man she loved, declaring their love to the endless blue sky. She looked like a fairy tale in her gown of pale, shimmering gold; so ethereally beautiful that Kieran could scarcely believe she was real.

The church blessing would have to wait a while, until the bride and groom could get back to England for a holiday, and Gerry could officiate. That at least would make it up to Brenda and Nanna Craine for the lack of a gigantic white wedding; and make Kieran feel that he was really and truly part of this family that had embraced him for so long. But for now, the whole family was able to watch them exchanging vows, thanks to Oz and his webcam. Even Ros and Lars were able to toast them with cocoa at base camp on their Himalayan climbing expedition.

339

Afterwards, they toasted the marriage with chilled guava juice and a banquet of the freshest seafood any of them had ever tasted. But Belle hardly ate a thing. The excitement was too much. So many things had gone wrong for her and Kieran, and some of them had been her own fault; yet now, at last, the one thing that really mattered had gone right. They were man and wife.

'Do you think you'll stay here in Dubai then?' asked Oz. 'You've got it nice and cushy.'

'Beats Cheltenham in December,' agreed Mona. 'Except when it's our wedding anniversary of course!' she added swiftly.

'Who knows?' Kieran snuggled up to Belle and she laid her head upon his shoulder. 'A few months maybe. Or maybe a little longer. We've decided we're in no hurry to settle down and kids can wait for a few years yet – we're having too much fun!'

'They've also said I can stay on here at the shop if I want,' agreed Belle. 'But we'll just take things as they come, won't we, darling?'

'Sure will.'

They kissed.

'Well,' declared Mona, 'I never thought I'd hear Belle talking about taking things as they come. You used to be the biggest little worry-wart in the world. Ever! Now it's all wall-to-wall adventures.'

Now I've just begun the biggest one of all, thought Belle blissfully as night fell and she and Kieran lay curled up on their bed together, the balcony doors wide open, gazing out at the stars. I've gone and got myself married at last.

And that's what I call an adventure.

Be My Baby
Zoë Barnes

Lorna had given up her career as a midwife to have her own baby. Happily married to Ed, she had looked forward to telling him that Leo would soon have a baby brother or a sister to play with. But fate had stepped in and left her widowed with a young son and another baby on the way.

Eighteen months later, Lorna misses Ed as much as ever, but knows she must get out and make a new life for herself and her children. When her mum and dad suddenly find themselves desperate for somewhere to live, what could be more natural than for them to come and live with Lorna? It'll be a great opportunity for her to go back to her job, while they get to know their grandchildren.

But that's before the mishaps, the arguments over childcare, or the rows that break out when Lorna announces that she's met a hunky doctor and is ready to start dating again.

Praise for Zoë Barnes:

'bloody good read' *New Woman*

'Top ten book . . . feel-good escapism' *Heat*

'Zoë Barnes writes wonderfully escapist novels, firmly based in reality' *Express*

Split Ends
Zoë Barnes

Eight years ago, when Hannah was a struggling single mum, Nick Steadman seemed like Mr Right and Prince Charming rolled into one. Kind, strong, reliable – and the perfect step-dad to Lottie – what did it matter if his taste in trousers was more M&S than D&G?

OK, so their relationship's never been based on passion, but it has plenty of respect, friendship and trust. Trouble is, after eight years together they're beginning to realise that friendship isn't enough.

The solution? An amicable divorce. Which would be just fine if it wasn't so hard to explain to nine-year-old Lottie. And if Hannah didn't find herself a teeny bit annoyed at Nick's ability to move on so quickly.

Not that she isn't happy for him and his new lover. Of course she is. After all, they agreed they'd be mature, grown-up and rational about their separation. They may be divorced but they can still be friends.

Can't they?

Just Married

Zoë Barnes

Emma (née Cox) and Joe Sheridan have just got married. Emma has been in love with Joe since school – marrying him was the happiest day of her life. But now the honeymoon is over and Emma's having to cope with the reality of married life. She's living in a new town, has a new job and a new husband who hasn't quite left his bachelor days behind him. Then there's Emma's interfering mother-in-law who's expecting the patter of tiny feet before Joe's even carried her over the threshold!

Still, at least she and Joe are together at last. But Joe and Emma have never lived with each other before – and apart from the odd holiday – have never spent more than two weeks in each other's company. Setting up home together for the first time might be romantic, but nobody told them that living happily ever after takes a lot of hard work …

Love Bug
Zoë Barnes

Don't get bitten . . .

If love is a bug then Laurel Page is immune. Been there. Done that. Got over it. All she wants now is a quiet life. And while running a dating agency may not seem like the logical career path for a woman who has so fervently sworn off romance, for Laurel it's perfect. There's something deliciously safe about other people's romantic problems. Laurel's had enough drama in her relationships to last two life times.

And then Gabriel Jouet walks into her office. Tall, dark and oozing with Gallic charm, he's an unlikely client and almost enough to make even Laurel contemplate abandoning her vow of singledom. *Almost* . . . But Laurel's scars run deep: Cupid really would have to be stupid to pick on her again . . .